KRUGER'S ALP

D1650023

Christopher Hope

Atlantic Books

FOR MIKE KIRKWOOD

Who showed me the gaps in the laager

First published in Great Britain in 1984 by William Heinemann Ltd.

This paperback edition published in Great Britain in 2009 by
Atlantic Books, an imprint of Grove Atlantic Ltd.

The quotation by President Kruger (page 72) is taken from *The
Memoirs of Paul Kruger* (Negro University Press, New York, 1969).

1 3 5 7 9 10 8 6 4 2

A CIP catalogue record for this book is available from
the British Library.

ISBN: 978 1 84887 163 2

Printed in Great Britain by Clays Ltd, St Ives plc

Atlantic Books
An imprint of Grove Atlantic Ltd
Ormond House
26–27 Boswell Street
London
WC1N 3JZ

www.atlantic-books.co.uk

Pray, did you never hear what happened to a man some time ago of this town (whose name was Christian) that went on a Pilgrimage up towards the higher regions?

John Bunyan
Pilgrim's Progress

They took the hill (Whose hill? What for?)
But what a climb they left to do!
Out of that bungled, unwise war
An alp of unforgiveness grew.

William Plomer
'The Boer War'

We knew nothing of the theatrical element which is part of all revolutionary movements in France, and we believed sincerely in all we heard.

A. Herzen
Childhood, Youth and Exile

CHAPTER 1

As I walked through the wilderness of what remained of the world of Father Lynch and his 'little guild', I saw much to disturb me. Here was the last vestige of the parish garden where the bulldozers, earth-movers, grabbers and cranes had frozen into that peculiar menacing immobility giant machines assume when switched off; left as if stunned, open-mouthed, gaping at the human foolishness of wishing to stop work when they are strong and willing to continue. They stood silent, it being Sunday, resting from their merciless preparation of this new site for one of the enormous hostels of the huge University of National Christian Education, widely declared to be the largest in the southern hemisphere. I looked around me and found the work nearly complete. However, the machines had stopped eating for the moment; ours is a holy land and even the destruction of redundant churches halts on the Sabbath.

The advance of the university over the years had been slow but inexorable; at first, parcels of the extensive grounds of St Jude's had gone and, wisely, Lynch had not fought against this but had preserved his energies for guarding the church itself and his garden. His community of priests and lay brothers had been whittled away one by one. Bishop Blashford had conducted negotiations with the university so as to safeguard what he called 'an orderly withdrawal', with a skill which had won him the admiration of municipal councils across the country – and the commendation of the Papal Nuncio, Agnelli.

I stood in the destroyed church with the gaping roof. All religious ornaments had been removed, the sentimental paintings of lambs in emerald meadows, the wooden stations of the cross, the stained-glass windows of obscure martyrs, the baptismal font, the giant crucifix which had swung above the altar, the doors of the confessionals torn off so that now the little chambers gaped like disused lavatories. All gone – the golden tabernacle, the candles, the altar stone, the plaster Virgin in her sky-blue drapery and her brass circlet of stars, the wooden St Joseph with his surprising paunch, his bluff good looks and his blue sea-captain's eyes; all the gaudy, inappropriate prints of Italianate saints, all gone; the ruby

1

glass altar lamps in which the tiny flame glowed perpetually, the wooden altar rail at which Blanchaille had stood with his boat boy, Mickey the Poet, beside him, fumigating the first few rows of the congregation with pungent incense, the sacred cardboard hosts that stuck to the roof of the mouth for half an hour after Communion, the chalices, the sweet and rather yeasty smell of the cheap Jewish wine Lynch favoured for the Mass, the ciborium, the copes and chasubles stiff with gold thread, all the intoxicating plumage by which ordinary, irritable, balding men transformed themselves into birds of paradise and paraded to the strangely comforting sound of brass bells; all the absurdly delightful foreign paraphernalia with which a diminishing band of Catholics in a not very notable parish chimed, chanted, blessed and perfumed the start of each bright indifferent African morning. Only the pews remained now, the dark, polished mahogany pews, on the last two of which, at the rear of the church, I could make out still, small oblong patches of lighter wood where the brass plates had been; they were marked RESERVED, thus delicately designating the seats for the handful of black servants who used this church until Father Lynch had the plates removed, in the face of considerable opposition, in the days when these things were regarded as perfectly normal and fully in accord with the will of God and the customs of the country.

I saw that only Father Lynch's favourite tree, from beneath which the dying master of altar boys once conducted his famous picnics, was still standing. The Tree of Heaven, we called it, or *Ailanthus altissima* Father Lynch taught with desperate pedantry. Like Buddha, beneath the sacred Bo tree, Father Lynch sat – though there had been nothing Eastern about Father Lynch, who was small, thin and elfish and who told his boys that the name of the tree was highly misleading since its male flowers smelt pretty damn awful and its roots were a threat to the foundations of the church. It was beneath this Tree of Heaven that I lay down around noon and slept. And while I slept I dreamed.

In my dream I saw Theodore Blanchaille and he was not particularly well-dressed. But then he'd always been rather a sloppy character, old Blanchie, or Father Theodore Blanchaille as we learnt to refer to him, or Father Theo of the Camps, as he was known in the old days, or plain Mr Blanchaille as we must refer to him now, I suppose. He was wearing an old pair of khaki shorts, baggy, creased and much too big for him, and a weird kind of sailor's top of jagged dark blue stripes, squared at the neck. He was barefoot and sat in an empty room on a plastic chair. He was a big fellow carrying too much weight, but then he'd always been heavy, and I could see his belly pushing at the thin cotton shirt, and the plastic bands of the garden chair he sat in pressed against his lower back and made rolls of flesh protrude, meaty and tubular, stacked one above the other like bales of cloth. He was leaning forward with his elbows on his knees and reading a paper which was on the floor in front of him and turning the pages with his bare toes. He was holding a can of beans and occasionally he'd spoon a few of these into his mouth. No ordinary spoon this, but a square-tongued sugar spoon, silver-plated and made for the last visit of their Royal Majesties, King George VI and Queen Elizabeth, whose crowned heads in blue enamel tilted lovingly together above their coat of arms. As he read he wept and the tears landed on his knees and ran down the thick hair of his legs and stained the newspaper.

This struck me as extraordinary. A fellow who had been educated by the Margaret Brethren did not weep easily. But he was crying. Great shuddering sobs made the sailor shirt ripple and the tears glittered upon the thick hairs of his legs. His rather pear-shaped face wore a crumpled hopeless look, the big forehead creased. He bent his chin closer to his knees and with his free hand he clutched his hair which was dark and full of curls and strongly suggested his French blood given him by a Mauritian sailor father who left home shortly after his birth and never returned.

I saw the headline of the paper he held: Fiscal official in mystery slaying.

I knew he was reading about the death of Tony Ferreira who had been his friend in the old days when they were altar boys together under Father Lynch. This was to say in the time before Ferreira showed the signs of mathematical and financial abilities which were to carry him into the Civil Service and then to a high position in the Auditor General's office. It was extraordinary, given the advanced political education these boys received from Father Lynch, that any of them should ever go to work for the Regime, and yet two of them had done so. This boy whom Father Lynch in one of his wild prophesies had seen as a future visionary. Instead he became a Government accountant, of a very special and rarefied sort, but an accountant all the same. Someone had once asked Ferreira how he found it in him to go and work for the Regime and he simply shrugged and replied that he followed figures wherever they led. Figures were value free, they kept him out of politics and he found that a tremendous relief. Naturally his answer was received with

3

considerable disgust by those who knew him in the old days. Of course this was before an even more shocking betrayal when Trevor Van Vuuren joined the police.

The altar boys of Father Lynch were Theodore Blanchaille, Tony Ferreira, Trevor Van Vuuren, Roberto Giuseppe Zandrotti, Ronald Kipsel and little Michael Yates, afterwards Mickey the Poet. And I saw in my dream how in the old days they would occupy this very garden while Father Lynch sat beneath the Tree of Heaven; beside him on the picnic blanket two black boys, Gabriel and his brother Looksmart, the children of Grace Dladla, his housekeeper. I saw how Father Lynch reclined on an elbow and sipped a drink from a flask while he and the two black boys watched the white boys slaving in the sun, pulling up weeds, cutting back the bushes, raking, watering and desnailing Father Lynch's impossible parish garden. Gabriel and Looksmart Dladla were given bottles of fizzy orange to drink while Father Lynch leaned at his leisure, sipping iced cocktails from an aquamarine thermos flask. It did black boys good to sit in the shade and watch white boys work. It did white boys good to be watched. The mutual educational advantages of the experience should not be underestimated. This was among the many principles enunciated at Father Lynch's famous picnics.

Another was that it was given to each of us to discover the secrets of our own particular universe – but we should expect to be punished for it.

Another, that President Paul Kruger when he fled into exile at the end of the Boer War had taken large amounts of money with him – the missing Kruger millions. A glimpse of the purpose to which he had put these millions would be like a view of paradise – or at least as close to it as we were ever likely to get.

Another, that the Regime was corrupt, weak and dying from within – this at a time when our country was regarded as being as powerful as either Israel or Taiwan, had invaded almost every country along our border and even a number across the sea, some several times, always with crushing military victories.

Another, that destruction threatened everyone – this at a time when President Adolph Gerhardus Bubé had just returned from his extensive foreign tour of European capitals and initiated a new diplomatic policy of open relations with foreign countries which was said to have gained us many friends abroad and continued support in the world at large.

Father Ignatius Lynch, transplanted Irish hothead who never

4

understood Africa, or perhaps understood it too well, had been sent into this wilderness, he would say, indicating with a gesture of his small shapely hand the entire southern sub-continent of Africa, by error, misdirected by his boneheaded supervisors in Eire. A man with his gifts for the analysis of power, and the disguises which it took on, should have been retained at home as one who would recognise and appreciate the close bonds between clergy and rulers in his own country, or should have been posted to some superior European Catholic parish in Spain, or Portugal, or even to Rome, where his gifts might have been acknowledged. Being deprived of an adult, mature European culture where even babes and sucklings understood that the desirability of morality could never replace the necessities of power, and despite the realisation that Africa was not going to live up to his expectations, he worked hard at giving his boys a lively political sense.

Then, too, Father Lynch had alarming gifts for prophecy; he prophesied often, with tremendous conviction, of the future which lay ahead for his boys; prophecies truly imaginative, but magnificently inaccurate.

There was, too, this strange addiction to South African history, or at least to one of its distant and probably mythical sub-themes, the question of the missing Kruger millions, the great pile of gold which according to some legends Paul Kruger, President of the Transvaal Republic and leader of the Boer nation in the great war of freedom against the British imperialists at the turn of the century, had taken with him when he fled into exile as the victorious English *Rooineks* marched into the capital. This must have begun as a faint interest, a hobby perhaps, back in the mists of time, but what had been once a gentle historical investigation into a legend, which was very widely discounted by authorities, academic and political, became a passionate investigation into something which would supply the answer to the mystery of 'life as we know it', and was absolutely vital to their salvation, he told his boys – 'at least in so far as salvation could be defined or hoped for in this God-forsaken Calvinist African wilderness'. Father Lynch would express his belief with great finality, reclining on his elbow and sipping from his iced thermos beneath the Tree of Heaven as he watched his boys dragging at the leathery weeds.

I saw in my dream how Blanchaille sat in an empty room, with its bare parquet flooring and a few bad pieces of orange Rhodesian copper hanging on the walls, kudu drinking at a waterhole, and similar trifles, weeping as he read of the death of Ferreira, shaking his head and muttering. From somewhere outside the house, perhaps in the garden, I could hear angry voices raised, baying as if demanding to be let in and in my dream I saw who these angry ones were – they were Blanchaille's parishioners demonstrating against their priest.

Clearly unable to contain himself any longer, Blanchaille burst out with a choked cry: 'What shall I do? What the hell shall I do?'

And I saw in my dream four lines in small smudgy newsprint from the Press Association which reported that Dr Anthony Ferreira had been found dead in his ranch-style home in the Northern Suburbs. Police were investigating. Dr Ferreira had been his country's representative with various international monetary organisations abroad. Certain messages had been found written on the wall near the body.

It was possible to date this newspaper to the final days before the Onslaught because on the opposite page was a huge photograph of a darkened car window in which could be glimpsed the white blur of a man's face, and I knew at once that this was the picture of our President (our ex-President as he became), Adolph Gerhardus Bubé, on his celebrated foreign tour, the one which opened a new chapter in our international relations with the outside world. Ten countries in six days. It had been hailed at the time as a diplomatic triumph as well as a speed record. Photographs had appeared in the press: a man shielding his face outside the Louvre; an elderly gentleman in a hat on a bridge in Berne, a shadowy figure, back turned, feeding the pigeons in Trafalgar Square; a dim white face peering from the darkened windows of a black limousine speeding past the Colosseum . . . proofs of a triumph. It was the first time a president had been abroad since President Kruger fled to Switzerland in 1902. But Bubé's tour, alas, did not open the new chapter in foreign relations which the Government promised. He came home and we began digging in for the long siege. The Total Onslaught had begun.

Blanchaille had heard from Ferreira very shortly before his death. Of course his line had been tapped. The call had come out of the blue, but he knew instantly the familiar flat vowels and the unemotional voice: 'I'm sending you some money, Blanchie.'

'I don't need your money.'

'Oh, come on, of course you need money. I don't care what you use it for. Say some masses for my soul if you like, but I'm off. I'm through. Lynch was right, Blanchie. Something has been going on all these years. I've seen the books.'

Blanchaille did not wish to talk to Ferreira. He didn't like Ferreira. Ferreira had gone to work for the other side. He'd represented the country at the International Monetary Fund, he'd been co-opted into the office of the Auditor General. His speciality was currency movements, exchange control and foreign banking.

'You'll need this money, you'll need it to get where you're going. Don't be stubborn, Blanchie.'

'I'm not going anywhere.'

The eavesdroppers bugging the call handled their appliances in the customarily inept way. So many telephones, so many listeners needed. It was rumoured they took on students wishing to earn cash in their vacations. An unpleasant hum increasing in pitch and volume covered their piping exchanges. Ferreira's voice shrilled tinnily through the growing fog of interference. He was probably yelling his head off. 'I've had a revelation, Blanchie! I've found it – I've found the City of God!'

'Of what?' Blanchaille shrieked.

It was hopeless, the humming noise made the ear quiver. He knew then that the line had not merely been tapped, their conversation had been jammed.

The money came. There were hundreds, thousands perhaps. He hadn't counted it, wrapped in plastic film, crisp notes held tight with rubber bands. He hid it in a great tub of ice-cream in the freezer, scooping out the middle and sealing it with a plug of the peppermint chip and pistachio. It was the only food left in the house since Joyce had left, not counting the beans.

Now Ferreira was dead. The item itself in the paper was small, it might have been lost amongst the lists of divorces and the spreading columns of troop casualties on the Borders. The news of the Ferreira killing might not have been much but the stories surrounding it made clear the interest that it aroused. The young Secretary of the new Department of Communications, or Depcom, dynamic Miss Trudy Yssel, put out a statement deploring speculation about price falls on the Exchange and pointing out that the press must take a more responsible attitude and that this wasn't, after all, the Bubbles Schroeder murder case. This last a reference to one of the most celebrated murders in the country in which a pretty young whore named Bubbles Schroeder, who had slept with a number of people of note, was found lying in a grove of trees one morning with

7

a lump of limestone thrust into her mouth. And Yssel's boss, Minister for Parallel Equilibriums and Ethnic Autonomy, the formidable Augustus 'Gus' Kuiker who held, besides, the important portfolio of Cultural Communications, the Government's propaganda arm, took the opportunity to warn the press once again that the Government's patience was not limitless, that freedom was a privilege to be earned, not a licence for personal or political rumour-mongering. A further story reported the deaths of three brokers, Kranz, Lundquist and Skellum, and quoted the Chairman of the Exchange, Dov Solomon, as saying that an investigation had shown that these unfortunate accidents had no connection with one another, or with any other event. Blanchaille paid no attention to these attendant stories. It is probable that he detected no connection – but I saw in my dream that he would remember them later, when his investigative talents flowered as of course Father Lynch had prophesied they would.

Ah, the prophecies of Father Lynch! What is one to make of them?

Father Lynch had prophesied that Tony Ferreira was a natural visionary. Consequently he received the news of his interest in accountancy with what seemed like astonishing composure. He had taken to figures, he told Blanchaille once, because it kept his mind off his bruises. Now that was fair enough. Ferreira had been beaten since he was a baby. Indeed one of Blanchaille's earliest memories was seeing Ferreira arrive to serve early morning Mass with two eyes so swollen, so bruised, he could hardly see where he walked and had to take Blanchaille's arm as they made their way from the sacristy into the church, along the altar rail, through the gate and up the five grey marble steps leading to the altar. He could remember counting, 'here's one, now two coming up, here is three . . .' then they crossed the flat grey granite expanse and knelt together on the top altar step where Ferreira remained for the rest of the Mass too blind to move.

His father had been a bricklayer. Big head and a jutting lower lip. He drove a powder blue Pontiac with a pink plastic butterfly on the bonnet. Mrs Ferreira was white-faced, plain as a gate-post, cracked and peeling, whom Mr Ferreira carried everywhere with him like a club and used with terrible effect on his son when his own arm tired. Looking at them in their pew, the Ferreiras senior, he with pale hair on his sun-tanned arms and she solid, straight, wooden, with a blankness in their eyes as the Mass progressed, like two strangers who have darted out of the rain into church only to find they have

8

strayed into some foreign funeral service and must now patiently wait it out, masking their incomprehension in a slumberous passivity intended to suggest the appropriate demeanour. Hard to imagine them flinging themselves fist and boot on their only son. But Tony bore the marks.

Hemmed in on both sides his only escape was upward. Tony grew tall and elegant as if to repudiate his father's squat energy and outstrip it. With his father's thick pale hair and his mother's immobile features he was delicate, sensitive, smart. A war of attrition began as Tony set out deliberately to bait his father into extending himself by making plain his open contempt for his bricklaying business. Mr Ferreira responded, fighting back by opening branches, getting draughtsmen into his office; soon he denied he was a bricklayer and described himself as a quantity surveyor. He went on to employ other quantity surveyors and his picture even appeared in the papers as a man on the move in 'our thrusting, dynamic economy'. Father Lynch remarked on Ferreira's father's success, at which Tony nodded pleasantly: 'Yes, he's fully extended on all fronts now. His order books are bursting and he has substantial credit lines. The banks are falling over each other to lend him money.' When the big crash came Tony explained the reasons for it with gentle composure. 'It happens every day. He'd stretched himself to breaking point. Simply couldn't service his debts. Nailed by his own ambition. Crucified by his own success.' And then the final twist of the knife, elegant and terrible, Tony attended his father's bankruptcy hearing wearing a rich red tie and a glossy, heavily scented rose in his buttonhole and listened with rapt attention as the quantity surveyor's empire was dismantled brick by brick and thrown to his creditors.

Even Lynch heard of the crash.

'It seems your dad has been under fire, Tony.'

'Yes, Father. I'd say he's taken a good knock.'

'Snapped his head back, did it?'

'Decapitating.'

But why had Lynch described Ferreira as a visionary? The priest explained: 'They will tell you, the people who run this country, that they built the New Jerusalem in this brown, dry, prickly land. To see the lie behind the boast requires the eyes of the seer.'

Again: 'They will proffer the moral principles on which their empire is built, the keepers of the uneasy peace. Refuse their invitation. Ask instead to see the books.'

And: 'We are dealing here with questions of faith,' a favourite

9

opening, 'which in the neo-Calvinism followed by the Regime is in fact a matter of money. There's been no question of faith since Kruger left and his heirs forsook morality for power. We know this to be true. The difficulty will be in proving it.'

Father Lynch always had a line, a view. Mad he was, but reliable. I saw how desperately Blanchaille needed to consult the old priest long forsaken by his altar boys who not unnaturally believed they had outgrown him. The man I saw in my dream was cracking up. He wept and raved. Things were closing in. He sat in the empty house. Waiting, or hoping? His bags had never been unpacked since he arrived to take up his incumbency as parish priest in the new suburb of Merrievale. They waited for him now, by the door, three heavy tartan suitcases reinforced with leather straps. He had packed them when he left the camp and went to the priests' home in the mountains for rest and recuperation. He had carried them to his new post as parish priest in Merrievale. They contained clerical suits he never wore; books he did not read; boots, brushes, toiletries he no longer used; they were in effect the relics of a life he no longer led. Now and then he bought a new toothbrush, a pair of shoes, a couple of shirts whenever he needed them and left them behind when he moved on. But the cases he carried with him. Heavy, useless, but all he had to remind him of what, and to some extent where, he had been. He hadn't lasted long in Merrievale. His tenure as parish priest could be measured in three sermons and a siege. Outside his window his parishioners bayed for his blood. They waved banners and shook their fists, led by big-knuckled Tertius Makapan, the brick salesman. Word had it that Father Lynch was dying, but then Lynch had been dying ever since he'd met him. He'd made a profession of dying. 'I'm not long for this world, my boys!' he would shout from the shade of the Tree of Heaven. 'Get a move on!'

Lynch's love of easeful death wasn't quite what it seemed; it was rather as if he saw in it the chance of the transfer the Church had always denied him. Death might be the far country from whence no traveller returned – and if so he was all for it. Anywhere must be better than this. Hence the constant warnings: 'Hurry, my boys, I am not much longer for this life . . .' and 'Listen to these words of wisdom from a departing soul – the idealism of the Boer freedom fighters died with Kruger's flight into exile. What followed was not a success for Calvinist nationalism but a policy of "get what you can and keep it" – only remember to call it God's work.'

10

This urge to depart was more to be pitied than feared. Lynch knew that short of a miracle, or his own defection (and that meant air tickets and where was he to find the money?), he was condemned for life to this wild African place.

He suffered from dreams of money. Perhaps a rich relative would die and leave him a legacy? No, he was a practical man. But then again perhaps one of his altar boys would one day be rich enough to make a present to his old priest and mentor – enough to enable him to escape to what he called some serious country.

Perhaps this was the source of his fascination with the last days of the old Boer leader of the Transvaal Republic, Stephanus Johannes Paulus Kruger. Father Lynch knew the *Memoirs* very well, and he owned also what he claimed was the last surviving copy of *Further Memoirs of a Boer President*; a fat, red leather-bound book of reminiscences and prophecies apparently dictated by the exiled president to his faithful valet Happé in the old man's few remaining months of life in his rented house by the lake in Clarens, Switzerland, as the desolate, near-blind old lion mused over the future of his country and his people, broken by war and scattered in defeat to St Helena and Patagonia, Ceylon, Malaya, Madagascar, Mozambique, Angola and Tanganyika – a diaspora of Boers, the African Israelites, blown by history around the globe.

. . . And I shall use the short remaining time the Lord has been pleased to grant me to labour mightily, though conscious of my frailty and infirmity, to bring His people home to Him [Kruger promised in *Further Memoirs*], and since He has entrusted to my care the means whereby His will shall be accomplished I shall not rest until I find that place, 'the land', as the Lord said to Moses, 'which I have given unto the children of Israel' . . .

Father Lynch would interpret this for his altar boys, saying that by that 'place' Kruger undoubtedly meant a physical location, a home for dispossessed and faithful Boers who would not return to serve under the hated English, and by 'the means' Kruger certainly meant the treasure which had accompanied him into exile, the famed Kruger hoard, the gold millions of legend (taken in the form of ingots, bullion-bars or dust, who could say?) – from the inexhaustible mines of the Reef and smuggled out when the President fled.

This obsession with the millions came to outweigh all of Lynch's religious duties and the *Further Memoirs* became his daily office, his

11

'familiar bible' he called it, though it was widely believed among the altar boys he had written it himself.

It was precisely these unexpected ideas, combined with a complete lack of any religious scruple, which attracted to Father Lynch the boys from the nearby boarding hostel who were to form his little group of altar servers.

That Father Lynch was in disgrace with all the orthodox clergy appealed enormously to the wayward boys, handed by their parents into the care of Father Cradley, rector of the hostel: Ferreira, Blanchaille, Van Vuuren, Zandrotti, little Michael Yates, and, for a brief period, even Ronald Kipsel (afterwards the infamous Kipsel), these were the altar servers in Lynch's little guild. The boys detested the Church and yet were drawn to Father Lynch, for, after all, did the Church not hate Father Lynch? Wasn't it Father Lynch who insisted on integrating the two dozen black servants, washer-women and gardeners who knelt in the two final pews on either side of the nave, into the white congregation? Until ordered by Bishop Blashford to restore segregation immediately, because, desirable though a certain mixing might be in an ideal world and certain though it was that such things would one day happen – though not in our lifetime – the move was premature.

And was it not Father Lynch some years later who refused to introduce the new form of the Mass with its responses in English and its furtive handshakes and blushing kisses of peace, saying that although he understood the move was designed to counter dwindling congregations by giving the laity the idea that they were a vital part of the service, a move which he understood was known among theatre people as 'audience participation', he and his congregation were too old to change and he would continue to say Mass in the old Latin rite? Threats were made. They were ignored. And eventually the point was not pursued. After all, Lynch was an old man ministering to an elderly and diminishing congregation served by a little band of altar boys so bound by loyalty to the obstinate priest that they were probably beyond salvation.

And of course it was Lynch who, some years later still, when Blashford announced the Church's discovery of its new mission to Africa which meant reaching out to embrace its black brothers and sisters in Christ, retorted that having been ordered by his bishop to reverse his own attempt at integration some years before, he was not prepared to shame and humiliate his remaining black parishioners by ordering them back into the white pews from which they had been barred for so long. 'It is the nature of all power structures, whether armed or not, to present changes, however contradictory or cruel, as necessary progress towards the light,' Father Lynch, Parish Priest of St Jude's, taught his boys beneath the Tree of Heaven.

The church of St Jude, gloomy Catholic stronghold built of rough-hewn local stone with a wide-eaved heavy roof of grey slate, was set right next door to the young and rampantly spreading Calvinist university, a rock in a Rome-devouring sea, Lynch declared. It was from the nearby hostel for homeless boys that Father Lynch recruited his altar servers, for whom he promised many surprises in the years ahead, terrible surprises for his little guild. This was Father Lynch's way of dignifying his unpromising rag-bag of altar servers.

The hostel was presided over by another import, Father Benjamin Cradley, who came from England. He was soft, pink and mildly mannered and had come to them, as he so often said, from the Oratory. Of course they hadn't the faintest idea where that was. Some deep note in the resonant openness of the vowels suggested to Blanchaille a giant orifice, echoing cave or great clanging iron canal down which ships were launched. The Oratory! What a round, empty ring it had, that Oratory which had sent Benjamin Cradley to this wild hostel full of discarded boys in ill-mannered Africa. When you saw how little he understood of it all you realised how much the early white missionaries must have mystified and terrified the natives. What crusading ignorance was there! He sat up at high table, this fat man, happy to be on top of his little heap, this hostel for the children of the destitute, dead, divorced, distant and decamped families. It was a magnificently incongruous appointment. Cradley was not interested in where he was, or who these boys were, but gazed out into the middle distance through narrowed eyes, faint watery blue, continually screwed up against the cigarettes he chain-smoked, a few wisps of hair greased over the big forehead, the brass crucifix behind the belt moulded into the big belly pushed out before him, meditating not upon God but on the meal to come.

He wandered down the gleaming corridors of the hostel with a curiously beatific smile on his face, scattering cigarette ash and dreaming of dinner time. His large fleshy head with its neat sleek hair seemed too heavy for his shoulders and he always carried it cocked a little to the left, the heavily veined lids lowered over the eyes. This gave him a slightly oriental, half-devious look, underlined by an idiot simper quite at odds with that meaty, pink English face. When angered he flushed from the chin up and one could watch the blood pressure rising rosily like alcohol mounting in a thermometer. He was waited on hand and foot by two little nuns from some obscure Austrian order, the name of which Blanchaille could not remember – the White Sisters of the Virgin's Milk, or something exotic like that. Had it been? Anyway, they served and worshipped. Sister Gert, who was little and ugly, gnarled and nutty brown, looking not unlike Adolf Eichmann, and by her side the tall, plump, pretty Sister Isle, who spoke no English whatsoever but cooked, scrubbed, sewed and served with love and reverence verging on idolatory. Both of them called him 'Milord', and he spoke to them as one would to a pair of budgies: 'Who's a clever cook then?' and 'Father wants his pudding now – quick, quick!' And they tittered and curtsied and obeyed. They fussed about him at the head of the table, heaping his plate with fried potatoes and bending to flick away the ash which had lodged in the broad creases his belly made in his dusty black soutane. These two sisters in their white cotton habits and their short workmanlike veils, with their tremulous lips and their soft downy moustaches, and the way they chirped and flapped about their solitary, beaming, bovine master reminded him of tick birds attending to some old, solid bull. One day he remembered being delegated to clear the dishes at the head table and he stood close up watching Father Cradley digging plump fingers into a mound of Black Forest cake rather as a gardener drills the soil to take his seedlings, and then Blanchaille thought he understood why the Boers had gone to war against the English. He told Father Lynch.

'That is a misapprehension, boy. The English are capable of being lean, hard-faced killers just as the Boers are capable of running to fat. We should not judge things as they seem to be, or people as they look. If we all looked what we were the jails would be full.'

'The jails are full.'

'That's because we are in Africa. The jails here are built to be full. That doesn't remove from us responsibility for trying to get underneath the layer of illusion. Why is it, for instance, that although everyone here knows they're finished they appear not to have made contingency plans? You *do* all know you're finished? That you're on the way out? Your small white garrison can never hold out against the forces ranged against it. The end of your world is at hand.'

'It always has been,' said Blanchaille. 'We got in before you. We

14

had that thought before you arrived.'

'Yes, but yours is a nightmare. I'm telling you the truth.'

Even then, young and ignorant, he felt the presumption of an Irish priest talking of apocalypse in this knowing way. What had this old leprechaun with his thousands of years of history, still green and damp from the bogs of Ireland, to tell an African child about the end of the world? You were born with the sense you'd been perched on the edge of the African continent for about two-and-a-half minutes and in that time you'd discovered that you were white and blacks didn't like you; that you were English and so the Dutch Africans known as Afrikaners didn't like you; that you were Catholics and not even the English liked you.

No, there was nothing about the apocalypse which Lynch could teach him. Power was another matter. Proper Europeans, you learnt from history, had a sense and experience of power, of killing and being killed on a wide and effective scale which was quite foreign to Africa. Efficient slaughter they understood. Proper wars. Even Cradley understood that and responded to it. You saw it in his appointment of Van Vuuren to be head boy of the hostel, to keep order among steel lockers and wooden beds in the dormitories. Van Vuuren with his strong square jaw, jet-black hair combed crisply up to a great wave and sleeked back behind his ears, his hard pointed chin and his bright blue eyes, the amazing muscles and the ability to hit and talk at the same time. All this recommended him to Father Cradley as having an aura of moral leadership as a result of which 'we have decided to elect him to this position of authority.'

'We have elected him? Jesus! It's as if the early Christians elected one of their lions as Pope,' said Zandrotti.

Van Vuuren administered fair-minded, fair-fisted power. It was difficult to bear him any resentment. There were certain rules and he saw to it that all the others observed them. He enforced order with a terrifying cordiality while continuing himself to flaunt every rule and regulation. He was really a law unto himself. He smoked, he drank, he slipped away with girls, drove a car without a licence, slunk off to the movies with a half jack of vodka sticking out of his back pocket and sprayed large grey streaks into his black sideburns. And this apparent contradiction never drew any criticism from any of his victims since he rested so securely on what must have seemed to him a God-given assignment to do what came best to him, drinking and whoring on the one hand, and enforcing hostel authority on the other. Father Lynch had prophesied that Trevor Van Vuuren was heading straight for the priesthood.

15

A few years later he joined the police, a move which did nothing to deter Father Lynch's faith in his own prophecies, and if asked about Van Vuuren he would say that he was engaged upon taking holy orders, that he was a man who had dedicated his life to truth. 'His hands,' Father Lynch maintained, despite the fact that all who knew him never thought of him as having hands but fists, 'his hands will one day baptise children, bless young brides and succour the dying . . .'

It was Blanchaille who had become a priest, but Lynch would have none of it. He was at police college, he maintained, and when Blanchaille called on him in a dog-collar he declared that he thought it was a wonderful disguise.

Of Zandrotti he was rather more vague: 'An angel of sorts though of course without angelic qualities. But a go-between, a messenger, an interpreter moving between the old world and the new.' Angel? He was too ugly, a glance showed you that. Zandrotti was the son of a crooked builder with a great raw salami face, who wore creamy, shiny suits, had a great round head and a round body tapering to tiny pigeon-toes. The father Zandrotti came once a month to the hostel in some great American car to abuse his skinny little son, Roberto, with his long white face thick with freckles and his wild, spiky black hair.

Everyone lived in the suburban Catholic ghetto which occupied no more than perhaps a couple of square miles and included Father Lynch's parish of St Jude, the hostel for displaced boys, the Catholic School of St Wilgefortis run by the Margaret Brethren across the way, the bishop's house, home of the unspeakable Blashford, with its large lawns, its vineyards and its chapel which backed on to the mansion occupied by the Papal Nuncio, Agnelli, to whom Father Gabriel Dladla later served as secretary, while also serving as chaplain to Bishop Blashford. Around this ghetto reached the long arms of the new National University, claws they were, embracing it in a pincer movement. Father Lynch used to take the boys up to the bell tower and show them how the Calvinist enemy was surrounding them, 'Truly a cancerous growth, note the classic crab formation. It will consume us utterly one of these days.'

And then I saw in my dream how Blanchaille remembered himself and the other altar boys in the dark sacristy of St Jude where the altar boys robed for early morning Mass, for Benediction and weekly Wednesday Novena. Cramped like the crew's quarters of some old schooner, smelling of wax candles, of paraffin, of white Cobra floor polish, of altar wine, incense, rank tobacco, of the

16

pungent lemon and lime after-shave lotion which came off Father Lynch in waves as Mass wore on and he began sweating beneath his heavy vestments, and the terrifically strong brandy fumes from the old drunken sacristan, Brother Zacharias, of the socks and sweat of countless frantic altar boys dragging from the cheap boxwood cupboards their black cassocks, limp laced and always begrimed surplices, with a noisy clash of the frail, round shouldered wire hangers against the splintered plywood partitions. While from the robing room next door, so close you could hear the rumblings of his stomach knowing as it did that Mass still lay between it and breakfast, there came the smooth unceasing polished tirade of Father Lynch's invective as he briskly cursed the scrambling altar boys next door for the dirty-fingered, incompetent and unpunctual little poltroons they were. 'Oh, I shall die of hunger, or boredom, or both, at the hands of you little devils, far from home in this strange hot land, to be done to death by boredom and waiting . . .' Knock-knock went his black hairy knuckles on his biretta, 'Come along! Come along! What are you waiting for – the Last Judgement?' Those were the weekday Masses, early morning, low and swift.

In theory Brother Zacharias was there to assist the robing of Father Lynch. In reality he lay slumped in the chair most mornings nursing the hangover he'd got the previous evening from a colossal consumption of altar wine, cheap sweet stuff which came in thick-necked bottles with the Star of David stamped on the label, supplied by the firm of Fattis and Monis. Mass began a race between Father Lynch and his altar boys, as next door he struggled into his stole, maniple, chasuble, picked up the gold and bejewelled chalice, dropped onto his head with the finality of a man closing a manhole his four-winged biretta so that it rested on his jug ears and, swinging the key of the tabernacle on its long silver chain, he pounded on the plywood partition: 'Where is that damn server this morning?' And the server in question, frantically buttoning up his high collar and smoothing the lace that hung in tatters from the sleeves of his surplice, swooped out in front of him and led him down, out of the sacristy through the Gothic arch of the side chapel and on to the altar: *Introibo ad altarem Dei* . . . 'I will go to the altar of God . . . to God who gives joy to my youth . . .'

'– and employment to his priests,' Father Lynch liked to add.

On Sundays, in the olden times, when Father Lynch still had priests beneath him, before his clash with Blashford over his wish to integrate the pews, he had revolutionary dreams: 'Black and white, one Church in Christ,' Lynch said.

'More like a recipe for bloody disaster,' Blashford responded. 'Your parishioners will shoot you.'

These were the days before 'African renewal' or 'the mission to the townships', or 'the solidarity with our black brothers and sisters in Christ', with which Blashford was so closely associated in later years – it was before, in short, as Lynch said, 'the powers-that-be had looked closely at the figures'.

In those days then, on Sundays, there was in Lynch's church an occasional High Mass with enough priests to go around and of course Van Vuuren would dominate the altar as Master of Ceremonies, adroit, self-possessed; taller than most of the priests before the tabernacle, this smoothly assured MC moved, bowed, dispensed and disposed with expert precision. His command of the most technical details of the High Mass, the air of brooding concentration with which he overlooked the three concelebrating priests, his grave air of commanding authority and his expert choreography, moving between epistle and gospel sides of the altar, between chalice and the water and wine, between tabernacle and communicants, between incense bearers and bell boys, between altar and rail, was a marvel to see. His hands joined before his chest, the fingers curving in an elegant cathedral nave so that the tips almost touched his straight nose. The professional hauteur of it, the utter oiled assurance with which Van Vuuren managed such matters, always struck Blanchaille as a wonder and as being utterly at odds with the way he used his fists back in the dormitory in the hostel when he was about Father Cradley's business.

Thick creamy aromatic smoke rose from the bed of glowing charcoal on which they scattered the incense seeds, the smoke entered the nostrils like pincers, pierced the sinus passages and burst in a fragrant spray of bells somewhere deep inside the cranium. You never coughed, you learnt not to cough. Only the new ones coughed in the holy smoke. The new ones like little Michael Yates, who was Blanchaille's boat boy and was afterwards to become Mickey the Poet, martyr and victim of the traitor Kipsel, so tiny then that he came up to Blanchaille's hip and stood beside him holding the incense boat, the silver canoe with the hinged lid which closed with a snap upon the spoon at the flick of a finger. Father Lynch spooned incense from the incense boat, spreading it on the glowing charcoal in the thurifer where it crackled and spat and smoked. Van Vuuren, standing directly behind Lynch, sighted down his perfectly touching forefingers during the ladling of the incense and then with a contained nod, satisfied, dismissed Blanchaille and his boat boy. Both backed away slowly and bowed. Then Blanchaille adjusted the thurifer, lowering its perforated sugar-shaker cap down through the billowing incense, adjusting its closing with the complicated triple-chain pulley and then returned with little Yates to his place, swinging his smoking cargo before him slowly in a long lazy curve over his toe-caps. The fat puff of incense to left and right marked the furthest reaches of the swing. Van Vuuren wearing his elegant, economical, sober black and white cassock and surplice seemed in his plain costume almost a rebuke to the priests in their gaudy emerald-green vestments who lifted their arms to show the pearl-grey silk of their maniples, and turned their backs on their congregations to show the sacred markings, the great jewel-encrusted P slashed by the silver and oyster emphasis of the magic X. Van Vuuren carried more authority than all of them and it was about him, around the strong fixed point, that the other holy flamboyancies revolved like roman candles in the thickening aromatic fog of incense. Lynch had something of the truth in his prophecy about Van Vuuren because when you looked at Van Vuuren you knew, you said, he could have been a priest already. It was, Blanchaille supposed later, the air of authority that impressed, the sense of knowing what to do and when you had grown up among flounderers, it was an impressive sight.

All Father Lynch's boys, with the exception of Ferreira, lived in the hostel across the road from the Catholic High School of St Wilgefortis, a curious saint much celebrated in Flanders and generally depicted with a moustache and beard which God in his grace had granted to her to repulse the advances of would-be suitors. The school was run by the Margaret Brethren, a Flemish teaching order of brothers who, for reasons never known, took as their model of life the example of their medieval patroness, the formidable St Margaret of Cortona, who after a dissolute early life repented of her sins and began whipping into saintliness her flesh and the flesh of her flesh, her illegitimate son, the fruit of her seduction by a knight of Montepulciano.

Frequent and savage beatings she no doubt felt were deserved by this walking reproach to her saintly aspirations. At the same time she went about calling on the citizens of Cortona to repent, and given the lady's determination it was a call that would not be denied. As Margaret in the thirteenth century so did her Brethren in the twentieth, they beat the devil out of their boys with tireless piety and unstinting love for their souls and if this sometimes resulted in certain injuries, a simple fracture or bleeding from the ear, why then the Brothers laid on the strap or stick once more, happy in their hearts they were drawing close to their beloved patroness.

Education was not their aim but salvation. Their job was to unveil the plots and stratagems by which unsuspecting boys were led into mortal sin, to sudden death and to eternal damnation. Improper thoughts, loose companions, tight underwear, non-Catholic girl-friends, political controversy, these were the several baits which sprung the trap of sudden death and broke the neck of Christian hope. Yet they could be beaten, they were beaten, daily.

The boys of the Catholic school endured their years under the whip with sullen obedience. Like some small unruly, barbarian state crushed by an occupying army, they paid lip service. They bided their time. They worshipped the gods of their conquerors in public, and spat on them in private; sat, knelt or stood stonily through the obligatory daily prayers and Masses with heads bowed only to return to the worship of their own horrid deities the moment the school gates closed behind them. The gods of their underground church were genuinely worthy of worship. They were lust, loose-living, idleness, tobacco, Elvis Presley, liberalism, science, the paradise called Overseas, as well as those bawdy spirits whom some held were hiding in girls' brassières and between their legs and of which strange exhilarating legends circulated among the hidden faithful in the bicycle sheds, the changing rooms and lavatories. And of course what made these native gods more powerful, more adorable than any other, was the fact that they so clearly haunted and terrified the Margaret Brethren. The Margaret Brethren taught the knowledge of death, they cultivated the more advanced understanding of dying, of judgement, of hell and heaven. Education for them was the pursuit of a reign of terror. The dirty little secrets of the native gods which promised fun, excitement, escape, horrified them and they fought them tooth and nail.

If this strengthened the boys' sense of coming doom, of impending Armageddon, that was because they were so naturally adapted to it. They grew up with it, it came as no surprise to learn that the end of the world was at hand, though there was no way they could have explained this to the uncomprehending Flemish immigrants who simply couldn't understand how it was possible to be hated by anybody, except perhaps the French. The Margaret Brethren taught lonely, sudden violent death as the Wages of Sin. But white children of a certain sort, born in South Africa, then as now, knew of a wider and more general catastrophe, that the world was very likely to end in violence and sooner rather than later. One noted at one's mother's knee that the end of the world very probably was at hand and it was only a question of time before the avenging hordes swept down from the north.

Whether this was true or not didn't matter. It was believed. It was an article of faith.

And then there was the deep loathing which the Margaret Brethren instinctively felt for the wayward and disreputable Father Lynch, another of the highly impressive qualities about him that attracted to him his altar servers.·

Blanchaille was among the first. Blanchaille's mother lived three thousand miles away and sent him to the hostel when he was seven. She had been destitute and so the hostel, and the Margaret Brethren across the road, waived their fees and took him in in the name of Catholic charity. Blanchaille's father, a Mauritian sailor, had deserted his mother when she fell pregnant and never returned and yet she kept his name and passport, drew one for her son later which she renewed religiously, placing her faith in the French connection, clearly determined that her son would one day return to his motherland in triumph, like Napoleon. This foreign document embarrassed Blanchaille and he hid the passport for years. No one else had one. It looked strange and besides he wasn't going anywhere. No one was going anywhere. The others teased him about it, calling him Frenchie. But after he'd hidden it they forgot about it and began calling him Blanchie instead, a name that stuck. Trevor Van Vuuren appeared to have no parents but he had an elder brother who worked on the whalers and drove a bottle-green MG sports, which was all terrifically exciting. Zandrotti's father was a crooked businessman, a building contractor handling large commissions in the Government road programme. He made it his business to add rather too much sand to his cement and eventually catastrophe overtook him when bridges began collapsing across the country. A huge hulking man, he'd arrive in his blood-red Hudson Hornet to visit his skinny knock-kneed little son with his spiky hair and his ghostly pallor. Zandrotti Senior made these visits specifically for the purpose of abusing and ridiculing young Roberto. This so impressed the Margaret Brethren that they presented Zandrotti Senior with his very own scapular of the Third Order of St Francis, a devotional association to which they were vaguely attached for reasons never made clear except that Margaret of Cortona had been fond of it. His father, as Roberto later explained, had absolutely no culture and repaid the honour by making his mistress dance naked on a table for a visiting delegation of Portuguese Chianti merchants

21

wearing the scapular as a G-string. This story so delighted Father Lynch that he suggested that since the scapular had bounced up and down on what he called 'the lady's important point of entry', they should return it in the same wrapper to the Margaret Brethren challenging them to touch it to their nostrils and try to identify the fragrance, providing the helpful clue that they inhaled that very perfume which had so excited the saint's knightly seducer back in the bad old days when she was plain Margaret, just another unmarried mother of Cortona.

This love of the blasphemous jest was one of Father Lynch's appealing characteristics. Another was the conviction that he was dying and hence everything must be done in a hurry, a conviction repeated often but without any apparent sign of alarm since haste did not preclude style.

Kipsel seldom came to Mass and never to the picnics. Perversely as ever, Lynch praised his loyalty and predicted that Kipsel would go far in life.

Last in the group but first in martyrdom, poor Michael Yates, later Mickey the Poet. If there was any epitaph for him it was that he never knew what was going on. It might have been inscribed above his lost gravestone – 'He never had the faintest idea.' He was only to write one short poem, four lines of doggerel, which led Lynch to call him Mickey the Poet, and the name stuck. Lynch went on to discern in him, in that wild prophetic way, 'some gymnastic ability'.

Now I saw in my dream how Blanchaille grieved at the death of Ferreira. I saw him shaking his head and muttering to himself repeatedly: 'What shall I do? What shall I do? First Mickey the Poet, then Miranda, now Ferreira.'

Naturally he detected in these violent deaths real signs that the end was near, this fuelled his anxiety, deepened his general feeling of doom, of approaching extinction. It is common enough at the best of times in beleaguered minorities in Africa, this feeling of looming apocalypse. Blanchaille's people, a despised sub-group within a detested minority waited for the long-expected wrath to fall on them and destroy them. They didn't say so, of course. They didn't say anything unless drunk or tired or very pushed – and then they would say, 'Actually, we're all finished.' Or ruined, some of them said, or washed-up, or words a lot worse.

This was what in my dream I heard Blanchaille say again and again as he stared into his occupied garden. He knew, as I know, that as the years have passed more and more people have felt this

22

and they knew it to be true and the greater their perception of truth so greater became the efforts to disbelieve it, to push it to the back of their minds, to discredit it until at last, at the time of the Total Onslaught, it became a punishable offence to admit to the possibility. You could be punished, arrested, beaten up, imprisoned for defeatism in the face of the enemy, for after all there was by then a war going on. In my dream I saw Blanchaille place his hands on the window-sill and bow his head, his whole body bent as if something heavy pressed down on his back and he leaned forward rolling his forehead against the window-pane and staring into the garden, the very picture of a man oppressed, weighed down. He thought only of ways of escape. But from what and in which direction remained dark to him.

CHAPTER 2

And when in my dream I saw how Blanchaille stood at his window looking out across the garden towards the small knot of angry folk outside the front gate, I knew them to be his parishioners. They were the stony ground on which his seed had fallen. He had preached, he had warned, but the lambs would not hear, instead they banded together and drove their shepherd out. Tertius Makapan, in a mustard suit and luminous magenta tie, leaning against his dusty Toyota. A colossal man, a brick salesman, responsible for co-ordinating the attack on him; there were, too, his storm-troopers, Duggie and Maureen Kreta, Makapan's willing creatures, formerly the treasurer and secretary of the Parish Council (before the Council was reconstituted into the Parochial Consensus Committee, the consensus being that Blanchaille must go); and poor Mary Muldoon, mad Mary, who knew no better, or at least he had thought so until she had tricked him out of his key to the church and so allowed the Committee to lock and bar the place against him; and there, hanging back, his black housekeeper, Joyce, who had joined them quite suddenly one night. Simply abandoned the dinner she was cooking for him and left his steak smoking on the stove and went over to his enemies. Maureen and Duggie Kreta carried a large banner: PINK PRIEST MUST GO! They waved the poles and flapped the banner at him when they saw him at the window.

PINK PRIEST MUST GO! *Priest*? The use of the singular case annoyed him. Not that it was intentional, but merely echoed the Kretas' way of speaking. Maureen, round and determined with thick, rather greasy dark hair, and Duggie, some years younger, sharp face, thin mouth and full, blond hair. They rode everywhere on an ancient Puch autocycle wearing white peaked crash helmets and dark blue macs. They spoke to him as if he were a not very intelligent puppy. Thus Maureen: 'Father want to watch out for some of the guys in this parish who don't give a button on Sunday, look at the plate like it was something the dog brought in. In fact some of 'em only look in it at all like they're wondering what they can pull out. Father got to watch 'em like a hawk.' And Duggie, parish treasurer's briefings about lack of funds: 'Not two cents to

24

rub together most times. You have to raise some funds. The father before Father was a hot shot at raising funds. Charity walks. Charity runs. That was Rischa. Running priest.'

PINK PRIEST MUST GO!

Blanchaille wished to pull down the window and shout at them: 'Yes, pink priest going! White priest come, pink priest go. Green priest yes, black priest no!' It was like living in a bloody nursery. Well, he was going to oblige. With pleasure.

He was getting out just as fast as he could.

The need to escape had become for Blanchaille an obsession: if he asked himself what it was he wanted, he answered – rest, peace. Now at the time of the Total Onslaught this feeling was naturally strong, as it always is at the time of killing and much blood, among people of all colour and political persuasions, sad to say. The dead were to some extent envied. They were out of it at least. Those who had disappeared were considered to be fortunate also. Nobody knew where they had disappeared to and no one cared. It was whispered by some that those who had vanished were perhaps also dead but this was widely discounted – they were said to have 'gone pilgrim', meaning they were believed to be travelling overseas, thus distinguishing them from the truly dead soldiers who were said to have 'joined the big battalion'. In war time, said Father Lynch, morphine for the wounded, euphemisms for the survivors. So people bravely pointed out that in war time casualties must be expected and it was best not to question too deeply. It was devoutly to be hoped that the dead and those who had disappeared had gone to some happier place where they would at least be at peace. Now, when asked where this place was, some would have replied vaguely that it was somewhere overseas, others would have given a religious answer and pointed to the sky; a few very brave souls would have whispered quietly that perhaps they'd gone to 'that shining city on the hill' or to 'that colony of the blessed'; or to that 'rest-home for disconsolate souls', which legend held President Paul Kruger established for his homeless countrymen somewhere in Switzerland early this century. Despite threats of imprisonment issued regularly by the Regime, the legend of Kruger's heritage persisted, a holy refuge, a haven, funded with the golden millions he had taken with him when he fled into exile. The Regime scoffed at these primitive, childish beliefs and punished their public expression with prison terms. They were joined by the academic historians who regularly issued bulletins exploding the 'myth of the Kruger millions'. People you met were similarly dismissive, in fact it was not unusual to begin a conversation by remarking, apropos of nothing at all, 'Naturally I don't believe a word about the gold Kruger stole from the mines. Not a bloody word of it.' But everyone, people, historians, perhaps even the Regime itself, continued to trust in and hope for the existence of that much dreamed of distant, better place. Some became obsessed and fled. So it was with Blanchaille.

When he could stand it no longer Blanchaille applied for a long leave of absence. The Church of course, through a number of unhappy experiences, knew the signs. Bishop Blashford sent Gabriel Dladla to find out the reason.

'Is there a girl, we wondered?' Gabriel asked gently.

'There was a girl. But not here.'

'Yes, we thought there was a girl. Somewhere.'

The ease with which Gabriel followed him into the past tense chilled Blanchaille.

'There was a girl, a nursing sister, a Canadian. Miranda was her name. I met her years ago soon after I went to work in the camps or what she called the new growth industries, the growing heaps of unwanted people springing up everywhere in the backveld.'

'I would hardly call that an industry,' said Gabriel with a gently disapproving frown. 'The camps are a scandal, an affront to human dignity. A sin. The Church condemns the camps and the policy of racial Hitlerism which creates them.'

'It was one of her jokes,' said Blanchaille. 'She had a distinctive brand of humour. She had what she called a traditional job, a nursing sister in the township. She refused to dramatise the job. "I could be doing something similar in Manitoba," she would say, "It's nothing special." The difference between us, she insisted, was that I was doing something important but she was just doing a job. "Don't build it up. I'm not giving a performance," she said. She said I was at the forefront of things in the camps, learning how to process the people who had been thrown away; "Soon the whole country will run on this human garbage," she said. It was another of her jokes.'

'I don't see the joke,' Gabriel replied tightly.

'Nor in a sense did I. "That's your problem, Blanchie, you don't see the joke," she said.'

'The camps are an obscenity. Your work has been crucial in showing that,' Gabriel persisted.

'What about the townships?'

He shrugged. 'They're institutions. At least they're peaceful now. But the camps. . . !'

26

'And yet the Church goes in and supports them, cleans them, strengthens their existence.'

'Supports the people in them. An enormous difference. The camps are there. They're real. We have to work in the real world.'

'Look Gabriel, once there were no camps and that was the real world, and the Church lived in it; then there were camps and that was the real world and the Church lived in it. One day, please God, there will be no camps again and that will be the real world and the Church will live in it. No wonder they call the Church eternal.'

'I think it might be better if we left the Church out of this and talked of carnal matters.' Gabriel's tone was mild.

'What about the girl?'

'She seduced me.'

Gabriel smiled, 'Now, now, you mustn't try to shock me.'

'We made love several times in her car, an old Morris Minor, in the township after dark. It was rather like a tickbird mating with a crow, she in her white starched uniform and I in my cassock. Or like being locked in a room full of curtains fighting towards the light. After several experiments we discovered that the best way was to remove her underwear and lift her skirt to her chin and then I settled myself on her first lifting my cassock to my waist and dropping it gently so it floated around us, covering us, and we made love as it were in this warm, black tent, within the more intense darkness of the African night. It was a very private affair. Anyone walking past the car and shining a bright light on us would have seen nothing but a kind of Siamese twin, black and white and contracting strangely.'

Gabriel held up a hand. 'What ended it?'

'She was murdered.' Now he had the satisfaction of seeing the astonishment crease Gabriel's smooth face. 'She was pulled from her car in the township one morning as she drove to her clinic, and stoned. It seems mainly large pebbles were thrown. There were some half bricks as well, I believe. I went to identify the body. They pulled the big tray out of the fridge, and it wasn't her. The skull was crushed, you see, or perhaps you don't — unless you've examined head injuries on that scale. The features had shifted, slipped to the side like a floppy rubber mask. The face hung. It was so covered with blood, so smashed, she was unrecognisable. I remember thinking it was almost as if the mob that stoned her had wanted especially to destroy the head. The rest of the body carried very large bruises. I couldn't identify her in the strict sense but I knew, as one would know. And then the point began to get to me. You see, I realised that, Jesus! there must have been some of her patients in the crowd who stoned her. People whom she had nursed, saved their children maybe, and this was what they had done to her! And all around me I could hear the outrage beginning. Here was this woman who'd given her life to these bastards and here's what she got in return. Then a funny thing happened. I laughed. I faintly got the point. Miranda might have expected this official reaction. This predictable outrage. And I knew – she would have opposed it. In her book nurses died, like everyone else. Sometimes they got murdered, not merely here but in New York, or Blantyre, or Tokyo, and yes it was tragic but it was not special, it didn't happen for mystical reasons. But we wouldn't believe that. In our superiority, Miranda's death had to be notable. It had to mean something really nasty. In fact Miranda was too important to be allowed to suffer her individual death, she wouldn't be allowed to die, she had to live, for the sake of the propaganda we fed ourselves to enable us to go on saying that this sort of thing should not, ought not, *must* not happen. In our war of words Miranda's death was a big event. But in terms of her own spilt blood, hell, it didn't matter a damn. What mattered were the detonator words, "should," "must", "ought", which we can use to blow up the enemy. The enemy wants us little, ordinary, human, while we want to be big and important. We care about our position relative to the audience. We want to put on a good show. Everything depends on how things are looking on the stage. Making a performance. . . .'

'It's a pity in the way there is no woman – any longer,' Gabriel said. 'The Bishop is sympathetically disposed, in the new enlightenment which prevails after Vatican II. The sexual problems of his priests deserve loving consideration. Perhaps you read his piece in *The Cross*? However, in your case you might be better advised to apply for a transfer.'

'Right! I apply for a transfer – to the world next-door. Kindly inform His Grace.'

PINK PRIEST MUST GO!

Blanchaille did not consider himself particularly pink and he certainly no longer thought of himself as a priest, but he was in full agreement with the sentiment expressed in the crudely lettered banner the Kretas waved so enthusiastically – he was fully prepared, indeed he most devoutly wished, to go.

Gabriel Dladla had returned with the Bishop's reply soon after the siege began.

'I'm afraid it can't be done, Blanchie. This is your place now.'

'I'm finished here.'

'Finished? For heaven's sake, you've barely started.'

Gabriel had arrived wearing what he called his second hat. This wasn't a hat at all but referred to the car he was driving, a sleek black Chrysler belonging to the Papal Nuncio, Agnelli, whose secretary he was, as well as serving as Bishop Blashford's chaplain, choice appointments both indicating to a sceptical world that the Roman Church in Southern Africa took to its heart its black followers, indeed did more than that, set them soaring into the firmament, rising stars. Gabriel had come a very long way from the picnic basket in Father Lynch's garden when the two brothers, Gabriel and Looksmart, sat flanking the little priest. 'My two negro princes', he called them, as they sat watching the altar boys struggle with the weeds. Gabriel's was the only entry into the priesthood which had been approved. His brother Looksmart's attempt had failed when the new black theology took hold of him and he burnt the Bible on the steps of the seminary as 'the white man's manual of exploitation' and joined the political underground. Blanchaille's vocation had been derided and ignored. Only Gabriel's decision to become a priest had been applauded.

'He is only doing what any intelligent boy would do who wishes to rise. His behaviour would be entirely logical in Spain, or Portugal or Ireland. May we skip any tiresome talk of faith or morals? Gabriel intends to get ahead.'

Father Gabriel Dladla in his beautifully tailored dark suit and its pristine dog-collar, in his soft black fedora which he did not remove in the course of their interview, his chunky gold watch which he consulted with elegant economy in an unmistakable signal that the interview was nearing its end, with his whole air of intelligent, assured concentration with which he listened to Blanchaille but which did not suppress the faint air of impatience of a busy man with other, more important things on his mind. This was once the barefoot boy on the blanket translated in what seemed like a wink of time into a personage of weight and responsibility in the Church hierarchy. And it was with a wink surely that Blanchaille could move him back again to the blanket in the garden. He tried and failed. His eyelid fluttered. Gabriel remained the elegant, deft, important young person he was.

'Now I'm sorry Blanchie but I must be off. I have a party of visiting Italians to collect from the airport, guests of the Papal Nuncio. They're flying in from Rome. Do you know Rome at all? I adore Rome. Quite apart from the obvious connections in our case, it is the most surprising, rejuvenating of cities.'

'Gabriel, I cannot stay here. There must be another parish . . .'

'If you ever go, I recommend to you the Piazza Navona, a square which should be everyone's first glimpse of Rome, not even the tourists can ruin its perfect proportions . . .'

'Another appointment –'

'Another appointment? But this is your appointment and I am here to let you know that Bishop Blashford confirms you in this appointment. There is nowhere for you to be but here. Nowhere to go but back, back to Pennyheaven, this time for an indefinite stay.'

Blanchaille watched him walking down the garden path. The protesting parishioners cheered when he approached. Gabriel doffed his hat, waved cheerily to them and was gone.

Blanchaille phoned Lynch. The old priest cackled at the news of the visit. The electronic eavesdroppers chirruped and squawked along with him.

'Speak up, Blanchie, and keep it short. The line's heavily and ineptly tapped. The bastards never worked out how to use the equipment they import in such quantities from America.'

'I'm thinking of moving on.'

'Good. Knew you would come to your senses one day. Perhaps we should have a few words. Where are you?'

Blanchaille told him.

'My God, right in the sticks. What's that noise? I can hear people shouting.'

'Those are my parishioners. I'm under siege.'

Lynch's laughter was drowned in a shriek of static.

And I saw in my dream how Blanchaille's stay in the new peri-urban suburb of Merrievale as parish priest of the spanking-new church of St Peter-in-the-Wild had come to end in undignified confusion after just one month. The defection of his black housekeeper Joyce upset him particularly. She'd never got used to his arrival or the loss of the man he had replaced. How dreadfully unfavourably he must have compared with his predecessor, the youthful, energetic Syrian, Father Rischa. The Parish Consensus Committee had got to Joyce. They told her that Blanchaille was on his way out, they'd shown her the fatal mark of blood upon his lintel imprinted there by the Angel of Death who had passed that way and she'd shot off like a rabbit, an absolute winner in the Petrine stakes, in the thrice-crowing cock awards. Traitress. To hell with her!

St Peter-in-theWild was Blanchaille's first parish and his last. He hadn't been there two minutes when the complaints began.

'And what is the nature of your complaint, Mr Makapan?'

'History,' came the simple if unexpected reply from the brick salesman. 'Not only your own particular history, but your lack of understanding of the historical process in general and of our parts in it.'

Blanchaille's particular history – what was it? Unremarkable, really. A hostel boy, one-time altar server who had gone up to the seminary to become a priest. Why a priest? Because he wished to be like Father Lynch who understood the system of the Regime and sought to expose it. 'You are not priestly material,' Father Lynch had cautioned. 'You are raised with the puritan, primitive, moralising web of the system and cannot destroy it, but what you can do is to hunt down the guilty men and bring them to book. That is your real vocation. Blanchaille, the police college waits for you – answer the call!'

For once Lynch and the Bishop were in agreement. Blashford opposed his entry into the seminary and when the time came for Blanchaille's ordination, continued to oppose it, avoiding the duty to perform the ceremony by being indisposed. Instead Blanchaille was ordained by a visiting Hungarian archbishop who was deported soon after the event for gross interference in the domestic affairs of the country. Blanchaille had long suspected Blashford's hand behind the expulsion. Newly ordained, his first visit to Lynch had been disastrous. Lynch had stood him up in the pulpit and introduced him to the congregation as 'the boy you might remember having served at this altar for many a year, and is now a policeman engaged in important undercover work in the country, hence his disguise . . .'

Blanchaille had done no parish work. After six years of moral theology mixed with intense sexual agonies in the seminary, applying the purity paddle (a miniature ping-pong bat without the usual rubber facings) with a short, downward slap morning and night, whenever his errant member stiffened beneath his soutane, he went to work in the transit camps, the garbage heaps where the human rubbish, the superfluous appendages were thrown away; the huge shanty towns in the remote and barren veld set aside by the Regime as temporary homes for a variety of black people: there were in the camps the dependants, wives, children, grandparents of black workers in the cities; there were illegal immigrants who had taken work in the cities without proper papers; there were the aged, infirm and unemployable who had failed to fulfil the requirements of their contracts; there were shattered black communities which had been living, either by historical accident or with illegal intent, in areas designated as being for other ethnic groups, tribes, races, clans, formations laid down according to the principles of Ethnic Autonomy.

When Blanchaille went to the camps no one had heard of them, or of him. Soon everyone had heard of him. 'Father Theo of the Camps' the newspapers called him. Bishop Blashford warned him to avoid political involvement. Later Blashford was to call on Catholics to 'embrace the suffering Christ of the camps' and the Church moved in with force. But by that time Blanchaille had gone, had written his notorious letter to *The Cross* with its ringing phrase 'Charity Kills', in which he called for the camps to be bulldozed. As a result he had been transferred for 'rest and recuperation' in a spirit of 'loving brotherly concern', and under heavy guard, to the place called Pennyheaven.

Pennyheaven was an imposing country mansion of tall white fluted columns and heavy sash windows, red polished verandas, great oak floorboards a foot across, balding peacocks, an empty dry and cracked swimming pool, a conservatory where lizards basked, pressed against the bleary Victorian stained-glass windows. It had belonged once to Sam Giltstein, an old drinking buddy of Barney Barnato's. An individual, this Giltstein. When many of the Jewish mining magnates went over to Christianity early in the century, Gilstein, perverse as ever, resisted the movement into the Anglican faith and opted instead for the Church of Rome. When he died he left his inaccessible summer place in the high remote mountains thirty miles north of the capital, to the Church as a 'home for homeless clergy'. Many miles from the nearest village and halfway up the rocky mountainside at the end of an almost inaccessible dirt road, Pennyheaven had remained as remote and as distant from human habitation as Giltstein had intended it to be. No one visited Pennyheaven. To go there you had to be sent. To leave you had to be fetched.

Blanchaille was six weeks there waiting for his new posting. To Pennyheaven came priests for whom no other place could be found: priests not bad enough to expel, not mad enough to confine; ancient clerics awaiting transfer to geriatric homes, little trembling creatures sitting out on the veranda from dawn to sunset, trembling and dribbling, leaning over their sticks and turning weak eyes on the shimmering blue peaks; dipsomaniacs and men with strange cravings for little girls.

Blanchaille met there Father Wüli, a huge Swiss who described himself as the last of the great African travellers, who had come 'to rest in Pennyheaven between voyages of exploration'. What this in fact meant, Blanchaille discovered, was that Wüli was an inveterate escapee. He would stride miles across the mountains in his tough boots, his Swiss sense of direction carrying him to the outskirts of some town and there he would lurk among the rocks and kranses, leaping out to expose himself to terrified picnickers on the remote hillsides, his unerring compass on these prodigious treks, the needle that pointed him onward, leaping massively from his unzipped flies. Father Wüli would return from his distant journeys in a police landrover, blanketed against sudden display, looking very fit and quite unabashed.

He met there, too, Brother Khourrie, a little Lebanese who'd once been sacristan in a church by the seaside and who had led a blameless life until he was granted a vision of the Redeemer. Khourrie and Blanchaille sat on the veranda of the big house staring across the baking, shimmering country which ran away into the blue mountains: huge boulders stood stark among the thick burly vegetation. The nearby hills appeared to be made almost entirely of rocks, some split from the main mass, seamed, pitted, cleft, the colour of sand, lying among the thorn trees where they had rolled thousands of years before. Christ was a boy of about eighteen, Khourrie confided, in ragged shorts, carrying the T-piece of his cross slung across his shoulders, his arms outstretched and hanging over the beams to steady it. He was tall with blond hair worn rather long, and his skin was golden. He must have been lying down shortly before Khourrie saw him because sand had covered his back and stuck in the oil with which he had rubbed himself. He was gleaming and encrusted with sand and oil and sunlight. A shining man. Very gently and diffidently Blanchaille suggested it might have been a surfer he saw, but Khourrie was firm – to those with eyes to see he was plainly the Messiah. He had proof. The proof he produced was novel. He explained to Blanchaille that the Jews too had identified the Boy Messiah. That was why they had bought flats along the beach front and why they continued to do so in such numbers. Nearly all the flats which followed the curve of the sea shore were owned by Jews. The Jews always knew, said Khourrie. Naturally he'd reported the matter to the Church. Their response had been unforgivable. They had dispatched him to Pennyheaven. The reasons he was quite clear about, the Church and the Jews were in league. Neither wished it to be known that the Messiah had returned to earth.

After Pennyheaven, Blanchaille had been appointed to St Peter-in-the-Wild. The church was so new it still smelt of cement and the walls and ceiling were painted sky blue. The whole place was severely angular with pews of pale natural pine and a baptismal font at the back made of stainless steel, deeply shining, rather like the wash-basins found on trains. In a pulpit of steel and smoked glass with its directional microphone Blanchaille talked of Malanskop, his first camp. It had been, he said, a most terrible garden full of deadly melodies, a music of wonderful names: kwashiorkor and pellagra, enteritis, lekkerkrap and rickets. How they rolled off the tongue! How lovely they sounded! Children in particular found the music irresistible. They listened and died. Every day ended with perfunctory funerals. No less euphonious afflictions decimated the adults: tuberculosis, cystitis, scabies and salpingitis, cholera, typhoid . . . The red burial mounds grew up overnight beyond the pit latrines as if an army of moles had passed that way. Later the little graves were piled with stones to keep the jackals off and finally came the clumsy wooden crosses tied with string, the names burnt into the wood in a charred scrawl, dates recording the months, weeks, days, hours, in the brief lives of 'Beauty' and 'Edgar', 'Sampson', 'Nicodemus' and 'Precious'.

The Church half emptied after this first sermon. Blanchaille began to feel rather better about his new appointment. At the second sermon he tried to encourage the congregation remaining to recite after him the names of the camps and perhaps to clap the beat: 'Kraaifontein, Witziesbek, Verneuk, Bittereind, Mooiplaats . . .' The microphone gave a hard dry sound as he clapped his way through the litany. No one joined him. 'I want to suggest that in the foyer of the church we build models of these camps, of the shoe-box shantytowns, the tent villages, that we show their corrugated iron roofs, the towns built of paraffin tins, the three stand-pipes on which thousands of people relied for their water, the solitary borehole and of course the spreading graveyards. Everywhere the graveyards. We might use papier mâché.'

At his third sermon the congregation had shrunk to those few who he later realised constituted the Consensus Committee: Makapan, the two Kretas, and Mary Muldoon. Mary wore a hat with bright red cherries. Her flower arrangements, he noticed, had not changed since his first sermon. Before the altar the hyacinths were dying in their waterless brass vases.

34

'I wish to remember today, dear brethren, my third and final camp, Dolorosa, that tin and cardboard slum in the middle of nowhere which has since become so famous. In my day, the mortality rate for dysentery was a national record, the illness carried off three-quarters of the newborn in the first month after the camp was set up. People in their tin hovels with their sack doors died of despair, if they were lucky, before the more regular infections removed them. Dolorosa, as you know, is important because it caught the imagination of the country and the Church. It was called, in one of those detestable phrases, "a challenge to the conscience of the nation." Individuals arrived there in their private cars with loads of medicines and milk. Rotary Clubs collected blankets and bread. This charitable effort grew and teams of doctors and nurses, engineers and teachers made their way to Dolorosa. But more than anything else Dolorosa became the camp which the Church took up. It became, in the words of Bishop Blashford's episcopal letter, "the burning focal point of the charitable energies of the Catholic Church. . . ." A hospital was opened. Then a school. And a fine new church in the beehive style, this being judged as reflecting best the tribal architecture of the local people, was erected and dedicated. What was sought . . . What *was* sought? Oh yes, I remember, what was sought was "a living, long-term commitment" – they actually said that! Farsighted superiors in distant seminaries saw the potential. Could not such a place, these wise men asked themselves, provide a training ground for their priestlings? Give their chaps a taste of real poverty, they said, by billeting them on me for short periods. The spiritual directors of these seminaries took to visiting me by bus and helicopter. They brought tales of increasing interest among their novices. Inspired by the new direction the Church had found, these young men wished to live, for short periods, a sympathetic mirror existence with their brother outcasts, to embrace Mother Africa. A small pilot scheme was begun and proved to be extremely popular. It was likened to young doctors doing a year of housemanship. Parcels of young priests arrived simply crackling with a desire to do good and discover for themselves the vision of the suffering Christ of the camps. Well, of course, the word got round and before long other sympathisers and wellwishers asked if they too could take part in this scheme in a more practical way. It was one thing to drive down every weekend with a load of powdered milk in the back of the Datsun – but that was no substitute for actually "living in" . . . And if the priests were doing it, then why not the laity? The Church, keen to involve the faithful, agreed. Rather than to drive down to Dolorosa once a week with a fresh supply of saline drip, maybe people should get a taste of dysentery for themselves? A conference of bishops recognized the desire evident among the laity, and in their famous resolution called on them to "make living witness of their deep Christian concern for their dispossessed brethren by going among them, even as Our Lord did. . ." Well, you can imagine what happened. The accommodation problem at Dolorosa, and I believe at other camps, became suddenly very acute. Sociologists, writers, journalists, health workers, students, nuns, priests, all began crowding in. I found I had to ration the shanties, the lean-to's and huts. I had to open a waiting list. Soon we were doubling up on our volunteer workers, five or six to a hovel, three or four to a tent, up to half-a-dozen in the mobile homes donated by the Society of St Vincent de Paul on the proceeds gathered from a number of sponsored walks. Even so it wasn't enough. It became increasingly difficult to separate the races as the laws of the Regime required that we do, and harder still to keep the sexes apart, as morality demanded. Who hasn't heard of the tragic case of the Redemptorist Brother accused of raping an African girl behind the soup kitchen run by the Sisters of Mercy? Of the nurse who died of dysentery? Of the Dominican novice taken to hospital suffering from mal-nutrition? Of the infestation of head lice among a party of visiting Canadian clergy? For a while it seemed as if the whole project of "embracing the poor" was in serious doubt since the faithful seemed unable to resist the very diseases they came to relieve. As a temporary measure all inhabitants, both victims and volunteers, had to be moved into tents miles away from the infected zone while the entire shantytown was fumigated by volunteers from the Knights of Columbus wearing breathing apparatus supplied free of charge by a local firm. At the time the problem seemed insur-mountable but with that particular genius which has triumphed through the ages, the Church found a solution. The answer, as we now know, was the careful demarcation of areas of infection. This was achieved by driving sanitary corridors between the healthy volunteer forces on the outside and the infected slum people within; these were the so-called "fire breaks against infection", a kind of Hadrian's Wall of Defensive Medicine buttressed at strategic intervals by the SST's, camp jargon for the scour and shower ablutions, obligatory for all personnel passing between secure areas and infected zones. It was, according to the Bishop's Conference, a pioneering effort in disease control, a highly imaginative protective health measure sufficiently flexible to take into account the varying degrees of resistance (or lack of it) existing among the ethnic plurality of groups which made up the rich diversity of Southern African peoples . . .'

Blanchaille gripped the edge of the pulpit. His words no longer seemed to carry through the church. He tapped the microphone. Dead. The bastards had cut his mike. He peered at Mary Muldoon, the red cherries on her hat pulsed in the gloom. The rest of the parishioners stared back at him sullenly. 'It was at this time that I composed my letter to *The Cross*,' Blanchaille yelled. 'Perhaps you've heard of it? In it I said that if the people in the camps prayed for anything they should pray for the bulldozer. Enough of these smooth and resonant phrases, of plump churchmen talking of people living in a manner consonant with human dignity. Disease kills but so does charity, more slowly but just as surely. Flatten the camps, that is freedom! Release their inhabitants to a decent beggary, let them wander the countryside pleading for alms, calling on us to remember what we have done to them!'

It was his last sermon. After that the siege began.

And Makapan's second and general objection?

'You don't understand our role in history. We are not simply crude racialists of the sort you think – may I say perhaps even hope – that we are. We don't hate, despise, spit upon black people, not any longer. We recognise our failings. We reach out to embrace them.' He reached out his big, dusty hands towards Blanchaille's neck, he flexed the knuckles with the sound of distant rifle fire. 'You want to condemn us, but the prisoner has left the dock. The old charges against white South Africans have no force anywhere. Everywhere there is change. We are changing.'

Blanchaille shook his head. 'We are ruined. It's too late to change. It is time we left, got out.'

'Got out? But Father Blanchaille we have nowhere to go.'

'There are numbers of places – abroad.'

'Lies.'

'And stories of people who have disappeared.'

'Filthy slanders.'

'There is even talk of the formation of a government in exile.'

Makapan's hands descended on his shoulders. 'No more. Only your dog-collar protects you. There is no other place, no better place this side of the grave, than our country here. I will die for that belief.'

The thumbs, kneading his throat now, suggested that he would kill for that belief too. But Blanchaille was past caring. 'That is quite probable, Mr Makapan.'

Then in my dream I saw Blanchaille open the window and fix his eye on the figure in white; long white flowing robes like a nun, and a nursing sister's head-dress. Try as she might to hide herself behind the others she could not evade his eyes. This was his former black housekeeper, Joyce Nkwenzi. She had served Blanchaille's predecessor, the muscular Father Rischa, long and loyally, but she'd lasted with Blanchaille only until trouble struck and then left him, abruptly one evening.

Father Rischa had been popular. He had also been extremely fit. He'd left Blanchaille in possession of a house, empty but for a couple of pieces of very bad Rhodesian copperware and a larder full of inedible food: bean sprouts, soya-based products, nuts, grains, seaweed and porridge. It turned out he'd spent a lot of time organising footraces and sponsored walks and testing country runs along the rutted veld tracks from Uncle Vigo's Roadhouse to the African location several miles away.

'At first we looked at Rischa a little skew, if you know what I mean. We could hardly help it. When he was appointed here he seemed to spend hours in his tiny blue running shorts, his big thigh muscles sticking out, pounding up and down the sanitary lanes behind the houses. Thick black hair he had, and well oiled, the way they wear it, you know? He got a few stares in passing I can tell you, at least to begin with, but he was a good sport.'

The brick salesman's hands were big, square and yellow and he had a habit of knocking them together when speaking, perhaps developed over years of handling the samples stacked on his back seat, knocking off the brick dust. He evidently expected Blanchaille to be something of a good sport . . . 'When he left, he preached a sermon saying that he was happy to be going to the townships because he was going to search for those Africans who hadn't been ruined yet by the white man's diet of Coca-Cola and white bread and he was going to turn them into runners, he said. Look at the Kenyans, he said. Look at the Ethiopians. Aren't they excellent long-distance men? Well is there any reason why our tough boys in the bush shouldn't do just as well? He was going to organise camps for training them right there in the bush.'

'Why not? The bush is full of camps, Mr Makapan.'

'He was a fighter, was Father Rischa. He stuck up for his

country.'

'And the camps are full of starving people.'

'You don't have to tell me about the camps. I've done the weekly run like everyone else. The milk run, the medicine run. We know all about the camps.'

And then I saw the embattled priest, Blanchaille, glaring at the demonstrators at the bottom of his garden and he raised his hand pointing at the black woman: 'God sees you, Joyce Nkwenzi! You cannot hide.'

At the garden fence, Maureen and Duggie Kreta rattled their big banner. 'Shame! Leave her alone!'

'God sees you have deserted his minister!' roared Blanchaille. 'He will send you to hell, Joyce Nkwenzi.'

The girl's nerve broke and she threw herself down on her knees lifting clasped hands beseechingly towards her accuser in the window.

'There you will fry, faithless servant, like a fish in boiling oil – forever!'

With a shriek Joyce pitched forward on her face in the dust.

Blanchaille returned to his chair.

It was nearly midnight when Lynch arrived, slipping by the pickets at the gate with ease. Blanchaille embraced him, weeping a little. Lynch produced a flask and two glasses. 'Brandy. Stop that flood or you'll water the booze.'

'I'm leaving,' said Blanchaille.

'Not a moment too soon,' said Lynch. 'You've heard about Ferreira? Well, now they want you.' He took from his pocket a note typed on a sheet of cheap paper. He read out: 'Tell B. to get going. They're gunning for him.'

'Who sent that?'

'Van Vuuren.'

'Why should Van Vuuren care? He works for the Regime.'

'Don't see him that way. He's kept faith.'

Lynch wore a black coat and an old black beret. Blanchaille recognised the beret. He'd worn it when he'd taken his altar boys on a tour of the Air Force base near the school. The reasons for this odd Gallic touch had soon become clear.

On the windy airstrip, all those years before, he had made a speech: 'Every lad should get a view of his country's armaments. My beret is applicable since what we're going to look at is the new French jet. The French have supported our Government for many years. The Air Force is very proud of their new plane. It's a form of confidence building, they say. Between ourselves I suspect this display of weapons is similar to the impulse that makes some men expose themselves to little girls in public parks.' They trailed round behind him inspecting the sleek fighter. 'It is called a Mirage. Wonderfully appropriate,' Lynch said. 'It replaces the Sabre, which is obsolete. Not swords into ploughshares, you understand? But Sabres into Mirages . . .'

Blanchaille tried to remember how long it was since he'd last seen Lynch. Ten years? The black hair beneath the beret was peppered with grey and the face thinner, the chin more pointed, but for the rest he was the same, the beautifully flared nostrils, the prominent jug ears, the hard bright green eyes. 'I live alone now, since Brother Zacharias died of the cheap wine,' he said. 'The university encroaches, it swallows up more and more ground each day and you know that Blashford has sold my entire parish to the university? He says the money will be used to establish a new seminary somewhere in the country for black priests. He was advised by his banker to sell my church. Our old church. Has it ever occurred to you, Theodore, that the banks are at the forefront of innovation here? Remember how the banks introduced the new scheme for appointing black managers in their township branches? There was a lot of opposition to it from the white managers but head office decreed and head office was looking further ahead than the people here. Well you know how a little later the Church discovered its mission to the townships, the Church reaffirmed its historic role in Africa, acting, once again, on instructions from head office. In this case, Rome. It is interesting to see from where the power flows. It would be fascinating to talk more of this, but we can't. Ferreira is dead and you are suspected of being a connection in the case.'

'Why me?'

'He telephoned you. That's enough.'

'He was raving. He talked of the City of God.'

Lynch laughed and poured himself more brandy. 'Not God. It was a bad line, Blanchie. You had a lot of interference. What he said was not God but *gold*!'

'You're well informed.'

'I've heard the tapes, a friend of mine obliged.'

'Who killed him?'

Lynch shook his head. 'There are two possibilities which the police are following up. There was something painted in the room where he was found, scrawled low down on the wall. Three letters:

40

ASK followed by what might have been part of a *B*, or perhaps the number 3. The obvious organisations spring to mind. The Azanian Strike Kommando No. 3, the hit squad, I believe connected with the Azanian Liberation Front. The choice of the word Kommando being a deliberate gibe, a taking in vain of the name of the mobile fighting unit venerated by the Boers.'

'Well, it makes a kind of sense, I suppose. Tony was in the Government.'

'Not exactly. He was a Civil Servant. And besides, if you're going to assassinate someone why pick on an accountant?'

'Well, who then?'

'There is another lot, home based, with the same initials – the Afrika Straf Kaffir Brigade. Both are mysterious outfits – the Strike Kommando claims to have infiltrated the country to carry out executions of enemies of the people. The Straf Kaffir Brigade is a group of right-wing maniacs who claim to protect the white man's way of life, motherhood and freedom – whether all of those, or you take your pick, I don't know. Despite their name it is not actually blacks they're after, it's white men who they believe are destroying the soul of the Afrikaner. The Regime, needless to say, denies the existence of both groups. The Brigade has claimed responsibility for shooting up the houses of liberal lawyers, painting swastikas on the houses of selected targets like the local rabbi, which incensed him no end as it turned out he is a fervent supporter of the Regime. They go about generally making a nuisance of themselves.'

'I remember seeing the name,' Blanchaille said. 'Didn't they release syphilis-infected mice in several of these new casinos these entrepreneurs are opening in all the Bantu homelands, in the hopes of spreading the pox among white gamblers?'

'The same. They are demented. But why should even a bunch of madmen who ostensibly at least support the Regime, assassinate one of its officials? Equally, why should the Azanian lot murder Ferreira? He was no big noise, no minister, no target. It seems to me that the question we ought to ask is not which of these groups carried out the killing but why they should bother to remove a remote financial official who spent his time locked away with the ledgers poring over the figures?'

Blanchaille knew the old priest had to some extent at least answered his own questions. He suspected, as anyone would who knew Ferreira, that the answer lay in those figures.

'Do you believe in these organisations?'

'Believe? Of course I do! Whether they exist or not is another

41

question. But certainly I believe, just as I believe in the Kruger millions.'

'And the city of gold?'

'Naturally. It is a question of faith which I cling to with Augustinian ferocity. May God help you with your unbelief, poor Blanchie. Sadly I do not have time to explain my allusion.' He walked to the window and beckoned Blanchaille. 'Those lights over there – the flashing red and yellow neon, do you see? That's the Airport Palace Hotel. Ask to see the manager when you arrive. He'll handle things. Leave here as soon as you can.'

'What, now?'

'Certainly. The very instant your watchers settle down for the night.'

'But I'm not ready – not right now, anyway.'

'What? Not ready? Your sainted mother gave you your wonderful French passport. Your dead friend has supplied you with funds. Your bags are packed, I take it?'

Blanchaille nodded and pointed to the three tartan suitcases.

'What more do you want?'

He thought hard. 'I have no air ticket.'

Lynch tapped his nose and winked. 'Faith, my son.' He drained his brandy and rose. 'It will be taken care of. Now I'm on my way.'

'But you haven't said yet who you think killed Ferreira. Straf Kaffir Brigade, or Azanian Strike Kommando?'

Lynch regarded him unblinkingly. What he said next made Blanchaille's head spin: 'Or both?' he said.

Blanchaille went over to his chair, the same blue plastic garden chair on which he must have sat many a night and on which he was sitting when I first saw him in my dream.

'I am as much in the dark as you are,' Lynch said with a complete lack of sincerity. 'Now I must go. I'm not long for this world.'

'So you've said,' Blanchaille remarked sceptically.

'Can't be said often enough. Only this time I say it in hope. This time before the shades come down I see a gleam of something that may be –'

'Light?' Blanchaille put in helpfully.

'Gold!' said Lynch, 'and the deliriously exciting perception that history, or what passes for such in this dust-bin, may just be about to repeat itself. Remember, Theodore, red and yellow neon, Airport Palace – don't delay.' And with a grin the little priest stepped out into the darkness.

CHAPTER 3

Now in my dream I saw Blanchaille set off early in one of those typical highveld dawns, a sky of light blue plated steel arcing overhead. He wore old grey flannels and a white cotton jacket, grunting beneath the weight of his three bulky tartan suitcases well strapped, belted around their fat middles in thick-tongued fraying leather. He slipped quietly out of the house and set off down the dirt road. But Joyce, who was sleeping rolled in a blanket by the embers of the night fire, had sharp ears and shouted after him. This woke Makapan who was dozing behind the wheel of his motor car. Both came running after Blanchaille: 'What's this? Where are you going?'

'Somewhere where you won't be able to bother me.'

'But are you going for good?'

'For good.'

'You're running away then?' There was a jeering note in Makapan's voice. His eyelashes were crusted with sleep.

Blanchaille nodded. 'As fast as I can.'

Joyce said; 'Father won't get very far, those cases are too heavy. He'll have to walk slowly.'

'I expected you to stand and fight at least,' said Makapan.

'Where are you going?' Joyce asked.

'I don't know yet.'

Joyce became rather excited. Grasping one of the heavy suitcases Blanchaille held she tried to help him, half hobbling and half running alongside him. 'Are you going overseas?'

Blanchaille nodded. 'Perhaps.'

Makapan lumbered up. 'That's nonsense, man. You're starting to talk politics again. We're not that badly off. We're not finished. Even the Americans think there's life in us yet. I saw only yesterday in the paper how their Secretary for State for Political Affairs came all this way to tell us that it will come right in the end, that we're getting better all the time, that we will give political rights to other groups when the time is right, that we will be saved. There is no threat, not outside nor in, that our armed forces cannot handle. Even at the time of the Total Onslaught we hold our own. I assure you myself, and I am a captain in the Signals Corps. You do your military duty – even if it does sometimes harm your career prospects. My fight with you is religious, not political . . .'

Blanchaille understood this qualification.

In the time of the Total Onslaught of course everyone was in the armed services. For many years a quarter of a million young men capable of bearing arms were on active service or on reserve or in training. All immigrants were called up. However, the Regime decided this base was not sufficient and announced a plan to push this figure to one million men, by drafting individuals, old and young, who for various reasons had been overlooked in the years of the huge defence build-up. In a total white population of little over five million, this force represented a great army, at least on paper, able surely to withstand the Total Onslaught. However, it was also a considerable drain on the available workforce. The army had an insatiable appetite for more men because even the best strategic planners could not predict where the attack would come from next. The chief problem lay in guarding the borders which were thousands of miles long and growing longer all the time. There were, besides the national borders, the borders around the new Homelands, the former reserves in the rural areas which the Government declared independent and sovereign, and guaranteed that sovereignty by fencing them off. New countries meant new borders. New borders meant new fences. Entire battalions spent their period of military service banging in fence poles. Of course the Total Onslaught might also show itself from within, and as a result the huge black townships had to be encircled with wire and the resettlement camps fortified with foot patrols and armoured cars. Then there were Government buildings, the railheads, the power stations, the factories. Since these were frequently the targets of incendiary bombs and limpet mines, they required the strictest protection and the young men on active training might spend months on end sweating in desolate railway sidings or freezing by night outside the oil refineries waiting for something to happen. It seldom did, but then Total Onslaught required total preparedness.

The sons of the middle classes managed to defer their call up by going into university. Some emigrated, a few deserted and a tiny number pleaded conscientious objection and went to jail. But the great majority of young men went into the services and found the tedium quite lethal. Deaths from drink and drugs rose steadily; motor car accidents became more and more frequent and the number of deaths through careless, one might say carefree, handling of fire-arms, a form of suicide traditionally associated with the police in the old days, grew so alarmingly that the annual mortality rates actually overtook those inflicted by the Total Onslaught. In a notorious case, a young man named Gussie Lamprecht, a draftee lance-corporal in a coastal barracks, was enterprising enough to draw attention to this problem by telephoning a local newspaper, giving his name, rank and number, and promising that if their crime reporter would come to the beach he would see 'something very interesting'. As the reporter walked along the pier, he related at the inquest, he saw before him a figure on the beach, whom he now knew to be the deceased, lift a pistol to his temple and fire. He remembered that the incident had terrified an Indian fisherman catching shad nearby. He had taken a picture which his newspaper was refused permission to publish, photographs of Defence Force property being forbidden, and young Gussie Lamprecht though deceased was still regarded as Defence Force property. The case caused an outcry, worried mothers of draftees demanded that the Government take action. The Regime responded by forbidding publication of any further figures relating to accidental death caused by firearms and a delegation of mothers thanked the Minister concerned from the depths of their hearts.

A problem more intractable was the increasing shortage of manpower. To ameliorate the imbalance caused by the giant call-up, the Regime suggested a new deal, a kind of leaseback of uniformed labour at army prices. The army would liaise with various businesses and industries and Government bodies which would state their requirements which would then be assessed in terms of manpower available and then where possible specialised labour would be leased back to organisations in need. Contingents of soldiers were deployed whose training in civilian life approximated to the skills required. The word 'approximated' covered a wide range and so cooks and engineers might find themselves spending the period of their military training working through files in the Department of Inland Revenue and young accountants could spend years knocking in fence posts to take the electrified wire surrounding the Independent Homelands in which the ethnic identity of each black tribe was so fiercely protected.

'Is it true, in that place called Overseas, that white people and black people can meet as they please? You come and go when you like? No one tells you what to do? Everybody is equal?' Joyce asked.

'I have never been there, but I believe so,' said Blanchaille.

'Stop and consider, Blanchaille,' Makapan was pleading with him now, 'We haven't got on well, I know that. But if you stayed maybe we could work something out.'

'What do you fear, Father?' Joyce demanded.

Blanchaille's answer was intended to be brutally direct: 'Destruction.'

He saw the shadow shift across her eyes like a bird dipping across still water, felt her dissatisfaction at his answer, for it told her nothing, or rather it told her what she already knew, what everyone knew. What he had been expected to say was in which scenario he anticipated that destruction. There were three main scenarios with which every South African was by that time so familiar that they referred to them by numbers, rather as Americans will talk of 'taking the Fifth', meaning the Fifth Amendment, or university students will say they're hoping for a 'good second', South Africans would commonly talk of 'going for One', which translated meant that they favoured the first scenario for the end of things; this envisaged black hordes from the North sweeping down, joining the local Africans and obliterating the whites. While this view was still accorded some respect by traditionalists, being the most ancient of the nightmares, it was widely discounted. More people believed in the Second, in which the hordes would still sweep down, the local population would revolt but the whites would resist, fight them to a standstill and some sort of uneasy truce would prevail – until the next eruption. A minority of daring dreamers contemplated what they called No.3, which imagined the unimaginable, a defeat for the white forces who would retreat to the sea burning all behind them and die on the beaches, shooting their women and children first. It was this scenario which appealed so directly to the Azanian Liberation Front that their so-called Strike Kommando added No.3 to their designation. More recently another vision of the future conflict had begun to circulate in whispers and rumours and this scenario was doubly terrifying since it gave credence to No.3 while seeking to reassure the population that the white nation had found a defence against its possible defeat. Known as the 'Fourth Option' or more colloquially as 'the Smash', it suggested that nuclear weapons were being secretly prepared and if the worst came to the worst would be deployed, destroying the entire Southern Continent in an instant. Whispers of the Fourth Option had first begun to circulate at the last congress of the ruling National Party at which President Adolph Bubé had declared in his characteristic throaty growl: 'We wish to live in peace – but if attacked we will resist and we shall never surrender. We will never leave this Africa we love but if by some misfortune we are forced to go, rest assured we shall not go alone . . . This is not a threat but a promise!' The promise was met with wild applause from the party faithful and the newspapers interpreted the speech in the usual imaginative fashion with headlines ranging from PRESIDENT PLEADS FOR PEACE! to BUBÉ TALKS TOUGH! 'WE'LL TAKE YOU WITH US' WARNS PRESIDENT, to SOUTH AFRICA HAS NO NUCLEAR STRATEGY – OFFICIAL! This last referring to an off-the-record meeting between Bubé and various reporters after the speech in which he categorically denied that the Republic possessed nuclear weapons, or intended to manufacture any. The fact that he pronounced the first and the last *b* in bomb was regarded as highly significant and analysed at some length. Some papers suggesting that by putting peculiar emphasis on the word 'bomb' the President was signalling to hostile states to the north that they shouldn't take his denial too seriously, while still others argued against attaching too much importance to peculiarities of pronunciation pointing out that Bubé had been talking English, which was not his first language, and he had, in any event, an emphatic, gutteral way of speaking. Subtle observers reported that the fact that he had used English showed that he intended his warning to carry as far as possible. He had closed the meeting by consulting with a flourish his gold hunter, a time-piece of great beauty and fabled accuracy manufactured in Cologne, closing the case with a decisive snap which left no one in any doubt of his determination to protect the country's security at any cost.

Blanchaille's second answer to Joyce and Makapan at their dawn meeting was more specific. 'I am retiring.'

'Father is weak now. Joyce must carry his bags.'

Blanchaille was aghast. 'You want to come with me? When things got tough you went over to this man here. Now you've thought better of that and you return to me. What sort of behaviour is that?'

Joyce was not in the least abashed. 'I didn't know Father was going overseas.'

Makapan turned round and stalked off shouting: 'Overseas! What the hell do you know of overseas? No good can come of this. And you Joyce – don't make a fool of yourself. Stay with us. We will look after you. This man is mad. Don't listen to him. Don't go with him.'

But Joyce had now actually wrested one of Blanchaille's cases from him and was carrying it down the road. She took no notice of Makapan.

And so I saw how Blanchaille and the woman went on together. And in my dream I heard Joyce question Blanchaille, saying: 'Mr Makapan is a good man, but he is thick. He is thick in his head. He said Joyce must come to his side. If Joyce comes to his side then Father Rischa will come back and we will be happy again. Every night I sleep out in the cold waiting. I am tired of waiting. Why is Father going overseas?'

'I believe I will find a better place there.'

'And who told you of the better place?'

'It is written in a book.'

'Ah,' Joyce seemed pleased. 'In the book of the Lord?'

'No, it is in the book of the President.'

'Of the President Bubé?'

'No, of another President, of old President Kruger.'

'Has he also been overseas?'

'Yes. He was the only President who had been overseas until President Bubé went.'

'I have heard something of him. And the words in this book – are they true?'

Blanchaille hesitated. 'I cannot say if they are true, indeed it is said by some that this book does not exist. But if they are not true, these words, then they are interesting.'

'And what do they speak of, these promises in the book?'

'It is written that there is a place for hopeless souls who are tired of too much wandering. Good souls, African souls, who seek rest will find it in this special place.'

Joyce seized his elbow with such a powerful grip that he gasped. 'And what else?'

'There all people will be equal, there will be no segregation, no pass laws, no black and white skins, no separate lavatories, no servants' quarters, no resettlement camps. In that place friends who have disappeared will be found again and even some we thought were dead will greet us. There will be no police stations, no torture, no barbed wire, no guns, no soldiers and no bombs.'

'And in this place,' Joyce yipped excitedly catching the spirit of his peroration, and relying no doubt on her Bible reading, 'will we wear white clothes and golden crowns?'

'White clothes, certainly,' Blanchaille replied with all the conviction he could muster, 'but I cannot say about the crowns.'

'Yes. Golden crowns!' Joyce insisted with an expectant smile as if she were feeding clues to a not very bright child. She tapped her head. 'But not for *wearing*, maybe.'

At last he understood her. 'You mean *coins*. Golden coins! Krugerrands?'

Joyce nodded, satisfied to hear the words. 'That is what I remember of that old President, golden coins,' and she skipped before him like a child down the dirt road, despite the heavy suitcase she carried. 'Come on then. Let's go, my Father.'

My Father? Her temerity enraged him. First she had attached herself to Father Rischa, the sprinting Syrian, entranced by his popularity, then she left Blanchaille for his lack of it; she went over to the Parish Consensus Committee and now without a blink she had deserted them and returned to her original master in the mistaken belief that after all perhaps he offered the better deal. Look how she skipped ahead of him! Why she even lifted the suitcase onto her head in the way women carry water from the well and with it wonderfully balanced there she danced and jigged! It would do no good to talk to her of the difficulties of leaving without permission, without a ticket or passport. This was scarcely the time for discussion. But there were other ways perhaps. He had no intention of leaving before paying a few last calls, to Bishop Blashford in particular, perhaps to Gabriel. Ecclesiastical authority might do to Joyce what he could not. A momentary access of charity afflicted him at this point and he thought that he might have misjudged her, that perhaps she was a poor weak creature, easily swayed; but commonsense reasserted itself to tell him that this was nonsense, she was a ferocious woman determined on escape and mere legal detail would not deter her; that she had no permission or papers was no obstacle, for while she was with him, he was her permission, her passport, and her ticket. Her heavy body shook under her white skirt and blouse. Her head-dress was beautifully ironed. She endeavoured to look like a nun of the old sort, from the days before nuns began dressing like traffic wardens. If ever the situation changed and revolutionary firing squads roamed the streets executing their enemies, Joyce would be there, praying as the bodies hit the ground: 'He let me down, but forgive him, if you can.'

CHAPTER 4

And now I saw in my dream how the road which Blanchaille and Joyce followed took them past a great township on the edge of the city. Perhaps this was the township in which Blanchaille's friend Miranda had died, but if so he gave no indication of it. And outside this township, beside the usual scrolls of barbed wire so ornate they took on the look of some lean and spiky sculpture, the priest and his housekeeper saw police vans and Saracen armoured cars crowded in at the gates and armed policemen in positions on the roofs of the houses and in trees and on any high vantage point, training their guns on the township.

And then I saw a short, stocky man with a sub-machine gun under his arm step forward and introduce himself to the two travellers as Colonel Schlagter. This Schlagter was a burly capable-looking man, but that he was under some strain was clearly apparent from the tight grip he kept on the black machine gun, jabbing it at them and demanding to know their business.

'We are on a journey,' Blanchaille explained, indicating the suitcases.

Schlagter jerked his thumb at Joyce. 'Does this girl have a permit to be here? No one is allowed without a permit. Why is she outside? Why is she not inside with the others?'

'She's with me. She's my servant,' Blanchaille explained.

'O.K., in that case she can help you.' Schlagter turned to Joyce. 'I hope you got strong arms, my girl. There's lots of work for you here. Now both of you listen to me. This is the position. I'm commandeering you in terms of the State of Emergency, which gives me the right under the regulations to commandeer any civilians who in the opinion of the military commander or senior police officer on the scene may contribute to the safety of the State.'

'But what has happened? There's been trouble here, hasn't there?' Blanchaille demanded. 'I thought the townships were peaceful.'

Now this was a telling point because one of the proudest boasts of the Regime at that time was of the peace to be found in the townships. Full-page advertisements appeared in international newspapers: they showed happy scenes, a group of children playing

50

soccer; a roomful of smiling women taking sewing lessons; a crowded beer hall full of happy customers, and over the photographs the headline: YOU ARE LOOKING AT A RIOT IN A SOUTH AFRICAN TOWNSHIP. Trudy Yssel's Department of Communications ran this campaign with great success.

'The townships are peaceful. Don't you bother about that,' Schlagter snapped. 'Come along with me please.'

He led them into the township where before the huge and fortified police station a bleak sight met their eyes. In the dust there lay scores of people, very still, with just an edge of clothing, a corner of a dress, the tip of a headscarf lifting in the gentle breeze which carried on it the unmistakable heavy smell of meat and blood. Joyce put down the suitcase and drew close to Blanchaille, seizing his wrist in her terrible grip.

'Where have you brought Joyce? I believed in Father and where has he brought me?'

'We must do as he says,' Blanchaille whispered.

'We are caught here. Stuck forever,' Joyce replied.

'Less talk, more work my girl.' Schlagter indicated the fallen people in a matter-of-fact way, lifting his arms and drawing with his two forefingers an imaginary circle around them. 'The people you see here are guilty of attacking the police. Believing themselves to be in great danger my men, after several warnings, returned fire. Just in time, I can tell you. The Saracens held their fire. They were not called or the damage would have been far greater, particularly to peaceful people in their houses. I'm proud to say these officers contained the charge with rifle fire and well-directed barrages from their sub-machine guns, even though this is a comparatively new weapon, extremely light and portable but inclined to jam when fired in haste due to the palm-release mechanism which must be squeezed simultaneously with the trigger. It takes some time to get the knack of it. But it's no more than a teething problem, I can assure you. Now these casualties must be removed. You have a free hand. You and the girl will be covered throughout the operation so there's no cause for alarm' – this last was directed at Joyce who had begun sobbing. 'To your right you will see the front stoep of the police station which at the time of the murderous attack was occupied by only four black constables. Lay out the people there in orderly rows to facilitate counting and identification. Any problems, call on me.'

Priest and servant wandered among the fallen people, men, women and children tumbled into heaps or sprawled alone.

Blanchaille noticed the remnants of clothing, several old shoes, a petticoat and even an old kitchen chair scattered about. Most of the people had been shot recently for they were warm still and bled profusely. He'd never realised how much blood the human body could contain and how the violent perforations of heavy, close-range fire will make the blood gush and spread. And then, stranger still, there were others who showed no signs of blood, or wounds, not even a single puncture. But there was blood enough, soaking into the dust, making a pungent sticky mud which Blanchaille and Joyce stirred up still further with their feet, though they tried to be as careful as possible. The policemen from their vantage points sighted down their rifles.

'If we pick them up together that will be easier,' Blanchaille said.

'Do your own work yourself,' Joyce retorted.

Blanchaille began lifting the body of a young man, seizing his left arm and his right leg and carrying him across the stoep, hearing the blood drip as he shuffled across the open space. The man was a terrible weight. 'I cannot do it myself, nor can you. We must help one another.'

Joyce didn't even bother to look at him. She grabbed hold of the ankle of a plump woman with a gaping wound in her chest and simply dragged her across the ground in a slew of pebbles and dust. Blanchaille heard the woman's head bang on the edge of the wooden stoep as she hauled her on to the bare boards.

'Heads all the same way!' Schlagter yelled.

After that Blanchaille followed Joyce's example, seized a leg or an arm and turning his head away hauled the body to the stoep. Only the children he carried.

It was backbreaking labour and eventually Blanchaille could stand it no longer and went to Schlagter. 'There are so many, this is going to take a long time.

'Well, get on with it then.'

'Perhaps we could have some help?' Desperation made Blanchaille bold.

Schlagter shook his head. 'My men are on watch.'

'Watching for what? These people are dead,' Blanchaille said.

The Colonel smiled. 'When you've been in the police force as long as I have, you'll learn to be very careful before jumping to conclusions. These people may look like they're dead, I grant you that, but how do we know that some of them aren't pretending? Lying low? They're a sly lot these township people, I can tell you that from the years of working with them. What happens if some of them are just waiting until I order my men to put their guns down and go and start carrying the bodies? Then they jump up and attack! No man, I'm not taking any bloody chances.'

'These people are dead,' Blanchaille insisted.

'Says you! I'm in charge here and I'll decide who's dead or not.' Blanchaille went back to work.

'We will never escape,' Joyce snapped at him bitterly.

'Why should they want to hold us? Once this is finished we'll be out of here.'

'You think there aren't other townships, other bodies? They'll take us with them. Or perhaps they'll shoot us.'

She spat, a globule of moisture in the dust. What an odd collection of belongings littered the killing ground: there were quantities of shoes in different sizes and colours, some matching pairs as well as abandoned single shoes; there was a baby's push-chair, rusted, in blue leather, but still usable; there was, besides, a petticoat touchingly embroidered with pink lace, pink lace finely worked; a pair of spectacles with one lens smashed; a set of dentures, the teeth clicked shut, a bizarre solitary expression of naked obstinacy, the teeth presented an air of invulnerability which reminded him of that unyielding almost jaunty bravado that skeletons wear; and then, somehow most touchingly of all, there was the up-ended kitchen chair lying on its side as if someone had leapt from it only minutes before and left in a hurry. These small domestic details were more sad, and somehow more vocal, than the torn, shapeless bodies. The work was very hard. Joyce continued to drag the bodies to the stoep. He lifted some of them despite the strain and his aching muscles but he was now moving very slowly. Things changed when he came across a mother and child killed by a single bullet. The child was strapped to its mother's back in a red and blue blanket, tightly knotted. Their combined weight was too much for him to lift and he was forced, reluctantly, to try and separate the bodies but their blood had soaked the blanket and the knots would not budge. His hands slipped and reddened. With a snort of impatience Joyce came over and seized the mother's hands. He took her feet and between them they carried the bodies to the stoep. Joyce would have laid the mother out, face down, with the baby above but Blanchaille was revolted by the unnaturalness of this and gently turned the woman on her side so it looked as if mother and child were curled up asleep.

Perhaps this sign of gentleness softened Joyce, for she took up the next body with a brisk nod at Blanchaille, indicating that from now on they would clear the field together. Hoping this was the beginning of better relations, Blanchaille set the chair back on its feet, as if it would preside, become a witness, over their business. Joyce seemed to understand and approve of this gesture for there is always some comfort in extreme situations in the restoration of an even temporary normality. In the course of his work Blanchaille learnt something of bullet wounds. Learnt how the entry point may be smooth, how the speeding bullet may draw threads of clothing with it into the wound and the bullet, often encountering no obstacle on its passage through the body, burst out with ugly force from shoulder or neck. Or it might take a wildly eccentric course through the inner organs rebounding off bone to emerge in unexpected places, anything up to a foot above or below the point of entry. Head wounds could be particularly severe, seen from behind.

He went to Colonel Schlagter. 'You said that these people had been attacking your men.'

Schlagter eyed him warily, 'Well?'

'A lot of them have been shot in the back.'

'Christ man, what's that got to do with it?'

'Well it looks like they were running away.'

Schlagter shook his head. He laughed grimly. 'Front, sides, back – what the hell does it matter? Look, you've never been under attack. Let me tell you that when you're being attacked you don't stop to ask what direction the people are running in. Anyway, like I told you, they're a crafty lot. I mean for all you know some of them turned round and were running at us backwards. Have you thought of that?'

Blanchaille admitted that he had not.

When at last all the corpses were laid out on the long wooden veranda in front of the police station and an armed guard posted, 'just in case', Schlagter came over and thanked them for their work. 'You have been an indispensable help. You have served your country. All these people you see lying here will now be counted and photographed and their relatives will be brought to identify them, and afterwards they will be allowed to reclaim the members of their families. This is a strict procedure because the enemies of our country like nothing better than to inflate the figures of those killed and to claim that all sorts of people have been killed when they know this is a lie and a slander.'

The armed police were stood down and relaxed visibly. The Saracens left. Schlagter directed Blanchaille and Joyce to a stand-tap behind the police station building and asked them if they'd like to wash their hands.

Joyce washed first, holding her feet under the tap and then scrubbing ferociously at the blood stains on her white dress, folding handfuls of gravel into the material and rubbing it harshly, catching the water in a great scoop of her skirt like a prospector panning for gold and in this way she managed to reduce the vividness of the blood marks, but the stains remained.

Dust to dust, ashes to ashes, so the story went, Blanchaille reflected. Only it wasn't like that, not here. It was blood to dust and dust to mud and mud to water and away down the ditch with it. He watched as Joyce scrubbed at the blood which had caught in the cracks of her nails using the wet hem of her dress.

'I think they're going to let us go now.'

'You? Think! This is the new life you promised me. When I see how it starts, God knows how it will end!'

Blanchaille stepped up to the tap conscious of her rage, of her eyes boring into his back. He cleaned his face and his hands as best he could and rubbed rather hopelessly at the blood stains on his clothes but only succeeded in darkening and spreading them. When he turned again, Joyce was gone. He was not surprised and doubted whether anyone would have tried to stop her. Well, she would have a great deal to tell Makapan when she returned.

He walked to the front of the police station and, as he had expected, no one took any notice. He picked up his suitcases, one in each hand and one, bulky and uncomfortable, underneath his arm and began moving towards the front gate. Away to his right a group of policemen in shirt sleeves were playing a game of touch rugby using a water-bottle as a ball. The kitchen chair stood where he had left it, surveying the killing ground. He barely got out of the front gate before he collapsed, exhausted. He sat down in the dust on his suitcase beside the road.

And then I saw in my dream that a man driving a yellow Datsun estate stopped and offered him a lift. A short and balding man with a pleasant smile whose name was Derek Breslau. A commercial traveller for Lever Brothers dealing in ladies' shampoos. The inside of his car was so heavily perfumed it made Blanchaille swoon and he could barely find the words to thank him for his kindness.

'Don't mention it. Couldn't leave a guy sitting by the side of the road outside a bloody township. Normally I put my foot down and go like hell when I pass a township. You never know what's going on inside. Gee, you took a risk!' He examined Blanchaille's blood-stained, muddied clothes with interest.

'My bags are heavy and I can't go very far at a stretch.'

'Well, keep away from the townships.'

'It's a funny thing,' said Blanchaille, 'but I always believed that the townships were peaceful now.'

Breslau nodded. 'Well it depends on what you mean. If you mean the townships are peaceful except when there are riots, then I suppose that's correct. So I suppose you could say the townships are peaceful between riots. And I must say they're pretty peaceful after riots. If we need to go to the townships that's usually when we go. They have a period of mourning then, you see, and you got time to get in, do the job and get out again.'

'I suppose then you could also say that townships are peaceful before riots,' said Blanchaille, trying to be helpful.

Breslau thought this over and nodded approvingly. 'Yes, I suppose that's right. I never thought of it that way. But leaving all this aside, the truth is you can never be sure when the townships are going to be peaceful. You can drive into a township, and I have no option since I do business there, and find yourself in the middle of a riot. You can find yourself humping dead bodies or driving wounded to hospital. You can find yourself dispensing aid and comfort.'

'Aid and comfort?'

'Sure! That comes after the riots, usually, when they've laid out the victims and the relatives come along to claim them. It's an emotional time, as you can imagine. What they usually do these days is to get the priest up from the church and he gives each relative a blessing. Well one day I arrived just as the blessings had started. They didn't seem to be comforting people very much so the police officer in charge commandeered me and my vehicle and all my samples and he suggested that each relative should also get a sample of my shampoo, plus a blessing. Of course they weren't my samples to give, but on occasions like this you don't argue. Well, I stood next to the priest and he gave the blessing and I handed out the sample. Of course there was no question of matching hair types. I mean you can't stop the grieving relatives and ask them whether they suffer from dry, greasy or normal hair. I mean that's not exactly the time and place to start getting finicky. Can I drop you somewhere in town?'

Blanchaille mentioned the suburb where Bishop Blashford lived.

'Sure. Happy to help.'

'What disturbs the peace in the townships?'

Breslau shrugged. 'Everything – and nothing. Of course the

trouble is not having what they want, and then getting what they want. Like I mean first of all they don't have any sewage so the cry goes up for piped sewage and they get it. Then there's no electricity, so a consortium of businessmen organised by Himmelfarber and his Consolidated Holdings put in a private scheme of electrification. Then a football pitch is asked for. And given. And after each of these improvements there's a riot. It's interesting, that.'

'It's almost as if the trouble with the townships is the townships,' Blanchaille suggested.

'You can't not have townships or you wouldn't have any of this,' the salesman gestured out of the window at the blank and featureless veld on either side of the road. 'Cities have townships the way people have shadows. It's in the nature of things.'

'But we haven't always had townships.'

'Of course we have. Look, a township is just a reservoir. A pool. A depot for labour. I mean you look back to how it was when the first white settlers came here. You look at Van Riebeeck who came in – when was it – in 1652? And he arrives at the Cape of Good Hope – what a name when you think how things turned out! A bloody long time ago, right? What does Van Riebeeck find when he arrives in this big open place? He finds he's got to build himself a fort. He finds the place occupied, there are all these damn Hottentots swanning around. Anyway he sees all these black guys wandering around and he thinks to himself – Jesus! This is Christmas! What I'm going to do is sit in my fort, grow lots of vegetables and sell them to passing ships. And all these black Hottentots I see wandering around here, they're going to work for me. If they don't work for me they get zapped. So he sits there at the Cape and the black guys work for him. Afterwards he gets to be so famous they put his face on all the money. It's been like that ever since.'

'But he didn't have a township.'

'What d'you mean, he didn't have a township? The whole damn country was his township.'

Ever cautious Blanchaille got Breslau to drop him not outside Blashford's house, but at the foot of the hill on which the Bishop lived. The salesman drove off with a cheerful wave, 'Keep your head down.'

Blanchaille picked up his cases and began the slow painful ascent of the hill.

Puzzled by this conversation, in my dream I took up the matter with Breslau.

'Surely things aren't that bad? That's a very simplistic analysis of history that you offered him.'

'Right, but then it's a very simplistic situation. There is the view that we're all stuffed. We can fight all we like but we're finished. The catch is that if anyone takes that line they get shot or locked up or whipped. Or all of those things. That's how it was. That's how it is. Nothing's changed since the first Dutchman arrived, opened a police station and started handing out passes to the servants.'

'Can nothing be done to improve conditions in the townships?' I persisted.

Breslau laughed and slapped the steering wheel. 'Sure. As I told the traveller. Lots can be done. Lots is done. Ever since the long-haired vegetable grower arrived from Holland, people have been battling to improve the townships. But after the beer halls and the soccer pitches, the electric lights, the social clubs, the sports stadiums, the literacy classes and the best will in the world, the townships are still townships. And townships are trouble.'

'Even when they're peaceful?' I asked.

'Especially when they're peaceful,' said Breslau.

CHAPTER 5

They walked in the Bishop's official garden. Ceres, Bishop Blashford's ample black housekeeper, had allowed him to leave his suitcases in the hall and sent him out to join His Grace with the warning that he would be allowed no more than ten minutes before His Grace took tea.

Blashford, the unspeakable Blashford, his open face ringed by soft pale curls, had in his younger days played first-class golf: no doubt clouded the sports-writers' prediction that he would have gone on to international competition had the Church not selected him first. He was that rare hierarch, an authentic indigenous bishop, born and educated in the country. By choosing a sportsman for this important appointment the Vatican had shown that it understood where the springs of religious fervour truly lay. Now his neatly shod feet pressed the grass. He was wearing what he called his gardening clothes, a fawn suit and panama hat, by which Blanchaille understood him to mean not those clothes in which he worked in his garden but walked there before tea, a trim, elegant figure with a fair complexion which reddened easily in the sun. His black, heavily armoured toe caps glistened, the double knots of his laces showed like chunky black seaweed as his shoes broke free from the bunched wave of his flannels. There was a brief gleam of polished leather with each assured step he planted on the smooth unwrinkled surface of his beautiful lawn. The end of the official garden was bound by a line of apple and peach trees and behind them a thick pyracantha hedge showed its spikes. Heads held high, wagtails sprinted through the splashes of sunlight beneath the fruit trees, their equilibrium secured by the rocking balance of their long tails. They shared Blashford's dainty-footed confidence.

'Well, Blanchaille?'

'I'm leaving.'

'What?'

'Parish, priesthood, country. The lot. I'm in a position of a bride whose marriage has not been consummated. My ministry is null and void. In short, I'm off.'

'I've been expecting you to call. The volume of complaints from your parishioners in Merrievale these past weeks has reached an

59

absolute crescendo. Complaints had been laid with the police about political speeches from the pulpit. It was only with the greatest difficulty that I managed to persuade the authorities to allow the Church to deal with this in its own way.'

'You needn't have bothered. I also have friends in the police.'

'We all have friends in the police, Father. The question is will yours do what you ask them?'

He could feel the heat the Bishop gave off as he became angrier. He was vibrating like a cooking stove. He hissed from a corner of his mouth: 'It's not like leaving a party, you know. Or getting off a bus. Father Lynch is behind this I'm sure.'

'Father Lynch has never regarded me as a priest. He sees me as a policeman. I'm beginning to realise he knew what he was talking about. My relationship to the Church is that of a partner in an invalid marriage. The thing is null. I wanted to attack the Regime so I followed the only model I had – Father Lynch. I took holy orders. I would have done better learning to shoot.'

'Father Lynch is old, ill and not a little cracked. He flips about that decaying church of his like an ancient bat. He says masses in Latin to a band of parishioners as ill and decrepit as himself. He does so without permission. He keeps up the pretence of serving a parish where none exists. The building is scheduled for demolition. We are finding our way back into the world.'

Ah yes, the world. Blashford had been Bishop for as long as anyone could remember. Years ago he had been concerned with safeguarding the Church against the Calvinist aggressor, those who saw it as 'the Roman danger'. Then came Vatican II, and Blashford discovered 'the world'.

'Father Lynch always predicted that the day was coming when the Church hierarchy would be picked for their salesmanship.'

Blashford scowled. 'The church has been sold because it's redundant. Not only is the fabric beyond repair and the garden ruined, but only a handful of parishioners remain. There is no more room for all-white parishes, holy Mother Church embraces its South African responsibilities, she embraces her black brethren. Father Lynch, as I recall, refuses the embrace.'

The embrace. How long ago Lynch had foreseen that.

'Sitting in his garden long years ago, propped up on one arm with Gabriel and Looksmart Dladla on either side of him, he told us that the Church was ours now, we had better prepare ourselves for the embrace. Then he gathered us around him and he showed us the financial pages of the newspapers which were full of the new black appointments being made by foreign banks. Against fierce resistance from their white managers the head offices decreed that black managers be appointed to township banks. "Very soon now," he said, "we can expect the Church to follow suit. We have always taken our lead from the banks."'

Bishop Blashford joined his fingers together at the bridge of his nose in a prayerful gesture and spoke with a nasal twang into the tepee of his fingers. 'Lynch was headstrong, provocative, premature. Race relations in those days were primitive, it was only on sufferance that we allowed any blacks in our churches at all! You certainly didn't go round making a show of it, not unless you were looking for trouble. But then Lynch was always looking for trouble and you boys he gathered around him were gullible. He was an Irishman who never understood Africa, obsessed by myths and conspiracies. This madness over the Kruger millions, these holidays in fancy dress, these charades. Did you know that he continues to say Mass in Latin? Even though you boys are grown up and gone? Despite all my instructions?'

'He used to tell us that power was in love with secrecy but showed its public face in policies which arose quite arbitrarily or in reaction to outside forces, but were always presented to people as the result of due and deliberate consideration by wise minds. It's unlikely that Lynch would have seen the changes of the Vatican as anything more than panic-stricken measures taken in reaction to shrinking congregations. It was a case of swinging the stage around where they could keep an eye on the audience and getting them to sing along whenever possible. What is presented as the will of God is very often a response to a deteriorating market position, he said.'

'And where did it get you, this adulation of Lynch? You boys who surrounded him with your fancy dress revivals of the old Boer days and your talk of Uncle Paul Kruger? Where it got you was jail, exile, disgrace, death. That's what you got for listening to him.'

'But we never listened to him, that was the trouble. Ferreira was supposed to see visions. Van Vuuren was supposed to be a priest. I was scheduled to become a policeman. But maybe it's not too late. Maybe now he should be taken seriously.'

The Bishop stopped abruptly, he lowered his head, straightened his wrists and shook an imaginary putter, and then with utmost concentration he stroked an imaginary golf ball along the smooth surface of the lawn. This reversion to his old sporting ways suggested a certain tension. This was borne out when the Bishop at length straightened and said: 'There's blood on your shoes,' he looked more closely, 'and on your clothes,' he took Blanchaille's hand, 'and here, more on your hands, under the fingernails.'

'I was passing the township outside the city when I was ordered by the police officer in charge to help to remove the bodies of people shot during the riot.'

'There are no riots in the townships.'

Blanchaille held up his hands with their blood-stained fingernails.

'And what did he predict for Gabriel Dladla?' Blashford suddenly demanded.

'He never prophesied for the black boys. He said they were free agents, outside his range of understanding. Work with materials you know, he said. He would lie under the Tree of Heaven flanked by Gabriel and Looksmart Dladla, looking rather like those porcelain slave boys. You know the kind in turbans carrying bowls of fruit you sometimes see in old pictures? Look at what wins and know why, Lynch always told us. Be sure you select a winner you know, where you're connected. We weren't connected to the structures of Government power, we had no input there, but by the grace of God we had an example a whole lot closer, we had holy Mother Church herself! That would do, he said, as an analogue. All power institutions could be expected to adapt in similar ways. Their trick was to forbid individual alterations to the *status quo* while presenting their own changes as a genuine response to popular demands and altered circumstances, at the same time ensuring that such changes, as and when they were permitted to occur, safe-guarded their sole reason for being, that is to say, the retention of power. The capacity to praise today what you executed people for yesterday, and of course vice versa, always vice versa, and with complete sincerity is essential for the maintenance of power. He invited us to observe that the changes transforming the Catholic Church were undertaken by the very authorities who had forbidden those changes in previous times, to notice the vocabularies used, words like "renewal" and "reaffirmation" and "renaissance", and he invited us to apply what we learnt to the understanding of the way the Regime worked. The keywords for the Regime were "adaption", "evolution", "self-determination". What the words actually said were – O.K. Carruthers let the fuzzies out of the pens but shoot if they stampede. We saw the parallels. Church and Regime believed themselves divinely inspired, both regarded themselves as authoritative and both maintained that they held the secret of salvation. The parallels weren't exact but they were the best we had, he said. We would have to make do with them. And we did. The trouble was –'

Blashford interrupted angrily, 'The trouble was Lynch was mad and he never understood.'

Blanchaille shook his head. 'No, the trouble was we thought it was a game. Spot the connections. We enjoyed it but we didn't believe in it.'

The Bishop paused before a large and blowsy rose. Very deliberately he took the head in his hands and shook the petals so that they fluttered and drifted in the wind.

'This is a lovely garden. I remember it well,' Blanchaille said.

'You know my garden?' Blashford clearly deplored this news.

'I knew the other one better. The one behind the hedge.'

'I never knew I had another garden.'

The Bishop's official garden was very beautiful. The roses, large and blowsy, opened up their heavy red hearts and did not care where their petals drifted. Their perfume was heavy, meaty. Their bruised beefy solidity would have looked well on a butcher's slab. Sweetpeas thronged against the further trellis, the bougainvillaea foamed and dripped and six clipped lemon trees showed bright yellow fruit among darkly gleaming leaves.

But of course it was in the Bishop's other garden that the altar servers had grown up, the wilderness beyond the spiny hedge on the far side of the fruit trees, the neglected vineyard with its harsh, sour grapes, its choked lily pond, its loquat trees, its old disused well, its blackjacks and weeds. They met and smoked cheap American cigarettes, taking as their model the expertise of Van Vuuren who smoked with quite wonderful style and aplomb and adult poise. He was expert in making deep, lengthy inhalations which hollowed his cheeks and they watched fascinated as the jets of grey smoke expelled from his nostrils met and mixed with the single thick gust from his lips. They drank from quarter-bottles of brandy and vodka and dropped the empties down the well, too deep to hear the crash.

And they took girls there. He took Isobel Turner, first and foremost, not particularly highly rated it was true, in Ferreira's opinion 'no great shakes', but the only girl to show an interest. He walked her home from Wednesday Novena, coming to the Bishop's garden meant a lengthy detour but she didn't complain. A stocky twelve-year-old strutting by his side, her little heels clicking on the road, dark curls, large calves, short white socks, a very boyish, broad girl built like a little pony. She was known far and wide as Izzie for short, not a name to do anything for her femininity.

63

Somehow he summoned the courage to lead her into the garden, taking her hand and leading her beneath the trees and she following obediently with her little clip-clop. Once inside, the sharp rattle of undergrowth at their ankles and the moon high overhead, bright, severe and obtrusive like a naked light bulb in a small room, left him at a loss as to how to continue. He drew her beneath the trees where the shadows were and put his arm around her shoulders. They were so broad! He hadn't expected that. He took her hand instead and held it for long minutes, very tightly, and soon their palms were running with sweat. He was at a loss to know how to continue and in despair he said that perhaps they ought to be getting along. There was enough moonlight even under the trees to show her shoulders move in an indifferent shrug and he was conscious of having fallen below expectations. She pulled an apple down from the tree and crunched it right down to the core, ate that, then with a sigh which was more like a neigh, wheeled around and at a fast trot led the way home.

He went to the Bishop's other garden on a later occasion with Magdalena. The Magdalena who gave, the Magdalena who took up with the traitor Kipsel, who afterwards fled to London and was referred to in the papers as Red Magda, but at that time was no more than the amazing Magdalena who gave. Like crazy, without qualm, Ferreira had said. Like wow, Van Vuuren confirmed – his favourite expression of approval at the time. Blanchaille could remember him making the same response after Father Lynch had recounted the harrowing life of the great Italian composer, Gesualdo. Lynch's eyes had closed and a spasm of pain passed over his face.

'Wow? Van Vuuren. What is *wow*! It's hardly a reaction that answers the scale of the human tragedy I've unfolded, you young devil. One makes the mistake of talking about things European to you boys. One makes the mistake of thinking because you are white you must be European. In fact you are African boys. No, not boys but bombs, and in place of minds you have drawersful of high explosives on a short fuse. Not young boys, young bombs, that's what you are. Not listening, not learning, just sitting there waiting, fizzling, until the day you blow up and shower everyone with moral outrage.'

But with Magdalena, *wow*! seemed just about to cover it. He had invited her to Bishop Blashford's vineyard, his other garden, and she had nodded with complete enthusiasm. She had streaked blonde hair. Her face ended in a pointed chin. Her eyes were blue-grey.

He led her through the darkness with a churning stomach feeling rather like a young man who has come into a large fortune and has no idea how to begin spending it. She looked like a model, Van Vuuren had promised. So this was how a model looked! Clearly there could be no holding hands this time. He would grapple her to him. Kiss her. Remove her bra and fondle her breasts, maybe take them in his mouth. Why not? He was fifteen, it was about time. They would lie on the grass afterwards. It happened to be raining softly so perhaps they wouldn't, but if it stopped raining they could lie on her mac. That she wore a mac was evidence of her practicality and added to her charm. Would he try and take off her pants? He doubted it – but nothing was ruled out. They stood beneath the dripping trees and Magdalena drew him towards her and said: 'You're a pretty boy.' Her thin plastic raincoat crackled as she pressed him against her. There was something so practised in the kiss she gave him. Her lips were wet. With a stab of despair he noticed that the buttons on her mac were large and stuffed tightly through their buttonholes. This presented a smooth and shining armoured front. But she was well ahead of him and had no similar problems. Her hand reached up behind him under his shirt pressing into the small of his back. The other hand expertly opened his fly – smooth, fast, deft movements, and then she had his penis in her damp fingers and was lifting it over the elastic band of his underpants which slid painfully upwards to trap his testicles. But then she rubbed and rubbed and soon things grew warm and better. Then he groaned and spurted and all at once she laughed delightedly. 'But you're quick! The quickest I've ever met.' Not quite scorn in the laugh, but tones of someone pleased at their own handiwork and still willing to continue. He knew the matter wasn't closed as far as she was concerned. He also knew he'd come before he'd even kissed Magdalena. There might be more if he liked, he could feel it. It was up to him, he could feel that too. But of course it wasn't. What was to come had been and gone. The elastic cut more cruelly into his testicles. 'You're really nice,' Magdalena said, 'we'll do this again.' His own incompetence baffled and enraged him. Afterwards he picked a small bunch of the Bishop's grapes. Magdalena declined saying they were too sour, but he finished them anyway, sour or not, punishing himself. The perfectly ordinary, reasonable and agreeable reactions of human beings seemed closed to him. A few, like Magdalena, dwelt happily among them. And there was that girl he'd met when he was very much younger, somebody's big sister, whose he couldn't remember. He went to play with her, at her invitation. They played in the empty garage. Postman's knock and spin the bottle.

'How do you play?'

'If your number comes up you pay forfeits.'

'What forfeits?'

'Well, for instance, kisses or feelings, if you like. Otherwise hair-pulls and toe-stamps.'

He won a lot and took hair-pulls and toe-stamps and it was very many years later that it occurred to him what was being offered and why there was that strange, softly appealing note in her voice.

There was no possibility of normal, natural, obvious behaviour for him.

Instead he had, as Lynch said, moral crusades.

'You on our side believe in the multi-racial paradise in which Boer and Zulu lie down together like lambs. There are no longer any Kaffirs, coolies, Jew-boys, coloured bastards, hairies, rock spiders, Dutchmen, all the rich store of invective so vital to political debate – I mention too Rednecks and English swine – and no one notices what colour you are. You believe God is behind you in this. They, on the other side, believe that everyone has their own identity. Everyone deserves separate lavatories and if the crunch comes they will fight to the death, to the last man who will blow his brains out on the last beach, preferring death to dishonour and will go to heaven where there will also be parallel toilet facilities. We are all superior people, on both sides.'

Lynch spat on these dreams, sat beneath the Tree of Heaven spitting with amazing accuracy also into an old brass spittoon. Kruger had spat, with embarrassing frequency, he said, and he enjoyed learning how to do so. 'This society is one of deep criminality, its ministers have a tough job laying down the law, that's why if you want to be a priest, join the police force.'

The Bishop's other garden had been closed to Lynch's altar boys without warning. Three strands of barbed wire slanting inwards were fixed above the hedge and a great new lock appeared on the gate. Gabriel was given the key. The Garden of Eden had been closed, Father Lynch said, and the sinners ejected therefrom. The Archangel barred the way.

'We don't care a damn,' Van Vuuren said, 'he'll have to clear up our mess.'

'He'll have to pick up the french letters, the old cigarettes and clear the well of about a hundred vodka and brandy bottles.'

'He's ending up as just another garden boy,' Blanchaille said.

Father Lynch had listened to all of this with a faint smile. 'But he's in the Bishop's employ, isn't he? At his age and already an episcopal appointment! You keep an eye on Gabriel. That boy will go far.'

Bishop Blashford yawned and stretched. The interview was over.

'Perhaps Gabriel is around? I thought I might say goodbye,' Blanchaille said.

Bishop Blashford beat a retreat to the house where Ceres was waiting at the french windows. She held them open as he approached and once he'd slipped inside she quickly closed them to all but a few inches. Obviously Blanchaille was not invited to tea. 'You go up and see Gabriel,' Blashford shouted through the crack. 'He's our legal eagle. He'll get you whatever papers you need to make the application. There's no more I can do for you. Be it on your own head. Now, if you'll excuse me, I must go and wash my hands.'

'Your bags are outside by the front gate,' Ceres said and closed the french windows with considerable dignity.

CHAPTER 6

Blanchaille walked down the hill struggling with the heavy cases. He regretted vaguely having brought them. Books, socks, clerical suits he had never worn; the blue barathea blazer he was wearing when he entered the seminary, big lapels and double vents – quite out of fashion now . . . the weeds of yesteryear.

The sky above the crest of the hill was dark grey and becoming blacker with every moment. There was something huge and flamboyant about a highveld storm, an occasion of relentless melodrama. The sky grew heavy and crowded in over you. As the storm built, the air became more highly charged. The trees shook themselves. Birds would swoop and flee. The hush would begin to weigh. Occasionally a small wind would drift a few leaves past your ankles or slide past the eyebrows carrying a faint watery scent. The first flash would come, white as a slash of chalk across a blackboard and a crash that split the ear-drums. But it did not necessarily mean rain, something might happen in the atmosphere and the storm would wheel and miss you leaving you only with prodigious explosions, blackness and vivid fractures of light. All show, impressive but empty bluster, truncheon weather, crash, bash, wallop. Your hair stood on end but you didn't get wet. Yet you felt the threat, looked with respect at the towering darkness above. Not for nothing did the Regime sometimes broadcast important policy statements on radio and television during electrical storms, the words interspersed by static and thunder. When it did rain, the relief was palpable.

A large black car came bowling down the hill and stopped beside him with a shriek of brakes. The window descended with smooth electrical precision, and there was Gabriel. The interior of the car smelt of its blue vinyl coverings and the refrigerated whisper of its air conditioning. Gabriel didn't switch off the engine. The car waited, hissing faintly. Gabriel massaged his jaw, smooth, golden, smiling, a model of casual elegance.

'What's this, Blanchie? You'll be soaked if it comes down. You're a long way from home.'

Blanchaille nodded. Maybe he should ask his question now?

'I'd give you a lift but I'm meeting the Rome plane. Vatican bigwigs. Visiting firemen. Ah well – no rest for the wicked.'

'No.'

'Never be a bishop's chaplain.'

'No,' said Blanchaille, 'I won't.'

Blanchaille watched the big black car go purring down the hill. He hadn't asked his question. It was this: Looksmart Dladla had been warned to get out of the country by his brother. Fair enough. So then, if Gabriel told Looksmart the cops wanted him in connection with the Kipsel business, who told Gabriel?

As he reached the bottom of the hill the first drops fell but he was lucky enough to find a bus stop and gratefully took shelter beneath the corrugated iron roof, swung his cases up on the bench and himself up beside them while the rain sheeted down and ran rivers of red mud and gravel beneath the spindly metal legs of the shelter. Highveld rain was like no other, the drops were large and would sting the hand and batter the head, drilling into the earth, beating and upbraiding it. The highveld rain had weight and made each drop count, was a battering of the country, brief but overwhelming. The earth, so dry, was soon saturated in great pools everywhere, joining up into streams carrying off the top soil, rough brown surges hurtling down the gutters and thundering in the storm-water drains, and everything which had been settled was fluid and running. It never lasted of course. After the deluge the sun would come out and everything dried away to sticky mud and then to dust. But while it lasted the world ran free, and the mind with it.

Now in my dream, as the storm began tapering off, a figure stepped out of the rain and sat beside him on the bench. 'God Almighty, Blanchie! Did I not direct you to the Airport Palace?' Father Lynch's black raincoat was a sheen of wet cloth; rain gathered in the brim of his hat; when he spoke a hundred droplets exploded in the air before his mouth. 'You delayed. And now you may find the going harder. Bubé is gone!'

'So?'

'What do you mean – so? This is the most extraordinary news. At last the truth is beginning to emerge. Bubé has gone. Of course this affects your travel plans.'

'Why should it?'

'Why? Because the roads will be full of police. Theodore, for the first time since Paul Kruger's departure, a president has fled! Adolph Gerhardus Bubé has fled!'

Adolph Gerhardus Bubé, father of the nation. An intellectual who studied in his youth in universities in Holland, Germany and Belgium. One of the original founders of the old policy of ethnic parities, as it was then called, with his thesis 'Racial Separation with Justice', which became the Ur-text, the philosophical underpinning of the racial policy of equal freedoms or concomitant responsibilities, the vision of 'ethnic heartlands' each reflecting its distinctive tribal rhythm, each tribe breeding to its heart's content. It was from this thesis that many of the crucial ideas of modern South Africa originated, regarded as revolutionary once but now outmoded, its once striking maxims absorbed into everyday language, sentiments such as: 'There's no such place as South Africa', or as Pik Honneger, his most distinguished disciple put it, 'What's ours is ours, and what's theirs is what we are prepared to give them.'

Bubé's thesis had been required reading on Father Lynch's picnics. It was Lynch who pointed out how profoundly influenced Bubé had been throughout his career, as a young MP, as a distinguished Economics Minister and as President – by the birthrate. Bubé in his formal suits, with his paunch, his watch chain, his benign manner made speech after speech pointing to the burgeoning black population and he would appeal to his followers to remember the old Boer wife in the days of the Great Trek, during the wars of freedom and the oppression of the Boers by the British Empire. The old Boer wife, he said, had been a breeding machine, her womb was a weapon more potent than the Mauser, a holy factory in which there was renewed each month a new army, the white man's hope of a secure future in South Africa where he could thrive and prosper and protect his traditional way of life, his culture and his Christian God. But now the white birth-rate was spiralling down to zero growth while the black man was rearming in the belly of his wives. Tirelessly the President expounded his theme: 'White women, remember your duty!' HAVE A BABY FOR BUBÉ! the headlines ran. His supporters took up the slogan and ran through the streets chanting it, breaking into chemist shops, puncturing contraceptive sheaths and flushing birth control pills down the toilet and assaulting non-white persons for allegedly failing to respect pregnant white women. It was Bubé who funded the sterilisation campaign in the countryside, the secret radiation trucks, the so-called 'Nagasaki ambulances' which so terrified the rural population.

Lynch often expatiated upon the role of President Bubé, as he rested beneath the Tree of Heaven. 'It was our Adolph who reminded us that an earlier and better name for the Boer War was the Gold War. It was a war between Gold Bugs, who understood the importance of the metal, and the Boers who had still to learn this. The British Army came in on the side of the Gold Bugs – people like Werner and Beit, Himmelfarber etc. Let's not believe the story put out by men in an advanced state of dementia such as Cecil Rhodes, or Alfred Milner that they were defending the Anglo-Saxon race of which the English, God forgive poor Rhodes, were regarded as the most perfect flower, "the best, the most human, the most honourable race the world possesses . . ." This I quote to you from his *Confession of Faith*. Have you ever heard such rubbish? Reasons, you see – *reasons*. We must have reasons before the killing can begin. The Boers on their side under Kruger were fighting, they said, for the right to be free, for Calvinist Afrikanerdom, for the little man against the big, for independence, for truth. All lies, all lies. Gold it was and gold it has always been, the dream, the rumour, the hope and despair of the conquerors and of the conquerors before them, Arabs and Portuguese both. Stories of magical gilded cities, of Solomon's mines, of Monomatapa and Vigiti Magna lured them here. The Portuguese, the Dutch, the British and finally even the Boers, they all wanted it. Rhodes and all his fellow Bugs had the gold but Kruger owned the sacred soil from which it was mined. They thought that the Boers didn't want the gold. How absurd! It was the miners they hated. They saw them as the sub-life that crawled beneath the stone, so they averted their eyes, usually upward to God their Father and kept to the veld, content with their horses, their guns, a herd or two, the horizon endlessly receding, a host of servants and a wife in the back room breeding like a machine, claiming always simply that they wished to be left alone. The Boers were the Greta Garbos of history. The Boers didn't want the gold only so long as no one else had it. But they soon found the stuff had its uses. Before the war they were already building up their funds by illicitly buying gold stocks and amalgam from shady sellers. There were organised Government theft departments, that's what it amounted to. Contemporary observers were lost in admiration for the bribery, greed, corruption, the whole quality of the unblushing venality with which those involved enriched themselves in the Boer Republics. The lot of them. All those wily Hollanders surrounding Kruger, were rotten from the toes up. The Transvaal Government was supported by secret funds administered from secret accounts and with this stash fund the Krugerites bought votes, nobbled opponents, paid off old scores and enriched family and friends. When the war broke out they no longer had to buy their gold under the table, because they'd taken over the gold mines. They could take it straight out of the ground and put it into their vaults. So when they went to war with the British they said they were fighting for God and freedom and independence. But by then they knew that whoever got the gold had God and freedom thrown in buckshee. Even so, as Bubé points out in his thesis, men like Kruger and Rhodes were of the old century. Nineteenth-century men. And the quality of their hypocrisy and the nature of their corruption was a Victorian thing. The gold was a means, the way you paid for your dreams, financed them. The difference with us, the New Men, Bubé says, is that gold came first, the dreams later. You can see this change taking place at the end of the Boer War when even the most Christian fighting generals became bank robbers literally overnight. As the British marched into the capital, General Smuts was holding up the Standard Bank and the Mint and making off with a cool half-million in gold. Kruger saw it coming. His *Memoirs* make it clear that the discovery of gold was a catastrophe. It would 'soak the country in blood'.

The rain had stopped. Sheets of muddy water rushed past the two priests in the bus shelter. They could hear it thundering deep down in the storm-water drains.

'With Bubé's flight history comes full circle. It's the Kruger departure all over again. Heaven be praised!' Lynch's jug ears waggled in delight. Blanchaille noticed that the old man appeared to have lost more of his teeth. He grinned like an ancient baby. 'You're still planning to travel?'

Blanchaille nodded, 'Yes Father.'

'Oh you call me Father all right, but I'm not, you know. *Of course* you know! I'm more like an uncle to you boys. I like you, that makes me really different, close. Yes, I like you and mind you I'm probably the only one who does – and I nourish hopes for you all yet, though I look dark into your futures. But Father you call me! And what do you call your old President, the President Kruger? Why man, you call him Uncle, Uncle Paul! But that's all wrong. Sure it is. He's not your uncle, I am. He's your father, father of the nation, father of misfortune. Follow Kruger, find the truth. That's the line, Blanchie. Stick to it like glue as you're pitched into an uncertain future. Be sure and look out for your old Uncle Lynch because he'll be looking out for you. Take this. Trust me.' Lynch gave him a brown envelope on which an address was scrawled. 'You'll need cash.' The envelope smelt faintly of pistachio.

'You've taken Ferreira's money!' Blanchaille was outraged.

'I've simply returned the funds Ferreira bequeathed to you and which you unwisely left behind when you fled. I give it to you, after making suitable deductions. You can take a bus from here. At this address a friend is waiting. It's nine stages, and then you hop.'

Blanchaille counted the nine stages because he hoped against hope he might end up at an address different to that given on the envelope. It did no good. Nine stages brought him to the centre of the town, to the tall skyscraper known as Balthazar Buildings which housed the Security Police, the Special Branch and the organisation, so secret no one could be certain of its existence, known as the Bureau, under its phantom chief, Colonel Terblanche.

CHAPTER 7

Balthazar Buildings on Jan Smuts Square in the centre of the city –
notorious headquarters of the Security Police, scene of violent
incidents beyond number. Together with the usual offices it
comprised several hundred cells, interrogation rooms, as well as
offices of the Bureau for Public Safety, or, more briefly, the Bureau.
So mysterious that a Government committee found itself unable to
confirm its existence, despite the fact that a number of the
committee members were rumoured to be officers of the Bureau, or
Bureaucrats, as the knowing called them. Balthazar Buildings also
housed *Die Kring*, or the Ring, a secret society formed, according to
legend, at the turn of the century, at the time of Kruger's flight into
Swiss exile and dedicated to the preservation of the Calvinist ideal,
and the continuance, protection and furtherance of the Boer
nation. On the further fringes of the political spectrum, Blanchaille
remembered, there had been speculation that the Bureau and the
Ring were one and the same. Perhaps. There were many such secret
societies, all-male, dominated by devoted followers of the Regime,
dedicated to racial purity and in love with uniforms – the Phantom
Kommando; the Afrika Straf Kaffir Brigade; the Night Riders; the
Sons of Freedom; the Ox-Wagon Patriots – but the Ring, it was
said, controlled and dominated them all.

It had been claimed that the Ring was a fascist secret society.
Bubé had denied this, as had every president before him – all of
whom were members of the Ring. 'The English have their Rotary
Clubs, the Catholics have the Jesuits, the Bantu have their burial
societies – and we have the Ring. It is not a society, it is more like a
family gathering.'

It was with considerable trepidation that Blanchaille surveyed the
stone steps leading up to the great steel doors of Balthazar Buildings
and only by considerable effort of will did he tell himself that if this
was the place to which Lynch had directed him then he must have
his reasons. Across the road a boy was selling papers. PRESIDENT FOR
TREATMENT OVERSEAS? the posters ran. So Lynch had got hold of the
right story, at any rate. Blanchaille pushed the bell. Few who came
to Balthazar Buildings ever emerged unless they were led away to
waiting police vans, to court, to jail, to the gallows. Others left

briefly in flights from high windows, or tripped down staircases, or were found hanging from their cell bars by their belts or pyjama cords. This fortress housed the Russian spy Popov. Two TV cameras swivelled above his head and examined him silently.

The young constable who let him in was of the type Blanchaille knew well from school rugby matches against just such long-limbed, rangey sorts, full-grown men at twelve with moustaches to prove it. They smelt of sweat and onions and stomped you unmercifully whenever you went down with the ball. He gave his name. There he was in Balthazar Buildings along with the likes of Popov. He hoped Lynch knew what he was doing.

The story of Popov was widely known and loved and taught in school. Once a cipher clerk named Steenkamp was sitting at his desk in Balthazar Buildings on Sunday afternoon, hot and bored. He had just decided, by his own admission, that his job as a security policeman was at an end. The codes were beyond him and the amount of application required was simply too much for a simple man. And a simple man he was, this Steenkamp, the fifth son of a large and impoverished Karoo family, regarded by his superiors as a good policeman but unimaginative and perhaps a trifle slow. There was no hint then of the blaze of glory with which his career was to be crowned and was to make his photograph a familiar sight in every house in the country. Blanchaille had seen the photograph, everyone had seen the photograph. The mild empty eyes, the bored and unlined forehead which gave him the look of a man a decade younger than his forty years, the strong curling hair and the protuberant ears, the penalty of playing lock-forward for many years for the police team without wearing a scrum cap. It was this Steenkamp who one hot afternoon happened to look out of his window and see down below in the street a man taking photographs of him. He might have been picking his nose or yawning and there was this stranger in the street below taking pictures! He was down the stairs two at a time and he collared the impudent photographer who turned out to be Nikita Popov, a genuine, real, live Russian spy, and a full colonel in the KGB. It was a considerable coup and the President, wearing his other hat as Police Minister, went on television and thanked the Security Services for their watchfulness and said, 'Let this be a lesson to any other hostile countries who may have thought of infiltrating agents. The Security Forces are ready and waiting for them and will do their utmost to defend the country's integrity against the orchestrators of the Total Onslaught.' A police spokesman in turn thanked the Minister for thanking the police and the session ended in an orgy of mutual gratitude.

An anti-Regime paper caused a stir by suggesting the arrest was a fluke. The police issued a statement asserting that Steenkamp had known immediately that something deeply suspicious was going on since photographing police property was forbidden, along with army property, railway stations, harbours, electric pylons, atomic research centres and at least three hundred and sixty-three other items, from the servants of ministers to radio stations, which fell within the so-called 'Sensitive Subject Catalogue', regularly updated in the *Government Gazette*. As a general rule of thumb photographers should stick to photographing one another, unless one of them happened to be a banned person or a named Communist, in which case such photographs were also against the law. A few voices were raised inquiring how it was that a Russian colonel in the KGB should have entered the country in the first place and why he should spend his afternoons photographing police stations? But in a fiery parliamentary speech the Minister for Defence, the former army chief General Greaterman declared that the Russians were a devious and stealthy people and that such queries were clearly designed to denigrate the police and should cease immediately, or else. As for Steenkamp, he was sent to lecture at various police colleges and became a kind of saint for the new, young recruits who prayed that they too might one day strike such a blow for their country.

A photograph of Popov appeared which was to become 'the photograph': it showed a round, rather soft, boyish face with just a trace of a slant to the dark eyes, a sleepy, not unintelligent look, and, if you peered at it very closely, a gleam of utter astonishment in those eyes. Here was a living rebuke to those who accused the Regime of seeking Reds under the beds. Well, now the secret was out, they were in the streets taking photographs. The interest in Popov was enormous. It was presumed that he would be thoroughly interrogated, and then executed. A group of nurseryschool teachers canvassed the idea that the method of his execution should be one which would least disfigure his person. They argued that coming across Popov like this was rather like being given a giant panda, a rarity which should be preserved, perhaps put on display in a public place in a glass case where groups of school children could be taken to be shown the true reality of the Russian menace. 'Cut out his *derms*, stuff him and mount him!' sang the children in kindergarten

76

as they drew pictures of the spy, Popov.

Blanchaille waited in the lobby, a bare place with a desk and a few chairs. On the walls were the TV monitors for the closed-circuit cameras. Could the screams of the detained be heard from here? He strained his ears. Silence. There were two portraits on the wall. One showed President Bubé in tribal dress. Chief for the afternoon of some forsaken tribe upon which the Regime had visited the dubious distinction of independence and the President had gone along in ceremonial tribal finery to cut the umbilical cord. He wore a bulky fur hat, perhaps torn from a meerkat, and its tail curled about his neck. Over his shoulders hung a pelt, monkey probably, and beneath that another spotted skin, leopard perhaps. Various herbs and amulets dangled from his shoulders and sleeves and he carried a short stabbing spear and a cowhide shield. Even beneath this exotic head-dress his round owlish face in its heavy spectacles peered out almost piteously. Beneath the animal skins he could be seen to be wearing a dark morning suit and tie. He looked as if he were about to burst into tears. He would have made a speech to the gathered tribe standing upon a chair beneath a thorn tree.

> 'Dear Friends, it is nice to be here with you. I am from the Government and the Government's attitude is that we have to help people like you to have a better life in this beautiful country of ours. With that I will say goodbye and may you stay well.'

A similar speech was given by ministers visiting resettlement camps. But there it was followed by a hymn from the people – usually a lament.

On the opposite wall was the famous Kruger portrait. Blanchaille knew it well for Lynch always had a copy on his wall. Uncle Paul wore a top hat and his beard was thick and white with holes in it like a hedge that has been eaten away. Around his barrel chest was a broad green sash and on the right shoulder was a silver epaulette to take the sash – this epaulette was thickly fringed in tufty gold thread hanging in rich fronds. The old man's beard, so untidy, yellowly white, had the look of a fake. It seemed theatrical, stuck on, as if a powerful hand reaching below the ear lobe might with a sudden tug strip it from the powerful jaw with a medicinal screech. Perhaps the same might be done with the cotton wool eyebrows. 'Look to the past,' Kruger had written to his people as he lay dying in exile,

Lynch had taught, the African Moses warning his unruly people that if they forgot their God then they would perish and never find the Promised Land. 'The old Israelites built a golden calf,' Lynch said, 'these new ones build a stock exchange, they build a share portfolio, they build an army, they build themselves. They look to the future.'

The officer who entered was instantly familiar, the thick black hair glossed over the ears, the square powerful hands, the solid square jaw and his manner somewhere between that of some distinguished visiting specialist in the house of a dangerous case and a powerful athlete, a weight-lifter with a muscle-bound body unused to moving in a suit, and that strange, well-remembered faintly menacing mixture of formality and muscle power. But the smile was the same: open, pleasant, appealing. An utter contradiction stretching back to hostel days when he would half kill a boy for stepping out of line, then break every rule with affable, serene good nature and never a qualm.

'Hello Blanchie, long time no see.'

How long? At least ten, fifteen, years since Father Lynch, Van Vuuren, Ferreira, Zandrotti, little Mickey and Kipsel set off on holiday. They rode in an old Studebaker which Lynch had borrowed from somewhere, towing a caravan. It had been a Sprite, he remembered that, he could still see the flighty 'Caravans International' logo. The caravan was not for sleeping in, they had tents for that. Instead the vehicle was packed with large black boxes tied up with string. It had been a last holiday for Father Lynch and his altar boys. They were suspicious of the term 'holiday', knowing what Lynch had done to 'picnics'. It was all very mysterious but Lynch would say no more. All in good time. Officially it was put about that they were going to the Game Reserve. They would be exploring the flora and fauna of the Eastern Transvaal.

The Eastern Transvaal was a countryside vividly beautiful, of tangled greenery, plunging waters, thronging banks of azaleas which grew ever thicker as they approached the water; and then the crouching, tousled, tawny veld with its stinging sibilance where the thorn trees held up their fierce yellow heads in the hottest of suns. And it *was* hot. At noon the tall choked grass began ticking like a clock. The day wore on, wore out, and with the evening coming on the sky would turn a flushed pink, the colour of an electric bar-heater and the glow caught the undersides of the clouds and showed them pink and gold. The day didn't die but burnt away, faded suddenly with the last light in a smell of wood-smoke and the first crickets shrieking among the lengthening shadows.

Lynch had taken them to the Kruger Game Reserve, advising them to enjoy it while it lasted for soon work would start. They saw some lion, several buck, a couple of giraffe and then an extraordinary aged buffalo. This beast was indelibly printed on Blanchaille's memory; it was a buffalo seemingly determined to shatter its reputation as the most dangerous animal alive, terrifying when angered, capable of moving at amazing speed. When they drove up beside it, it stood there with its shuffling lop-sided bulk and its expression of weary but disconcertingly kind intelligence. The horns were a marvel, razor sharp, ready to kill, but seemed more homely than dangerous, appropriate, even graceful. They looked like the stiffened plaits on a little girl, they traced the outlines of a Dutch cap beginning in two thick round plaits clamped to the top of the skull, sweeping down and up in beautifully symmetrical curves into whittled points. Looked at another way they gave the impression of a frozen hairstyle, a stylised wig. The buffalo's forehead was broad, deeply lined and strangely white, perhaps this was where he showed his age. It was, if one could conceive of such a thing, a thinker's forehead. The eyes were not impressive, being small, bleared, brown beneath their heavy lids. A single stem of broken grass hung head downwards from the buffalo's mouth. If anything looked dangerous and menacing about the buffalo it was the ears, which were busy, angry, muscular. 'People will not believe it when you tell them you were frightened by a buffalo's ears,' Lynch warned.

The Elands River Falls gave its name to two villages, one beneath the waterfall and appropriately called Waterval Onder, and the one above called Waterval Boven. It was to Waterval Onder that Father Lynch came with his boys and his caravan on that one and only holiday and just outside town the camp was set up. The mysterious cardboard boxes were unpacked and were found to contain the uniforms of Boer soldiers, leather trousers you wrapped around yourself called *klapbroek*, bandoliers, muskets and hats. The boys became Boers and the caravan became a railway saloon and Father Lynch, in yellow straggly beard and cotton wool eyebrows became, of course, President Kruger. For it was here at Waterval Onder that the Boers had their last glimpse of their leader, of the Old Lion, before the railway line carried him out of the country forever. Lynch pointed out that the building of this line had long been Kruger's dream. He wanted a rail link which ran from his capital through the Eastern Transvaal and into Portuguese East Africa and the friendly port of Lourenço Marques, a line which avoided the hated dependency on the ports in the rest of the country held by the British. As it happened, he proved to be the most valuable piece of freight it ever carried. Outside Waterval Boven, President Kruger old and ill (Lynch in the part) sat once again, watched by Denys Reitz and his brother Hjalmar (Blanchaille and Van Vuuren), reading his Bible in the railway saloon (played by the Sprite caravan), 'a lonely, tired man' Reitz observed.

Lynch made them walk the distance between Waterval Onder and Waterval Boven which, although only some eight kilometres in distance, was virtually straight uphill and Lynch pointed out to them the one and only stretch of railway still to be seen there, built by the South African Railway Company in 1883. He took them to the tunnel cut through the rock beside the pretty Elands River Falls to help reduce the gradient and he pointed out the old stone bridge with its graceful arches along which the trains had trundled as they crossed the aptly named Get-Lost-Hill stream. How much had been lost crossing that stream! The presidential train had strained up the steep gradient of one in twenty, crossed the border and steamed into the port of Lourenço Marques where the Dutch cruiser, the *Gelderland*, lay riding at anchor in the blue swell of the Indian Ocean. And the gold went with him on 21 October 1900.

In bullion or minted coins, in gold dust or in bars? And in what guise? And how much? Father Lynch stood on the quayside in Lourenço Marques and stroked his fake beard, and wondered aloud. His boys in their slouch hats and their crossed bandoliers sweated beside him in the moth-eaten uniforms, the stage property of some defunct theatrical company which Lynch had raided for these old khaki cast-offs, *velskoens* and reproduction muzzle loaders. And did the millions really go at all? Or was it another story? They wanted to ask but dared not. Lynch stood there comfortably enough in top hat and fake beard but his boys were deeply embarrassed by the looks they were given by the black Portuguese who giggled behind their hands and pointed.

'Jesus, what a bunch of tits we must look!' he remembered Ferreira fumed.

Blanchaille answered Van Vuuren, 'How long? Not since we were living history.'

'Living history! We were dying of embarrassment,' Van Vuuren said. 'He claimed he was trying to make us understand the roles we played.'

Blanchaille remembered how they had shuffled and glowered and banged their rifle butts on the ground. 'I never felt a bit like a Boer.'

'Lynch never cared about our feelings. He made us pretend because he knew that's what we did best. Lynch wanted us to understand that our lives were all play-acting. There was nothing real about them. He wanted us to see that all we lived for was to pretend to be what we weren't. Your role, Blanchie, has always reminded me of St Paul. You remember the trouble with St Paul, don't you? He spent all those years persecuting Christians for being Christian and then he got converted and spent the rest of his life persecuting them for not being Christian enough. And for that he was canonised by his grateful victims. God's policeman, old Paul was. And you're another. Why do you think Lynch always insisted that you'd gone to police college and refused to accept that you were in the Seminary? The dogmatic, policeman-like qualities in you, were what he saw. Look at your life! You went into the camps and you gave the Regime hell for treating people like garbage. You attacked the Church, your own church, at every turn for failing in its responsibility. Then you took to touring the country like a wandering madman demanding that the camps be bulldozed. Then you were given a church and you stood up in the pulpit and addressed your parishioners like the investigating officer. You stood up there to unmask the villain, like the tiny Flemish tax inspector or the seemingly genial ex-nun in the detective yarn unmasking the totally unsuspected killer. You expected them to stand up and confess. Instead, like Makapan, they lost their tempers and besieged your house. Well, what did you expect? You've lived the investigating life, you've taken the high moral ground, you've gone after the culprits, the criminals. Your vocation is to bring the guilty ones to book, you're the holy detective, the righteous sleuth. And where's it got you? Nowhere. It's done nothing for you – except to ruin you. You've taken the drugs this country offers moral outrage, angry condemnation – and they've wrecked you. You're on your last legs and you're going down, you're going out.'

'And you? I suppose you know better,' Blanchaille said angrily.

'I joined the police because I believed I would find out what was really going on. You know what it's like. Under the Regime everything important is called a police matter, history is a police matter. All presidents as far back as Babbelas and Breker have also held the portfolio of Minister of Police. You know the argument –

the State is an instrument of God. Its security is a matter of divine concern. The police are the mediators between the Almighty and the citizen. I believed it. We all believed it.'

'Of course.'

'But Blanchie, what if it isn't true?'

'You mean it isn't true?'

'Not entirely. That's the thing. Nothing is entirely true. Or entirely anything. I began to learn that as a rookie cop when they put me on surveillance in a department called "foreign friends". Now that alone was an eye-opener. I thought we didn't have any foreign friends. Or need them. Or want them. We were the Albania of the South. Our foreign policy was to tell everyone to go and get stuffed. But that's wrong! We've got loads of foreign friends. That's why President Bubé went on his whirlwind foreign tour. He wasn't foisting himself on his hosts in the capitals of Europe. He was returning calls! We do have foreign friends. Lots. And I was detailed to watch over them. Once they came singly: businessmen, politicians – here to collect their bribes to arrange shipments of materials we needed like planes or football teams. But soon we had so many foreign friends they took block bookings and came on chartered flights calling themselves the Patagonian Hockey Team and were taken away in buses with darkened windows. I got assigned to one of these teams. The papers usually got the story after the new arrivals had been spirited away and ran headlines like: VICTORY FOR GOVERNMENT SPORTS POLICY: PATAGONIANS TO TOUR! This led to world-wide protests and the Patagonians would flatly deny that any of their teams was playing in South Africa. By then the 'team' had disappeared. I looked after a team who wore baseball caps the wrong way round, with the peaks down their necks. Or yarmulkas. And they'd get drunk with the township girls and cause us a lot of trouble. They worked in a camp in the mountains outside the capital. It turned out that the language they were speaking was Hebrew and they were scientists of some sort. I went to my superiors and said, "Look there's a colony of Jewish scientists working in the mountains." "Nonsense," my superiors said. "They're not Jews, they're Israelis. And this conversation did not take place." I was sent to another camp about five miles away. This one was a very different kettle of fish. It was full of Chinese. Now wasn't that strange? I mean we don't even have Chinese laundries and here is a colony of Chinese working in a strange factory. I went to my supervisors. "Look here," I said, "what are all these Chinese doing? I thought we didn't like Chinese. I thought the

Regime had taken a vow of No More Coolies! Ever since their bad experience with the indentured labourers on the gold mines early this century." "There are no Chinese," said my superiors, "only Taiwanese and this conversation did not take place." Then I was taken off people and put on to things. I was posted to security on the atomic research station out there in the mountains. I missed the voluble scientists and the quiet, hardworking technicians but you go where you're sent. The atomic research station was getting large shipments of equipment. I happened to see the inventories. They took delivery of something called the Cyber 750-170 which is an interesting computer. Because its main strength is multi-channel analysis, it's used for sorting through the hundreds of cables collecting data from a test-blast site. Other shipments to the research centre included vibration equipment and ballistic re-entry vehicles. Oh, I almost forgot, there were supplies of some gas too, Helium 3 it was. I thought about this. You put together the scientists, the technicians and the equipment and you come up with something that explodes.'

Blanchaille began to understand. He knew the rumours, the unmentionable stories.

Van Vuuren's blue eyes widened. 'Go on, Blanchie, take a guess.'

'A bomb! The bastards are building a bomb. Now the question is – are we working on a large dirty weapons system, or small, relatively clean devices? Neutron bombs, say? Or field launching systems. Yes, tactical battlefield weapons. Or both? That would give flexibility. Large bombs against hostile forces on our borders, or on the capital of an enemy, or on the capitals of states supporting that enemy. Then the smaller, cleaner, weapons for specific jobs, say the 155 millimeter cannon, capable of lobbing nuclear shells. But what's the gas for? This Helium 3?'

'It's used to make Tritium. That's a form of hydrogen used in thermo-nuclear weapons.'

'What a lot you know about this sort of thing,' Blanchaille said.

'I remember hearing about it first years ago from Kipsel, Silberstein and Zandrotti and the others in their bomb-making days. No, I did not interrogate them, that affair was before my appointment to Interrogation, or Twenty Questions, as they call it here. But I read the report of Kipsel's confessions. Even though all they were planning to demolish were a few pylons, Kipsel was never one to do anything by halves. He got Silberstein to swot up on everything from fireworks to weapons in the megaton range.'

Blanchaille nodded. 'Lawyers read.'

Van Vuuren looked cagey. 'They were young. They confused yearning with faith. They really believed the revolution had started. Zandrotti was convinced.' Again the odd look, almost embarrassment. 'Poor old Zandrotti.'

'We were all young and we all believed. What else could we do?'

'Sure, sure.' Van Vuuren regarded him steadily. 'From what I've told you, then, you conclude that we're building a bomb, or rather the Taiwanese are building us a bomb designed by the Israelis who are selling it to us wholesale?'

'Seems like it.'

'You know of course that the Regime deny that we possess any nuclear weapons – and when mysterious explosions occurred in the southern hemisphere the Regime rejected American claims that we were testing nuclear weapons. They said it was atmospheric disturbance, or the American instruments were faulty. Then they said a meteorite landed in the Namib Desert. So what do we surmise from that?'

'That they were lying.'

Van Vuuren's blue eyes widened still further. 'Certainly not. We agree that there was no explosion. From there we go on to state categorically that we have no nuclear weapons.'

Now it was Blanchaille's turn to stare. 'But you said –'

'No. I didn't.'

'But I heard you.'

'You couldn't have done. This conversation never took place.' Van Vuuren took a photograph from a desk drawer and fanned himself with it absently. 'What is the official policy towards the Russians, Blanchie?'

'The Russians are our enemies. They are after our gold, our diamonds, our minerals, our strategic positions, our sea-lanes. We do not talk to the Russians, have never talked to them, will never talk to them.'

'Excellent answer. Now have a look at this.' Van Vuuren handed him a small black and white photograph, rather grainy and blurred, as if taken from a distance. In the foreground two men were walking together, behind them a busy street with trams. 'Paradeplatz in Zurich where the banks sell gold like hot rolls in a baker's window. Do you recognise the men?'

Blanchaille studied the grainy photograph. The two men were deep in conversation. The older man wore a black Homburg. The other looked younger, was bare-headed, fair-haired.

'Never seen either before.'

'The man on the left in the hat is a Russian. The official, accredited roving representative of the Bank of Foreign Trade in Moscow, on secondment to the Wozchod Handelsbank in Zurjch. The other man is Bennie Craddock, an executive of Consolidated Holdings and the nephew of its Chairman, Curtis Christian Himmelfarber. Here is another photograph of Craddock, this time in Moscow. Notice anything?'

The photograph showed Craddock standing in a snowy Red Square surrounded by what appeared to be curious bystanders.

'Yes,' said Blanchaille, 'he seems to be crying.'

'Odd, isn't it? Why go all the way to Moscow for a cry? It's as odd as the spy Popov's behaviour when he was arrested outside this very building. He was reported to be very, very angry. It puzzled me. That he was upset I can understand, even anguished, but *angry*? No, I can't make sense of that. And I can't clear up the mystery by asking anyone. What strikes me about this investigation is that there are more and more mysteries and fewer and fewer people to question. I've had the urge, increasingly hard to resist, to call off the whole damn investigation and start praying. It starts with Ferreira. Somebody has been telling stories about Ferreira. He dies. Shares fall on the Exchange. People disappear leaving behind only the stories we go on telling about them. Craddock has not been seen since the photograph was taken. And his uncle, Himmelfarber, is abroad. So many people are overseas. Have you noticed? Minister Gus Kuiker and his Secretary of Communications are out of the country. The President is said to be travelling overseas for medical treatment. Even you will soon be gone.'

'You could ask Popov yourself, you've got him here. "Why the rage Nikita?" you could say.'

'I heard why – from Himmelfarber. Popov's gone. He was spirited away by the Bureau and now he, like it, may or may not exist. You see how isolated I am, Blanchie? Even those who assigned me to investigate the murder of Tony Ferrcira have gone. I had no shortage of instructions. First to put me on the case was the President himself. It's his prerogative when he wears his other hat as Minister of Police so I went to it with a will. President Bubé implied that Minister Kuiker might have had some involvement. As I knew that Gus Kuiker is a rising star in the Regime, tipped to succeed Bubé one day, or even replace him, I put this down to professional jealousy. After all Kuiker took over Bubé's baby platform. The President went around the country encouraging white women voters to breed; but Kuiker took positive steps to reduce the opposition birth-rate and he used science. He made it his aim to reduce the non-white breeding potential by one half and he got the boffins involved. All Bubé did was to encourage white women to have more babies. Whereas Kuiker hit the enemy where he lived –in the womb. He got the reputation of a modern whizz-kid. Bubé never forgave him. But Kuiker didn't care.'

Of course Kuiker did not care. Augustus Carel Kuiker, Minister for Parallel Equilibriums, Ethnic Autonomy and Cultural Communication, cared only for success. Kuiker with the thick, ridged, almost stepped hairstyle, a rugged jaw and heavy, surprisingly sensuous lips. He looked like a rather thuggish Charles Laughton. Blanchaille recalled Kuiker's speeches, how he tirelessly stomped the country reeling off figures. The total population was already over twenty-seven million, it could rise to thirty-eight million or more by the year 2000. The number of whites was dropping. Zero population growth might be all very well for the rest of the world but for the Europeans of the southern sub-continent it was suicide. The percentage, now about sixteen, would fall to eleven after the turn of the millennium. The Government, he announced, might have to introduce a programme. It would not shrink from introducing a programme. This programme might well involve penalising certain groups if they had too many children as well as offering sterilisation and abortion on demand. He felt sure that many black people would welcome abortion on demand, and even, he hinted with that famous frown wrinkling across his forehead, also by command. He was not afraid to speak plainly, if non-whites were not able to limit their own fertility, then the Government might have to step in to find a way to help them do it. This was not a threat but a promise. The Regime might also have to remind white women where their duty lay. Requests were not enough (this was a clear jibe at Bubé). Despite countless fertility crusades, tax incentives for larger families among whites, the ratio of black people to white people in the country was still five or six to one, and rising. The Government looked with new hope to the extraordinary advances in embryology and fertility drugs, much of which was due to the pioneering work of the brilliant young doctor, Wim Wonderluk. There were those who were clearly breeding for victory, who planned to bury the Boer. Well the Government would not stand by idly and see this happen. If offers of television sets and free operations did not work, then other measures must be taken. Soon rumours reached the capital that vasectomy platoons were stalking the countryside, that officials in Landrovers were rounding up herds of young black matrons and giving them the single shot, three-monthly contraceptive jabs. There were stories of secret radiation trucks known as scan vans, far superior to the old Nagasaki ambulances Bubé had sponsored, raiding the townships and tribal villages and the officials in these vans were armed with demographic studies and at the first sign of a birth bulge would visit those potential centres of population growth after dark and give them a burst of radiation, enough, the theory was, to impair fertility. A kind of human crop-spraying technique. People said it couldn't be true until they remembered that anything you could think about could very easily be true. Kuiker was as forthright in his address to white women, 'our breeders of the future' he called them and he talked of introductory programmes of fertility drugs for all who wanted or needed them. Teams of researchers were working with selected females of child-bearing age on Government sponsored programmes to increase the white birth-rate without excluding the possibility, difficult though it might be, of obligatory implantation of fertilised ova in the selfish white wombs of women who had put golf and pleasure before their duty to the country. Pregnancy was good for the nation. He compared it with the military training which all young men had to undergo and pointed out that nine months' service was not too much to ask of a woman. Gus Kuiker was clearly going places. He caught the public eye. He didn't look to the past, he looked to the future which could be won if allied to technology. 'Breed or bleed' had been his rallying cry and he asked the eminent embryologist, Professor Wim Wonderluk, to prepare a working document encompassing his plans for the new future. Yes, Blanchaille knew all about Kuiker. Knew more than enough to be going on with.

'Why have you got me here? I was heading out under my own steam. It would have been easier, cleaner.' Blanchaille stood up knowing the policeman was not ready to release him.

'Two reasons. Mine and Lynch's. I wanted to make you take another look at things you thought you knew all about. I don't want to be left alone with my mysteries. You're going out. Fine. So maybe you'll be able to use some of what I show you to get some answers out there in the outside world. That's my reason. Lynch's was more practical. He knew you'd never get out without my help.'

'Why not? How many have gone already?'

Van Vuuren's look was cold. 'Not all those who disappeared have left the country. Getting out is not what it was. It has become a police matter. Things got difficult when Bubé and Kuiker issued instructions that disappearances were becoming too frequent and a close watch was to be kept on ports and airports.'

'Then disappeared themselves.'

'Yes, but the orders are still in force,' Van Vuuren said.

Blanchaille sat down again. 'O.K. What else do you want to tell me?' he asked warily.

'Turn around,' Van Vuuren ordered, 'and watch the screen.'

On a television monitor behind him there appeared a group of men sitting at a long table, six to a side, all wearing earphones.

'A delegation from the Ring are meeting a delegation from an Italian secret society known as the *Manus Virginis*, the Hand of the Virgin. The Hand is some sort of expression of the Church Fiscal. This lot arrived in the country claiming to be a male voice choir and they all have names like Monteverdi and Gabrielli and Frescobaldi. The Hand appears very interested in investment. Each chapter or cell of the Hand is called a Finger and takes a different part of the world for its investment which is done through their own bank called the Banco Angelicus. On the other side of the table is the finance committee of the Ring. They read from left to right: Brother Hyslop – Chairman; Brother van Straaten – he's their political commissar; Brother Wilhelm – Treasurer; Brother Maisels – transport arrangements. Don't laugh. Getting here in style and doing it in secret is very important to them. Brother Snyman – catering and hospitality. Since the Brothers regard themselves as hosts they put themselves out for these meetings, they bring along wine, a good pâté, a selection of cheeses. Headphones are for simultaneous translation.'

'But why are you monitoring the Ring? All the major figures in the Regime are members of the Ring, so why get you to spy on it?'

'Because though all members of the Government are in the Ring, not all members of the Ring are in the Government.'

Blanchaille looked at the heavy men on both sides of the table with their earphones clamped around their heads like Alice-bands which had slipped, and thought how alike they looked with their big gold signet rings, hairy knuckles, gold tie-pins, three-piece suits, their burly assurance. Here were devoted Calvinist Afrikaners who spat on Catholics as a form of morning prayers, sitting down with a bunch of not only Catholics, but Roman *wops*! To talk about – what?

'Money,' said Van Vuuren. 'Highly technical chat about investments, exchange controls, off-shore banks, letters of credit, brokers, money moving backwards and forwards. But how are such meetings arranged and, more importantly, *why*?'

'Ferreira would have understood,' said Blanchaille. 'But I don't. What is the connection?'

'I think,' said Van Vuuren, 'that the connection isn't as odd as it seems. The philosophical ideas behind the Ring are not too dissimilar to those practised by Pope Pius X. He fired off salvos at the way we live. He attacked the ideas about humans improving themselves. He pissed on perfectability. He lambasted modern science and slack-kneed liberal ideas. So does the Ring. They have more in common than we think. Perhaps we do too.'

Blanchaille stared at the men on the screen. 'I still can't believe what I'm seeing.'

The picture faded into blackness. 'You haven't seen anything,' said Van Vuuren. 'Now come along and look at what we have in the holding cells.'

CHAPTER 8

The holding cells were below ground, arranged in tiers rather in the manner of an underground parking garage, Van Vuuren explained in what to Blanchaille was an inappropriate and chilling comparison. And why 'holding' cells? Van Vuuren was also quick to counter the notion that this was intended to distinguish them from 'hanging' cells, or 'jumping' cells. The policeman seemed, surprisingly, to regard this suspicion as being in bad taste.

Van Vuuren led him into a long concrete corridor: air-conditioning vents breathed coldly, a thin, flat hair-cord carpet on the floor, abrasive white walls, overhead fluorescent light-strips pallid and unforgiving. Down one side of the corridor were steel cell doors. At the far end of the corridor, in front of a cell, stood a group of uniformed officers. Senior men they must have been for Blanchaille caught the gleam of gold on caps and epaulettes. They seemed nervous, slapping their swagger-sticks against their thighs. One carried a clipboard and he was tapping his pencil nervously against his teeth.

'We'll wait here and watch,' said Van Vuuren.

Then I saw in my dream, marching around the corner, two more policemen and between them their prisoner, a powerful man in grey flannels and white shirt, at least a half a head taller than his captors. As they approached the cell door the policeman with the clipboard stepped forward and held up his hand. 'We are happy to inform you, Dr Strydom, that you are free to go. There is no further need to hold you. Your name has been removed from my list.'

The reaction of the prisoner to this information was sudden and violent. He gave the clipboard carrier an enormous blow to the head. The two men guarding him fell on him and tried to wrestle him to the ground, but he was too big, too strong. The uniformed policemen with the swagger-sticks joined in and a wild scrum of battling men seethed in the corridor. The prisoner laid about him with a will and reaching his objective, the cell door, opened it, rearing and lashing out with his feet, kicking backwards like a stallion at the policemen clawing at him. 'Now write down my name in your book,' he roared at the unfortunate clipboard carrier who was leaning shakily against the wall and then leapt into the cell, slamming the heavy door behind him.

Glumly the policemen gathered themselves together and wiped the blood from their faces. From behind the cell door Blanchaille could hear the prisoner's voice raised in the National Anthem:

'On your call we may not waver, so we pledge from near and far; So to live, or so to perish – yes we come, South Africa-a-a-r!'

'That's quite a patriot you've got there,' Blanchaille said. He couldn't help smiling, 'Balthazar Buildings is a place from which generations of doomed prisoners have tried to escape. I think I've just seen a man fighting to get in. The world is suddenly stood on its head.'

'That man is Wessels Strydom, once a leading light in the Ring which he left claiming it had been undermined by the Communists. Strydom said that the Regime was going soft on the old enemies, Reds, liberals, Jews, internationalists, terrorists. He expressed the feeling that control was slipping away from God's people. With a group of like-thinking supporters he formed what they called the *Nuwe Orde*. This organisation aims to expose betrayals of the Boer nation, by direct action. The military wing of the *Nuwe Orde* is the Afrika Straf Kaffir Brigade. You've heard of their punishment squads who deal with people they see as threatening or sullying the old idea of purity? Their ideas of punishment are juvenile but no less painful for that, mind you. They'll hang about a house where they know blacks and whites are holding a party and slash tyres; a little while ago they devised a plan of releasing thousands of syphilis-infected white mice in one of the multi-racial casinos; they're not above kidnapping the children of social workers or trade unionists who they feel are betraying the Afrikaner nation; or breaking into cinemas and destroying films they disapprove of; or shooting up the houses of lawyers (Piatikus Lenski, the liberal defence lawyer was a favourite target); or preparing to mate with their wives in front of the Memorial to the Second Mauritian Invasion in response to the falling white birth-rate, a huge breed-in of hundreds of naked male members of the *Nuwe Orde* and their carefully positioned wives all preparing for insemination at a given signal. They want a homeland for the Boer nation and eventual independence. In this new homeland only white people will be admitted. The idea is to remove all dependence on black labour. They'll do their own housework, sweep their streets, run their own factories, deliver their own letters, mow their lawns. They'll be safe, separate, independent. They've bought a tract of land down on the

South Coast. The sea is important to them as a symbol, it's something that they have to have their backs to.'

'Would they be capable of killing?'

Van Vuuren shrugged. 'You're thinking of the writing on Ferreira's wall, aren't you? So were we. That's why we hauled this Strydom in. Frankly it was a terrible mistake. I'm not saying that the A.S.K. couldn't have killed him but Ferreira was dealing in highly complex matters concerning the movement of funds through very complicated channels which none of us understood. Certainly not this Strydom. He could barely read his own bank account. And he doesn't care about those things, he cares about race, about history, about being right. Arresting him has proved to be a terrible mistake. We can't get rid of him. We don't need him any more, we don't want to hold him, there's nothing he can tell us, but he won't go! And it suits the *Nuwe Orde* to have him here. It makes it look like the Regime is really taking them seriously, locking him up like any black radical. You can see how determined Strydom is. He literally fights his way in back into his holding cell. The thing to remember about the *Nuwe Orde* is that it is actually a very old order.'

Now I saw in my dream how Blanchaille and the policeman Van Vuuren moved to another cell and peered through the thick glass spyhole in the door and Blanchaille recoiled at what he saw. For there, lying on the bunk, was Roberto Giuseppe Zandrotti, the anarchist. He recognised immediately the spiky black hair, the long, thin chin, the freckled, ghostly white face. 'I don't believe this. He's in London.'

Van Vuuren shook his head. 'We had known he was planning to return secretly to the country. We knew when he would arrive and, most importantly, what he would be wearing. The information was top-grade. So accurate Zandrotti never stood a chance. Blanchie, he came back disguised as a nun, of the Loretto Order, to be precise. Imagine it if you will. There's this double-decker bus trundling through a green and leafy suburb, all the passengers peering out of the window and paying very little attention to what some of them afterwards thought of as perhaps rather 'swarthy' a sister who sat there on her seat keeping her eyes demurely downcast and most of her face hidden behind her large wimple. Imagine their surprise when three large men in hairy green sportscoats and thick rubber-soled brown shoes jump aboard the bus and begin attacking this nun. Apparently the conductor went to her assistance and was struck down with a blow to the temple. He lay sprawled in the aisle,

92

bleeding, and all the coins from his ticket machine went rolling beneath the bus seats.'

Blanchaille imagined it. He saw it. He heard the jingling flutter as the coins spun and settled beneath the seats.

'Anyway, these three guys wrestled with the nun who hoofs them repeatedly in the nuts until they pick her up and carry her down the aisle head first. The other passengers see that this nun isn't what they thought because the headdress has been torn off and they look at the hair and the freckles and the beard and fall over themselves with amazement – this is a man! There was no end of trouble afterwards stopping them talking to the papers, and the conductor, he was well into negotiations to sell his story to something called *Flick*, a flashy picture magazine, when he was stopped at the last moment.'

Of course escaping from jail in clerical dress had a long history. There had been Magdalena who got out disguised as a nun. A less appropriate garb could not be imagined. From that day nuns leaving the country were abused by Customs officers still smarting over the one who got away. Then there had been Kramer and Lipshitz who bribed their way out of their cells dressed as Cistercian monks. But for a wanted man to return to the country in clerical dress, to certain arrest, that was beyond comprehension. The exit permit on which Zandrotti had left the country on his release from jail specified arrest should he return.

'Unless, of course, he wanted to be caught,' suggested Blanchaille.

'It makes no sense. But you know Roberto, and you know his way of thinking. Jesus, he must have wanted to be caught! There is no other explanation. He let it be known in London, in certain quarters, that he was going home – knowing the details would get back to us. They did. We even knew his seat number on the aircraft.' Van Vuuren unlocked the door and drew Blanchaille into the cell.

Zandrotti had always gone his own way, opposed not merely to the Regime but to every authority he encountered. His schemes for that opposition were novel, intriguing, entirely characteristic, quirkish, outrageous, quite impractical and wonderfully diverting. Zandrotti's plan for immediate revolution was a message, passed by word of mouth to all those opposed to the Regime, that on a particular day at a particular time each man, woman and child would fetch a stone, the biggest and heaviest that could be carried, and place it in the middle of the road and then go home and wait for the country to grind to a halt. Zandrotti's grand coup at school had been the occasion when he broke into the cadet armoury and stole a supply of .303 rifles and full sets of uniforms, khaki shorts and shirts, boots and puttees and caps, with which he dressed and armed a platoon of black school cleaners and drilled them on the school playground for all the world to see. The sight of black men marching with rifles caused panic in the neighbourhood. Zandrotti was expelled from the Hostel and they remembered how he was driven away in Father Cradley's grey DKW, sitting in the back fervently making the Sign of the Cross. The rector was a notoriously bad driver and they watched Zandrotti's mock gibbers of terror, helpless with laughter.

His star appearance was in the dock at the Kipsel trial. The trial of the so-called Fanatical Five. It wasn't Five for long. Looksmart Dladla had fled, mysteriously warned a few days previously by an unknown source. That left just four: Kipsel, Mickey the Poet, Magdalena and Zandrotti.

The number was further reduced when Mickey the Poet hanged himself in his cell. What a miracle of athletic agility that had been, what a wonder of tenacity! Michael Yates, little Mickey the Poet, short, blond, barrel-chested, the build of a youthful welter-weight with powerful forearms and lengthy reach (which perhaps helped in the miracle of his death). But Mickey wasn't a boxer, he was a poet, not by practice but by acclamation. He was known for four quite hopeless lines: *Bourgeois, bourgeois, bourgeois fool/ Little capitalistic tool/ What you ask, will end white rule?/ Ask the children in the school!* With these few lines of thudding doggerel Mickey acquired the sobriquet 'the Poet', and met his end. For not very long after that came the township disturbances when the school-children rioted and Mickey's words seemed amazingly prophetic, if not a straight case of incitement, and his little poem was printed in an anthology of revolutionary verse and was much quoted abroad. And then there was the photograph of Mickey with the 'Liberation Committee', as the leaders of what later became the Azanian Liberation Front were known. A famous photograph showing Mickey standing between Athol Ngogi and Horatio Vilakaze, and with Achmed Witbooi, Oscar Amandla and Ramsamy Gopak, all raising clenched fists and singing. Mickey said he had gone to the meeting by mistake, someone had told him it was a jazz concert, that he never knew. *He never knew.* Another brief epitaph for his gravestone. He never knew when he was approached by Kipsel for a lift what it was that Kipsel carried in the brown leather briefcase. Mickey's ignorance was invincible and nothing that the State Prosecutor, Natie Kirschbaum, said could pierce it. With wonderful simplicity Mickey informed the judge that since he hadn't the first idea of why he had been arrested but since the prosecution seemed to have a number of explanations, he planned to call the entire prosecution team as witnesses for the defence and to cross-examine them carefully on all aspects of his case. The surprised judge adjourned the hearing to consider the application and promised a decision the following day. It caused a sensation. POET TAKES ON PROSECUTION! the headlines read.

The next day never came for Mickey the Poet. Some time during the following twenty-four hours Mickey had attached a strip of towel to his bedstead and the other around his neck and strangled himself. The incredulity with which this was greeted stopped the trial while evidence was heard of Mickey's last hours. The shock of his death was only surpassed by the wonder of its achievement. The defence lawyers produced a statement in which Mickey complained of electric shocks, beatings, and frequent threats that he would be thrown from a high window in Balthazar Buildings. Mickey, it seemed, had demanded to see, as was his right, the Inspector of Detainees, but this had not happened. He had then, it was alleged, gone to bed, tied the towel around his neck and choked himself. Sergeant Betty Paine was called to the witness box to explain why the Inspector had not called. Sergeant Paine's job was to take down statements from prisoners when they complained that they had been tortured and, as she added charmingly with a little flick of her blonde head, to hand this to the interrogator so that he might determine whether indeed there was a case for reporting the complaint to the Inspector of Detainees. However, when the Inspector arrived he was told by Sergeant Paine that the prisoner, Michael Yates, was 'out'. The judge was puzzled by this and asked for the meaning of the word 'out'. Did Sergeant Paine mean 'out' as in 'out for the count,' or 'out for lunch', or 'out of order'? Or perhaps 'out like a light'? Presumably she did not mean 'out to tea' or 'out on the town'. There was laughter in court at this and the judge threatened to clear the galleries.

Sergeant Paine replied that political prisoners were the responsibility of the Security Police who were interrogating them. The police held the keys to the cell and entrance was by permission only, one could not simply go barging into a detainee's cell unannounced or uninvited at any old hour of the night, and although it was true that the officer in charge had given permission for the Inspector of Detainees to call on Yates, as it happened she did not have the keys that night and there was nothing she could do. Rather than hurt the Inspector's feelings she had told him that Yates was 'out'. Sergeant Paine told the court that she dreaded such requests and did her best to please, she even kept a sign on her desk which read: 'Please don't ask to see the prisoners as a refusal may offend . . .' Well, the judge enquired, if the Inspector of Detainees had not seen the prisoner, then presumably Paine had done so, since she had taken down his statement on her Brother electric typewriter. Did he strike her as someone who had been assaulted by interrogating officers? She gave a rather flustered glance desperately towards what were known as the choir stalls, the front benches of the court where the prosecution witnesses from the police sat. A security branch man was shaking his head vigorously at her. The defence counsel protested, claiming that the witness was being prompted from the wings. Sergeant Paine shrilly denied the charge and burst into tears and the judge cautioned the defence for hectoring the witness and permitted her to step down.

And that was the end of the inquiry into the strange death of Mickey the Poet.

The next day Kipsel turned state witness and gave his evidence in a hoarse whisper. He took all the blame on himself: he had persuaded Mickey the Poet to drive him, it was his uncle who ran the compound where the explosive store was situated, it was he who persuaded Looksmart to draw the map of the township and it was through her love for him that Magdalena had allowed herself to be persuaded to take part in the operation. And Zandrotti? Why, he hadn't really been involved at all, he'd merely winked, smiled and sang a couple of verses of the National Anthem.

Kipsel was given a suspended sentence and discharged.

While he was giving evidence to a hushed courtroom, Magdalena turned her back on him and Zandrotti shouted angrily that he should keep his explanations to himself, better a bungling saboteur than a traitor. For this he was removed to the cells beneath the court room.

He received five years.

Magdalena was given three.

A few weeks later, after apparently bribing a wardress, and disguised as a nun, Magdalena escaped from jail and fled across the border. The disguise she affected led to a tremendous row between Church and State. President Bubé in a warmly received speech to his Party Congress warned that the Roman danger was growing, and called on the Pope's men and women to put their house in order. He hinted at Church connivance in Magdalena's escape and its tacit support of terrorist groups. Bishop Blashford, speaking for the Church, responded by ordering a central register of all working nuns, 'genuine sisters' as he called them and disclaimed any connection between the renegade Magdalena and the true Brides of Christ who, he said angrily, dedicated their lives to serving God and their fellow men and took no part in politics. At the same time he warned that violent opposition to the Regime would continue while they maintained their hideous racial policies. He took the occasion for attacking as well their authoritarian methods of birth control, the dumping of unwanted people in remote camps in the veld, and the crass folly and blatant inhumanity of the Regime's political arrangements. He drew parallels with Nazi Germany and went so far as to compare President Bubé with Hitler, a time-honoured insult and much appreciated throughout the country where Blashford earned enthusiastic praise from the anti-Regime opposition but equally delighted President Bubé's followers, so much so that in the traditional response he publicly thanked the good Bishop for the compliment, since after all Hitler had been a strong man, proud of his people and his country. Both men came out of the confrontation with their public prestige much enhanced and behind the scenes it was said they were both good friends and often went fishing together.

The anarchist's eyes were red-flecked milky pools surrounding pupils dark and hard as stones. And I saw in my dream how hesitantly Blanchaille approached him, not knowing what his reception was likely to be at the hands of his old friend not seen for so long, so cruelly used, for after that terrible trial it had been Zandrotti alone who faced the assaults of his jailers, cruelties not refined but oafish, coarse, persistently callous, and above all, juvenile. The young warders had waged a campaign of humiliation against him, Blanchaille heard on his weekly visits to the prison; they would apple-pie his bed, piss on his cigarettes replacing them limp and wet in the pack, tear pages from the books he was reading and allocate him cells from which he could hear the singing of the condemned men on death row. Lovely singing it was too, Zandrotti told him, day and night, right up to the last moment, this male voice choir of killers waiting for the end. They would sing special requests, the warders joked with Zandrotti. It had been his idea of hell, Zandrotti told Blanchaille afterwards when he was free, to be locked in a small room with the intellectual equivalent of the police rugby team. Beside that horror the fires of conventional Roman hell cooled to an inviting glow.

Blanchaille drove him to the airport after his release, the anarchist clutching a few clothes, a little cash and an exit visa which ensured he would depart from the country forever within forty-eight hours. 'They opened a little gate in the big prison gate and pushed me out clutching my money, in this badly fitting blue suit, carrying my passport and an exit permit and told me, God bless, old fellow. God bless! Can you believe that?' All he wanted on the road to the airport was news. He had none in the years inside. He greeted the news that Magdalena was regarded as dangerous by the Regime with a whistle of appreciation. But he was amazed to learn that Kipsel was still alive, had not done the expected and hanged himself, or shot himself.

Apparently Magdalena had helped Zandrotti when he reached London. Blanchaille had no idea of his situation there except for one report that showed his old perverse sense of humour operated still. He read of the anarchist being hauled before an English court for persistently photographing everyone who entered or left the South African embassy because, as he explained to the magistrate, this was a custom in his own country where everyone expected to be photographed on street corners by agents of the Regime not once but many times during their lives and he wished to continue this ancient custom in exile.

Now he lay in a bunk in the cells of Balthazar Buildings, strangely quiet, supine, and yet with a gleam of defiance which contrasted oddly with his air of defeat.

'Ask him why he's here,' Van Vuuren said.

'What brought you back, Roberto? And looking so holy, too. The flying nun. Mother Zandrotti of the Townships . . .'

The prisoner favoured him with a fleeting smile. 'I met Tony Ferreira in London. He was staying at this hotel and we went down to the bar. He was in London on the last leg of a world tour. He got very drunk in the bar, kept falling to his knees and reciting bits of the Litany. You will remember the sort of thing – "Bower of Roses, Tower of Ivory, Hope of Sinners", and so on. You know the lyrics, I'm sure you could sing it yourself. But in a bar in London surrounded by English Protestants, it can be rather alarming. Anyway the barman, thank God, ordered him to stop or leave . . .'

'But why did Ferreira want you back here?'

'He didn't. That was the last thing he wanted. The bastard slandered his country!'

'Slandered his country! God almighty, Roberto! What sort of rubbish is that? Where did he want you to go?'

'To the other place. To Geneva. Oh hell, you know, Uncle Paul's place.'

'What else did he say?'

'I don't remember.' The anarchist's eyes swam on their veined pools. 'Ask him yourself.'

'Ferreira is dead. Murdered.'

The anarchist shrugged. 'So they say. Well, not before time. I would have killed him myself.'

Blanchaille tried to control his astonishment. 'What did he do to you?'

'He tried to destroy everything I've ever believed in, hoped in. He pissed on it! He crapped on it! Rubbed my nose in it, between invocations to the Queen of Heaven . . .'

'But what did he say?'

'Don't remember.'

Van Vuuren interposed. 'That's all you'll get from him, the forgetfulness is strategic.'

They withdrew. The prisoner showed little sign of recognizing their going until they reached the door when Blanchaille said, 'Goodbye then, Roberto, and I'm sorry to meet you in this place.'

The anarchist sat upright and waved his fist in fury. 'I'm sorry for you, yes, because if you're going where I think you're going, then you're going to die of sorrow! Don't be sorry for me, Blanchie, save it for yourself. I'm still here.'

Outside in the corridor Blanchaille asked Van Vuuren: 'What does he mean – he's still here?'

'Just what he says. Here, in jail, he is Zandrotti, known as such, wanted by the police and dangerous enough to apprehend, torture, perhaps kill. These threats confirm his existence, his importance, not least to himself. Here and perhaps only here he is Zandrotti still. We are the police, this is the infamous prison, Balthazar Buildings. Everything is what it is expected to be. I don't know what Ferreira told him in London but clearly it made him so desperate that prison seems infinitely preferable to all other alternatives . . . But let's get something clear, we don't want him. We're not holding the anarchist Zandrotti, despite what the papers say overseas and the silent vigils in front of our embassy demanding the brave soul's release. No, he is clinging to us. It is he who won't let us go . . .'

Blanchaille was becoming more weary and confused by the mysteries which though they had a certain bizarre interest were not getting him very far along the road to the Airport Palace Hotel and his flight to freedom and he respectfully requested to be allowed to continue his journey.

'One last port of call,' Van Vuuren promised, 'and then you can go.' He paused outside a cell door and lifted the steel cover from the spyhole and invited Blanchaille to look inside. 'Recognise him?'

'Naturally.' How could he not do so? The large fine head, the grizzled steel-grey curls, the powerful dignified bearing of the man who had done more than anyone else to advance the cause of liberation in Southern Africa, Horatio Vilakaze, arrested soon after the fateful picture had appeared showing Mickey the Poet apparently in attendance on the liberation leaders, back in those exciting days before death, dispersal, imprisonment, exile, house arrest and age had split and destroyed the original organising committee of the Black Justice Campaign. How long ago? Years, years and years. It did no good to count them.

'Vilakaze is perhaps the saddest of all our cases,' Van Vuuren said. 'We don't have to go into the cell, we can listen to his speech from out here,' he flicked a switch and the old man's powerful voice reverberated along the chill, empty corridor.

'Brothers and sisters, comrades, freedom will be ours!' He held up his arms as if to still the cheering crowds and when the applause which must have rung between his ears like brass bands had died away he rallied the faithful thousands only he could see and hear. 'Within the country our forces are massing, our fighters are brave, the Regime shrinks from them. On the borders the armies of our allies gather like locusts to sweep on our enemy and defeat him. Together we will overcome, we will drive the oppressor into the sea, God is with us!'

Van Vuuren killed the vibrant, echoing words. 'Too sad to hear. That was his last great speech before he was arrested. He was speaking to thirty thousand supporters, and he can't forget it. It preys on his mind, he reruns the speech a dozen times a day. That was before the young men took over. He is a great man.'

'It didn't stop you arresting him.'

'Yes. We did arrest him, but only after we had been approached by a number of his friends anxious to spare him the humiliation of ejection from the movement he had helped to found. So yes, you can say we arrested him, but really we took him in.'

Took him in? *Took him in!* What a terrible thing to say. As if this place had been a home for strays, a dogs' home. Or an orphanage. There was in this something he could not accept. Something so awful it didn't bear thinking about.

'You're saying that it was an act of charity?' He could hear the incredulous ring in his voice.

'Something like that. And a mistake, too. Once in custody there was no releasing him. We tried once, sent him back to his people who wouldn't have him. They're hard-nosed, young, efficient elements who want power, who want to succeed at any cost even if it means some weird, subtle deal with the Regime, and to them old Vilakaze with his talk of armies and locusts is an embarrassment . . . they're happy to use his name, to keep the Free Vilakaze committees going all over the world, the silent vigils, the marches, the petitions calling for his release but what they won't stand for is for us to let him go. We've been warned – put him back on the street and he's a dead man,'

Back in the reception area with its portraits of the presidents, Blanchaille said, 'I think I begin to understand what you're up against. Once the police were there to arrest people they considered a danger to the State. This was our world. Ugly, perhaps cruel. But dependable. Things have changed. These people, Strydom, Zandrotti, Vilakaze, they don't know where they are anymore. Except when they're in here. What you've got here are specimens from another age. This isn't a prison, it's a museum.'

Van Vuuren reflected. 'And a hospital. They pose no threat to the State. The only people they're a danger to are themselves. These people shouldn't be here. They're not criminals. They're failures. They shouldn't be in jail. They should be sent somewhere for treatment. Some special hospital for incurable failures.'

'I believe there is,' said Blanchaille.

Van Vuuren joined his hands together in a pious gesture of the altar server of long ago. 'Let's hope so.'

CHAPTER 9

Van Vuuren loaded Blanchaille's cases into a small, powder-blue Volkswagen Golf. There wasn't room for the cases in the boot and he put them on the back seat. 'Don't worry about the car, just leave it at the airport. Its owner, I'm afraid, has no further use for it. It comes from our pool.'

'Goodbye,' Blanchaille said dazed by all he had learnt.

'Good luck,' Van Vuuren replied. 'I take it you see things a little differently now?'

Blanchaille felt embarrassed. Van Vuuren had made himself difficult to dislike. 'Why do you stay on?'

Van Vuuren looked uncomfortable. He shrugged. 'Duty, perhaps.'

'Duty? To what? To whom?'

Again Van Vuuren was silent but he gave Blanchaille an odd, rather mocking glance and waved him away. 'You're under police protection. It's about as good as being anointed.'

In order to reach the airport one takes the national highway, a great curving road much of it a long, gentle climb. It was getting dark. A stony, glittering moon rose swiftly, glared briefly and was gone. Just as he cleared the city it began to rain. Rounding a bend he found his way blocked when three men in orange oilskins stepped into the road and flagged him down. His bright lights reflected back off the brilliant orange plastic and dazzled him so that he had to shield his eyes. The men stepped up to the window: 'Theodore Blanchaille?'

'What do you want?'

'Please get out of the car,' said the first policeman.

'We're giving you something,' said the second policeman.

'Please take off your clothes,' said the third policeman.

The door was opened and Blanchaille was helped out. A large green and red golf umbrella was unfurled and held over his head. The first policeman reached into the car and dragged out Blanchaille's three cases.

'What are you doing with those?'

'We're relieving you of them.'

'But it's all my stuff.'

'You won't be needing it where you're going. Now in return we have three things to give you. A change of clothes, good advice and proper papers.'

The first policeman went over to his car and returned with a large cardboard box. This he unpacked carefully and took from it a white suit. There in the pouring rain, standing beneath the umbrella, Blanchaille was forced to remove his clothes and don the new white suit. There was a red woollen tie to go with it, silk shirt, a crimson spotted handkerchief for the breast pocket and slim, pale, pointed Italian shoes with cream silk socks.

The rain stopped, the wild moon reappeared. Blanchaille gleamed coldly in its light.

'That's better,' said the first policeman. 'Now you look like somebody.'

'I am to give you some advice,' said the second policeman. 'You're going out, you're leaving, you're going to visit the outside world, you will need to be prepared. Remember things aren't quite so simple there, people worry about different things, about inflation and unemployment. They worry about whether to have their children vaccinated against whooping cough. They argue about the environment and the rights of women and they fear the extinction of the world by atomic explosion.'

And then the third policeman stepped closer to the now resplendent priest looking like a plump, prosperous riverboat gambler in his white suit and after checking his passport, handed him his exit permit. 'Although we all know you are leaving, the point of this permit is to ensure that you take a one-way trip. There is no return.' Then stepping even closer he whispered in the fugitive's ear in a voice so low I could not catch them, the directions he was to take once he arrived safely at his final destination.

They put him back in his car, they stepped away from it in unison and they waved him on, three wet policemen, shining in the fierce moonlight.

I saw in my dream how Blanchaille went very little further that night but pulled over onto the side of the road and with his head swimming with all that had happened to him that day, and having first carefully folded his new jacket and put it on the back seat, he slept.

In the first light of the new day he started the car and set out to complete his drive to the airport. This gently rising country he knew well, here it was where the huge army camps were situated with their big red notices warning of electrified fencing and the regular watch towers. And on the other side of the road lay the military cemeteries, entered by way of giant bronze gates cast in the form of wagon wheels through the spokes of which he could glimpse the orange crosses on the graves. Orange crosses were a particular feature of the military graveyard. No other colour was suitable. White, brown, pink, black, yellow and even red, all carried racial or political connotations which were judged to be undesirable. After all, since the Total Onslaught began it had not been only Europeans who gave their lives for the mother country. People of many colours including large contingents of black storm-troopers, Indian cooks, coloured drivers, Bushmen trackers, served in the armed forces. So it was orange, the dominant colour of the national flag, colour of the original Free State, the substantial feature of the African sunset, that was found in military memorials.

Here was the Air Force base which they had visited as boys with Father Lynch, when the priest had worn his beret as a mark of cordiality to celebrate the French connection, 'an entirely appropriate symbol, I think, and a gesture of esteem for one of our most faithful arms suppliers, the old Sabre Jets are gone and the new French fighters are in.'

'Not swords into ploug'shares, Sabres into Mirages . . .' Blanchaille muttered.

Along these perimeter fences he saw the early morning Alsatian patrols, the dogs held in a U-shaped metal lead with their trainers running behind them. It was rather reminiscent of guide dogs leading the blind. Here were endless miles of military suburbs named Shangri-La, Valhalla, El Dorado, Happy Valley.

The first of the great national monuments was the burly granite sarcophagus raised to the memory of the early Trekkers, grey and powerful on a low green hill and looking like nothing so much as an old-fashioned wireless, a giant Art-Deco piece, a great circular window intersected by deep parallel grooves where the loudspeaker would have been, hidden behind its wire and wicker screen. The monument sat in its massive bulk on the hill, forever.

Next, the monument to the dead of the concentration camps which the British ran in the Boer War, a huge, weeping, gilded Boer mother dipping her poke bonnet over her starving children who buried their faces in her ample lap.

Next, the monument to the first invasion of Angola, the bronze soldier posed behind a captured Russian artillery-piece mounted on a lorry, everything precise in all its details, the 122-millimetre rocket launcher, the famous 'Stalin organ', capable of firing salvos of forty rockets at a burst. The soldier and artillery-piece and lorry were on a raised grassy bank surrounded by a mass of flowers, a kind of floral gunpit, banks of white madonna lilies bloodily speckled here and there with clumps of red hot pokers.

Here was the monument to the dead of the abortive Mauritian landings, perhaps the first military invasion organised by private enterprise, the money having been put up by the large mining companies which had found themselves under fire for lack of patriotism and wished to provide assurances of good faith to the Regime. It had been a monumental error, the soldiers had come ashore from their landing craft under the most terrible mis-apprehension that the way was clear and that a coup would simultaneously topple the Government. Came ashore at the wrong time on the wrong day, and under the very guns of a section of the army out on manoeuvres who had observed the seaborne invasion with incredulity from their fortified emplacements and then opened fire with gusto laying the invaders face down on the beach in a grotesque and bloody mimicry of holiday sunbathers. The dead were remembered by a towering block of marble. The early morning sun hit the golden orange lettering in which their names were incised, row upon row.

And here were the military camps which stretched as far as the eye could see. Huge townships in the veld. Once the country had had a civilian army, when people left their jobs and served time in the forces. Now at the time of the Total Onslaught the length of military service was indefinite and people took off their uniforms for brief periods and served time in their old offices, in their firms and factories.

All this great military complex spread before Blanchaille was an expression of unshakable faith, an affirmation of survival, a substantiation of the vow that white men would survive in Southern Africa whatever the odds. It affirmed the covenant between God and his people that they would serve him and he would preserve the nation. The country was run by the national party in the national interest, the national borders were safeguarded against the national enemy, the arms the people carried were the arms of God. This was the war-music of the Republic. This was the song of the mourning Boer mother, it was the message broadcast from the granite wireless, it was the symphony played on the Stalin organ.

Blanchaille was within sight of the airport. He could see the hangars, he could see the planes on the tarmac, he passed the

Holiday Inn, he slowed down and looked about him for the Airport Palace. Two black men appeared running towards him holding up their hands and shouting. He slowed and rolled down the window. The men seized the window-frame panting, their eyes rolling, 'Sir, you must go back. Everybody must go back. There are soldiers in the airport. Crazy men. They have guns, they're shooting. Turn back, turn back!'

But Blanchaille knew he'd come too far to turn back, whatever the danger. 'Do you know the Airport Palace Hotel?'

'Yes, yes, we know it.'

'Can I walk there from here?'

'You can walk, but you must pass through the soldiers. And they're shooting. They are crazy and roaring like lions.'

Blanchaille got out of the car. He gave the keys to the men. 'You go back, but I have to tell you it's no safer behind me. Go. Take the car. I won't need it any more.'

They told him to keep walking down the road and he would find the hotel, he would hear the shooting and he would know he was there. And the roaring, he would hear that too.

Blanchaille set off. As the men had predicted he heard the firing first but quickened his pace. It meant the hotel was close.

The Airport Palace was built of steel and green glass. It was surrounded by a brick wall and outside this wall were the soldiers. He knew at once who they were. They weren't regular troops, they wore an unusual uniform, black three-cornered hats, bottle-green tunics with gold buttons, grey riding breeches and knee-high boots and they ran here and there, firing their rifles, shouting, weeping and groaning. It was these groans the fleeing men had taken for roars. They carried the traditional Boer muzzle loader and their firing, though noisy, was wild and inaccurate. They fired into the air and they fired into walls and they had to stop to reload each time, to prime the guns and to fire again. This was the ceremonial President's guard who accompanied Adolph Bubé on all official occasions. Their uniform was modelled on the guard of honour which had greeted the President on his celebrated visit to General Stroessner in Paraguay. He had gone home and designed the uniforms himself. Blanchaille remembered the headlines at the time: BUBÉ VISITS STROESSNER! A few years later the visit was returned: STROESSNER VISITS BUBÉ! Stroessner and Bubé presented each other with medals: PRESIDENT BUBÉ HONOURED BY REPUBLIC OF PARAGUAY – FREEDOM MEDAL FOR BUBÉ. AFRICA STAR FOR STROESSNER!

The soldiers ran here and there, wild-eyed and sweating in their heavy uniforms. They reminded Blanchaille of marionettes. They seemed out of control, demented with fear. There was a cast-iron gate in the wall. Blanchaille banged on the gate and called for someone to let him in. The soldiers ignored him, charging about in their stiff-legged tin-man way.

An elderly man limped to the gate, drying his hands on a tea towel.

'Name?'

'Blanchaille. I think I'm expected.'

'You used to be called Father Theo of the Settlements?'

'Of the Camps, but now it's plain Blanchaille.'

'What kept you?'

'It's a long story. I'd like to come inside. Are those real bullets those guys are firing?'

'Oh no. The President's guard were never provided with live ammo. In case they got tempted, see? No, they're just shouting and shooting and running around like chickens who've had their heads cut off. They've lost their President, you see. They're supposed to guard Bubé and Bubé's gone, and it has sent them round the bend. They're like deserted robots. The man who used to wind them up has gone away. Come inside. Come inside and meet the girls.'

CHAPTER 10

Now I saw in my dream the reception of the plump renegade
Blanchaille by the ancient porter of the Airport Palace Hotel, a
certain Visser, once a colonel in a tank corps fighting Rommel's
troops in the desert war Up North. Something of a trace of military
bearing remained about the doddering fellow who worked now
unbeknown to the world as concierge, doorkeeper, porter, cleaner
and barman at the Palace. He promised his guest 'interesting
stories'.

To Visser there attached a tale no less tragic than the hundreds he
had heard across the bar of the Airport Palace Hotel from sad
pilgrims about to quit the country. Except Visser would never
leave, he said. If he did he would shrivel up and die he claimed, not
realising he had been as good as dead for years. For it was Visser
who had started the once-famous Brigades of Light when he
returned from the war and found enemy sympathisers poised to
take power. From the stage of the Sir Benjamin D'Urban Memorial
Hall on the South Coast with the Indian Ocean seething outside the
windows, he told his audience of ex-servicemen that they had been
betrayed. While they'd been fighting Up North the new Regime had
been blowing up bridges and knitting woolly socks to send to
Hitler's troops. Was it for this that young men had risked their lives
in the desert war? He called on them to go home and set a lighted
candle in the window to burn for liberty. And thus the Brigades of
Light had been born. The name conjured up dedicated fighters for
freedom. It turned out to be a group of newly demobbed,
enthusiastic young men who went about at night in large cheerful
rather drunken groups and stuck pictures of flaming candles on
letter boxes and gates. It was good fun while it lasted but the raids,
as they were called, soon deteriorated into nightly gallops and

drunken binges. At Christmas their flaming taper was confused with that of the Carols by Candlelight organisation which collected for a host of deserving charities. After this discipline deteriorated. The exuberant ex-soldiers threw stones on corrugated iron roofs, rang the bells and ran away, or peered at young women undressing in their bedrooms. It was hardly the liberation force Colonel Visser had hoped for. For a while he managed to rally his troops. Duty platoons went to election meetings and fought with supporters of the Regime, collecting black eyes and bloody noses and feeling that at least they were doing something, though they knew in their hearts that the Regime was unstoppable. The wilder souls dreamt of burying rifles on the lonely beaches, there was even talk of secession but it didn't last. The young men went to work as accountants, got married, took up Sunday rugby. Colonel Visser issued increasingly desperate orders from Brigade headquarters but it was useless. He disappeared from public view and there were rumours that he had been hideously disfigured in a car crash and was hiding in some obscure Cape resort attended only by a faithful black servant; there was talk that he had emigrated to England where he entered a closed community of Anglican brothers; but instead he had come here, to the Airport Palace Hotel, despite its name an obscure hostelry for souls on their way out – and to be found in no hotel directory.

That Blanchaille should have been welcomed by an elderly military man who promised him a selection of tales not without historical interest to be told by a collection of 'rather special' ladies, might have surprised Blanchaille had his experience in the holding cells not destroyed his remaining reserves of surprise.

Visser talked to Blanchaille of the old connection between the Regime and the Nazi movement as he conducted him to his room and from there to the bar. 'Why did they support Hitler? On the basis that my enemy's enemy is my friend. Tradition played a part as well. The Kaiser had supported Paul Kruger against the British in the old days and that was a pretty good precedent for his descendants to do the same. There had been German support for the Boer fighters for freedom. *Ergo* – the later liaison between the Austrian housepainter and the hairy little rockspiders who run our country. A marriage of true minds.'

The hotel was huge and empty, built of steel and glass and filled with the hiss of the air-conditioning. The tinted windows did not open. Brown chocolate carpet climbed the walls. Visser stood behind the bar, a great polished bank of teak surrounded by a brass rail, and I saw in my dream how he summoned the first of the four girls whom he described as hostesses dedicated to the refreshment of guests at the Palace 'with a selection of stories and even an exhibition or two', he said. The first of the storytellers was Freia.

Freia was blonde, she wore denim shorts, Visser described her as 'our conductor'. She did not look like it. Her hair was scraped back and held in place by a blue Alice-band, she was crumpled and yawning and had obviously been sleeping. Across the front of her tee-shirt was the map of Switzerland cunningly placed so that there rose up from it the twin alps of her breasts. She ordered 'the usual' from Visser, a green cocktail in a frosty glass and licking the sugar from the rim with a sharp pink tongue, she began in a voice dreamy and lilting as if she recalled something recent and strange, but which Blanchaille soon understood from the expert timing and sardonic emphases of her delivery to be a story often told.

'I used to be a tour conductor. I worked in the townships in the days when we still ran tours. I was in Gus Kuiker's department – you know Gus Kuiker? Augustus Kuiker, the Minister? My job was to show tourists around, the official tourists who get invited out here, ageing film stars, American senators, elderly prima donnas, industrialists, pop-singers, tennis players, members of Anglican investigative commissions.' Freia laughed, drained her glass and held it out for a refill. 'I remember my last tour. Eighteen English footballers and one of their big men from British television, Cliff Irving, a pointy fellow with a sparse beard, balding, small bright black eyes, hands like soup-plates. They'd been bribed, of course. They're all bribed. When they come out here the townships are on every itinerary. Obligatory. There were, besides, a few Japanese businessmen, good loyal friends. It's the pig-iron they come for, or did, years ago. We'd stopped looking on them as little yellow devils with funny eyes and saw them as honorary white men. Loaded with cameras, of course. And a batch of Israelis in funny hats. We weren't supposed to know they were Israelis. They were described as a Chilean judo team. A smattering of Germans, industrialists or bankers, came too. The soccer tourists from Britain were ageing hacks for the most part, best years behind them, anxious to make more money in three weeks than they'd ever made before in their lives. Nice enough fellows, but forever making speeches. At the drop of a hat they'd tell you that they were really interested in pushing back the barriers of racial segregation, playing township teams, coaching barefoot piccaninnies, and so on. They climbed

110

aboard loaded with coolbags full of beer because they'd just been to the brewery which sponsored their visit and put them on show. They were ticking nicely by the time they got to us and the famous TV sports journalist had trouble calming them down. First stop was the 200-megawatt generator which could supply millions of kilowatt hours, all the Japanese taking notes, very impressed to learn we were supplying electricity not only to our own industries but to big power stations hundreds and hundreds of miles away in independent countries to the north. Everybody needs our power. We told these countries. "Look, you deal with us. Or nothing. You either pay or you shut up." My tourists always glazed over when I hit them with pig-iron and electric power figures. But they had to get the sell. Not easy for me, with everyone gazing dutifully out of the windows at the cooling towers, except the Japanese. Pretty boring stuff I have to admit. Someone always asked why the power station was surrounded by barbed wire, fields of lean, cruel, spindly stuff like some dangerous crop. Well, you explained that it had to be there otherwise these guys came in and blew it up. You had to have the wire and the dogs and the night patrols, and so on. Then we drove through the town proper, I mean what can you say? Thousands upon thousands upon thousands of tiny brick and tin houses. There it is, staring you in the face, it lies there in the veld and the tourists stare at it for a while like they can't believe what they're seeing, and I remember one of the footballers said it was worse than bloody Manchester. So at this point we were trained to talk about murder. You sat back in your uniform and your perky cap in your seat next to the driver and turned the mike up and hit them with the murder rate. More people killed hourly in our townships than in New York on a good hot summer's night, more than in Guatemala! That was always good for a bit of a sharp intake of breath. They always believe that Guatemala is really the killing ground of the world. Down the dusty streets we trundled with the barefoot kids charging after us. The soccer players would get into the spirit of things and we'd open a window or two and encourage them to throw coins out to the kids, and perhaps a few sweets. Or they'd throw signed photographs of themselves. We passed the Umdombala Cash Store and the Dutch Reformed Church. Usual thing, polished blond wood, glass, with that thin skinny little black metal chicken on the steeple that's supposed to serve as a weather vane. One of those horrible little buildings that they put up, all sharp angles and shiny edges and you're supposed to get the feeling of upward thrust of flight, but the base is so broad and heavy it's like a fat space rocket that can't take off. And then we'd stop at the local cash store and we'd let them buy brightly coloured kaffir blankets. They had an absolute fascination for these sorts of native goods. They liked blankets and beads and wire work. We didn't hide things. We took them past the police station, they were always interested in that, and you know the police stations in the townships are always barred, with enormous gates and acres of barbed wire, with the armoured cars drawn up in front of the charge office and the parade ground with the flagpole and ornamental cannons. They all noticed the sportsfields and we'd make the point that the police would often invite neighbouring children to come and play with them, kids from the township, and if they were tough, well they had to be, that they were really not as bad as they had been painted, after all they were policing one of the murder capitals of the world. You'd get people who simply wouldn't let the murder rate drop, who'd say, "I still believe it's Guatemala that's the murder capital"; and you'd say, "Look, maybe thirty or fifty people a night die in Guatemala, whereas here we're way ahead of anything like that, we're in a different league here". Then, to redress the balance as it were, we'd stop at the kindergarten run by a buxom little nun, Sister Edith. Sister Edith's crèche was a very popular tourist stop. She'd call the kids out and they'd sit on their little wooden benches in their blue smocks and their large yellow sashes and they'd sing for the tourists, beautiful singing, wonderful intonation, and you could tell that Sister Edith spent a lot of time polishing up these tiny choirs of hers. They used to sing laments usually. They seemed to be awfully good at laments those little kids. I remember one – it went "My mother has gone to Egoli . . . my father comes no more . . ." ' Freia sang softly to herself, a mournful, achingly despairing little air echoing around the bar. 'We'd have to tear ourselves away from Sister Edith's singing kindergarten and I would generally drive them past the big hospital where the stab cases were recuperating, lying out on the big old stoep, paralysed from the waist down after being attacked by local hoodlums with sharpened bicycle spokes lunging at the spinal cord. And these young cripples would wave and smile as we drove by and show that they still had a lot of spirit. Next stop, millionaire's row, places like Mr Masinga's mansion and we'd make the point: look, no matter what you've read about starvation and so on in the townships, you will see that these people are actually thriving, that they are actually getting on bloody well. That men like Mr Masinga could have bought anybody on that bus, German, Japanese or Israeli, five times over. But remember, this isn't

Clacton or Bremerhaven, this is Africa! With that, off to the beer hall where the municipal authorities brewed their own beer, tremendously popular and fantastically healthy for the workers who absolutely lapped it up at a few cents for a great big plastic bucket of the stuff. Occasionally we saw a fight and I'd let them sit through it. Why hide the unpleasant side of life? After all they're adults. People fight all over the world when they've had too much to drink, not just our blacks. Then on to the pride of the township, the sports centre with its football pitch and its cycling track and the footballers would get excited because they would be playing there, or at least they expected to, but these bandit tours were often cancelled in mid-course when the centre-forward was arrested in a black brothel, or the sponsor got cold feet, so there was always an air of unease in the first glimpse of the soccer stadium. We'd watch a black cyclist in full gear making a circuit of the track in his Coca-Cola cap and his Barclays Bank shorts and his Raleigh bike. Finally we drove past the funeral parlour with all the coffin prices clearly displayed and the Christmas Club where you pay off so much a month to make sure that you get buried. So much for a funeral with car, without a car, and priced according to mourners, just like a roadhouse. The tourists were always fascinated and would ask questions like, why are these people sitting with bundles of blankets on their laps? And then of course it gradually dawned on the innocents that what looked like bundles of blankets were in fact dead babies. You should have seen their faces! I couldn't help smiling. Suddenly they realised that they were in Africa! I mean I don't have to tell you this, Father Theo of the Camps – but this was the place where you got babies dying like flies because of these epidemics sweeping through the new-born of the townships like Herod's soldiers. And then you'd get one of these Japanese – you know how it is, they'd photograph anything! – and one of them would pull out a camera and ask if he could take a shot and we'd say, look, you know, *look*, if you don't intrude on a mother's grief then it's okay. If you've got a telephoto lens then go ahead, but no going up close and snapping right in their faces, have some respect for the dead, this is Africa and Africa is cruel but we want to maintain civilised standards if at all possible . . . But why am I telling you this? You're Father Theo of the Camps –' Freia widened her big green eyes in mock astonishment.

'Was,' Blanchaille contradicted her. 'Was once.'

'Well, anyway, why tell you? You've seen more of infant mortality than I ever will. But that's my piece and you're welcome to it. Now it's Happy's turn. She'll give you a different view of things.'

Happy, tall, black, appeared with Visser leaning gratefully on her arm. She took a seat between Freia and Blanchaille and ordered a highball. Her hair was drawn up in a great dark crown and seeded with what looked like pearls. Her fingernails were painted pink. Her manner was strident, even aggressive and Blanchaille shifted uneasily. Freia caught his eye and winked. 'Takes all sorts,' she whispered sympathetically, 'that's the trouble.' Happy glared. Freia fell silent. Blanchaille sighed and turned to Happy. He was being punished with parables.

'I worked in the house of my Minister from about the age of fourteen onwards. Because my Minister was powerful I learnt things and because I learnt things I went places. My Minister's department decided that it was no good dealing with our northern black neighbours as we'd done in the old colonial times with the white men lording it over blacks. In the new age black must speak to black and so I became a negotiator, that's to say I dealt with heads of state and political officials in the enemy states to the north. Since as you may know, they buy the works from us – power, food, transport, arms, everything from nappies to canned fruit – I used to say to them, look, this is our price, take it or leave it. Sometimes I'd get a lot of opposition. Some big hero of the African revolution, chest clinking with medals, would meet me at the National Redeemer Airport and say: "Jesus Christ! You're black, Happy, you're one of us, how can you help them to bleed us to death?" And I'd say, "Man – we take forty thousand mine workers a year from you, and if you don't like the arrangement and the price per head we're quoting then fine – don't send them. Or maybe you'd prefer that instead of remitting their salaries to you *in toto*, direct, we might consider paying the poor bastards individually and in that case half your national income goes out the window . . ." Allow me to present you with a photograph of my Minister.'

Before he could refuse Happy thrust a photograph in his hands. Involuntarily he glanced at it: 'Kuiker, of course.'

This delighted his audience who clapped their hands and echoed him: 'Kuiker, of course.'

The face of a pugilist, of an all-in wrestler. The flesh kneaded into thick ridges around the jaw-line, eyebrows and lips; nose flat and wide, a bony spur run askew and bedded down in thick flat flesh. The full lips in their charateristic sneer, even when compressed.

114

MINISTER KUIKER WEARING HIS SARDONIC SMILE, the papers said. Thick dark hair combed back from the forehead in stiff, oiled ridges running over his ears and down the back of his neck. He had a taste for shiny suits and bright ties and a paradoxical reputation for unyielding conservatism combined with modern pragmatism. He was solid, powerful and dangerous, this man, the marbled eyes, the petrified hair, the enormous capacity for Scotch, the truculent ties and the cheap fashion jewellery, gold tie-pins with their diamond chips, the skull rings with red-glass bloodshot eyes he affected on both hands. Gus Kuiker was widely tipped to succeed President Bubé when the old man went. His only rival, young 'Bomber Vollenhoven', was seen as too inexperienced and too liberal. Kuiker was the mastermind behind President Bubé's lightning foreign tours and the man responsible for plucking a young statistical clerk by name of Trudy Yssel from a lowly job in the President's Department for Applied Ethnic Embryology and appointing her to the post of Secretary to the Department of Communications: YSSEL NEW SUPREMO AT DEPCOM, the papers said. KUIKER'S PROPAGANDA OFFENSIVE!

In the picture Kuiker gazed belligerently ahead. It might have been a police mug shot.

'Where was this taken?'

'Here.'

His eyes must have held the question which of course there was no need to ask, and his hosts were too tactful to answer. There was only one reason why anyone stopped at the Airport Palace Hotel. Blanchaille felt conscious once again of his naïvety. Well, he could not help that. He had been raised to believe such things were impossible. Only Lynch had disagreed. But then Lynch had been mad. Now it seemed increasingly that Lynch's madness was being borne out. It also, and this was ironic, seemed to bear out the charge of the Old Guard within the Regime, that the New Men, of whom Kuiker was a leading representative, would cut and run when things got tough.

The Old Guard believed in shooting. The New Men believed in certain adjustments. 'I was one of these adjustments he had in mind,' said Happy, 'when he talked about necessary adjustments to racial policies. He talked of ethnic autonomy, of equalised freedoms, of positive tribalism, of the thousand subtle easements of policy which, my Minister Gus Kuiker would say, were necessary to relax the corset of rigid white centralism and to allow us to reach and embrace the future, as we must if we were to survive. Did the white man think – our Minister would ask – that he had a right in Africa because he had been there for three hundred years? Nonsense! The Portuguese had been in Africa for five hundred years, and where were they now? They were back in Lisbon on the dole. Therefore, in answer to the question – what shall we do to be saved? – the Old Guard would have replied, shoot to kill. But ask the New Men and they would tell you, do anything necessary. What kills them is to be condemned for acting for reasons of expediency when they believe as much as their predecessors, the Old Guard, that they act out of divine necessity. Watch out for Minister Kuiker, in whatever guise you find him. He has been abused by his own people and that has made him crazy.'

Now I saw in my dream that a pretty Indian arrived and took her place at the bar. She wore an apricot silk sari. Petite and teetotal, she drank only orange juice and announced herself to be a Moslem and a Marxist. Her name was Fatima. She spoke so softly Blanchaille had to strain to hear the words. Soon he wished he hadn't.

'I hope to replace the present Regime with a people's democracy,' Fatima said mildly. 'And as a result of my beliefs I was placed in preventive detention. My interrogators, who were all men, at first found themselves unwilling to inflict pain. That is to say, they didn't like to beat me since it flew in the face of beliefs deeply instilled into them that large men do not go around hitting women, and perhaps because of the fact that I am particularly small boned, they were actually unable to raise their fists to me. However, after a certain time they stripped me, secured my hands and legs, and attempted to torture me by introducing various objects – pen tops, broom handles and finally fingers – into my vagina and anus. The reasons why they did this were complicated. I presume that since they weren't attempting to extract any information from me, they must be trying to humiliate me, I being a slender girl and they being large and muscular white men and I suspect that they had read that Asian girls were naturally reticent and modest. But I wasn't prepared to allow myself to be humiliated and this put them in a difficult position. I also pointed out to the men assaulting me that without exception they had large erections which were quite discernible beneath their blue serge trousers. Perhaps for this reason I was returned to my cell and later discharged. It seemed to me that sexual excitement had begun to replace serious political discussion. This was some time ago. By now these interrogators have probably done away with prisoners and replaced them with perverse solitary sexual acts. Not only did the revolution I envisaged seem impossible, but it had become impossible to even pose the question or the threat. I came here where at least I can help people to leave this world behind them.'

Blanchaille did not enjoy hearing his course of action so described but did not feel it was time to say so. Instead he babbled inanely to his hostesses of their extraordinary lives.

Freia shrugged. 'Characteristic.'

Blanchaille persisted. 'No, no. Wild – and awful.'

'That's their characteristic,' said Happy.

'If you wish to hear an extraordinary story we'll call Babybel,' said Fatima.

Babybel was by far the most beautiful of the four girls. Hair rich and auburn, the tiny lobes of her ears so delicate they were almost translucent; she wore a pale blue towelling robe which set off quite beautifully the soft, smooth milkiness of her skin. She'd been swimming, or at least relaxing by the pool, she said, until the sun became too much for her. With her fair skin she couldn't take too much sun and, besides, the noise of the President's demented guard firing away had driven her inside. She ordered champagne. 'She always drinks champagne,' said Freia.

'Nothing but the best for Babybel,' said Fatima.

'Tell Blanchaille your story,' said Happy.

'Despite appearances to the contrary, I am coloured. You may not believe this but you would see it immediately if you were to meet my brother, Calvin. When we were small we were at school together until one day they came and looked at Calvin. Inspected his brown skin and curly hair and said – Calvin must go! Go to the school up the road, a school for coloured children, for Capey children. I cried, I clung to him. Calvin did nothing. He went. But he whispered to me before he went, "My time will come." As I grew older and people noticed my looks Calvin evolved his plan, built it out of his very pure and uncompromising hatred for what had been done to him. "You will be my white poodle, Babybel," he said to me, "I will manicure, powder, preen you and I shall take you for walks through the suburbs where rich men will stop to stroke you and then, on an order from me, you will sink your teeth into their hands." It began when I left school and under Calvin's direction I made myself available to certain men, powerful in the Government. "You are jailbait, pure jailbait, my little Babybel," Calvin said to me. As I lay with these big *meneers* in bed, Calvin would reveal the truth. At first, in his boyish enthusiasm, he might hide in the cupboard and jump out shouting – "I am the fruit of your union. I am the child you are making!" But as time went on he grew more subtle, he worked with letters, photographs, video tapes and he drove these powerful men, my lovers, to distraction, to suicide, to ruin. I was quite happy with my role as the flesh with which he baited his hook for I believed in the incorruptible anger, let me say the immaculate hatred, buried in Calvin's heart, I considered it as something commendable, noble even. Alas, Calvin became too subtle. "Equipment *costs*," he told me. He went to the banks. Worse, he went to the Bureau. He was funded by those who ruined his life. What begins as pure revenge ends as investment, in our country. Calvin began to rule. He had become one of the big *meneers*.'

The ladies around the bar were in complete agreement and called on Visser for fresh drinks and even Fatima gave a bleak little smile as if only Babybel's story approached her own in revealing the cruel and rich lunacy of everyday life among ordinary people in the days of the Total Onslaught.

'And so I came to the Palace, to this home for homeless girls.' Here she fluttered her delightful eyelashes at Blanchaille who understood what a potent lure she must have been to the big Government men she seduced.

'But explain one thing to me,' Blanchaille begged. 'Who brought you here?'

'We'll explain that, and a whole lot more to you in your all too brief stay with us,' Fatima said. 'But that question is to be explored with delicacy, so let's say that to a certain friend we were virgins pretending to be whores. It is he we have to thank for revealing this to Freia, Happy, Babybel and me. He sent us here, where we would be useful to those on their way out.'

'But that's enough of us,' said Babybel. 'tell us your story now.'

And Blanchaille told them how he had left his parish of Merrievale and passed through the township which was called peaceful. He told them of his call on Blashford and Gabriel and of his time with Van Vuuren in Balthazar Buildings, and of the meetings between the strange Italians and the members of the Ring. He told them of his visit to the holding cells and of seeing the man Strydom; of his sorrow and bewilderment at meeting his friend Zandrotti, now paralysed by some terrible knowledge obtained from Ferreira in London. Ferreira! who knew nothing but figures; of poor Vilakaze, condemned to make the same old speech to an audience who had long ago deserted him.

And they marvelled at his tale – except for Happy, that is, who laughed a trifle harshly.

And this talk went on far into the night and of those details I can recall there was in particular the explanation of the secret Italian organisation Blanchaille had seen at work in Balthazar Buildings.

The *Manus Virginis* had been founded in Portugal in 1924 by a reprobate Lisbon cleric, a dissolute, lustful man, who'd more or less abandoned all his priestly duties, stolen the gold and silver from his church, and taken to pursuing women. His name was Juan Porres and he lived as if he believed, he once flagrantly said, that 'salvation lies in the laps of women'. Then one night as he lay sleeping beside his latest mistress, a short hairy creature of stupefying ugliness named Puta (or Petra) who was said later to be related distantly to the dictator Salazar, the Virgin Mary appeared to him and demanded that he mend his ways. She declared that from that moment on he would no longer be Porres the defiler of women, but the protector of their honour, and in particular the honour of the Virgin Mother. She advised him to invest his ill-gotten money in the Portuguese Marconi Company and devote the profits to the 'honour of the mother'. The Virgin afforded him several visions, in one of which she appeared with her hand extended over the globe of the world with her fingers resting on what Juan called in his memoirs 'troubled and vexed spots'. The next morning he put aside his ugly mistress and went into the street where he met a banker whom he converted to his cause. From this small beginning Juan Porres formed his association of militant groups of priests and laymen divided into sections, which spread with amazing rapidity throughout the world. Their aim was personal sanctity combined with financial integrity. From the late twenties these 'fingers', as they came to be called, grew from a mere dozen to sixty or seventy and their influence could now be felt all around the world. The 'honour of the mother' was later to be interpreted as referring not merely to the sanctity of women, but to the general safety of Holy Mother Church. Membership to the *Manus Virginis* was open to anyone, men, women, priests and laymen, but membership was strictly secret and the organisation had considerable autonomy within the Church, its controlling bishop had his headquarters in Rome and reported directly to the Pope. The organisation had changed little over the years. Members still practised various forms of mortification of the flesh. They used the hair shirt, the whip and the bracelet, a steel chain placed around the leg or upper arm and tightened daily. The *Manus Virginis* continued to have interests in certain aspects of the welfare of women, in particular the preparation of anti-abortion literature, homes for unmarried mothers, and in marriage guidance counselling, but the emphasis over the past thirty years had really been in the field of finance. The *Manus* was to money what the Jesuits had been to education, the fiscal troops, the militant accountants, the sanctified economists. The *Manus Virginis* claimed to have reconciled the age-old contradiction between money and religion, God and Mammon. They invested quite simply for God and the greater honour of the Church. Strategic charity it was sometimes called, or tactical philanthropy. God repaid their investment with high returns and 'the divine portfolio', as the investment plan was known, had made the Hand grow extremely rich. The appeal of the Hand was that it allowed ordinary men and women everywhere to lead secret lives of heroic self-sacrifice and obedience, and to experience the effects of grace with which God rewarded his followers in a form which they could recognise, called 'divine funding', namely cash. The beautiful simplicity of the doctrine had made the attraction of the Hand extremely potent. The tactical charitable investment of the organisation was seen by its members as a form of holy warfare which was directed from its secret headquarters in Rome. Of course there were links with other secret societies, with various Masonic Lodges in Italy, with the Mafia and with other sympathetic organisations. It was an interesting fact to be noted, said Happy, that while secret societies turned inwards and away from the general public their mutual interest in power often enabled them to overcome the animosity they might feel for other clandestine groups. The Hand of the Virgin had its own bank, the Banco Angelicus, from which its investment policy was co-ordinated throughout the world. The Bank provided a useful receptacle for funds which did not seek public attention. It was said to play banker to various secret organisations including the South African Ring, and even, it was said, to the Vatican itself. It was a policy of the Hand of the Virgin that tactical investments should be made in regimes broadly sympathetic to the beliefs of western Christian civilisation. Funds were often used to stabilise regimes, and even large companies which, in the opinion of the *Manus Virginis*, deserved divine support. Where the funds for investment came from was no longer important once the money had passed into the bank, for in the Banco Angelicus there was no such thing as tainted money. All was for the greater glory of God. The Banco Angelicus manipulated its extensive investments through a series of offshore companies in Panama and Bermuda, and had especially close links with many South American dictatorships and was increasingly involved in Third World countries where growing Catholic communities were established.

'Naturally the Church claims to know nothing of the activities of the *Manus*, much as our Regime claims to be unconnected with the Ring. But how else would Church and Regime talk except through such organisations?' Fatima enquired, with eyes modestly lowered.

'There are other conversations which go on in Balthazar Buildings,' said Happy. 'It's probably just as well you didn't witness in any of them. There are, for instance, the talks between the Regime and Agnelli, the Papal Nuncio.'

Blanchaille nodded dully. Of course . . . why not? First they spoke through proxies. Those were the talks he'd witnessed between the Italians and the rough guys from the Ring. No doubt talks followed between the principals involved. He realised the girls had not offered him a drink. Now he knew why. They were plying him with information more potent than any booze. He felt as high as a kite.

'Of course, you see the Church has a great deal to teach the Regime about change. The Regime is now in the position not unlike that of the Church some years ago. Both are preaching to a shrinking audience, changes are to be made if that audience is to be kept. Some of the old slogans must be abandoned, slogans like "death before adaption", "separation is liberation", "tribalism is the future!". These had to be revalued, reassessed, reappraised and reviewed. Just as the Church's ringing affirmation of its mission to the townships and its irresistible embrace of its black brethren was not unrelated to a good hard look at the market. The Regime realised that if it was going to survive it was going to have to start allowing black people into white parks and removing discriminatory signs and stress the positive side of ethnic identity and equal freedoms. Those in power liked to present this as conscious choice, as liberalisation, but in fact it's a form of desperate accountancy.'

Blanchaille nodded. 'I do remember now how it was some years ago when you could go to a Catholic church and study in a Catholic school, recover in a Catholic hospital and never hear a single query raised about whether Jesus lived in the big house or in the servants' quarters, and to blurt out the question was to be threatened with divine punishment and beaten with a strap loaded with halfpennies and cast into the outer darkness. Then suddenly one day you found a whole lot of people were shouting at you for not applauding the

121

Church's eternal commitment to the liberation of Africa, and you were so deafened that it took a while to realise that you were being shouted at by the very people who beat you in the first place.'

'That's right,' Happy said. 'It's the figures again, you see. In the middle of this century the number of Catholics in the white West, in Europe and North America was over half the world total, but before much longer European Catholics will be a minority – the majority will be found in places like Asia and Africa. Not surprisingly, certain conclusions have been drawn . . .'

And so that night passed with talking and stories, rather too much drink and too little sleep, and the next day as well. Conversation and information was exchanged between the fleeing ex-priest and the kind hostesses of the secret travellers' rest known to lost souls as the Airport Palace Hotel, and their mentor, the man they referred to affectionately as their 'Commanding Officer', the elderly barman, Colonel Visser, who had founded with such great hopes the Brigades of Light.

Fatima spoke to him of recent travellers who had stopped at the Palace Hotel *en route* for some long-desired home in the faraway mountains, and mentioned startling names such as Ezra Savage the novelist, Claude Peterkin the radio producer, and Gus Kuiker and the Secretary of the Department of Communications, Trudy Yssel. Blanchaille had great difficulty in believing it, not knowing where truth ended and wishful thinking began.

He asked them how they had come to the Airport Palace Hotel and each described an encounter with the mysterious stranger who revealed to them that they were virgins pretending to be whores; this stranger had various names, Jack, or Fergus, or simply 'our friend'. Well before he heard that he spoke with an Irish accent Blanchaille knew who their saviour had been. Even before they had shown him in their little 'museum of mementoes' (in reality the ladies' cloakroom) an old black beret which he instantly recognized as the one Lynch had worn to the airbase. The implications only struck him later.

He was also given directions to his final destination. Geneva was the starting point and then old Kruger's house by the lakeside in Clarens, near Montreux. But this, it was stressed, was only the beginning. From the official Kruger house he must climb to 'the place itself'. Happy showed him grainy black and white photographs of what she called 'the place itself' and bad though the shots were, he recognised the wild turrets of mad King Ludwig's castle Hohenschwanstein, but said nothing, being loath to injure such simple, shining faith in the former Government negotiator. Having examined, in one of Lynch's living history classes, both Paul Kruger's official former residences and found them no more than a large bungalow and a simple farm respectively, it was impossible to credit that the old President's tastes would have run to anything so fanciful. 'Paul Kruger belonged to the Dopper sect of especially puritanical Calvinists, we can expect his last refuge to reflect his didactic, moralising spirit,' Father Lynch had explained. 'It is comical to reflect how his enemies might have played on this in the Boer War; consider – the British might have brought the war to an early end if they could have convinced the old man that the sight of white men shooting each other gave unalloyed pleasure to the natives . . .'

Fatima's directions were as unpersuasive: 'Above the lake and to the left,' she said. 'Start at Clarens. Where Kruger finished.'

So they made him ready for the journey. Babybel insisted on pressing his white shirt, because, she said, if a man was leaving for parts unknown with literally nothing but the clothes he stood up in, he would want to put his best foot forward. Visser agreed, saying that Blanchaille faced an ordeal ahead, a battle, a formidable enemy. When one entered the Garden of Eden, he explained somewhat mysteriously, one faced not merely the snake, but the apple, and there were circumstances in which apples were more subtle than serpents.

It was Freia who injected a note of realism into these conversations by revealing that Eden was hardly Blanchaille's destination. He was going to England. Indispensable Freia! Owing perhaps to her training as a township tour guide she had checked his ticket and revealed that he was flying to London with a thirty-six-hour stopover before his flight to Geneva. Why not a direct flight? Blanchaille protested, but there was nothing to be done. Besides, said Visser, the police themselves had booked his ticket and must have known what they were doing. *Only* the police knew what they were doing. They comprised the holy circle. Since the police in this instance were personified by Van Vuuren, whose status as a policeman was increasingly mysterious, Blanchaille hoped he still fell within the holy circle referred to by Visser. Blanchaille hoped he knew what he was doing.

As if to console him, Babybel gave him a necklace of golden Krugerrands, pierced and threaded on a string which she told him to wear at all times and promised him that it was a key, the use of which he would know when the time came.

And then, in the evening, I saw how they personally escorted him from the hotel to the airport, stepping over the bodies of the Presidential Guard which lay scattered on the streets and pavements like soldiers from a child's toy box. Whether dead or drunk, simply asleep or resting, he could not tell. Then I saw with what tears the girls fell upon his neck and kissed him goodbye. On the plane he was given a window seat beside an Indian gentleman. At ten o'clock the plane took off. Peering towards the bright lights of the airport as they began to taxi, the sight of Visser and his four girls waving from the roof of the building was the last he saw of Africa.

CHAPTER 11

On the non-stop flight to London Blanchaille sat beside Mr Mal who explained that he was a fleeing Asian. Blanchaille said he thought that Asians had stopped fleeing Africa, but Mr Mal replied that Africa was still full of fleeing Asians, if only you looked around you. Mr Mal had fled from Uganda to Tanzania, from Tanzania to South Africa, and he was now fleeing to Bradford. He spoke of Bradford in the terms of wonder American immigrants must once have used about California. In his opinion the Asians were the Jews of Africa. It was amazing, Blanchaille thought, just how many people claimed to be the Jews of Africa. President Bubé in a celebrated speech claimed that distinction for the Afrikaner; Bishop Blashford was not above claiming it for harassed Catholics in the days when they were often persecuted by the Calvinists as 'the Roman danger'. President Bubé issued a statement declaring that the Catholics could pretend to be Jews or Methodists or Scientologists for all he cared, but while subversives threatened the country under the cloak of religion, he would show no mercy . . . (this a reference to the flight of Magdalena dressed as a nun). Let them go around in prayer shawls and yarmulkas if they liked, the security forces would root them out. Newspapers discussed this animatedly. CAMPS FOR CATHOLICS? the headlines wondered excitedly, and BUBÉ PLANS POGROM? What did the real Jews of Africa call themselves – with so many people competing for the title?

There was a large party of deaf-mutes travelling on the plane, pleasant young people who seemed quite unaffected by their disability. Blanchaille watched a young man in blue jeans and a red shirt carrying out an animated conversation with his girlfriend. He was a walking picture show. He held his nose, pulled his ears and seemed able to rub his stomach and pat his head simultaneously. He also did impressions: a boxing referee counting his man out, the drunk in the bar thumping his chest angrily, he opened bottles, he snatched a hundred invisible midges out of the air, hitched a ride, sent semaphore signals across the cabin. His fingers, his hands, his busy silent tongue that lapped against his open lips were altogether an eloquent and loquacious display. His hands and fingers flew, pecked and parroted, swam in the air, signalled, sang, played the old game of scissors, paper and stone. They were an excited aviary those flying hands, moving hieroglyphics, they signalled the meanings which words, if they had tongues of their own, would picture to themselves. His girl appeared to listen to him with her nose. Frequently her eyes applauded. He almost envied them their ability to talk so openly without fear of being overheard. He wished he knew why he had been routed through London. Beside him Mr Mal dozed, and cried out in his sleep of the pleasures of exotic Bradford.

Nothing prepared Blanchaille for the shock of finding her waiting at the barrier.

She took his trolley from him despite his protests and led him through the automatic glass doors into the thin uncertain sunshine of the English spring. He gazed at her, the thick blonde hair was pulled behind the pretty ears and expensively waved. Her perfume enveloped him in waves of warm musk. Magdalena looked chic and well cared for. He watched her small, square, capable, deft hands on the steering wheel. He couldn't believe he was sitting beside her again.

'This is kind, Magdalena. But not necessary, really.'

'Not kind or necessary. Blanchie, it is absolutely essential!'

He sat back in the car and watched the huge clouds passing low overhead like enormous aircraft showing their massive bellies. The sky in England seemed very low. That was his only observation to date. Magdalena had hugged him mightily and noted his weight increase. 'Too much beer,' she said affectionately.

In the old days Father Lynch had remarked on the abundance of Magdalena's affections. She resembled her biblical namesake, he said, and much would be forgiven her for she loved much, or more accurately she loved many. That was true. The altar boys had heard of Magdalena's powers as one hears of a wonderful cave of diamonds from which everyone is free to help themselves; of a hill of cash; a love goddess one dreamed of, panted after and never expected to get and who suddenly announced she was giving away the lot, for the asking.

Van Vuuren had announced the miracle: 'There's a girl called Magdalena. She gives.'

'How much?'

'Everything.'

It seemed inconceivable, a colossal lie. One could not accept the alarming hugeness of this claim. How much did she give? And what exactly did that wild generalisation mean? Did she pet? Did she French kiss? Did she allow her bra to be removed? Was it possible to go any, well, further?

'Piss off,' said Van Vuuren. 'You're an unbelieving lot. I said the lot. I mean the lot. Everything.'

'How do you know?'

'How do you think?'

'You didn't? Just like that.'

'We don't believe you.'

'I don't care. But you can try for yourselves.'

And they did. Zandrotti first, followed by Ferreira and both returned glowing from the encounter, enchanted and absolutely converted, aflame with new faith and zeal. In her arms they had passed from uncertainty to deep belief. She was a miracle, a blessing! Kipsel confirmed, and Van Vuuren looked knowing, the veteran. Blanchaille held out in his scepticism. His unbelief was of Augustinian proportions and he prayed that it be strengthened with each fresh report of his friends' success, with Zandrotti's tears, always emotional, in recalling how amazingly easy it had been, *she* had been. She had just opened up and took him in and there he was, doing it like he'd been doing it all his life.

'What – without precautions?'

'Sure. When are you going to do it, Blanchie?'

'Soon.'

'How soon?'

'Just soon.'

'You're chicken.'

'No, I'm not. Look, all right, it happened with you but it doesn't necessarily follow that it will happen with *me*.'

And it did seem to him too fast and too far. Too implausible. Sexual intercourse was something that clearly required longterm planning, something worked up towards, a large project studied in the old *Chambers's Encyclopedia* of 1931 which he found in the hostel library and which dwelt in detail on the fertility rites of remote tribes in New Guinea. Not something you nipped in for on a Saturday afternoon. But it was for Saturday afternoon that it had been arranged and he was to be driven there by Van Vuuren, Zandrotti, Kipsel and Ferreira, in Van Vuuren's brother's bottle-green MG. It occurred to him that they feared that unless they took him there themselves he might not go, he might just say he'd been . . . He denied it vehemently but knew it could well have been true.

To Blanchaille's horror Magdalena's parents were at home,

something which deterred his grinning sponsors who began a swift retreat and left him with the miracle herself, a broad-shouldered, solid, commanding, shapely girl with a mature manner and a shrewd assessing look in her blue-grey eyes. Backing out with embarrassed grins his friends mumbled shamelessly about 'getting home', probably regarding the afternoon as lost. Suddenly the parents also left, claiming with what Blanchaille considered false sincerity that they'd remembered an urgent appointment at the bowls club. Blanchaille was contorted with shame and rage; could the parents of the easiest girl in town play bowls? Surely they knew why he was there and were not going to allow it? Could they remain slumped in deck chairs over their brandies after playing a couple of taxing lengths on the green without a care in the world about what their daughter was doing with her young friend?

Obviously they could.

Magdalena had sized him up with a practised eye. Blanchaille thrust his hands into the pockets of his grey raincoat which he had worn, not against the weather, but simply because it hid the frightful khaki shorts all the hostel boys were made to wear. What happened next was a blur. She did not ask him to sit down (speed was always her strength), she crossed the room, kissed him hard, so hard she lifted him off his heels. In his confusion he thanked her but she did not seem to require thanks. Indeed, seeming to regard all conversational niceties as superfluous she pushed him down onto the sofa and attempted to spread him out. The fear of her parents returned. His own unpreparedness plus some foolish juvenile desire to preserve at least a vestige of the romantic formality made Blanchaille resist her advance, bracing his legs, refusing to straighten the knees. Magdalena left off pushing and went to the heart of the matter by loosening his belt, lifting his shirt, easing him, fingering him, making him ready. All this with the one hand while the other, on his chest, pinned him firmly to the sofa and then directing his hands beneath her skirt, obliging him to lower her pants, wriggling expertly as she sloughed them off and planted herself upon him. Blanchaille attempted to say something but his tongue had thickened in his mouth and all that came out was a low gurgle. He thought afterwards that perhaps what he'd meant to say was something like: 'Shouldn't we at least close the curtains?' But the moment was gone, passed before he knew it. She moved once, twice, three times and Blanchaille was afloat in that warm sea he'd just entered.

And just as suddenly cast ashore. Someone who has invested so

128

much reading time in such concepts as 'ejaculation' cannot but expect far more. But to have come and gone before one knew it! Brief and involuntary. Behind almost before it began. Like a hiccup. 'We might have been shaking hands.'

'Hell, Blanchie, you're a born romantic,' Kipsel said.

And then some time later, once again, in Blashford's other, unofficial garden.

What could one say of Magdalena? Everybody's girlfriend once, twice, and then she took off like a rocket into the political firmament, out of reach of mere altar servers, numbering among her lovers such heavy figures as Buffy Lestrade the Hegelian radical lecturer, and no more contact was made until Kipsel rediscovered her and carried her off to blow up pylons in the veld. Afterwards the trial, the betrayal, and the extraordinary escape. Magdalena, the saboteur turned demure nun in her audacious dash for freedom from beneath the very nose of the Regime, became a legend.

Once in London she came to be rated amongst the six most dangerous enemies beyond the borders. Connected with the Azanian Liberation Front, romantically linked for a time with one of its leaders, Kaiser Zulu, she was branded a convinced and radical believer in the violent overthrow of the Regime. Rumours and legends constantly appeared in the press. Red Magda they called her. He remembered Magdalena's mother had made an attempt to save her. She announced that she would go abroad and talk to her daughter, call on her to repent. Various well-wishers raised money. Her local bowling club of course, a building society, and several newspapers ran the campaign to raise money to send this brave mother to save her daughter from the clutches of a terror movement, notorious for its cruel atrocities throughout the southern sub-continent. The usual photographs of flyblown and swollen corpses of murdered nuns, frozen in typically blind poses of hopeless entreaty, were shown, the pathetic stumps of what had been arms and legs pushing against the concrete air. Those shockingly familiar pictures the newspapers so loved, of decaying remains pictured against the dusty landscape of Africa which seemed in a strange way to lend a curiously gentle, eerily inoffensive aspect to the once-human husk, as if the horror melted away amid these vast indifferent surroundings and the bones, the hide, the carcass spread-eagled in the veld like a lion kill, or a drought victim, was another of the necessary sights of Africa. Except these were holy remains. The papers said so. Sacred clay. Relics. Powerful muti. As those who killed them and those who photographed them knew, in Africa the only good nun was a dead nun.

Magdalena's mother's visit of redemption went badly wrong. She got on famously with Kaiser Zulu, who, she said, reminded her of her old cookboy, and she was pictured singing choruses of 'Down at the Old Bull and Bush' in some tourist nightspot and told reporters, on her return, that her daughter wasn't as black as she had been painted. Angry letters filled the newspapers from readers demanding their money back.

RED MAGDA'S MOTHER DUPED! the headlines yelled.

The sunshine lay shyly on the grey-green fields beside the motorway. Blanchaille's first glimpse of England showed it to be small and tightly woven. The fields fenced everything within view. Nothing out of eyeshot, everywhere contained, ordered, bounded. The jumble of houses to left and right, three small factories, a smudge of development eating away the green and then the countryside spluttering out in a last fling of parks and trees as the houses began in earnest, but still, even to Blanchaille's untrained eye, recognisably houses, double storeys, detached, heavily planted in muddy yards, in the strange green smallness of the countryside.

Magdalena drove well, fast, her small, pretty hands in speckled yellow gloves calm on the wheel. The road swept upwards and ran as an elevated motorway into the solid, metalled city with its row upon row of semi-detached dwellings. It struck the stranger, the sandy tongued foreigner, blinking with lack of sleep, this sudden mass of building. It asserted itself, this solid, glued immobility of London, everywhere packed, joined, touching, far fewer single houses now and these were bulge-fronted, pebble-dashed, red tiled roofs. And then blocks of them, stuck solid, identical, joined irretrievably and running on for streets seemingly without end. He shivered. Magdalena must have seen this for she smiled.

'You thin-blooded African creatures, travelling north without coats. You could freeze to death here. Even in summer.'

'I brought nothing, nothing except what I stand up in.'

'You're unprepared then, in many ways. I'm glad to see you, Blanchie. But I have to tell you I really don't know what you're doing here. Your clerical career was both wild and original. You upset the Church, your friends, the Regime and you did it damn well. We all depended on you, watching from here. You were useful there. I'm afraid you may be at a bit of a loss here.' She lit a cigarette, the grey smoke blurred and clung to the furry coat she wore. She smiled, perhaps to soften the force of her remarks and showed sharp white teeth, but when he protested he had not come 'here' in any sense but was merely passing through he was cut short by a growl of displeasure.

'This place is hell. I can't tell you what I've been through. People told me I was lucky to have missed the balance of payments crisis. They say that was worse. The English are a strange race, obsessed with economics and they seldom bath. You've no idea how I suffered when I first arrived. When I came the country was governed by a series of pressure groups who went around shrieking at one another about incomprehensible causes. The daily obsession of the country was the value of the pound. "Pound up a penny" the headlines screamed, day after day. "Pound down a half penny!" Nothing else counted. Nowhere else featured. Wild rumours swept the land. I remember going to the opera when suddenly through the stalls and around the banks of boxes ran the whisper: "Pound lost three points against the dollar!" Pandemonium! Strong men tore their hair, women swooned. And given the lack of washing facilities, to which I've already referred, you can imagine what a malodorous demoralised crowd they were. Like an elderly woman with a guilty past they are beset by their desire to confess, on the one hand, and deny it all, on the other. They regret, repent and deplore all they've been, never realising that it's only their past that makes them worth knowing.'

She lived in Sealion Mansions off Old Marylebone Road. A squat, solid, peeling green-painted block smelling of wax, dust and the sea. From the fishmonger's opposite there drifted an aroma, a cocktail of brine, shell and sand wafting across the street. A corridor of fragrance crossed the road between fishmonger's and entrance foyer along which the sea tang drifted from the boxes of silver fish, wide-eyed in their beds of crushed ice.

Also staring up at the flat were two men in raincoats. The sky was clear.

Magdalena's flat was luxurious but small. A little entrance hall, a sitting-room, a bathroom, bedroom and kitchen. The bedroom was done in apricot silk.

'You're looking for a shining city on a hill, a sort of heaven, but you won't find it, Blanchie. Not here, at any rate.'

'I'm not looking here.'

'Then why stop over?'

'I tell you, I don't know.'

He admired her bedroom. She seemed pleased. It was her lair, she said. An odd term. Above the circular bed hung a large painting

131

in which two opposing forces shaped like tattered kites clashed violently. Red and black, two antagonistic whirlpools, fighting cocks, shredded and bloody, whirling and tearing at each other. Or perhaps two circular saws meeting tooth-on and the very sounds of their grinding collision were reflected in the shards of green and yellow paint with which the outer edges of the canvas were pierced.

She made him scrambled eggs and she ordered him to sleep in the large circular bed. He awoke in the late afternoon with the soft grey light in the room and found her above him, straddling him, naked. Her hand on his chest pinned him on the bed.

'Stay. Don't go on.'

Stay where? What did she mean? Sleepily he asked for an explanation but she drew him up into her and then fell to work from above, deftly rolling him from side to side and so their love-making began. Or not love-making really, but a struggle of sorts, without words, hot and desperate. She darting her head down to kiss him, his temple, foot, hand, sharp stinging kisses and he responding, no not responding but retaliating, giving little nips to lobes and elbows so that she squealed when she came, her hands gripping his buttocks and ramming herself home again and again, long after it was over. And still she would not release him and it was to be done again, their pubic bones jarred like shunting engines. He was bruised now. How hard she was down there, how rough! But she forced him over and over until he came at last, briefly, again, hopelessly, quite exhausted now, lying with his face in her neck and beginning to feel the pain in his back. She must have scratched him, the sweat ran into the score marks her nails had made and stung, but still she did not let up and since he was now past any sort of movement, slid from him, came out sideways, sliding, lubricated with sweat and turned him over now, mounted, reared up, placing precisely the lip of her vagina against his coccyx, rubbed herself there, scouring, grinding herself until she came to her climax, her breath hoarse in his ear.

He did not hear her leave. Perhaps he slept, briefly, or even passed out, but when he at last left the bed to look for her she'd gone.

He sat in the bathroom, his penis still achingly firm, throbbing to his heartbeat. The cool porcelain of the bath edge cooled him and he tried to relax, to clear his mind, to will the thing to fall and droop, an old seminary trick this. It had been an attack, a series of attacks. But why should she attack him? She had always had rough and ready ways, he remembered this from as far back as their first love-making. But this was an attack. Mounted attack, yes. There had been something angry, desperate, despairing in their encounter. And there was the speed with which it had happened. Almost a rush.

He tried to clear his mind. In the seminary there were tricks taught by the Monitor for Moral Instruction, Father Pauw. He had yellow teeth and green eyes and what he called a prodigious working knowledge of the fleshly ills. His lecture 'The young priest and the early morning erection – some observations', was a classic of its kind. 'You will find it,' he said, 'a common complaint amongst young men, particularly in the early days of their ministry, that the member has a mind of its own. You rise in the morning to find it's risen before you, a curse, a weapon which it cannot use against others and so often seeks to stab its owner. To treat this, first evacuate the bladder, then pray. If unsuccessful, reach for the paddle, the purity paddle.' This instrument was a piece of polished wood, rather like a miniature ping-pong bat. It was to be used often. It was indispensable. Seven sharp slaps put the flesh in its place, disarmed the enemy within.

He sat on the bath and took his red and angry throbbing weapon in his hand; his heart thumped in unison. Damn Magdalena! What the hell was she playing at?

He ran the bath and lay in the warm water. Threads of blood drifted by, fine ribbons and spirals floated in the water. The blood was real enough. How had she known he was coming? Why had she fallen on him so savagely? Where was she now?

When darkness fell and she had still not returned he dressed and went downstairs and across the road to the fishmongers where the two men in raincoats stared up at the building, waiting for him.

CHAPTER 12

Now I saw in my dream the truth of the supposition widespread in émigré circles amongst the refugees who have fled from the Regime, though this continues to be officially denied, that there are paid agents abroad who shadow, observe, report on, harass, hinder and even silence those individuals they fear.

Across the road from Magdalena's flat, outside the now empty, Arctic spaces of the fishmonger's window, the two men, one tall, one tiny, stood in the shadows. As he crossed the road towards them Blanchaille knew as soon as he set eyes on their raincoats, on their stiff and unyielding moustaches and heard their flat accents, that here were countrymen.

They stepped close to him and pressing him on either side said: 'Theodore Blanchaille, if you know what's good for you, go back.'

'Who are you?' Blanchaille asked.

'We are unwilling agents of the Regime,' came the prompt reply. 'Poor men who a long time ago booked on what was then known as a Pink Pussycat Tour of the Fun Capitals of Europe, and we looked forward to enjoying ourselves in Montparnasse and on the fabulous Reeperbahn. We were promised the time of our lives in the strip joints of Soho and the canalside brothels of Amsterdam. Here, look –' and he took from his pocket an old, creased, much thumbed and garish brochure showing a naked girl straddling a large pink cat which had orange whiskers and wore a monocle: 'Hiya fellas! Get out on the tiles! Just wear your smile. . . !' The naked girl pictured wore a tight, strained smile. Blanchaille looked at the ridiculous cat, blushed at the noisy old-fashioned dated enthusiasm of the invitation. It was all tremendously sad.

The large one folded the tissue-thin brochure with reverence and returned it gently to his pocket.

'We were ordinary blokes,' said the little one. 'Out for a good time. I was a butcher.'

'And I was a school inspector,' said the large one. 'And we saved long and hard, I can tell you. I mean, hell, it's no small thing, getting at our stage of life the promise of a really good time. We were in a button-popping hurry to inseminate the entire continent of Europe. Well, would you do otherwise? We planned for months, we scrimped, we bought Hawaiian shirts with orange suns and canary yellow sweaters to wear, just like Minister Kuiker who set the tone around that time, being the only person of note to venture outside the country publicly.'

'We dreamt of Dutch *vrouws* and silk beds. We saved every cent and when the big day came we kissed our wives goodbye and stepped onto the Boeing with hope in our hearts.'

'And stiffening pricks.'

The little one looked up at Blanchaille, unabashed, shrugged his shoulders and gave a bitter smile. 'Off to sleep with coloured girls.'

'Off to smoke dagga.'

'To go fishing on Sundays.'

'Get drunk on religious holidays.'

'Watch dirty movies and gamble into the small hours.'

The big one sighed wearily. 'But what we got was duty. We're stuck here, in the shadows.'

'This is hell,' said the little one. 'I thought a Free State Sunday was hell, but this is hell.'

'Who are you?' Blanchaille demanded.

'We're called Apple Two,' the big one explained, looking embarrassed, 'so-called because it stands for both of us.' He raised two fingers.

'But who is Apple One?'

The watchers shrugged. 'Don't ask us.'

'What sort of a name is that?'

'It's a code name. We can't give you our real names. Our orders were to stand out here and watch the flat until further notice.' The little one looked apologetic.

'Who gave the order?'

'Apple One. We were to watch the flat until you left,' said the big man.

'And then we were to tell you to go to the Embassy. Don't be hard on us, we don't like this job. We didn't ask for it,' said the little one, clutching Blanchaille's sleeve. 'We stepped off the plane in London and the Embassy car was waiting. We thought, Christ but this is odd! Why should our Government come and meet us? Anyway we took it as a gesture. We told ourselves they were just being hospitable. Little did we know. We were driven into town, chatting happily like any group of tourists in London the first time, lightheaded with that sense of freedom that comes to all South Africans who discover that the outside world really does exist, and we pulled up in Trafalgar Square at the sign of the golden springbuck and I remember turning before we were hustled through the swing doors, I remember seeing the fountains, the pigeons, the tourists mooning about, Nelson up on his column . . . my last glimpse of freedom.'

'What happened?' Blanchaille asked.

The two watchers in the shadows sighed and drew their coats around them. 'We were commissioned, into the security forces. It was explained to us that we should put duty above pleasure. Our air tickets would be refunded, they said. Our families had been notified that we were heroically responding to the call of our country abroad. With manpower shortages in security, as in all other industries, we were to be given the chance of serving our motherland by helping in the surveillance of suspected persons abroad.'

'Do you know what's happened to Magdalena?' Blanchaille asked.

'She left some time ago,' the large one said.

'Better not ask where she was going,' said the little one.

'Where was she going?' Blanchaille persisted doggedly.

'To the Embassy.'

'Where is the Embassy? How do I get there?'

'Go to Trafalgar Square. Look for the sign of the golden springbuck,' said the little one.

'Blanchaille,' said the large one, 'don't be a fool. Get out. Go back to our country. There's nothing for you here. Believe us, we know. This is hell. It's a small, rather dingy, gloomy northern country. Everything is dead, the only signs of life are to be detected in the police, the army and the monarchy. Go back to where there are real issues to fight for.'

'I wasn't thinking of staying here. I'm in transit.' Blanchaille replied. 'I'm only here for forty-eight hours, and believe me, that's not my idea. I'm heading for Europe. There are certain mysteries I wish to solve.'

'That's worse,' said the little one. 'That is the dark continent, Europe. It's littered with the bones of Africans searching for the answers to certain mysteries.'

'Then I'll follow the bones,' said Blanchaille. 'See what they tell me.'

The watchers shrugged. 'Rather you than us,' they said. 'Don't say we didn't warn you.'

And I saw in my dream how Blanchaille, having exchanged some of his money into British currency with the watchers, who gave him a good rate 'just for a feel of home', and having been pointed to the nearest tube, made his way down into the earth.

He was not prepared for life below ground. The elevator taking him down was very old and shook and its revolving belts squealed and cried like a man in agony. A hot wind carried on it the smell of metallic dust that blew from the yawning black holes at each end of the platform. A few desultory late-night passengers moped disconsolately in the shadows. Advertisements lined the sides of the tunnel. Most seemed to be taken up with lingerie and the delights of early retirement.

Blanchaille heard a terrible noise, a shouting, a screaming and howling as if troops of banshees were approaching, their cries emphasised by the hollowness of the deep underground. The waiting passengers seemed to know what was happening because he saw them scurrying for the far dark corners of the platform. With a great burst of shouting, singing, clapping, a strange army of young men arrived. They wore scarves and big boots, waved rattles and flags. The posse of policemen guarding them had trouble keeping them under control. Red seemed to be their colour, red bobble caps and scarves and shirts and socks, streamers and pennants.

They were marched to the far end of the platform, laughing and threatening to push each other onto the rails and terrorising the passengers. No sooner were they in place when the second army was ushered on to the platform and marched down towards the opposite end of the station, also with whistles and klaxons, hooters, cheering and whistles. Their colour seemed to be yellow: yellow hats and yellow flags. When the Reds caught sight of the Yellows pandemonium broke loose. Individuals broke free from both sides and hurled themselves at each other, kicking and clawing at one another and police and dogs struggled to keep them apart. Clearly the Reds and the Yellows were sworn enemies. The Reds shouting out, 'Niggers, niggers, niggers!' and the Yellows replied, 'Yids, yids, yids!' Blanchaille was reminded of the tremendous battles which took place between Fascists and Jews on the anniversary of Hitler's birthday on the pavement outside the beer cellars in the capital. The hatred they clearly felt for one another was so reminiscent of the life he had left, that for a moment he was overwhelmed with feelings of homesickness, even a kind of strange nostalgia. A train arrived and the Reds were allowed aboard. The Yellows were held back on the platform. No doubt they had their separate train.

As Blanchaille arrived at Trafalgar Square station I saw how a succession of young girls came up to him. 'Business, business,' they said repeatedly. This puzzled Blanchaille who could not imagine what girls so young could be doing in such a place, so late at night.

The crowds pressing around him as the escalator rose slowly towards the light wore ecclesiastical costumes as if got up to resemble old religious pictures. He saw a bishop, a scattering of cardinals, a bevy of virgins in blue veils. It was only when he peered closely that he saw their stubbled chins and realised they were all men. They clustered behind Blanchaille on the escalator whispering, perhaps to each other, perhaps to themselves, perhaps it wasn't even they who spoke but only voices inside his head, but from wherever the words came they scandalised him. Their talk was of organs and orifices, of anal chic, of comings and goings, of tongues, testicles, of ruptures, lesions and sphincters, of AIDS, herpes and hepatitis, of pancake make-up and the versatility of latex, of leather and the ethics of climactic simulation and of the lover of some unfortunate creature who had lost her life, head smashed with a heavy hammer when it was discovered that she was not he pretending, coiffed and beguiling, but the very her she had been pretending to be. 'Come over to our side ducks and get the feel of life!' These ribald remarks caused a great deal of mirth among the knot of purpled cardinals whose faces, he saw, were painted dead white with large black eyes so that they looked like Japanese actors. The long staircase creaked its way upwards to the dirty patch of light above. Of course it was all too likely that these scenes took place only in his imagination and the crowds around him were perfectly ordinary people returning from walks in the country, and scout outings and the girls so desperate for business were collecting for charity. But that his imagination should run in these channels at such a time worried him deeply.

And then he was up in the Square. He saw the column with Nelson on top of it. He saw the fountains, he saw buildings which reminded him very much of the campus of the Christian National University with its predilection for the neo-Grecian temple style and then directly across the road he saw the sign of the golden springbuck. (You must note here, if you will, how typical were Blanchaille's feelings of excitement and ignorance, the feelings of an innocent abroad. Had he known it, the dangers he imagined in the underground were as nothing compared with the perils which now faced him.) He gazed up at the large corner building, the Embassy squat and solid, that old box of ashes and bones as it was called by that celebrated dissident, the Methodist missionary Ernest Wickham (and he should have known, since he was widely credited with having burgled the Embassy and taken away sensitive papers which were later passed to the Azanian Liberation Front). A daring triumph, but shortlived, for a little while later Wickham received a parcel from a favourite Methodist mission in the Kalahari, where much of his fieldwork had taken place. Wickham made the mistake of opening the parcel and was blown into smaller bits than would fill a small plastic bag, given that hair, teeth, bones and odd gobbits of flesh were dutifully collected notwithstanding. The bomb, it was suggested, might have come from the Pen Pals Division of the Bureau which had long exploited the exiles' weakness for welcoming parcels from home. (It should be noted here that the Regime had since commemorated the work of Pen Pals Division of the Bureau with the issue of a special stamp showing on an aquamarine background a large plain parcel wrapped in brown paper and neatly tied up with string. In the lefthand corner the keen-eyed observer will spot the tiny letters 'PP', which, he will now know, do not stand for postage paid.)

Sitting in a high window of the Embassy was Dirk Heiden, the so-called South African super-spy, a sobriquet well earned. This formidable man worked himself into the top job of the Students Advisory Bureau, a Swiss-based organisation promoting the aims of radical students abroad, particularly exiled students from the South African townships, a post which he held for some eighteen months in which time he took part in freedom marches in Lagos against the racism of the Regime and was photographed taking a sleigh ride in the Moscow snow. From his office in Geneva he monitored the activities of resistance groups, anti-war objectors and other dissidents abroad, tailing them, taping them, photocopying documents and insinuating himself into the clandestine councils of various radicals abroad who seemed as free with their secrets as they were with their brandy. As a result of his reports many at home were beaten, imprisoned, stripped, manacled and tortured. Hciden had returned home to the kind of triumphant reception normally accorded only to rugby teams or visiting pop-singers who had defied the international ban against appearances likely to benefit the Regime. But his hour of glory over, he fell prey to the boredom which so often affects those who have lived too long abroad. He grew fat and listless, developed a drink problem, was arrested for firing his pistol at passers-by, pined for his tie-maker and his old sophisticated life, and so his superiors returned him to an overseas post, a chair in the window of an upstairs room in the Embassy where he peered through the glass searching the Square for familiar faces.

Heiden sat in a chair by the window, so still he might have been dead. His weight had continued to increase, his facial skin was stretched tight and shining over the bones, it had the texture of rubber on a beach ball blown up to bursting point. He stared out of the window because it was his job to look at people who visit the Square below, look for faces he might recognise, for it is a well-known fact that South Africans abroad will come and stand silently outside their Embassy, prompted perhaps by the same impulses that bring early morning observers to wait outside the walls of a prison where a hanging is to take place, or crowds to stand outside the palace walls when the monarch is dying.

In another window on the same floor sat the Reverend Pabst, 'the holy hit man' they called him once, but a shambling wreck now, surrounded by empty cane spirit bottles and scraps of food. His career had been simple and brutal. God had instructed the Regime that His enemies should be identified and exterminated. Pabst went to work. A fine shot and a quick and efficient killer using his bare hands and no more than a length of fishing line, he had a considerable tally of victims to his credit. Sadly, unknown to himself, he had also killed, besides enemies of the Regime, certain members of the Regime, quite possibly tricked into doing so by other members of the Regime. He could no longer be allowed to roam loose. He sat in a chair with a small sub-machine gun in his lap. He would cradle it beneath his chin and sometimes even suck the snout-like barrel, pressing gently on the palm-release trigger. The gun was not loaded of course, and the door behind him was locked and bolted. Sometimes he would hurl himself at the window, mowing down imaginary hordes with his wicked little gun only to fall back in his chair with a streaming nose or broken tooth. The windows were thickly armour-plated. The old man would dribble and grin, dreaming of past assassinations.

Blanchaille passed by these dangers quite unknowing. It is not surprising. He was not known and would not have known the watchers in the windows. And besides, I saw in my dream that he had eyes for only one thing, a man on the other side of the busy street. He knew him instantly, despite the grey clerical suit, the dog-collar. His old clothes!

Blanchaille called his name, hopping from foot to foot on the edge of the Square while a steady stream of traffic surged between them. At first the man appeared not to hear. Blanchaille called again, and then, because the man appeared to be about to escape, without thinking he charged into the traffic. A large tourist bus narrowly missed him. He stumbled and almost fell beneath the wheels of a taxi, the driver squealing to a halt and cursing him. But he reached the other side and seized the coat of the man now hurrying down the Strand, seized him almost at the same instant as the watchers in the windows above saw him and positively identified his quarry (with what consequences I dread to think!) as Trevor Van Vuuren.

CHAPTER 13

Now that the absconding priest, Theodore Blanchaille, met and talked with the policeman, Trevor Van Vuuren, is not in doubt. Where opinions differ concerns the motives which brought Van Vuuren to London and the fate he suffered there. The official version put out by the Regime is well-known and straightforward. Van Vuuren visited London in pursuit of the renegade cleric, Blanchaille, because he believed the man had information which might throw light on the murder of Anthony Ferreira. His quarry, realising that the law was closing in, lured the policeman into a trap.

That is why there are still those who talk of Van Vuuren 'The Martyr'.

I saw things differently in my dream. I saw Blanchaille and Van Vuuren, arm in arm, making their way down the Strand. An odd picture they were, closer than ever to Lynch's predictions, for Blanchaille resembled a ruined Southern gambler in crumpled white suit and heavy stubble with his strange seal-like shuffle, the feet thrown out in a wide flipper shove, and Van Vuuren was the muscular priest beside him. They proceeded slowly down the street, the weightlifter and the punchbag. And so the short night passed.

They passed a bank which looked like a church and opposite it a station which looked to him like a palace and beside it a cinema showing a pornographic movie. Blanchaille had never seen a pornographic movie, he'd never seen a cinema advertise pornographic films. This one was called *Convent Girls*, and showed three naked blondes in nun's wimples running across a green field. 'Hellfire passions behind the convent walls!' How he envied the potential of European Catholicism! No wonder Lynch had felt cheated in Africa. Blanchaille remembered the convent girls of his youth, shy creatures in sky-blue dresses, white panamas and short white ankle socks, shepherded by swathed and nimble-booted nuns patched in black and white, nipping at their heels like sheep-dogs. Van Vuuren was dressed in his friend's old cast-off clerical suit, rather dirty charcoal with ash-grey V-necked vest and dog-collar far too large for him so that it hung below his adam's apple like one of those loops one tosses over a coconut in a fairground. He had not shaved and the black stubble gleamed on his chin in the early light, that pale English dawn light which comes on rather like a wan bureaucrat to give notice that the day ahead will once again be one of low horizons and modest expectations.

I heard their conversation which I record as accurately as possible.

'Thanks for waiting.'

'After seeing you plunge into the traffic in that suicidal manner I had to wait. If only to see if you made it.'

'I had to make a run for it because I saw the look on your face when you spotted me. I thought you were going to bolt.'

'I was. You don't want to be involved with me. I'm bad news, Blanchie.'

'Why are you here?'

'Because my people sent for me.'

'I couldn't believe it when I saw you. I said to myself, that's Trevor, but it can't be. He's at home.'

'This is home for me, Blanchie.'

'Who are your people?'

'The Azanian Liberation Front.'

'The ALF – your people? Since when?'

'From as far back as I can remember. I went with the Communion wafer still sticking to my palate, straight from my last Corpus Christi procession, and told them I wanted to enlist. I had a meeting with old Vilakaze, he was still boss in those days. I must have been the first, perhaps the only, white schoolboy member of the Azanian Liberation Front. When I was ready to leave school the Front said to me, go back and work for the Government. Join the police. Fall asleep in the arms of the Regime. We will wake you when you're needed.'

'What? All this time, Trevor, an agent for the Front?'

'All this time. A special sort of policeman, just as Lynch predicted. I kept the faith, like I told you. In my own way. Then, a couple of days ago, soon after I had seen you in Balthazar Buildings I got a message from London. My job was over. I could come home. I took the plane. When I arrived at the airport there was another message waiting for me. I was to go to the Embassy. It seemed strange. The Embassy is one of those places I would have expected to avoid. But then I'm a soldier. I take orders. The Front says go and I go. Even so, I was surprised no one met me at Heathrow. I didn't expect a band and streamers, but I thought someone might have shown up. So I came here, expecting someone familiar. But not a sign of anyone, until you came along. Don't take this amiss, Blanchie, but you were hardly what I expected.'

'Why do you say you're bad news?'

'Well, I should have been met, you see. Something's very wrong.'

'I was met.'

And Blanchaille told him about Magdalena, about their meeting at the airport, about her flat, omitting the details of her extraordinary attack on him, about the watchers outside the fishmonger's.

'Apple Two,' said Van Vuuren and laughed. 'Who do you think Apple One is?'

Van Vuuren was pale in the early morning light. Blanchaille was put in mind neither of the policeman he had been nor the priest he now resembled. Blanchaille could smell the fear on him. He was sweating though it was still cool in the dawn, breathing heavily, lifting his face, the nostrils flaring and sniffing deeply as if by the couple of inches this gave him he might find pure air easier to breathe. Blanchaille was reminded of a buffalo he'd once seen looking for water, plunging into a swamp and drinking and drinking until he moved in too far and could not pull himself out. Half-submerged, with his curved horns pointed above the water line, the beast struggled to free himself only to sink all the more securely into the mud until only the line of his back and the flashing horns were visible and the long wet muzzle with just the nostrils clear, sucking at the air, taking in a little water each time with a rivelled hiss. A little more water each time and the brown eyes blinked and bulged helplessly as the animal slipped deeper. It fought for each breath, a gurgling hiss of air and water passing into the nostrils. Then the buffalo gave a convulsive jerk, let its body sink and angled its head up in the air fighting the nostrils clear; he heard the clogged snuffle, more laboured, more lengthy, the watery intake and then, suddenly, nothing – just an ear and the horns and the silence. Why did Van Vuuren make him think of that?

'Who sent for you?'

'Kaiser himself.'

Blanchaille didn't pursue the subject.

'I can still remember my last Corpus Christi procession,' said Van Vuuren. 'I see us all gathered outside the railway station getting ready for the march to the Cathedral. The Children of Mary in blue cloaks and white veils; a platoon from the Society of St Vincent de Paul, male pillars of the Church in their grey flannel suits and their neat side partings; nuns running excitedly to and fro with their veils fluttering in their faces, all freshly scrubbed and shining with anticipation of the treat to come; young men and women of the various religious sodalities, very pink and pious and most disturbingly calm about it all. Contingents, squads, whole battalions of priests forming up beneath the banners. A small group of White Fathers appeared in that strange outfit they wore that gave them a slightly sporting look, like female bowlers; and of course Franciscans with their bunching brown robes, tightly roped around the waist; and throngs of tiny boys and girls who'd made their first Communion that morning, girls in bridal flounces with flowers in their hair and little boys in bow ties all carrying baskets of flowers with which to strew the streets. We were all formed up in a procession and at the head was the Bishop, the unspeakable Blashford, decked out in gold vestments and flanked by assistant priests and served by an army of altar boys, incense bearers, boat boys, bell ringers and acolytes, all attending His Grace who was bearing aloft the gold and silver monstrance with its small circular glass window behind which you glimpsed the sacred host, the white and sacred heart of the golden sun, the rays of which were suggested in the jagged, spiky ruby-tipped petals of the monstrance, a sight to dazzle and astound the faithful. Behind the ranks of altar boys, the great crowd of assistant priests in white surplices. I remember how the onlookers began to form, how they used to crowd the streets which were usually very empty on Sunday and watched with blank incomprehension as the Corpus Christi procession in all its gaudy Roman glory snaked forward, chanted, sang, knelt, shuffled up from its knees and staggered on again. Fluttering above the Bishop and the monstrance was the silken canopy supported on four poles by members of the Knights of De Gama wearing broad sashes and white gloves. The crowds gawped. The white people looked stern and unimpressed; behind them the blacks giggled and pointed and shook their heads at this fantastic spectacle of mad pilgrims in curious costumes following their gorgeous leader beneath his wind-rippled canopy. The white spectators put their hands in their pockets and struck attitudes of contempt. The Africans gave little outbreaks of spontaneous applause, as if they were watching a varsity rag procession and admiring the different floats. I remember they saved their best applause for the little band of black Christians who traditionally brought up the rear of the procession, usually wearing religious costumes of their own design, long white flowing albs, shimmering chains of holy medals clinking on coloured ribbons worn around the neck, roughly cut wooden staffs in their

hands. These wild prophets received a special police escort. Occasionally there were fights as a group of white bystanders isolated and assaulted some chosen black spectator, raining blows and kicks upon the victim for reasons you never understood – I mean you could hardly stop and ask. And the police moved in and rescued the fallen man with the customary arrest. Every so often, you remember, we stopped and knelt. I can still smell the hot tar. The old hands spread a handkerchief. Sometimes horses had passed that way and you could smell the dung. There were oil stains right there in the middle of the road. There we knelt in the middle of the city, on a bright Sunday morning, the whole great procession reciting the rosary, a vast murmur rising and falling. Do you remember how the spectators often shrieked if the holy water sprinkled by the priests accidentally touched them? And they would wave away the fog of incense with their newspapers. You remember how they used to cough and give artificial little explosions of irritation to show how much they disapproved of it all? And you remember how embarrassed we were? I was anyway. I knelt there and prayed that the buildings would topple and cover me. We had to endure *hours* of it! pretending that nothing strange or bizarre was happening, that this was what you did every Sunday morning, you got dressed up in crazy clothes and went out and knelt in the middle of the road while the traffic policemen kept the cars away. You remember the traffic policemen? They stood at the intersections and wore those black jodhpurs, black tunic, grey shirt, the sunglasses, and the black peak cap. They said the uniform was modelled on that of the SS. I knelt there and prayed for the earth to open or the sky to fall, or for bolts of lightning to obliterate the entire procession in an instant, or for bombs to go off, or for a madman armed with a sten gun to burst upon the scene and mow down every living soul. I prayed for a message: "Lord, tell me what to do." And the message came back: "Join the ALF, my son. It is the only act of faith left to you. You kneel here on the hot tarmac, foolish, exposed, embarrassed. You are that comical thing – a white man in Africa. Repent whilst there is still time, join the Front . . ."
It was a religious conversion. The Front ordered me into the police force. I knew my friends would see it as an act of treachery, but I could live with that. Let my friends think of me as the traitor-policeman. Let them spit at me. I could take it. For the Cause. For the Front! Actually, at the time I think I was suffering from a kind of religious mania. Luckily it had no outward sign. I mean it didn't issue in fainting fits or speaking in tongues or stigmata or levitation

or uncontrolled miracles. All of that would have been rather inappropriate in a police officer, as you can imagine. And there was a short period when I experimented with flagellation, making a small branched whip with half a dozen tails securely attached to a short wooden stock and I beat myself with this whip but there were immediate difficulties. Probably few people know it, but it's not possible to direct the whip so as to avoid marking oneself on the neck or wrist, and these are places where the weals might show and so arouse suspicion. And then I had myself a hairshirt made of horsehair and wool and wore it next to the skin for over a week. Not very practical either. It was hot, you see. I'd sweat. And the sweat would saturate the hair on the shirt and the shirt clung to me underneath my tunic and gave me a very odd shape. One or two of my colleagues asked if I was putting on weight. It was a very odd time for me.'

Now I saw in my dream how Blanchaille and Van Vuuren, though unaware of it, talked and walked their way up the Strand, around Covent Garden and by degrees into Soho. And it was in Soho that they first noticed the black cab trailing along behind them and saw that it carried none other than their old mentor, Father Ignatius Lynch.

And Blanchaille remembered the famous black beret in the Airport Palace, and knew why it was there before him.

Stories abound concerning the conversation Blanchaille and Van Vuuren had with their old master at that strange meeting in Soho, once they had recovered from their astonishment. How they noted his tremendous excitement as well as his weariness. (This is hardly surprising when you consider the old man had achieved a lifetime's dream in escaping from Africa, helped no doubt by the pistachio-flavoured banknotes he had borrowed from the money poor Ferreira had left Blanchaille.) Yet having made good his escape from Africa at last, why come looking for them? Lynch cut short such enquiries. In fact, as I saw in my dream, he did most of the talking, telling them for the last time that his time was short and he was not much longer for this world and as if to emphasise it, he kept the taxi waiting, meter ticking over. Indeed, he implied that they might not be much longer for this world either. He reminded them that they were babes abroad, that neither had ever been out of the country before except for their living history lessons he'd provided years before. He said they wouldn't ever have known that they were now in Soho had he not told them, and grave dangers awaited them.

147

All his talk was of death, while the meter ticked. And for once it seemed true, this expectation of his own end. He was smaller, thinner, more frail than they had ever seen him before. It was by a fragile, grinning, big-eared wraith that they were addressed in a Soho street.

He told them about the strange suicides of the brokers Lundquist, Kranz and Skellum, which he described as the most extraordinary acts of self-destruction since Mickey the Poet strangled himself with his own hands.

'The broker Kranz died by hanging himself during a lunch given by the Woolgrowers' Association of which, for obscure family reasons that need not detain us, he was a director. It had been a very good lunch apparently and they got down to coffee and liqueurs when Kranz himself was, in the words of one witness, "as merry as hell". Setting off to the bathroom his last words were – again I have this from the family, "Keep the bottle coming around – I'm off for a splash", and then walking, or rather weaving, happily from the room, a large brandy in hand, he disappeared. The glass of brandy, now drained, was found in a basin in the men's lavatory and suspended from the window directly above the toilet, hanging by his own belt, was the unfortunate Kranz. It seems there were a number of puzzling bruises and contusions on the body for which no explanation could be found. Certainly it seems unlikely that Kranz could have injured himself like that, but the inquest finally decided that Kranz in his drunken state had probably clambered up on the seat of the lavatory and then onto the cistern itself, attaching the belt to a steel window frame. However, being drunk, he was clumsy and hadn't tied the knots correctly and he fell, or so the story goes, perhaps he fell several times only to clamber up again, stubborn fellow that he was, and try again. Everyone agreed that he had shown quite remarkable determination.

'Lundquist showed the same intensity of purpose as his colleague Kranz. For we must believe that this small man lifted his heavy executive chair, weighing half as much as he did, and using it as a kind of battering ram smashed a hole in the window large enough to pass through and so plunged to his death one hundred and fifty feet below. A wonderfully neat worker, too, this Lundquist. For although the body was badly broken, as you would expect after such a fall, it seems he had not been cut once by the wall of glass through which he had smashed in his feverish desire for extinction.

'Of Skellum, the third suicide, it must be said that we have an act of self-destruction which deserves the palm. Here we had a man with a brilliant military record who was invalided out of the service suffering from shellshock. This was caused by a terrifying experience when the patrol he was leading was ambushed and lay under continual mortar fire for a full day and Skellum saw his companions killed beside him one by one. Not surprisingly this experience left him with an uncontrollable fear of sudden and violent explosions, a backfire, a slammed door, a firework, even a loud cough would reduce him to a state of gibbering terror. Yet this man so overcame his fear as to bounce into his office one morning bright and early, close the door, put a .38 pistol to his temple and blow his brains out, falling forward onto his desk, thereby unintentionally summoning his secretary who came in with her notebook thinking that her boss wanted to dictate some letters.

'Now these dead brokers might have been remembered for nothing more than their suicides,' Father Lynch concluded, 'had it not been for the fact that each had seen Ferreira shortly before his death. Ferreira had revealed to them that their dealings in gold and industrial shares for ostensibly reputable clients, were really deals on behalf of dummy companies set up by the Ring. Kranz, Lundquist and Skellum had been dealing for the Ring. And it in turn had been dealing for the Hand of the Virgin, you will know that organisation of devout Catholic freemasons. Unfortunately the Ring felt entitled to a decent commission. And they forgot to mention it to the Hand.

'The Bank of the Angels called in the accounts, checked them over – and had a convulsion. But the real culprits, the Ring, slipped out of reach of the Fingers by the simplest and time-honoured expedient in these matters, it blamed the brokers who had handled the deals. If there was money missing, the Italians were informed, then Kranz, Lundquist and Skellum were the guilty men. The Hand reached out. It reached for necks.

'It was now that Ferreira called in the brokers. The only way the brokers could save themselves, Ferreira told them, was to co-operate with his enquiry. Give him details of the shares purchased, sums remitted, names of contacts. And naturally the brokers fell over themselves to comply with this request. They firmed up Ferreira's case so tight you could have built battleships with the steel in it. And then Ferreira goes and gets murdered. Maybe the Azanian Kommando did it, maybe the Afrika Brigade – what did it matter to Kranz, Lundquist and Skellum? Did it matter what the writing on the wall really meant? To them its message was clear enough. It said "You next". So they panicked. Who wouldn't? They began off-loading shares, too many, too fast. Maybe they planned to skip? Or buy their way out of trouble – who knows? The market turned downwards. And there followed the sensational suicides. Truly, the only miracle left in our country these days is the wonderful and mysterious ways which men find to take their own lives. Of this, poor Mickey the Poet is the patron saint and initiating martyr. We can but pray that they find peace at last in another place, as we pray we all may do one day.'

'And may we pray that the Regime, the Ring and the Hand one day roast in hell?' demanded Van Vuuren, angrily.

'Certainly we may pray for no such thing,' came the prompt reply, 'but we can always hope.'

And then Blanchaille asked him this question: 'Father Lynch, you've cleared up one of the mysteries in this business. We know why share prices fell. But tell us – who killed Ferreira?'

'Read the writing on the wall,' replied the little priest. 'You're the policeman, remember, work it out.'

'But we read the writing on the wall and it told us that either the Straf Kaffir Brigade got him – or the black radicals, the Azanian Strike Kommando No. 3. But a lot of other people could have had a motive. Like Bubé, or Minister Kuiker and Trudy Yssel, or the Israelis, or the Taiwanese, or the Ring, or the Hand or just about anybody who believed Ferreira knew enough to sink them *and* he intended to publish it . . .'

Lynch inclined his head. 'Certainly, or it could have been the Papal Nuncio, or Himmelfarber, or the Bureau or the *Nuwe Orde*. So many suspects, so many motives. No good to go down that road. Perhaps the answer to at least part of the mystery is staring us in the face, providing we read the writing on the wall, providing we know how to read the writing. For has it not occurred to you that the letters ASK 3 might not have been left there by any of the persons or groups we have mentioned?'

'I'm sorry,' said Van Vuuren. 'I don't understand. If they didn't write the letters, who did?'

'Why Ferreira himself, of course,' said Father Lynch.

Well you can imagine the impact of this revelation. They fell to whistling and clicking their tongues in admiration and Van Vuuren sufficiently forgot himself to utter a few choice oaths, of which 'Well, I'll be fucked', is the only one I recall, and followed this with an apology.

And Lynch accepted their compliments with that curious little smile which made his jug-ears lift and the corners of his mouth twitch as they always did when he was pleased. 'No, no! Merely part of the training of one who has read deeply in the history of the Church's relations with the State, where murder cannot always be allowed to blight an otherwise intelligent, well-meaning policy. It is possible for martyrs, poets, inquisitors, poisoners, canon lawyers, bankers, cardinals to connive, plot, campaign to arrive at a mystery which will thrill the devout and balance the books. Well in this case, never mind the devout, and as I've told you before – examine the books. Have the courage to face what stares you in the face.'

Then Lynch read to them from his favourite book, withdrawing it from an inside pocket of his cassock with a fluid movement, *Further Memoirs of a Boer President*, the familiar bible, the mysterious tome edged with gold in a red leather cover.

> In the mountains above and somewhat to the left of the town of Montreux we found the place we sought and kneeling down with my valet, Happé, supporting me, I gave thanks when I saw it; dead though its chambers now lie, still its voice, it shall live again when our people come, as over the years they shall assuredly come, sick for home, to this home from home . . .

Then Lynch warned them again that his time was short, and so was theirs. They were marked men and one of them, he could not say which, would not see another sunrise. And when they protested that he could not possibly know this for sure, he said nothing, just stepped back into his taxi and tapped on the glass and told the cabbie to drive on. When they ran after the cab as it gathered speed demanding to know how anyone would find them in London, he rolled down the window and asked them how they thought he had found them so easily. It would be no trouble to their enemies, they could find them whenever they liked simply by looking in the right place, just as one found characters in a book, simply by looking them up.

CHAPTER 14

Blanchaille looked at Soho with big eyes. Van Vuuren looked hardly at all, turning his gaze inward, as if he knew what was to come.

So they went, the priest and the policeman, the egg and spoon, through the little streets, this once great mixing place of European peoples, now all gone, leaving behind them only their tourists and their restaurants and a profusion of continental erotica. He looked at it with professional eyes, Blanchaille told himself, trying perhaps to explain his interest, as a centre dedicated to sin. It looked to him, Van Vuuren replied, like a dump – over-rated, over-priced, dull, tawdry and sad. Blanchaille stared at the hawkers, the barrow-boys, the suitcase salesmen. A fat man with one sleeve rolled up offering gold watches strapped to his arm like chain mail flashing in the sun, was trumpeting the bargains of a lifetime and waving the highly coloured guarantees like flags. Arab men with pot bellies and tight, flared tailored trousers walked around with their hands in their pockets, staring boldly at single women; a girl winked at him from a balcony; in the dull entrances of crumbling buildings he saw the name-plates of cheap cardboard inscribed in shaky ballpoint – MYRA, MODEL, WALK RIGHT UP. He peered through the bead curtains across the doorways of the 'adult film parlours' which gave them an oddly oriental look. A striptease club displayed pale cracked photographs, faded by infrequent suns, showing a female chorus line presenting their buttocks to a delirious audience. Blanchaille was ashamed to find himself hesitating fractionally, drawn as it were, downwards.

THE BARE PIT – SIX LOVELY LADIES IN FANTASTIC COMBINATIONS/DAY-NITE NUDES NON-STOP!!! Some had pound notes tacked to their pubic mounds. One carried a whip. Another was wearing nothing but an iron cross. Two oiled female wrestlers grappled in a miniature ring. A largish and very pale redhead was immersed, for some mysterious reason, in what looked like a giant goldfish bowl. But it was an empty black leather chair in the centre of the stage which looked truly obscene.

A burly and very black man blocked their path and invited them to step below and see for themselves the loveliest things in the universe, at the same time introducing himself to them as Minto, their guide to the pleasures of The Bare Pit. Van Vuuren attempted to brush him off but Minto was persistent and took his arm in what was clearly a very persuasive grip and, as Blanchaille realised when he saw pain succeed annoyance on the square handsome features, one that succeeded in its intentions.

'Run, Blanchie, run!' said Van Vuuren.

But there was another man, taller, very wiry, who declared himself to be Dudley from Malta, with a little black moustache and no less fierce a grip.

Of course Van Vuuren would have flattened them both, one, two, bang, bang, in his former life. Perhaps the clerical garb restrained him because he put up no struggle as they were marched downstairs.

It was dimly lit below stairs, a bar at one end and a stage at the other, the twenty or so rows of seats between furnished in red plush, redolent of ancient excitements of old men: of tobacco, sweat, aged underpants, hair oil, disappointed hope, stale beer, old socks, bitter anger, and various unidentifiable, recent stains. In the front row sat several large gentlemen.

Blanchaille remembered what he had read of such places, of the old men who came down here to watch women strip and masturbate beneath their plastic raincoats. One had read of such accounts since childhood, they were a part of the contemporary portrait of Britain, where all the people not on strike were on the dole, or on pension; where child murder was widely practised; few people bathed; income tax was 19/6d in the pound and nobody ate meat any longer. The Regime taught this in its schools. His French mother confirmed at least the last: 'The roast beefs,' as she used to call the English contemptuously, 'have no roast beef any longer.' Blanchaille's mother had never been to England, but then that hardly mattered. England was a repository, a store of rumours of decline from which the world could draw at will for stories to frighten children. It had no other use but to remind one, horribly, of what your country might become if the Total Onslaught succeeded.

Minto and Dudley from Malta introduced Blanchaille to the proprietor, a small and stout individual with black hair gleaming lushly in the concealed lighting around the bar. He was called Momzie. Without hesitation he poured Blanchaille a Scotch and soda and patted the bar stool beside him. 'May as well make yourself comfortable while those gentlemen over there have their little conversation with your friend.'

Minto and Dudley marched Van Vuuren up on to the stage. The props the girls used in their show were still there, the black leather chair, the wicked whip of grey rhino hide, the giant goldfish bowl of rather milky water, the wrestling ring. Van Vuuren was roped to the black leather chair.

'I think these people intend to injure my friend,' said Blanchaille.

'I hire out this place when we're not busy,' Momzie said. 'People want somewhere where they can have a quiet chat. It's money up front and I don't care who uses it as long as they watch their hours. I've got a show to run here and sometimes they're inclined to overshoot.'

The men in the front row weren't wearing plastic raincoats. They were young. They wore a variety of costume, sports jackets, tweeds and safari suits. One of them was a black man wearing a pale blue suit. They looked at Van Vuuren with special interest. From his seat on the stage he gazed defiantly back, but the footlights must have made it difficult to identify them at first.

'I see it now,' he said, 'a deputation from my old Department; Brandt from Signals, Kritzinger from Interrogation, Breda from Surveillance, Kramer from Accounts – well, hell's bells Jack! I never dreamt you were operational, or did you get promotion, or did they send you over to see the strippers for a Christmas treat, or something?'

'You fucked out on us, Trev,' said the man called Kramer from Accounts, 'and now you're tootling around England tricked out as a poncey priest. It's not right, Trev.'

Now Van Vuuren noticed the black man in the pale blue suit. Even from where he sat at the bar between Minto and Dudley from Malta, his drink untouched, Blanchaille saw the horror on his face.

'Oscar! What in Christ's name are you doing here?'

The man in the blue suit stood up. 'Things are complex,' he said. 'I could ask you the same question.'

'But you guys sent for me. I've come home, Oscar. Tell them! Why didn't you meet me at the airport?'

'We didn't expect you, Trevor.'

'But damn it to hell, Oscar, I *work* for you.'

'No, you work for us,' said the shaven-headed man called Kritzinger from Interrogation.

Van Vuuren was straining at the ropes now. 'What the hell is going on? Oscar what is someone from the ALF doing in this hole with these vultures from my Department? These guys shoot people like you, Oscar. Where is Kaiser? Does he know you're here?'

Oscar nodded. 'He sent me. He said to tell you hello –'

'And goodbye,' said Brandt from Signals.

The front row laughed heartily.

'I want to see Kaiser,' Van Vuuren demanded.

Oscar shook his head sorrowfully. 'Kaiser isn't in any condition to see you. He's suffered a major set-back, has Kaiser. He won't be dealing any more. From now on I'll be dealing.'

'And that means sitting down with these people?'

'Like I said, Trevor, things are complex. I don't expect you to understand because you don't see the whole story. But on certain issues the Azanian Liberation Front and the Regime have common interests that override the struggle.'

'Such as?'

'The disappearance of Bubé, the strange disappearance of Gus Kuiker and Trudy Yssel, the murder of Ferreira.'

'– the defection of security policemen,' said Kramer from Accounts. 'We're going to piss on you, Trev, I promise you.'

'The growing habit of certain people to whizz around the world like they owned the place. This threatens to destroy a delicate network of discussions, talks, negotiations, painfully achieved agreements between those who have the health of our country close to their hearts,' said Brandt from Signals.

'You fucked out on us, Trev,' repeated Kramer from Accounts.

The big men in the row of seats laughed loudly.

'The British have a great sense of humour,' said Momzie.

'Those people aren't British,' Blanchaille said. 'They're from my country, they're South Africans.'

Momzie ignored him. 'They like especially men dressed as women making jokes about foreigners. Speaking as a whole.'

'It is true,' said Dudley from Malta, 'speaking as a whole, and speaking of the English now, the English love to laugh at all sorts. It is one of their greatest gifts. They laugh even at themselves.'

'Yes,' agreed Minto, 'but what they don't like is other people laughing at them.'

'Even more hilarious do the English find than drag artists,' said Dudley from Malta, incoherent with excitement, 'speaking very much as a whole, are drag artists who make jokes about foreigners, Japs, frogs and whatnot.'

'There is something the English find even funnier than that,' said Minto defiantly.

'No,' said Momzie with heavy menace. 'There is nothing they find funnier than that.'

155

'Yes, yes,' Minto persisted. 'Yes there is and I know what it is!'

'What is it?' Momzie demanded. 'And this better be good.'

Minto beamed. 'They like even more than men dressed as women making jokes about foreigners, men dressed as women making jokes –'

'For God's sake get on with it!' Dudley groaned.

'Making jokes about foreigners . . . in *lavatories*!' crowed Minto triumphantly.

They seemed to recognise the justice of this, but Momzie was not giving up yet. 'Oh yes, how do you know?'

'Saw it on TV.'

That clinched it. They all nodded. Clearly there was no further argument.

'We watch a lot of television,' said Momzie. 'Ours is the best television service in the world.'

'Have you watched any of our television?' Minto asked.

But Blanchaille was watching Van Vuuren. 'Please,' he said, 'those guys are going to hurt my friend.'

'Balls,' said Momzie. 'We're here, aren't we. We're here to see fair play.'

Van Vuuren had stopped struggling against the ropes. 'I can't believe I'm hearing this.'

'You aren't,' the man called Oscar said bluntly. 'This conversation never took place.'

Kramer came over the Momzie. 'Do you have somewhere more private where we can continue our discussion. A cellar maybe?'

'This is a cellar,' said Momzie.

'There's the liquor store,' said Dudley from Malta.

'There's not much room in there,' said Minto.

'Going to cost you extra,' said Momzie.

The front row stood now, picked up the black leather chair and, in a procession which had a triumphant air about it, carried the prisoner from the stage. Blanchaille tried to intervene but Momzie produced an ugly little pistol from beneath the bar and hit him across the mouth. After that Blanchaille made no attempt to move but sat there watching the blood from his mouth dripping into his untouched whisky.

'This place of mine is in heavy demand, being an easy walk from your Embassy,' said Momzie proudly. He went on to tell the story of how he had recruited Minto and Dudley.

'I met these guys when we were on a tour through the regions, or at least they were. They were walking a troop. What's walking a troop? I hear you ask. It's like taking a show on the road. You march a bunch of slags around the place from hotel to hotel and you nail a customer or two. He's out there for a few days in the sun and isn't with his wife and wishes he was, or is and wishes he wasn't. It's hard work and pretty thankless. You get girls who fuck around just for the hell of it. And some of them won't keep accounts and they really begin to believe they are on holiday. They shoot off here and there and you spend half the day running after them like a fucking collie dog chasing sheep. I suppose you can't blame them, the holiday atmosphere gets to the girls. I can tell you there's nothing worse than a whore on holiday. These guys got so tired chasing after their pigeons they tried to lay it on me. Lay it on Momzie, shit that's a joke! I read them like a book. I told them – look get out of the provinces, I mean regions, as we got to call them now, and come up to town. I need a bit of knuckle on the door, I said, and you want a bit of peace and quiet after years of pushing fanny around the place. So here we are, as happy as sandboys in The Bare Pit.'

'This is the land of opportunity,' said Dudley from Malta.

'I'm proud to be British,' said Minto.

One would like to draw a veil over subsequent proceedings. Alas, in dreams veils cannot be drawn.

And so I saw them carry the prisoner into the cellar, in the chair, like some mutant pope, and there they beat him, stamped on him, stabbed him. Though whether he died when they stabbed him or was dead when the knives went in, I cannot say. Also they pissed on him, as Kramer had sworn they would do, showing that he had not been speaking metaphorically. They actually, together or singly, urinated on him as he lay in his blood among the broken whisky bottles the fumes of which were suffocating in the small room and the air soon became fetid – which I agree is not really surprising when you remember that there were several strong men taking violent exercise in a small space; a crude, enthusiastic, messy, bludgeoning assault of boots, fists, bottles. It resembled nothing so much as the violence which passes for pleasure in the lower divisions of the rugby league. Even in this instance they reverted to type. They whooped, stamped, yelled. It was foul play. It was the foulest play imaginable. But it was damn good sport! Those who speak of rugby as a game believe they are making a joke. I can tell them they've seen neither the game or the joke – for neither is involved. What we are talking about are matters of life and death, not of who should live, or who should die, but who should decide! We are talking of sacred matters.

All this I saw through Blanchaille's eyes. He watched the men come out of the liquor store, smelt the spirits on them and imagined in his naïvety that they had been drinking and this accounted for their strained, pale faces, their laboured breathing, the slightly giddy looks, and the stains on Oscar's blue suit. He watched as the money was paid 'for the hire of the hall', as Momzie called it. A handful of small gold coins on the bar counter.

'Who else but these guys pays in Krugerrands?' he asked proudly, scooping up the hoard. 'But then again, who better? Ain't they got the market cornered?'

It was only when Dudley from Malta complained about the heat that they realised something had happened.

Minto went over and tried the handle.

The explosion blew off the door of the liquor store and carried away Minto, still attached to the handle. Momzie and Dudley from Malta screamed as they tried to beat back the flames with their jackets. The bottles of booze shattering like brilliant bombs. The body on the floor glowed like a lamp, and exploded, lighting up its own disfigurements, the smashed face, the knife wounds. A hot gust of alcohol, sweat and, yes, urine, hit them. And Blanchaille, finding himself unattended, took the dead man's earlier advice and ran.

CHAPTER 15

And so it was that I saw Blanchaille retrace his steps and I saw how despite his terrifying experience, once back in Magdalena's flat he cooked eggs. In the midst of tragedy, of bereavement, scorched by the fiery vision of Van Vuuren's pricked and broken body, he had not expected to feel suddenly, ravenously, hungry. But there it was. The fleshly appetites were unrelenting, the Margaret Brethren had warned their boys, which if not constantly beaten into submission would command the frail human creature and bend him to their will.

Now we know that the stories of how Van Vuuren met his end were eventually to differ widely. The Regime acted quickly to claim him for their own. He became the faithful detective murdered by agents for the Azanian Liberation Front. The Front further complicated matters by admitting responsibility for the 'execution', declaring that the police-spy's fate was a warning to any other agents of the Regime who attempted to subvert the forces of liberation. The Regime in turn announced that brilliant undercover work by Captain Van Vuuren had revealed a deep split within the Azanian terror group resulting in the demotion of its president, Kaiser Zulu. The Front in a statement called this a typical lie of fascist adventurers and claimed that President Zulu was enjoying a well-deserved retirement in a home for high state officials 'in the country of a friendly ally', somewhere on the Caspian Sea. The Regime then posthumously awarded to Van Vuuren its premier decoration, the Cross of the Golden Eland with Star, an honour previously accorded only to visiting Heads of State, that is to say, to General Stroessner of Paraguay, the only Head of State to pass that way in living memory. The national poet composed an ode in honour of the dead policeman. This was the former radical poet, Pik Groenewald, who after years of self-imposed exile in Mexico City plotting the destruction of the Regime had a vision one night of a lion attacked by army ants and returned home immediately and joined the tank-corps where besides valiant service in the operational areas he composed a series of laments upon his previous treachery which he dedicated, with apologies, to President Adolph Bubé. Groenewald's 'Ode to an Assassinated Security Branch Officer' played cleverly on the flammable connotations of Van Vuuren's name, in the celebrated line *Flame to the fire they fed him/Blade to the vein they bled him* . . . And it was quoted in Parliament to spontaneous applause.

Blanchaille of course, as I saw, knew the true story, knew that by some peculiar chain of logic both the Regime and the Front derived profit from the death of Van Vuuren. That this knowledge did not drive him to anger or despair but left him ravenous is testimony to the toughness of human nature or to the growing self-awareness of the fat ex-priest from the camps that nothing was what it seemed.

What a place this England was! Blanchaille stared at the English eggs, they were not like African eggs, they were pallid, waterish little things by comparison with the garish orange, cholesterol-packed bombs from the hot South. But he cooked three or four, even so, and a mound of bacon and ate without stopping, shovelling the food into his mouth and plugging it there with chunks of thin white bread, running a very fine line between sustenance and suffocation. In the cupboard beneath the sink he found half a bottle of Chianti and finished it off directly. It was as if there were spaces inside him he must fill, not simply hungry spaces but vulnerable sections which he must protect.

Afterwards he lay in the great white tub, soaking there beneath the benign gaze of the Duke of Wellington upon the wall, beneath Magdalena's stockings, hanging above him from a cunning arrangement of lines, and looking, through the steam, like skinny vultures perched upon telephone wires. Magdalena's depilatories, her soaps, her shampoos, some sort of nobbled glove affair, presumably meant for rubbing dry skin from the body, her back brush and sponge and bubble bath, all waited with the air of things that know their owner will not be returning. He lay in the bath and let the grime of the past hours float from him and begin to form a brown ring around the bath. Strangely comforting, this evidence of life, human dirt.

As he sat on the side of the bath drying his hair the doorbell rang.

Beside the door hung a photograph. It showed Magdalena in Moscow. She wore a white fur hat and a white fur coat. Beside her were the onion towers of the Kremlin. She was smiling radiantly. The photograph was a trophy. It showed how far and how successfully Magdalena had gone in the service of her cause. The picture was unassailable proof of her credentials as a radical, as a leading member of the Front, as one of the prime enemies of the Regime in exile. It insisted upon this achievement. And yet there were certain matters unexplained, certain questions he wanted to ask Magdalena which could not be answered by that photograph. 'I have been to Moscow', the photograph trumpeted. 'Few of you have been further than Durban!' True. But not enough.

It took him a few moments to recognise the man at the door. The hair was still as unruly as ever, growing now even more thickly above the ears. The eyebrows were more bushy than he remembered but the lips were the same. Oh yes, they were the same rather bulbous lips, wet from continuous nervous licking, the nose broad, the eyes soft waterish brown, and there it was, the characteristic pout with the lips pushed outwards into a little 'o', surrounded by soft white down. A fish pout. Kipsel!

'Hello Blanchie, long time no see.'

That was that. No apology, no cringing and fumbling explanation, no sign of regret or mortification. Merely – 'Hello Blanchie, long time no see.' Blanchaille stood back from the door and let Kipsel enter. And there he was in the room, that same Kipsel who had grievously betrayed everyone he knew, had fled the country in utter despair, the man who had had the gall to go on existing after the treachery, which even those who benefited from it had condemned. Why had he not done the only decent thing and slashed his wrists or hanged himself from a stout beam? Instead Kipsel had gone out and got a job, in a northern university, and taught sociology. Of all things, *sociology*, that quasi-religious subject with its faintly moralistic ring. Perhaps more than anything the choice of the subject he taught had scandalised friend and enemy alike.

'Why have you come?'

'Because there was a question I wanted to ask Magdalena. I've turned it over in my mind for so many years now but I can't come up with an answer. There is something I don't understand. I'm not sure she's got the answer. Or if she'd tell me if she knew. Or if I want to hear it. But I know I want to ask the question.'

'You can ask me if you like.'

'That's kind. But in the first place I didn't expect to see you. And secondly, you won't do.'

'I'm all you've got. Magdalena isn't here. I don't know where she is. She met me at the airport yesterday morning. She brought me here and then she disappeared.'

'What are you doing here?'

'Just passing through. My ticket gave me an unrequested stop-over in London and I fly out tonight. Is that your question?'

Kipsel shook his head. His eyes were large and liquid. 'No, that was plain curiosity. The real question goes back much further. To the days I spent in jail, and before that to my interrogation in Balthazar Buildings, after the business of the pylons. The official story is that I gave the police information about everybody connected with the explosions. I told them everything. In exchange I got a deal, I got immunity from prosecution. Only I didn't! Do you hear, Blanchie? And for one bloody good reason. I didn't have to tell them. They knew! They knew already! About me, Mickey, Magdalena, Dladla – everyone! For God's sake, they even knew what brand of petrol we used, they had copies of the maps, recordings of our phone conversations . . . You name it, they had them. So I changed tack. I accepted everything – except where it concerned Magdalena. I confirmed everything they had was right – and dammit, it was! – except for the girl. She had known nothing of our plan, of the bombs, of the Azanian Liberation Front. She had been duped. She came along for the ride. She was only there because she loved me. That's what I told them. I tried to save Magdalena. I am *not* Kipsel the traitor. But if not me, then who?'

Blanchaille looked at the pale, trembling creature before him. The round, downy cheeks quivered. Kipsel's extraordinarily thick eyelashes rose and fell rapidly and his round mouth shone as his tongue licked the blubber lips. His hands flapped. He looked more like a fish than ever. A fish drowning in air.

'I understand your question. If you didn't tell the police, who did?'

Then the two friends flung their arms around each others' necks and embraced. Lost in the world, how they rejoiced in each other's company. Blanchaille told Kipsel of his arrival in London, of his meeting with Magdalena, of the visit to the Embassy, of the encounter with Father Lynch in a Soho street, of his warning and of Van Vuuren's brave death in a Soho cellar. At this news Kipsel broke down and wept unashamedly. I heard, too, how Blanchaille told his friend of the two watchers outside the fishmonger's and their strange name: Apple Two.

'I also have a question,' said Blanchaille. 'Who is Apple One?'

And Kipsel replied. 'Perhaps when we answer mine, we will answer yours.'

CHAPTER 16

Blanchaille knew the man at the airport bar as a fellow countryman from his accent. But he could also identify him from a picture he had just seen which showed him strolling along a Paris street. It had been printed in the English newspaper he bought on arriving at the airport. He was relieved to see that he drank brandy.

Is not the choice of strong drink one of the easiest, not to say one of the most pleasant ways of rising painlessly on the social scale, of impressing friends and confounding enemies? Or for that matter, of refuting the notion, lamentably widespread even in this day and age, that South Africans are only interested in beer and shooting kaffirs, and in either order. There is even a calumny, sadly current still, that a famous South African lager I must not name (suffice it to say that the beer in question is a product of a brewery owned by the Himmelfarber empire) is supposed to have run an advertising campaign with the slogan SHOOTING KAFFIRS IS THIRSTY WORK. Now the truth is not (as some Government apologists maintain) that the campaign in question was run many years ago and is now thoroughly discredited. Nor that Curtis Christian Himmelfarber himself led the campaign to deface the posters, altering the wording to something less likely to incite racial hostility and with his own hand struck down the forgotten manager who first coined the infamous slogan, although it is a satisfying tale. Misunderstandings abound. There is even argument about the precise wording of the slogan. There are some who maintain that what it really said was : Is SHOOTING THIRSTY KAFFIRS' WORK? Whilst others say it read: THIRSTY KAFFIRS IS SHOOTING WORK. Whereas in fact the truth is that the original slogan read simply: SHOOTING IS THIRSTY WORK, but unseen enemy hands across the land at a pre-arranged signal added the offending words, either with the intention of discrediting our country in the eyes of the world, or of embarrassing C.C. Himmelfarber who with his giant enterprise, Consolidated Holdings, had always been a stalwart champion of the progressive forces for political change in the country, or both. None the less the malicious legend lingers on and so when you come across a South African drinking not beer but brandy in a bar at Heathrow airport, as Blanchaille and Kipsel did as they waited to be called for their flight to Geneva, even if one does not particularly wish to meet another fellow South African at the time, a feeling of patriotic pride and relief suffuses the frame.

The so-called 'kaffir beer' scandal was a typical example of the concerted campaign waged by overseas dissidents, hostile forces and illegal organisations such as the Azanian Liberation Front, against the honest efforts of the Regime to offer justice to all its population groups. Such black propaganda was in turn just another adjunct of the universal campaign to destroy the white man in Southern Africa, which came to be known as the Total Onslaught.

It was to counter this campaign that the new minister of Ethnic Autonomy and Parallel Equilibriums, Augustus Kuiker, vowed to devote himself when he was appointed Deputy Leader of the Party by the President, Adolph Bubé. It had been Kuiker who replaced Hans Job when that decent man was driven from office by a scurrilous whispering campaign soon after he had succeeded the flamboyant but ailing merino millionaire, J.J. Vokker, when sudden ill health forced him to step down. This change had been the subject of a very cruel joke. 'Who will replace a Vokker?' went the question. 'Only a Hansjob!' came the reply and the whole country doubled up with ribald laughter. Even those who should have known better held their sides. It was then that the formidable Kuiker was appointed and the laughing had to stop. 'Our Gus', people called him, and shivered. The face of granite, the lips of a cement-mixer. It was Kuiker who had appointed Trudy Yssel to the newly formed Department of Communications with the brief to put our country's case abroad with all the punch she could muster. It was regarded as a brave move.

It was a very curious combination; Kuiker the granite man at home, but curiously, even distinctively, colourful abroad, with his taste for bright Hawaiian shirts aglow with orange sunsets and rampant palms, and the new Secretary to the Department of Communications, Trudy Yssel, young, pretty, tough as hell, shrewd and decidedly modern. There was always something stubbornly old-fashioned about Gus Kuiker. He was large, lumpish even. Trudy was svelte and auburn. He looked like a prize fighter, with a big bone-plated forehead, cauliflower ears, a doughy nose, fleshy and rather sensuous lips. But they were a formidable team, it was widely agreed, and of their determination to change the face of internal and foreign propaganda there could be no doubt. As far as Gus Kuiker was concerned, Trudy Yssel could simply do no wrong. What's more she was funded to the hilt. She seemed unstoppable.

As Blanchaille and Kipsel arrived at Heathrow Airport the newspapers they bought told a very strange story. DEPCOM MYSTERY DEEPENS. WHERE IS TRUDY?

Kipsel studied the paper. The Kuiker/Yssel affair was now making international news. The English papers printed an account of an interview given by a spokesman in Kuiker's Department.

Reporter: Can you give us any idea about the location of Trudy Yssel?

Spokesman: It is not in the public interest to disclose any further information.

Reporter: Would you comment on rumours that she has left the country?

Spokesman: The rumour is without foundation.

A few days later, after Trudy Yssel had been sighted in Philadelphia, another news conference was given.

Reporter: Will you confirm that Miss Yssel is now in Philadelphia?

Spokesman: I cannot confirm or deny that report.

Reporter: Do you admit that she is abroad?

Spokesman: I have not said that she is abroad.

Reporter: But she's in Philadelphia. Therefore she must be abroad.

Spokesman: You should learn a little more about your own country before leaping to conclusions. There are other Philadelphias nearer home.

Reporter: Whichever Philadelphia she may be in, what is she doing there?

Spokesman: I will not be cross-examined like this.

Well, of course, the invitation was impossible to resist and a search was immediately launched and indeed another Philadelphia was found, closer to hand, in the Cape province, a small town consisting of no more than the usual bank and church and a few hundred puzzled inhabitants who lined and cheered when the reporters from the nation's press arrived in their Japanese estate cars and their big Mercedes to interview everyone from the mayor to the town's oldest inhabitant, Granny Ryneveldt, aged 103, who declared that she hadn't seen such excitement since Dominee Vasbythoven ran off with his gardener and joined the gay community in the Maluti mountains. However, there was no trace of

Trudy. Everybody had heard of her, of course. But nobody had seen her.

It didn't matter. The Regime made capital out of the reporters' double discomfiture. Journalists, they said, should get to know their own country better and not always look overseas for glamorous stories. Various sanctions were hinted at if the newspapers did not take up this suggestion. Then ministers of the Dutch Reformed Church expressed their outrage that the affair of the renegade minister, Vasbythoven, had been dragged up once more. For their part, several liberal English clerics preached sermons against the hounding of the unfortunate minister, reminding their congregations that homosexual practice between consenting adults was widely regarded as acceptable in the outside world and they lauded Dominee Vasbythoven who had shown his bravery not only by taking as a lover one of his own sex but someone of another race which showed him to be not only sexually liberated but racially balanced and they pointed out that this was no small feat for a man whose great-great uncle had been Judge-President of the Orange Free State, when it had still been a Boer Republic. Here again the Regime waded in with warnings to the opposition press against attempts to slander the memory of the Boer Republics when, led by Uncle Paul Kruger, the Boer Nation with God's help had fought for its freedom against the wicked imperialist colonialist oppression of the British. Anti-Government papers were warned for the last time to put their house in order.

The English papers overseas, beyond the reach of the Regime, agreed that Minister Kuiker and his protégée Trudy Yssel had disappeared. They also agreed that large sums of Government money appeared to have gone missing with them. They printed a photograph which showed the missing pair in a Paris street. She carried several shopping bags and smiled vivaciously. He covered his face with one hand, but was instantly recognisable. Behind them walked two men in dark suits. One of these men now sat drinking at the bar.

The only other drinkers were a small group of oriental businessmen who drank from globular tankards foaming pink cocktails garnished with sprigs of mint and cherries, leaning forward above the liquid and tasting it with tongues and fingertips, giving excited little barks of encouragement. A small girl carrying an enormous soft green cat with wild eyes and a forest of woolly whiskers wandered around the footrail with tear-stained face obviously searching for her parents. All around was the teeming flux of anonymous travellers departing for a hundred destinations.

The drinker who aroused this rhapsody of patriotic memories in Blanchaille was painfully thin, his sports jacket hung on him, a loud tweed of blues and greens with an ugly stiffening of the bristles which had the effect of making the colours of the cloth shimmer, a sickly rainbow effect. His complexion too was strange, a light grey translucency tinged with pink. He'd been drinking for some time, Blanchaille judged, and despite the flush that warmed the bony face, it was the air of desiccation that struck him, as if a kind of internal emaciation had taken place, an interior drought, a profound dryness which no amount of watering could end. He had crisp, slightly oiled sandy hair through which the scalp gleamed bleakly. Altogether he had the look of St John of Capistrano, formidable Inquisitor-General of Vienna, a portrait of whom had hung in Blanchaille's class-room many years before.

His message to Kipsel was succinct: 'Cop.'

Kipsel did not thank him. 'I warn you Blanchie, when shown a South African security man competing urges threaten me.'

'Which?'

'Do I hit out, or throw up?'

At the bar the oriental businessmen had replenished their tankards and were lapping away happily at the pink stuff. The little girl had been given a bowl of crisps by the barman and sat eating steadily, gazing out into the seething concourse with tearful eyes. Blanchaille introduced his friend and himself to the solitary drinker.

'Jesus!' said the drinker, 'Not Kipsel the traitor?'

'No,' Kipsel said firmly. 'Not Kipsel the traitor.'

'Ernest Nokkles,' said the drinker, 'passing on to Geneva.'

'So are we.'

'Let me get you a drink,' said Blanchaille.

'Brandy,' said Nokkles. 'A large one if you will. The bloody English tot is about as much as a nun pees with her knees crossed. And Coke with it. I always have it with Coke. The bastards here drink it neat, y'know.'

'How are things at home?' Kipsel asked.

'Do you mean militarily or economically?'

'I didn't know there was a difference.'

'They're linked, but they're different. Militarily we're all right. Hell, there's nobody who's going to touch us. Frankly I think we're in more danger from the drought. But if you consider the Total Onslaught, then there's no doubt about its having an effect. Slow but cumulative. We might crack one day. But despite that, the Big

167

Seven reckon we're doing O.K., financially.'

The Big Seven were those groups which between them controlled almost every area of life and dominated the Stock Exchange. The gold mining companies of course and various major industries – armaments, insurance, drink and tobacco together with the Government control boards that regulated everything from transport to citrus. Seven was a mystical number. The Big Seven represented the aggregate of national interests.

The profile which emerged of your average South African was a dedicated smoker who took to booze in a big way, kept himself armed to the teeth but was sensible enough to insure against the risk that either cigarettes or drink or terrorists might blow him away, and paid for this lifestyle with gold bullion. For the rest he did as the Regime told him, travelled as the Government directed him and died when and where the State demanded it. This handful of huge conglomerates owned everything and they also owned slices of each other and were all held, in turn, in the capacious lap of the Regime which allowed and even encouraged these cliques, cartels, monopolies to operate and indeed took a very close interest in them to the extent of inviting their directors to sit on various Government boards, boards of arms companies and the rural development agencies. Private business responded by asking Government ministers to take up seats on the boards of the gold mining companies, army officers were invited to join insurance companies, tobacco groups and breweries. Complicated interlocking deals were set up between the State and the great conglomerates, a famous instance of which was the Life Saving Bond which allowed families of soldiers to purchase a special insurance policy on the life of their loved one for a small monthly premium. 'In the event of deprivation', as the preamble to the policy put it, the next of kin received a 'Life Saving Bond' certificate which showed the value of all their contributions to date. The premiums which had accrued were then 'sent forward', which meant the sum was invested in 'armaments and/or other industries vital to the war effort', thereby giving all soldiers a second chance to serve by helping to ensure that the country's weaponry was the best possible. The casualties joined what the field padres called the army invisible, or simply the Big Battalion, known familiarly as the BB. 'Oh, he's serving with the BB' became a common way of skirting around a tragedy and won for those who spoke the words a new respect. The Regime encouraged positive thinking and inspectors ensured that the attractive blue and white Bond Certificates were prominently displayed in the home. Every month a draw took place and the family with the lucky bond number won for themselves a tour of the forward operational areas, plus a visit to the site of some celebrated victory (combat conditions permitting) and invariably returned strengthened and resolute. The newspapers and television followed these visits with great interest and press stories appeared and television reports showing pictures of Dick and Eugenia and their children, Marta and Kobus, proudly wearing combat helmets they'd been given, trundling through the veld in an armoured troop carrier. 'My Day in the Operational Areas' was an increasingly popular title in school examination papers.

'The English,' said Nokkles, 'are bloody awful snobs. And racialists. They also have their kaffirs, you know. It's just that you can't tell them apart. Being English they all look alike. But they have them. Oh yes, they have them.'

He swallowed his brandy with relish, clicking his tongue. But no amount of drinking would irrigate that consuming desert within Ernie Nokkles.

A man in a dark green anorak and a big woman in a pixie cap, its straps pulled down hard over her ears and knotted cruelly beneath her chin, both of them buttoned everywhere, plumply encased, walked up to the little girl and removed her from the counter. 'We've been calling you on the loudspeaker,' the woman said between clenched teeth. And then bending over the little girl she administered several stinging slaps, saying at the same time and in rhythm to her blows: '*Why didn't you listen?*'

'And child beaters, too,' Nokkles said. 'What do you think?'

'We think that you must be Trudy's detective,' Blanchaille said.

'That,' said Nokkles with a contemptuous downward twitch of the lips and a sideways flick of the head, so sudden Blanchaille thought for the moment he might have spat on the floor, 'is a newspaper lie. I am not a policeman. In fact my function is quite vague. I fall within the remit of a number of officials – there's Pieter Weerhaan, Dominee Lippetaal, as well as Mr Glip, and then of course there is Ernest Tweegat and Dr Enigiets. Actually I work for all these people, and of course for Miss Yssel. This for me was a fairly recent move. By training I'm a population movement man. I came from the PRP, the Population Resettlement Programme. I only got this Yssel job because someone went sick and I was shoved in. Believe it or not, I began working as a rookie years ago in Old

Ma Dubbeltong's Department, as it then was, of Entry and Egress; that was the original outfit, that was the egg which this new-fangled Department for Population Settlements came from. The PRP is really just old wine in new bottles. Anyway when I was there it was a damn sight tougher than anything today. God! My boss was old Harry Waterman, my hell what a tartar! Screaming Harry we called him. Well, say what you like, credit where credit's due, he was largely instrumental, along with Ma, in formulating policy for what we now call population settlement. Screaming Harry was a blunt official, no fanciness about him. Nothing elegant. A straight guy, a removalist of the old school. Look, he'd say, you've got all these blackies wandering around the country or slipping into the towns or setting up camps wherever they feel like it and squatting here and there, and they've got to be moved. Right? They've got to be put down in some place of their own and made to stay there. Now you never beg or threaten when you're running a removal. It doesn't matter if you're endorsing out – because that's what we called it then, endorsing out – some old bastard who doesn't have a pass, or an entire fucking tribe. First, you notify deadline for removal, then you get your paper-work right, you double check that the trucks are ordered up – and then you move them. As I say, old Harry Waterman was a plain removalist. None of these fancy titles for him, like Resettlement Officer or Relocation Adviser, as they like to call themselves now, these clever dicks from Varsity. No, everything was straight talking for Harry. As the trucks come out of the camp which you're removing, Harry said, you put the bulldozers in and flatten the place. End of story. It's quick, clean, efficient. You know something?' Nokkles gazed earnestly at Blanchaille and Kipsel. 'I don't know if it's not a lot kinder than the boards of enquiry and appeal and so on which dominate the resettlement field today. After all we all know in the end, after all the talking's done, they're going to have to get out. So why lead them on? The only talent you need to be a removalist, old Harry was fond of saying, is eyes in the back of your head. Front eyes watch the trucks moving out, those in the back watch the bulldozers moving in. A great guy, old Harry. Dead now. But he never understood the new scheme of things. I believe you have to move with the times. So when the call came, I was ready. Fate spoke. "Ernie Nokkles," it said, "will you or will you not accept secondment to this new Department of Communications run by this hot lady said to be going places under the aegis of Minister Gus Kuiker?" And like a shot I answered back, "Damn sure!" But I am not, and never was, Trudy's detective.'

170

'What were you then?' asked Kipsel.

'Her aide, confidante and loyal member of her Department,' said Nokkles proudly. 'What I wanted was to help her and the Minister in their great task.'

'Great task,' Kipsel repeated scathingly. 'Trudy Yssel tried to carry the propaganda war to the enemy abroad, she wanted to coax, buy, bend overseas opinion about the true nature of the Regime. It was her task to show them as being not simply a gang of wooden headed, rock-brained farmers terrified that their grandfathers might have slept with their cooks – no – they were to become human ethnologists determined to allow all ethnic groups to blossom according to their cultural traditions within the natural parameters recognised by God, biology and history.'

'I don't know what you mean,' said Nokkles. 'But if you're saying she wanted to save us, I say *yes*. She and the Minister wanted to lead us out of the past, back into the world, into the future. And that's what I wanted too.'

'And what do you want now?' Blanchaille asked gently.

Nokkles looked around quickly. He dropped his voice. 'I wish I was back in old Ma Dubbeltong's department again. But that can't be. Look, you guys are going to Switzerland and I am going to Switzerland. We're countrymen abroad. So why don't we travel together? I mean we don't have to agree politically, just to keep company a bit – not so?'

'Sure, we'll go along with you, but you might not like where we're going,' said Blanchaille.

'We're heading for Uncle Paul's place,' said Kipsel.

The change in Nokkles was dramatic. He stood up and drained his glass. He picked up his bag. 'God help you then. That old dream's not for me.'

They watched him walk away, blindly shouldering his way through the crowds. They're ruined, these people, Blanchaille thought. They don't know who they are or where they're going. Once nothing would stop them doing their duty as they saw it and that was to defend their people and their way of life. And they were hated for it. Good, they accepted that hate. But then the new ideas took over, they got wise, got modern, took on the world. Once upon a time nothing would make them give up the principle that the tribe would survive because God wished it so – now there's nothing they won't do just to hang on a little longer. Uncle Paul's other place is a bad dream, it takes them back to the *velskoen* years, the days of biltong and boere biscuits, of muzzle loaders, Bibles, of creeping backward slowly like an armour-plated ox, out of range of the future. Some no doubt wished to go back, as Nokkles did, wanted to go back to Old Ma Dubbeltong's department, back to the old dream of a country fit for farmers, where a man was free to ride his acres, shoot his game, father his children, lash his slaves, free from drought, English, Jews, missionaries, rinderpest, blacks, coolies and tax-collectors. But back there waited the hateful legend, the impossible story, the triumphant British, the defeated people, the exiled president, the store of gold, the secret heaven somewhere in Switzerland, the last refuge of a broken tribe.

'What do you think?' Kipsel asked.

'I think he's Trudy's detective and he's lost Trudy. All he's left with is what she taught him. He's dead. He's spinning out of control. He's like a space probe gone loco. Nothing can save him unless he finds another mother-ship to lock onto, or another planet to land on. He's spinning into space. And space is cold and big and blacker than Africa.'

On the plane service was polite but cool and they didn't get a drink until they asked the stewardess. 'It's a short flight, we prefer passengers to ask,' she told them. 'Except in first class.'

At one point the curtains closing off the first class cabin opened to reveal Nokkles sprawled across two seats. He was drinking champagne and his hand rested on the neck of the bottle in a protective yet rather showy manner. In the way that a man might rest his hand on the neck of an expensive girl whom he wishes to show off to the world. It was a gesture of desperate pride. It turned its back on Boers and shooting kaffirs and beer. It looked outward. It was confident, modern, worldly. Much had been invested in it.

CHAPTER 17

Of their arrival at Geneva Airport there is to be noted only that Ernest Nokkles was swept into the arms of that growing number of castaway agents abroad, all now increasingly anxious about the disappearances of their various chiefs and determined to reattach themselves to centres of influence or persons of importance whenever they appeared.

My dream showed me Nokkles, awash in good champagne, immediately claimed as he left the Customs area by three men who introduced themselves as Chris Dieweld, Emil Moolah and Koos Spahr. Two members of this burly trio claimed to have been recently attached to the office of the President, had travelled with him as far as London in search of medical treatment and there he had given them the slip. And I saw how these big men shivered and trembled at their loss.

Chris Dieweld, Emil Moolah and Koos Spahr surrounded Trudy's detective demanding to know what news he had brought. Dieweld was big and blond with a great cows-lick combed back from his forehead like a frozen wave, Moolah thin and springy with a mouth full of gold teeth and Spahr, bespectacled, with a round expressionless face and astonishingly bright blue eyes, gave no clue to his expertise with the parcel bomb. Nokkles knew Spahr as one of the men on Kuiker's security staff. The others he thought he knew vaguely from photographs of the President in foreign parts. Dieweld, he vaguely remembered, had disgraced himself by fainting when a demented maize farmer had attempted to shoot the President at the official opening of the Monument to Heroes of the Mauritian Invasion.

Nokkles' first question was about Bubé. The President was in Geneva, he had it on the best authority. Trace the President and surely the others could not be far away?

The security men looked glum. They too had heard of the President's visit to London. They had heard he was on his way to Geneva. They had met every plane. But the old fox must have disguised himself because he eluded them.

'Remember,' said Moolah, 'the President visited most of the European capitals during his celebrated tour and was never once

173

recognised. What chance did we stand?'

As for Blanchaille and Kipsel, they stood on the moving pavement carrying them towards passport control and Customs, gazing with fascination at the advertisements for watches sculpted from coins, or carved from ingots, the offer of hotels so efficient they operated without manpower and the multitude of advertisements in cunningly illuminated panels alongside the moving pavement showing deep blue lakes and icing sugar alps. Most of all they stared at the multitudinous shapes and forms of gold to be purchased, ingots, coins, pendants, lozenges; some cute and almost edible came in little cubes, fat and yellow like processed cheese. How extraordinary that so much treasure should be produced from the deep, black, stony heart of their country.

This reverie was broken by a chauffeur in smart green livery who carried a sign reading 'Reverend Blanchaille' and announced that he had instructions to transport them to 'the big house on the hill', where a friend awaited them.

Who were they to argue? Alone and unloved in a strange land? However close to the end of their journey they might be (for after all 'the big house of the hill' was a tantalising description) offers of friendship from whatever quarter were difficult to resist.

It is a sign of the desperate state to which the once-powerful security men had been reduced that they, seeing Blanchaille and Kipsel escorted to a great limousine, should have decided to follow them, despite Nokkles' warning that these men were deluded pilgrims come to Switzerland to seek Kruger's dream kingdom and that they were in real life a disgraced traitor and a renegade priest. As Chris Dieweld put it: 'We're lost without someone to follow.'

The chauffeur pointed to the grey Mercedes keeping discreetly behind them. 'We'll lose them,' he promised.

The road ran for miles along the lakeside. The lower slopes of the mountain were thickly crammed with vines, every inch of land terraced to its very edges, the dense greenness tumbling down to the roadside, vine leaves stirring in the passing breeze their car made. Then on the other side of the road the vines continuing their downward plunge to the very water's edge. Up ahead were larger mountains folding one into another and covered in a thick dark fur of vegetation. It amazed him, the roughness of this vegetation, its harsh contours. No doubt it was different in the winter when the snows softened and smoothed away the detail, but now, under the sun hot and high, under a light-blue sky, there was a rough, wiry, raw determination about the way these shrubs and trees clung to the mountain side, a lack of softness, an absence of prettiness that reminded him very strongly of Africa. After running some way along the lakeside they began climbing steeply. The driver pointed to the town of Montreux below and to a small tongue of land jutting out into the lake, that was the prison castle, Château Chillon, very famous. They climbed through the thick fuzz of bush and forest, the harsh unlovely vegetation. Here and there boulders broke through the dark green and nearer the summits were ridges of grey stone, mountain skulls, patched and balding. And even higher still was the snow, even in this June heat, last year's snow, icy grey.

And here was a grand house, a castle within its own walls, but no rearing bulk of dull stones, more of a *Schloss*, a château, white-washed, trim and solid. Then they were driving through the great wrought-iron gates with their chevrons and swans intricately worked, along a gravel drive up to great oaken doors.

Their host in his big solid house at the end of a long drive, behind high walls and wrought-iron gates, awaited them on the steps. With his hand outstretched, wearing the dark business suit, the well-shaped smile so familiar from a thousand press photographs and television, with his head cocked to one side, sparse grey hair neatly combed, the round intelligent face with bright eyes that gave him the look of an intelligent gun dog, the characteristic quick shrewd glance from behind thick lashes, the quiet, formidable air of authority. It was very difficult for them to suppress their astonishment.

'What? Himmelfarber, you!' Blanchaille said.

Kipsel said, 'It really is another bloody exodus. It's a diaspora. If Himmelfarber the mine-owner has left, then it's all finished. Everyone will leave. You won't be able to move anywhere overseas for fleeing South Africans.'

'But I haven't left,' said the mine-owner. 'This is merely my summer place. I spend the African winter here.'

Blanchaille turned on his heel. 'Have a happy holiday,' he said.

'I have a proposition,' said Himmelfarber.

'We're not open to any proposals,' Blanchaille said very firmly.

'We may as well hear what he has to say,' said Kipsel, 'now that we're here.'

'Let's talk inside,' Himmelfarber led them through the house into an enormous lounge furnished in white leather with thick pink carpets on the floor, a large generous room looking through french windows onto the lawn and large circular lily pond. Himmelfarber stood at the bar at the far end and poured them drinks. A little fruit punch, he said, of his own making, light and refreshing.

On the walls of this room were blow-ups of black and white photographs of miners working below ground, drilling the rock face, or loading the ore, coming off shift. Happy pictures of a classroom full of new recruits learning Fanagalo. Other photographs, far more disturbing, showed men terribly mutilated, crushed and bleeding; they also saw corpses lying on sheets in what must have been a morgue, rows of them, they stared at the ceiling wide-eyed and with quite terrible, unfrightened detachment. Why should Himmelfarber keep these reminders about him?

Blanchaille considered the entrepreneur. Curtis Christian Himmelfarber was the brilliant son of a brilliant family. The family had been established by the remarkable Julius Himmelfarber, a penniless Latvian emigrant to the South African goldfields who had founded a great mining empire. Old Julius had been an intimate of Cecil Rhodes and Milner, a drinking companion of Barney Barnato, a sworn enemy of Kruger who had called him '*Daardie Joodse smous*' . . . that Jewish pedlar . . . Julius Himmelfarber had bought Blydag, his first mine and one of the premier producers of all time, for a little more than was now paid for one single ounce of its gold, and the foundation of a great financial empire had been laid.

Frank Harris, the noted Irish philanderer on a visit to South Africa shortly before the Boer War began, had been favourably impressed.

Harris had met Julius Himmelfarber and liked him well enough to leave a portrait of him: '. . . cultured, urbane, very pointed in conversation, a gentle Croesus, a philosopher miner, a flower of the Semitic type, markedly superior to your Anglo-Saxon sportsmen.' But then Harris, of course, had held a long-standing prejudice against the Anglo-Saxon sportsman, for, as he told Cecil Rhodes in a bizarre meeting which took place on top of Table Mountain while Rhodes presumably gazed from this fairest Cape in all the world towards distant Cairo, it was perfectly understandable that God in his youth should have chosen the Jews for his special people, for they were after all an attractive, lovable race. But that later he should have changed his mind in favour of the English, as Rhodes contended, showed that he must be in his dotage.

Curtis Christian Himmelfarber, who was now handing out drinks in the pink and white room to Blanchaille and Kipsel, would not have been described by Harris as the flower of the Semitic type. In any event, the Himmelfarbers had long since severed the con-

176

nection. Curtis Christian was an Anglican and this faith, along with his mines, had been part of his inheritance. The change in faith had taken place when his fierce grandfather, Aaron, always a mercurial man, the ne'er-do-well of the family, had persuaded investors that a local mine under his control was capable of producing richer amounts than anyone had suspected, and displayed samples to prove it. Alas, a surveyor's report revealed that the mine was likely to produce far less than promised and Aaron found himself in jail, awaiting trial. It was there that he underwent a spectacular conversion at the hands of a travelling Baptist minister. Naturally the entire family followed suit. They did not long stay with the Baptists but moved instead, down the years, by degrees, with a stately assurance that reminded one of a luxury liner heading for its home port, from the choppy seas of Baptist rhetoric into the calmer, shallower waters of the Church of England and in these pacific waters had floated ever since.

The Himmelfarbers were the closest thing to a Royal family the country had. Each member of this family received adulatory notice in the media. Everyone in the country was familiar with the little vagaries of the Himmelfarbers. There was Waverley, C.C.'s wife, tall, tanned and fit. She appeared often at fund-raising dinners, drove jeeps for famine relief, organised milk for the townships and free school books for the kids. There was Elspeth, the eldest daughter and the 'serious one', a lawyer. There was Cookie, the madcap gadabout youngest, with a taste for high living and drugs, a kind of painter, and reportedly a great strain on her parents. And then of course Timmo, the son and heir, dashing, eligible, often pictured behind the wheel of a racing car, or in his yacht off Cape Point. Photographers had accompanied him on his first day of military service. That service was later to be marred by a scandal when it was rumoured that Timmo, who had trained with a crack paratroop squadron 'The Leopard's Claw', had been excused jumps over hostile territory. The chiefs of staff took the unusual step of refuting the rumour and reported that young Himmelfarber always jumped with his comrades and, what was more, he had one of the highest 'score' rates (the name given to the jump/kill ratios), in the entire regiment.

'I see you're examining my photographs,' said Himmelfarber. 'These pictures, you know what they are? They're photographs of my workers and show the full extent of their employment. The dangers of mining are not disguised. Accidents at the rock face, drilling accidents, men hurt in rockfalls, or ramming, that is to say when loading the trucks with gold-bearing rock. I wonder if you have any idea what a mine looks like underground? Imagine a buried Christmas tree, the trunk is the mine shaft plunging down hundreds of meters. Off the shaft the stopes radiate like branches. At the far tips of these branches is the thread of gold. Think of it rather like tinsel that you drape over the branches of your Christmas tree. Gold mining is deep, dark, hot, dangerous work. You must break a great deal of rock to claim a little of the glitter, a couple of tons of ore give you little more than twenty grammes of gold. I keep these pictures on my wall to remind me where I come from, how I live and what it costs.' Himmelfarber brought their drinks across. 'This is a good light punch. I hope you'll enjoy it. Fruit juice spiked with rum and lemon, mixed with a little pomegranate, satsuma segments, some passion fruit and thin shavings of watermelon. Shall we drink to the health of our President? I believe he needs our good wishes,' Himmelfarber smiled, and raised his glass. 'But that's another story. I haven't got you here to talk about poor Bubé.'

'Why are we here?' Blanchaille demanded.

Himmelfarber looked surprised. 'To listen to a few stories of my own. Such as the story of Popov.'

'Do you really mean that?' Kipsel demanded incredulously. 'Do you know the true story of Popov?'

This is where Blanchaille waded in. 'Now just a moment,' he said. 'Let's get this straight before you start swallowing everything he tells you. Himmelfarber here and his firm, Consolidated Holdings, have propped up successive governments for as long as anyone can remember. Himmelfarber buys defence bonds, sits on armaments boards, advises the Regime on its business deals, he even plays golf with Bubé.'

'That's one way of looking at it. I also fund the Democratic People's Party, I'm a public supporter of racial freedom and Consolidated Holdings is one of the most enlightened employers in the country. It has more black personnel managers than any other, it was the first to employ Indian salesmen, our coloured cost accountants are internationally known and bright young Liberals join us in the sure knowledge that their ideas will be welcomed and acted upon.'

'For God's sake, Ronnie, you're not going to stand there and swallow that stuff, are you? Why don't you ask him about Popov?'

Kipsel's eyes widened. 'You knew Popov?'

'Knew him! Himmelfarber ran him!' Blanchaille shouted.

178

'I asked Mr Himmelfarber, Blanchie, let him answer for himself.'

Himmelfarber placed four fingers over the rim of his glass and put his mouth to the liquid and laughed softly, a frothy resonance. 'Now you see the trouble with our holy friend here. He's very much the obsessive South African type. He's more of a danger to our country than the entire Total Onslaught. And d'you know why? It's because he combines this horrible puritanical streak on the one hand with an absolutely crusading ignorance on the other. Your friend Blanchaille suffers from the characteristic South African disease. He wishes to blame people. No, Mr Kipsel, I can't promise you the true story of Popov. But I can give you my version.'

'That will do,' said Kipsel, and he helped himself to more punch.

'But before you can understand the importance of Popov, you must listen to my story of why we love the Russians.'

'Do we love the Russians?' Kipsel asked.

'In our own way, yes we do. We have something in common which completely overrides our political differences – our gold sales. This is only natural since the Soviet Union and the Republic between them possess most of the gold in the world. It's obviously in our mutual interest to regulate the supply of that gold to the world markets and thereby to control the price. Remember that every fluctuation of a few dollars up or down is a total gain or loss of millions to our economies. Let me give you an example of the sort of co-operation I have in mind. For years gold sales were handled in London. But we found that successive British governments were becoming too damn inquisitive about our sales. So we pulled out. London till then was *the* gold market, the next moment we were gone. On our side naturally it gave the Regime great pleasure to kick the Limeys in the teeth, it's an extension of the Boer War, of course – I quote to you President Bubé's choice remark: "We've got nothing against the British – it's the English we hate." The Russians also had their reasons for pulling out. They said they were concerned about security at Heathrow. But they weren't really worried about the stuff being stolen, although it happens from time to time. What they really objected to was having people sniffing around their gold because word might get out about the amount they were selling. So off we went to Switzerland and there, with the price doubling and redoubling like crazy, we had a high old time in our Zurich years. In fact so much gold was sold that the Swiss threw caution to the winds for once, and seeing a chance of making even more money the Government slapped on a sales tax, something a little over five per cent I seem to recall. It's a long time ago now.

179

Well, that was a very bad mistake. It wasn't that we objected to the Swiss becoming even richer but having that tax meant that the dealers had to show how much gold they were selling, from which could be calculated the amount that we were putting onto the market. We were right back where we were before. And the amounts of gold we were making available were in danger of being anticipated, even discounted. Even then we might have hung on, but the price crashed as it does every few years and the Swiss dealers, who had grown fat in the good years, dragged their feet over selling our newly mined metal at a much lower price than in the old good gilded days of yore. So back we went to London with some of our business. We and our friends. Not all our business. Never again all of it. What a welcome! Kisses on both cheeks from the Bank of England, no unseemly taxes, or too close a scrutiny of sales – our friends were most insistent about that – and everything looked like sweetness and light.'

Blanchaille turned to Kipsel. 'You hear what he says? He admits to working with the Russians and he expects us to clap. And yet we know people who did the same thing and were hanged. Look at the first commandment of our country: the Regime kills people who help the Russians. That's the rule. Everyone knows it. Everyone obeys it. Go up to the man in the street and ask what will happen if you help the Russians and he'll draw his finger across his throat. He may even kill you himself. People live and die according to the rules the Regime makes – so how can they change them?'

'Why not? If it suits them,' Himmelfarber demanded brutally. 'They're their rules.'

'But what about Popov, the spy?' Kipsel asked. 'You still haven't said.'

'He was no spy,' said Blanchaille. 'He was a Russian banker who got arrested by mistake. Van Vuuren showed me that.'

'Correct,' Himmelfarber acknowledged. 'First inkling I had of it came in a call from Zurich, the Wozchod Handelsbank, and my contact Glotz on the line, screaming at me: "Just what the hell have you done? You stupid, fucking Boers! You morons! What in Christ's name have you done with Popov? I've just had Vneshtorgbank on the line – that's his headquarters, Bank for Foreign Trade in Moscow – absolutely frantic! They say their man has gone cold. Do something!" Well? What could I say? Nothing – at the time and just as well, too. Imagine his reaction if I told him – yes, look I'm sorry about this Ivan, but your man is at the moment languishing in a cell in Balthazar Buildings having been beaten within an inch of his life. Because he was, you know. The Security Police got so drunk when they realised they'd caught a live Russian that they didn't refer the matter to the Bureau, as they should have done; instead they gave poor Popov the treatment. They strung him up by his toes, they tied him to a broomstick and gave him the catherine wheel, they put an uncomfortable voltage through each testicle. Then they threw a party. They went to the press and issued self-congratulatory statements. Popov by this stage was past knowing or caring. He didn't tell them much. He *couldn't* tell them much! His English has never been any good and he was in a state of profound shock. Besides that he'd lost his false teeth which fell out when these buggers dangled him from an open window on the tenth floor. They frightened him to within an inch of his life and that put paid to any chance of communication. Fear and the lack of teeth ensured that Popov was talking to no one. But as far as the papers were concerned, as far as the rest of the country was concerned, our boys had caught a Russian and of course the Regime had to play along with it. They had to confirm that their brilliant Security Police had pulled off the most extraordinary capture of a Russian spy, they made him a full colonel in the KGB and they went round saying proudly how clever they'd been. Well they had to, hadn't they? The Government had been warning for years that the Russians were working to destroy us, that they sent their spies into the country all the time, that they had armed and supported the black armies on the borders, that their agents had infiltrated the townships, and the resettlement camps, that their submarines cruised off our coasts and that they were working day and night for the destruction of our country. Now they'd gone and proved it! Well, I had to take some hard decisions. I started taking flack from both directions. The Regime wanted to know what I was going to do about smoothing relations with the Russians. The Russians were muttering darkly about treachery and threatening to end co-operation on gold sales. The Regime, while publicly ordering its ministers to dance in the street, was telling me that I was the only one who could sort out matters with Moscow. In the end I did what I had to.'

'What was that?' Kipsel asked.

'I sent my nephew to Moscow.'

'Just like that?'

'He's been before.. Popov was the Russians' man here. Bennie was our man there.'

'Bennie?'

'My nephew. A bright boy, Craddock. A few years ago I was

181

happy to make him a director of Consolidated Holdings. He's been running missions to Moscow for years.'

'What happened in Moscow?' Kipsel asked.

'He was arrested the moment he stepped off the plane.'

'You shopped him,' declared Kipsel wonderingly.

'It was my duty,' said Himmelfarber. 'I had to give Moscow something to hold. He was a kind of deposit against the safe return of Popov. We knew it was necessary.'

'We?' said Kipsel.

'Those of us who will seize the chance of a change in our country. Real change! Consider, Ronald, our previous history. Once the Regime consisted of men who believed themselves chosen by God to bring light to a dark place. They were known as the Dark Men, or the Old Guard. In time they were replaced by a new breed, the so-called Men of Light, or New Men. Now the New Men believed also that God had chosen them, but they also believed that the country couldn't be protected by faith alone. They must be protected by rocket launchers and useful business contacts as well as the proper deployment of troops on the borders. Of course the New Men are no longer frightened of the outside world. They want to carry the fight to the enemy, they want to meet the world and beat it. They refuse to see the options closing one by one. They want to get out and do things. It was the New Men who were behind Bubé's foreign tours, and I'm not just talking about the European tour that got all the publicity, the six capitals in five days, or whatever it was. No, I'm talking about the tours, the secret tours that have been going on for years, the clandestine diplomacy on which the President has been engaged for almost a decade now. Why, if I told you the number of countries he had visited you'd be absolutely amazed. Then there's also been a publicity campaign mounted by the Department of Communications and the quite stunning work which Trudy Yssel has done, buying into, buying up, and buying off opinion makers in the West. I tell you there's not a place from the Vatican to the White House where Trudy, yes little Trudy Yssel from the back-of-beyond, a poor little country girl who went to school barefoot, is not welcomed and fêted. Fêted! Do you see the nature of things? Do I make myself clear? Do you see the chances to which I refer? The old ways have gone, or at least are going and others are being adapted. Yes, of course we still believe in God. Yes, of course, we still believe that under certain circumstances a platoon ambushed must fight to the last man for the glory of the country and to add substance to the ancient belief that the entire

182

country would do so, in need. Yet gradually the realisation has come about, that what we need is not God and bombs, though they may be very useful, but gold. And we have it! By God, we have it and we use it. Hell, can either of you imagine what it's like to turn on your TV and see one of our warlike black presidents in one of the states to the north of us threatening to blast us off the map of Africa and know that not twelve hours before the same guy has been pouring you a whisky and soda in the VIP's guest-house and inquiring after your wife and kids? That's progress! The Regime sees the options and uses them, that's all,' said Himmelfarber, 'and so do I.'

'You're saying it's possible to do a deal with the New Men?' Blanchaille asked.

Himmelfarber gave the wolfish smile of one who has scented the approaching kill. 'I don't know about dealing with the Regime. That comes later. But sure, I'll deal *for* them. I already did. More than once. Let me give you one example. The Regime has a lot of trouble securing various supplies which we regard as essential. A little guy from the Department of Commerce comes to see me. Can I suggest a way for our country to acquire certain strategic supplies overseas? Well that's a bit of a problem because you see foreign countries don't exactly like the idea of penetration by South African interests, still less by South African Government agencies. So what did we do at Consolidated Holdings to resolve this difficulty? Well, we did our buying using a group of Panamanian companies which could not be traced back to us. And having bought our way in to certain target industries abroad we left the local management structures very largely intact and operated through a series of interlocking boards. This was a wise move because it's always better not to disturb the people on the ground. But since you have your own directors in there and these directors are linked, and controlled, say from your New York office, you maintain a fairly useful oversight of your operation. Perhaps you might buy a forest in Scotland, because we need pit props in good supply, or a British insurance company, or take over American interests in coal, copper, uranium and so on. Look, believe it or not, and I'd probably be shot if anybody knew I'd told you, but so vital does the Regime consider this programme of strategic acquirements that they're investing millions in its long-term strategy for buying up or buying into key interests abroad. Somebody has to do it for them.'

'But you'd still consider yourself an opponent of the Regime?' Kipsel asked.

'Greater opposer is there none,' said Himmelfarber, directing his eyes heavenward. 'My family has opposed this Regime and all its neolithic predecessors. Consolidated Holdings is in the forefront of the struggle to reform the labour laws, electrify the black townships, promote the inter-racial arts and encourage more black mothers to breastfeed. Yessir, we are opponents! But as opponents the question we must ask ourselves, if we are serious, is do we merely wish to condemn the Regime, or do we want to destroy it? Look, I work with the Government on certain ventures, but that doesn't make me a Government man. I also make donations in an indirect fashion to the Azanian Liberation Front – but that doesn't make me a guerrilla. It's really just a question, as I say, of exploring all the options. This is now Government policy. And believe you me it's going to sink the bastards! Already it has started. Yssel and Kuiker are gone. When you get people using a lot of money, travelling, living well, it's perhaps not surprising that they begin to acquire expensive tastes. They start enjoying certain wines, they become fascinated with a house with a particular view. These things happen. As for President Bubé, I've no reason to doubt that he's abroad because he's ill and he's seeking treatment, as the reports say. As to the rumours – well, I also know that when gold sales were switched from London to Zurich a number of Swiss dealers competed for President Bubé's friendship and co-operation and made concrete signals of their gratitude when he was able to help them. But before you jump to conclusions let's consider that in a way perhaps his motives might have been good. According to the rumours we hear, any money that President Bubé may have acquired has been set aside as a kind of insurance fund against the day when, possibly for military reasons, the Regime finds it cannot any longer operate safely from home base and they have to set up somewhere abroad. In other words, Bubé has set aside funds for the establishment of the Government in exile. Now why should this be a scandal? Surely it's not an ignoble gesture. It might even be quite sensible. You see what forces in the end will destroy them? They will smash on their own logic.'

'Yes,' said Kipsel. There was a strange light in his eye. 'I follow you now. What you're saying is that if you are genuinely committed to exploring all options, then among the options you're going to have to consider is the one that has you disappearing down the plug hole.'

'You've got it,' Himmelfarber beamed, clearly believing that in Kipsel he had found a recruit. 'I appeal to you. Leave off this foolish travelling. Come back with me. Come back home and make the new changes work for us. The old consensus is smashed. The bastards are on the run. They say they're being modern. In fact they're merely terrified. They say they want to look ahead. In fact they daren't open their eyes.'

'Join them,' said Kipsel, 'join them and then destroy them – isn't that it?'

'Exactly.' Himmelfarber was clearly exulted by the thought. 'You understand.'

'Indeed I do. I have friends who did the same thing once. To me,' Kipsel said. He stood up. 'Come Blanchie, it's time we were on our way. I'm sorry but I suppose by rights I belong to the Old Guard. I will never be a New Man.'

And Blanchaille, his heart pounding with relief and gratitude, followed his friend through the french windows and down the drive before the astonished Himmelfarber could collect his wits.

'Thank God!' muttered Blanchaille. 'For a few moments I thought he had you. You see what he does to people, don't you? You see his own miners on the wall and how he's destroyed them. You think of the bright-eyed idealists who go to work for Consolidated Holdings in its Art-Deco palace in the capital with their new suits and their dreams of multi-racial progress. Of how they will become personnel officers and drive their new BMWs proudly home to the townships at night to show that they have succeeded in a white man's world because they work for kindly, liberal, rich, decent Curtis Christian Himmelfarber.'

'Think of his nephew,' said Kipsel.

Behind them C.C. Himmelfarber stood in the window screaming: 'Preachers! Prudes! Sermonisers! My God, if there's anyone worse than racists – it's people like you!'

'Of course we should never forget what Himmelfarber gets from this for dealing on behalf of the Regime,' said Kipsel, unexpectedly revealing how sure his grasp of the complexities of the mine-owner's position had been. 'What he gets out of it is increased clout with the Regime and he gets business put his way. Perhaps most important of all, he gets a number of channels for exporting his own funds abroad, currency regulations hold no fear for him, if they ever did. Since he's doing business abroad on behalf of the Regime, secret, valuable business, he can transfer as much capital abroad as he wishes. He can build up his interests in Europe and in America. Should he ever have to leave his native country he wouldn't have to pack more than a travelling bag. It's just another option, you see.'

'You know,' said Blanchaille as they neared the end of the drive, 'it's always the same with the Himmelfarbers. I suppose Julius, the founder of the whole firm, was all right. But C.C.'s great-grandfather, Julius Himmelfarber, kept on best terms with the Boers right throughout the war, kept supplying them with gold. And when the British marched into Johannesburg he was on best terms with them too. Now you have C.C. with his liberal politics and his Government contacts. He really does mean to destroy them. And if he does, he wins.'

'And if he doesn't?' Kipsel asked.

'He still wins.'

A grey Mercedes travelling at speed spat gravel at them as it raced up the drive. It carried Ernest Nokkles and Chris Dieweld, Emil Moolah and Koos Spahr.

'For a moment back there I thought Himmelfarber was getting through to you,' Blanchaille said.

'I suppose it's betrayal that sticks in my gullet. We're old-fashioned, Blanchie. That's why we're finished. We never got the point of it all. As true as God sometimes I think we knew about as little as Mickey the Poet. It's a joke, really.'

'Yes, I think it is a bit of a joke,' said Blanchaille sadly, recalling his lost love, remembering Miranda's words. 'I'm beginning to get it now. If it's any consolation, you can say you were betrayed by your enemies. Now the New Men can expect to be betrayed by their friends.'

Kipsel gave him a strange, twisted look. Blanchaille did not know whether he meant to laugh or cry. 'But, Blanchie, that's just it! The joke. There are no New Men.' Then he laughed. 'O.K. now where?'

Blanchaille remembered Lynch's last words, '. . . to the left and above the town . . .' but the beginning, as the girls at the Airport Palace had told him, was Clarens and the official Kruger house by the lakeside, preserved as a national monument by the Regime. 'Where Uncle Paul finished seems as good as a place as any to begin.'

Kipsel continually turned back to stare behind them, though Blanchaille implored him not to do so. Himmelfarber was best forgotten. He was even then presumably pouring punch for his new guests.

'The men in the Mercedes, Nokkles and others, who were following us,' Blanchaille said.

'I thought we'd lost them,' said Kipsel.

Blanchaille shook his head. 'People like that will always find their way to Himmelfarber.'

What proposition the mine-owner put to Nokkles and his colleagues can only be guessed at – whether they returned to work in South Africa on Himmelfarber's behalf, or remained abroad to look after the Swiss end of his operations, or were dispatched on secret missions to buy coffee plantations in Brazil, or weapons systems in Germany, or computers in Silicone Valley, or excavation equipment in Scotland on behalf of shadowy Panamanian companies, I cannot say. But having entered into Himmelfarber's employ, certainly it was the last that anyone ever saw of them.

CHAPTER 18

She stood upon a platform, dais, podium, rostrum, elevation of some kind, he could not tell precisely what it was, looking back, as if petrified by the bright light which hit her. Raised above her adoring public clamouring to touch her, she was surrounded by dignitaries who sat in gilt chairs in rows behind her on the stage. Of course she was not petrified. She was loving it! Smiling proudly, radiantly.

It took Kipsel a moment before he recognised her photograph in the French newspaper in the Café of The Three Poets, where they paused on the road to Clarens. (He did not know it then but she was in fact standing upon the stage of the newly-completed Opera House on the Campus of the University of National Christian Education which had so recently eaten up the defunct parish of Father Lynch.) That too he did not know. Nor did he know that at that same venue, some nights before, at the official opening of the Opera House with a production of *Madame Butterfly* in the presence of the new President, young Jan 'Bomber' Vollenhoven, terrible scenes had been witnessed when the famous soprano, Maisie van der Westhuizen, 'our Maisie', appearing in the title role, arrived on stage to find the front rows packed with orthodox Jews in yarmulkas waving placards reading SAY NO TO MAISIE'S NAZIS!, and she rushed from the stage in tears and disappeared forever. But that was another story.

In a stunningly low-cut evening gown with plaited shoulder straps, aglitter with diamonds, she wore a high choker around her neck, as well as some sort of ribbon and medal, an official military decoration pinned below her right breast. Her head was turned away from the camera, chin slightly raised and the frozen look was no more than a pose she had struck. And for what possible reason? Not vengeance, as with Lot's wife, who also looked back, but fame! And yet it could be said she stood so still, she seemed so studied in her stillness that she might have been stone, or a pillar of salt. Kipsel had the impression he was witnessing some tableau in which an actress impersonated a woman he knew, or had once known. Among her adoring audience were men in uniform, saluting. Others, in evening dress, were raising glasses to her in excited acclamation. The women present were wearing big picture hats identifying them immediately as wives of Government ministers. They gazed in rapture at their heroine upon her raised platform and she half-turned graciously as if she had been on the point of leaving this gathering or reception or perhaps tumultuous welcome, or whatever it was, and stopped for a final wave, turned once again, perhaps to acknowledge the applause of the crowd and it was in this half-turn that the flash caught her.

Kipsel had found the newspaper rolled around a long stick in the cordial manner of continental cafés, and unfolded it idly as they sat among the remains of their excellent lunch, fillets of fera, a succulent fish found in Lake Geneva. The photograph was on the front page. Kipsel passed Blanchaille the newspaper and asked for a translation of the headline.

Blanchaille, barely able to contain his horrified astonishment, pointed out to his friend that although he descended from a Mauritian sailor and his mother had had high ambitions for him in the France she had never seen, although he carried a French passport, his knowledge of the language was elementary. None the less, after much muttering in a voice from which the tones of horror could not be eradicated, he stared at the headline: LA GRANDE ESPIONNE SUD-AFRICAINE RENTRE.

'Big, grand or great South African spy returns,' Blanchaille offered reluctantly.

'Returns?' said Kipsel wonderingly. 'That means she's been with them all along. It is Magdalena – isn't it?'

'I'm sorry, Ronnie.'

Inside the paper there were more pictures. They showed Magdalena's secret life in colour photographs. Here was a picture of her spymaster, Brigadier Jim Langman, taken in Magdalena's garden, Blanchaille announced after some deciphering. It showed the Brigadier in what appeared to be a uniform of his own making, a rather strange tan tunic with great big buttoned breast pockets and a collar of exceptional size. Brigadier Langman sat on the swing in the garden. The swing was painted lemon yellow. Langman wore black shoes and white socks which clashed noticeably with the tan uniform. He gazed soulfully out of the photograph, a round, fleshy face with soft, rather pouchy dark eyes with a glint to them that reminded Blanchaille of an ageing watchdog. Brigadier Langman's nose was large, veined, his moustache curved out and downwards from each nostril to bracket the corners of his mouth. What was the Brigadier doing, perched on the swing in this odd uniform? No matter. It made a startling photograph in what was an amazing series. Here was Magdalena taking the sun by her poolside. Here she was at pistol practice wearing ear-protectors, the tip of her tongue clenched between her teeth in an effort of concentration, her tailored jumpsuit covered in zips, her hair caught behind her head in a bow. Here was Magdalena in Red Square, white fur collar around her ears, the same photograph which hung on the wall in her flat. Here was Magdalena in a recently bombed refugee camp somewhere north of the border wearing military uniform, identification disc pinned to her chest, inspecting the damage following a South African air raid. Here was Magdalena with a group of black students in Mombasa, a row of grins and clenched fist salutes. Here was Magdalena arm-in-arm with Kaiser at an Azanian Liberation rally in Hyde Park and here she was again at a barbecue in a suburban garden in the company of a number of men whose very long shorts, bullet heads, stony eyes, the curious way the hair was shaved well above the ears and vigorously oiled, revealed them to be policemen. Here was a photograph of Magdalena's favourite weapon, a Beretta Parabellum which it seemed she now carried everywhere in a hand-tooled leather case. The reasons were clear, even with their limited French. The Front for the Liberation of Azania, enraged at its humiliating penetration, had sworn revenge. Its eradication squad, the mysterious Strike Kommando No. 3, had vowed to kill her. Here was a photograph of Magdalena attending the christening of the youngest child of Kaiser's cousin, in St Martin-in-the-Fields, where she had become the child's godmother. Was there no end to her capacity for deception? It seemed not.

Now I saw Kipsel struggle to an elbow and with glazed eyes begin to speak: 'Look, let's get this straight – I never set out to be what I am. Hell, no! I mean a guy starts off at home as a rugby player, most guys do, but if he's got more than a smidgen of brain someone comes along who tells him there's more to life than playing ball, there's politics which is just as dangerous, intellectually satisfying and pulls girls who start thinking about these things from an early age being more mature than boys. So before I knew it I was investigating the living conditions of our cook and pressing my old folks to increase her wages – and this while still at school, such is the pace of political development. At university, well, you find yourself leading a protest march on the police station, or picketing the profs for free medicals for black lab assistants, you go on marches, join demonstrations, engage in sit-ins and get arrested when failing to disperse after being ordered to do so by a police officer, but after a while it palls, or at least disenchantment sets in, you don't feel that you're really doing anything, you're simply not scoring, so you get active, you start a trade union for gardeners and you dream of becoming a para-medic in the starving homelands. Jesus! you even send for the home-tuition course and you run a literacy night-class for black taxi-drivers and *still* you don't feel you're connecting. I mean there's no one cheering in the stands and so you become desperate for action, and of course you're reading like mad, Marx and Dostoevsky and Gide and Fanon, and you suddenly realise that what is needed is the lonely gesture of self-affirmation, that freedom is to be seized in a single act, authentic existence must be deliberately chosen, so what do you do? You get a few guys together and form a secret revolutionary cell, that's me and J.J. Bliksem and Len Silberstein and Magdalena, but not Mickey the Poet, he was never in the cell, he was just roped in to drive because Silberstein's stupid bloody Volvo wouldn't start on the last morning of our campaign. Off we went, clutching our dynamite snitched from the explosives store of the gold mine where Silberstein's uncle was compound manager, and found some power pylons in the veld outside town. They had to be outside town because we didn't want to hurt anyone. We drew the line at casualties, hell we drew the line at everything you can think of! We wanted to make an impact but we didn't want blood, or maiming. I mean we were naïve middle-class people, we gave up our seats to old ladies on buses, so we weren't about to scatter arms and legs across the place. Silberstein laid the charges because he'd leant how to do it having been a sapper during his military service. I helped him. Back at the car Magdalena engaged Mickey the Poet in conversation and took him for a walk. Mickey said in court that she seduced him and I believe him. It was her usual response when conversation flagged, and that when the blast went off she told him these were the reverberations of his inner being. Mickey would believe anything. But I noticed that next night when we had to go off and blast the electrical pylons in the black township Mickey was unavailable to drive us and Silberstein had to borrow his father's car. We went to bomb the other pylons after a pretty heated argument. I said two was enough but Silberstein and Magdalena said it would expose us to a charge of racial division if we hit white stuff only. As the Regime decreed separate lavatories it was only right that we hit separate black pylons; anything else would look like crude anti-white prejudice. The next morning the police picked me up. They knew everything; they knew Silberstein's uncle, they knew how many sticks of dynamite, dammit they even knew poor Mickey's poem. They played me tapes of the fool Silberstein's telephone conversations. After we got back from the township bombing he spent hours phoning people around the country hinting at what we'd done, telling them to read the papers in the morning, like it was a picnic we'd been on, or a party. I didn't think to ask myself how they knew. I just knew they knew and I tried to save Magdalena. They locked me in a room upstairs at the police station with the curtains drawn with a Special Branch killer called Vuis. He hit me until I fell down. Then he kicked me. In those days they didn't bother to be subtle, no electrodes on the balls, no strangling with the wet towel. Fists and feet, drowning, doorways, steep stairs, high windows. They didn't care if the marks showed. Dammit, they *wanted* marks to show! That was one of the perks of being a security policeman, you got to hit people often. Tried to tell them that Mickey had nothing to do with the explosions, but they laughed. Told them not a syllable about Magdalena and they beat me some more. For interrupting! You see, they knew the lot! They didn't want my confession, true or not. They wanted to be left alone to go on with the beating. Arnoldus Vuis was also captain of the police hockey team; on his days off, he told me between punches, he played left back. It's funny what you remember when you're bleeding heavily and seeing double. We used electric detonators on the pylons. Silberstein read all about them, that's the useful thing about lawyers, they read. Captain Vuis knew about Silberstein's reading. He knew about things even I didn't know about, like the fact that it had been Looksmart Dladla who did the recce and supplied the map of the power pylons in the township. They slipped there, of course, because Looksmart happened to have been hauled in before the attacks on the electric pylons and when the dynamite went off he was being savagely beaten and had his head banged against the wall, so he could not have been present. His alibi was unshakeable. They had to release him temporarily and were about to pick him up when someone tipped him off and he skipped to Philadelphia. Anyway, I shopped myself and Silberstein, reckoning we were for the high jump anyway, but I said nothing about Magdalena and I defended Mickey as best I could.'

Here Kipsel broke down and began to stab Magdalena's picture with his fork and Blanchaille had to lead his friend from the café before the proprietor became too angry.

'I wasn't the traitor. Magdalena was with the Regime all the time. She set me up, and you. And even Kaiser. Christ! But Kaiser must feel sick.'

'So do I,' said Blanchaille, 'Magdalena was Apple One. It's so obvious it hurts.'

'Well,' said Kipsel, 'maybe at last we know something.'

'Maybe,' said Blanchaille.

But it wasn't much and it came too late.

CHAPTER 19

They wandered about in the general area of Clarens until they struck the little road set back from the lake and lined with large nineteenth-century villas, one of which they knew immediately from a hundred slides and photographs Father Lynch had shown them over the years. Then, too, there was the familiar flag flying from a first-floor balcony. It was growing dark, the sun was setting behind the further mountains lighting the clouds from below so they seemed not so much clouds as daubs of black and gold on the deepening blue of the sky. Even though there were lights in the upper storey of the house, the shutters on the lower floors were closed. The last of the tourists had departed. They would not gain entry until the following morning.

As it happened there were a number of garden chairs and a small, circular steel table at the bottom of a short flight of stairs which led from the front of the house into the garden. Here, though cold, they slept until some time after midnight when they were roughly awoken.

They knew him even though he wasn't wearing one of his Hawaiian shirts with the golden beaches, the coconut palms and the brilliant sunsets, even though he carried a revolver which he waved at them ordering them into the house.

Once inside, Blanchaille marvelled at his outfit. A raw silk suit extremely crumpled as if it had been slept in, no tie, shirt collar twisted, his laces undone as if he'd just shoved his feet into his shoes before coming outside and wafting off him good and strong were waves of liquor. He'd been drinking, drinking most of the night, Blanchaille guessed. He was aware of a hallway, the smell of polish, photographs on the walls, Kruger everywhere, and to his right a staircase which carried the large warning: *No Admittance to the Public*. At the top of the stairs stood a woman in a blue dressing-gown.

'What have you got there, Gus?' she asked grumpily.

They recognised her immediately, of course, that slightly imperious, dark, faintly hawk-like profile – those handsome rather beaky good looks, the eagle priestess, Secretary of the Department of Communications, Trudy Yssel.

'Oh Ernie Nokkles where are you now?' Kipsel whispered.

'Spies are what I've got here,' said the big wild man.

'Tourists,' Blanchaille countered.

'Normal times for that. Normal opening times. It's rare that pilgrims, whatever their fervour, camp in the grounds. Isn't that so, Trudy – isn't that so?' he appealed to the haughty figure in blue above them.

'I'd say, from the look of them, you've picked up a couple of bums, that's what I'd say. Who are you boys?'

They told her.

'Not *the* Kipsel?'

Kipsel sighed and admitted it.

'And I know you,' said Kuiker to Blanchaille. 'You used to be Father Theo of the Camps.'

'And you used to be Gus Kuiker, Minister of Parallel Equilibriums and Ethnic Autonomy.'

Above their heads Trudy Yssel laughed harshly. 'You really picked a couple of wise-guys this time. As if we don't have problems! When will you learn to leave well alone?' She spun on her heel.

'Come on, Trudy,' the Minister implored. 'Give a man a break. I caught 'em.'

But she was gone.

Another woman bustled along the corridor. Frizzy grey hair and a cross red face. She carried a broom and a pan. She looked at Kipsel and Blanchaille with horror. 'Now whom have you invited? I told the Minister that he can't have any more people here. This house isn't designed for guests, it's a museum. I'm sorry but they must go away, they can find a hotel, or a guest-house. The Minister must understand, we can't have no more people here.' She began sweeping the floor vigorously.

'I'm sorry, Mevrou Fritz, but you see, these aren't guests,' said Kuiker, 'These are prisoners.'

'Prisoners, guests, it's all the same to me. Where will the Minister put them? I keep trying to explain to the Minister. This house is not made for staying in. It's made for looking at. Every day at ten I open the doors and let the people in to look. They look, sign the visitors' book and leave.'

'I'll lock them in the cellar,' said Kuiker.

Kuiker took his prisoners down into the cellar, which turned out to be a warm and well-lit place built along the best Swiss lines to accommodate a family at the time of a nuclear blast and was

195

equipped with all conveniences, central heating, wash-lines, food and toilets. Kuiker producing a length of rope, ordered Blanchaille to tie Kipsel to the hot-water pipes and then did the same for Blanchaille, despite the complaints of Mevrou Fritz who pointed out, not unreasonably, that she would be extremely put off when she did her ironing by the sight of these two men trussed up like chickens, staring at her. Kuiker's response was to turn on her and bellow. His face turned purple, the veins stood out in his neck. Mevrou Fritz flung aside her broom and fled with a shriek.

Kuiker whispered rustily in Blanchaille's ear. 'Soon the house will be open to tourists. You will hear them passing overhead. Examining the relics, paying their respects to the memory of Uncle Paul. Make any attempt to get attention and you'll be dealt with. That's a promise.' And to prove it he struck Blanchaille across the face with his pistol.

They sat trussed like chickens all day. At one stage Mevrou Fritz came in and used the ironing table, complaining increasingly about their presence and of the trouble which the arrival of Gus Kuiker and Trudy Yssel had caused her. 'This is Government property. I'm here as a housekeeper, I see to it that the tourists don't break things or take things. I sell them postcards. I polish the floors. I dust the Kruger deathbed and I straighten the pictures. It is dull and lonely work, far from home and the last thing I expect is to have to share my extremely cramped quarters with a jumped-up little hussy who's too big for her boots and a Government minister on the run who spends most of the day drinking. And now I have prisoners in the cellar.'

Blanchaille and Kipsel were not fed. They were released from their chairs only to go to the lavatory and then only under Gus Kuiker's gun.

Later that night Trudy Yssel lay in bed. Down the corridor from the small spare bedroom they could hear the continual low grumblings of Mevrou Fritz now relegated to this little corner of the house, as if, she said, she were a bloody servant, or a skivvy.

Minister Gus Kuiker poured whisky into a tooth glass. Trudy Yssel looked at him. It was hard to believe that this unshaven drunk was the Minister confidently tipped to succeed President Bubé. But then she considered her own position. Despite the attempt to maintain appearances, the carefully groomed nails, the chiffon négligé, the impeccable hair, it was hard to believe that she was the Secretary of the Department of Communications.

'What do you recommend, Trudy?'

Trudy looked at him pityingly. 'Why ask me? You brought them in here. Now you deal with them. Why couldn't you have left them in the garden? Then they would have come in at the official time, with all the other tourists, looked around and left. None the wiser.'

'Maybe they're spies,' said Kuiker. 'Maybe the Regime sent them to find us.'

'Well, that doesn't matter now – does it? You've found them. They know who we are. Worse still, they know *where* we are. What's to be done?'

'Get rid of them, I suppose,' said Kuiker.

The blood had dried on Blanchaille's face and on the ropes that strapped him in. He blamed himself for not anticipating something like this. Kipsel was hard put to find anything to say that would cheer him up. When Kuiker arrived the general mood of gloom darkened still further. He pulled up a chair and sat opposite them, he swung his pistol around the finger guard in a manner so casual Kipsel would not have expected it in a police trainee. He was very drunk. His midnight blue dressing gown was monogrammed with a great *G* gulping down a smaller *K*. The stubble on his chin was longer and tinged with grey. His feet were bare and the pyjama trousers which protruded beyond his dressing-gown creased and rather grubby around the unhealthy whiteness of his ankles.

'Why are you here? Who sent you?' Kuiker demanded.

Blanchaille ignored him.

'If we'd known you were holed up here we'd never have come,' said Kipsel. 'Come to that – what are you doing here? The papers said you were in Philadelphia.'

'We were betrayed in Philadelphia. That black shit Looksmart dropped us in it. He and that oily priest bastard brother of his got together and destroyed us in America. Years of work wiped out in a few minutes. Our plans broadcast all over the bloody country. Now, at home, they've turned on us. We heard today that there are warrants out for our arrest, it seems that the Regime, desperate to find somebody to blame has settled on us. It is we, it seems, who have been rifling the treasury, absconding with public funds, hiring executive jets and wining and dining our way around the world, all for our own selfish ends. They are saying that we went abroad once too often and were seduced by foreign ways and luxuries. But they, *they* stayed at home, they are the only ones who remained pure. They will preserve racial amity, only they can withstand the Total Onslaught, they have never been corrupted. They are no longer pretending that we are in Philadelphia, they have officially an-

nounced that we are on the run and what's more the bastards have
taken credit for making the announcement, for setting up an enquiry
into the misuse of public funds, for the dismantling of the
Department of Communications, they have resurrected the dead
official, Ferreira, they have announced that this good and faithful
official discovered the beginnings of this rotten business, as if small
peculiarities in the movements of Government funds which we
handled are worth twopence compared to the much larger, one
could say total, distortion and perversion of reality the Regime has
organised against us.'

'Do you know who killed Ferreira?'

'Who? You mean *what*! What killed Ferreira? I'll tell you what
killed Ferreira. Curiosity killed Ferreira, and ignorance and the
refusal to operate within the parameters of the practical. The mind
of an accountant. The insistence on perfection, his own perfection.
The stubborn desire to go by the book. His book. *His* books! The
refusal to recognise that we were just proper people doing what we
could to change things for the better, to win our country a place
again in the world. To fight. And we had to fight because we were at
war, see. And you can't behave like you're in a monastery garden
when you're at war with the rest of the world. But ignorance and
pig-headed fucking stubborness chiefly – that's what killed Ferreira.
He wouldn't listen, he wouldn't learn, he wouldn't adapt. So he
died.'

The Minister lurched forward waving his revolver and perhaps in
his rage might have killed the prisoners had not Mevrou Fritz
bustled in at that moment with a fresh pile of ironing and
complained that the prisoners were beginning to smell.

'They'll stink a lot more when they're dead,' said Kuiker.

Kipsel kept perfectly calm. 'This place as such is of no importance
to us, it's a shell, a ghost house. We only came here because it's the
start of our mission. We're not fighting the war against you. We're
looking for the other Kruger House, we're retiring.'

Kuiker made a sound, somewhere between a belch and a laugh.
'There is no safe house, no garden of refuge, no asylum, no home
for the likes of you – or me. And shall I tell you how I know? For one
very good reason. If there were such a place you can be damn sure I
would have found it by now.' He swayed and almost fell, ran a hand
through his hair, pounded himself several times on the chest and
hawking phlegm turned abruptly on his heel they heard him
clumping upstairs.

That night when Kuiker got into bed he said, 'There's no

persuading them. They're mad. I tried to explain this is the end of the road. This is where we turn and fight. But they seriously believe in some promised land. We'll have to finish with them.'

'Let me try,' said Trudy Yssel.

Early next morning she fetched the prisoners from the cellar. Blanchaille and Kipsel were unshaven and smelt badly and after days without food they were weak on their feet. But Trudy smiled at them as if she were taking them on a picnic. Before the first visitors arrived at Uncle Paul's House she wanted to take them on a little tour, she said. She wore a spotted blue dress with pearl ear-rings and was unnaturally cheerful, relaxed and chatted to them as if she might have been any houseproud wife showing off her establishment and not the mistress of a hunted Government minister with a price on his head and she the disgraced and vilified civil servant accused of spiriting away thousands upon thousands of public money.

'Don't you think, Father Blanchaille, that the tour is nowadays the chief way we now have of communicating information to busy people? We have a tour of the game reserve to learn about animals. We tour the townships to show our black people living in peace. We tour the operational areas of our border wars to discover how well we are doing. Talking of war, do you know I have toured forward areas where it felt as if the war had been turned off for the day, like a tap, or a radio broadcast, or a light. You expected when you got back to your tent at night to find a small note on your pillow saying –"The conflict has been suspended during your visit by the kind agreement of the forces concerned", but of course you knew that wasn't so when you heard of American senators caught in the bombing raid, or a group of nuns from one of the aid organisations like "Catholics Against Cuba", had been ripped to pieces by shrapnel. Follow me, gentlemen. Don't hang back.'

The place was kept spotless, a gleaming polished purity, it seemed to them that Mevrou Fritz must have caught the Swiss passion for cleanliness. It smelt of elbow grease, it smelt of floor wax. It was heavy, dark, depressing and virtually empty. Their footsteps echoed on the smooth boards. 'Of course none of the furniture remained when the old man died. It was sold off. The house now comes under the Department of Works and they've replaced what they can with copies, or pieces of the period. But it's still pretty bad. A bit of a tomb really. When the old man died his body was taken back to South Africa, again on a Dutch warship, and given a hero's burial. That was the end of his association with Switzerland. There was no money left here, the furniture was sold off, the house given up and any talk of the missing millions was simply a myth. And it remained, as General Smuts said, merely something "to spook the minds of great British statesmen". The time has come to stop talking of these dreams. We must wake up. We've been woken up, the Minister and I. We're considering our position. When we're ready we will move.'

'I think you're on the run,' said Blanchaille.

'You're in hiding,' said Kipsel. 'We read the papers.'

'Bullshit,' said Trudy pleasantly. 'This house is Government property. As Government people we're entitled to stay here.'

'You said you were getting ready. For what?' Blanchaille asked.

'Our President is expected shortly. Once he arrives we'll be in a position to put certain thoughts to our Government at home. We plan to hold talks with our Government.'

'What makes you think they'll talk to you?'

She smiled again. 'We would rather talk to them than to the world press.'

'Blackmail,' said Blanchaille.

'We won't be blamed for having done our duty. When we've cleared our name we shall return in triumph.'

'And until then?' Kipsel asked.

'We will wait here. In the Kruger House. You believe in the sad story of a rest home for the refugees the Old President set up. You should be the first to understand the use we put this place to. Uncle Paul would have understood.'

'You don't understand what has happened back home,' Kipsel said. 'They've dispensed with you. When Ferreira found the figures, publicised them and died, he blew the matter wide open. The Regime stepped away from its anointed Minister and his favourite. First they covered for you. But now they're joining the crowds calling for your blood. You should be going where we're going.'

'There is no place where you're going,' said Trudy. She led them into a small bedroom. 'This is Uncle Paul's death room. Here is the actual death bed. Well no, not the actual death bed, but a replica.'

They saw the dark wood of the bedstead. The sturdy head board, the starkly simple bulk of the bed with its white linen counterpane. On a small bedside table stood a vase of pink carnations. Thick green drapes in the window and fuzzy white net curtains strained the sunlight to a weak, pallid wash. A huge old-fashioned radiator stood in the corner and a large carved chair stood very prominently by the bedside. The seat and back of the chair were decorated in bold floral patterns and surmounted by crossed muzzle-loaders. This was a recurring emblem throughout the house, the Boerish equivalent of the fleur-de-lis. Other popular symbols about the house were powder horns, ox wagons and lions. Lions had always been associated with Uncle Paul. Hadn't he wrestled one to death before his thirteenth birthday? Or outrun one? And had he not been known as the Lion of the North? Or was it of the South? Blanchaille couldn't remember. All presidents had been identified with larger powerful beasts, or weapons. President Bubé had been known as Buffalo, or more colloquially as 'Buffels Bubé', while the young and thrusting Wim Vollenhoven, 'Bomber' Jan Vollenhoven as they called him, the Vice-President, continued the old tradition.

Trudy sat on the bed. Blanchaille was struck by the ease with which she committed this sacrilege. Here indeed was one of the new people. He pushed open the french windows and stepped on to the veranda where the flag gave its leathery rattle.

'Our belief, our brief, our mission was straightforward. In this matter of putting across our country's position we should attack. Fuck sitting on our arses any longer. Get out there and sell the bastards our bag of goodies. Don't try and win through to the big men overseas, spot the young ones in advance, pick them when they begin to come up the tree, and gamble. Don't expect the foreign newspapers to print nice stories about you, the only reason they like producing stories about you is because you're so horrible. So don't wait for them to tell your story, buy a space and tell it yourself. If possible buy the fucking newspaper, radio station, investors' bulletin, whatever. If that won't do then buy the owners lunch, dinner, drinks as often as possible, have them around to your place for confidential chats. If governments are against you, fly their MPs over, show them the game reserves, the war zones, the beer halls, peace in the townships. Play golf with them. Did you know we were the ones who got Bubé to play golf with the newspaper owners? We made him take lessons, even though he moaned like hell at the time. Well, today, they're saying back home that we stole the money for the golf clubs. They say it was Government money. Well of course it was bloody Government money! Where else would it come from? And what's more the Government knew it was Government money, because that was the deal. I said to them, I spoke to half the damn cabinet, that half of it which matters: Kuiker, the President himself, Vollenhoven and of course General Greaterman, the

Defence Minister. I said to them, look, I want permission to go ahead on a propaganda offensive. O.K. they said. Wait, I said, till I finish. It's going to cost a bomb. If I need to send an editor away with his mistress to Madeira, then I'll do it. If I have to bribe a newspaper editor, then I need the funds immediately. No questions asked. If I need to hire an executive jet to fly a party of journalists into the country via Caracas or Palm Springs or anywhere else on the globe, then I want the wherewithal to do it – without anybody raising an eyebrow. Bubé was there and he wanted to know how much this campaign would cost. I gave it to him straight. Millions, I said. He took it on the chin. I should start as soon as possible and the funds would be forthcoming. So I went ahead, and I stress this, with full official backing. And I've done so from that day to this. They all knew. President Bubé knew. Vollenhoven knew. Greaterman knew. And approved. The money was raised from various departments so as not to cause too great a dent in individual budgets. So much from Defence, so much from Security, so much from Tourism, everybody had to cough up their share and the money was then transferred to Switzerland and passed through various Swiss banks. And let me here say a word for the Swiss banks which have been bloody unfairly slandered. We have a great debt of gratitude to the Swiss banks. They have raised loans for us when nobody else would and we were damned hard up for foreign capital. They've safeguarded difficult deposits, overseen delicate payments and observed the strictest confidentiality in sensitive matters such as the volume of gold sales. To suggest that we bribe certain Swiss banks to hold secret funds is a gross lie. And a nonsense. They did it for nothing. Well, for a small holding percentage. And even there we get a discount from them. No, I won't hear a word said against the Swiss banks. Where would South Africa be today without them?'

'Why were you denounced then? Why have you made a run for it? Why are you hiding out here?' Kipsel demanded, scratching blearily at the thick stubble on his jaw, and shivering slightly in the early morning damp rising from the lake.

'We were fingered by the Regime! They were frightened to own up to a mission they had sanctioned. They wanted scapegoats.'

'And the story about the missing money, the Swiss accounts, the house in Capri, the apartment on the Italian Riviera?'

'The houses were part of the job, safe houses for our people, reception centres for new recruits, entertainment bases for important visiting VIPs who didn't want the world to know that they were spending the weekend with South Africans. The houses were used in the course of operations, they weren't holiday cottages, you know. As for the money we're supposed to hold – what money?'

Blanchaille looked out across the big green lawn to the lake. It was on this balcony the old man had sat, the Bible open on his knees, peering blearily across the water at the big blue mountains on the other side. The locals had paused, he knew, as they passed by and pointed up at the famous old exile, Uncle Paul on his balcony. The lake lapped at the bottom of the garden. The gulls made their skidding contact with the water, claws angled for the landing as if not knowing for certain where they were putting down until they had actually landed, distrustful of the medium. The old man had sat on his chair, solid as the mountains, deep as the lake. Perhaps he had seen and admired this tireless energy of the gulls, this compulsion to take off and land, but that energy always tempered by caution, their wildness calmed into life-preserving habit. Away to the right was the town of Montreux, it crowded down to the water's edge along a gentle crammed curve of densely packed buildings on the shore, pretending to be a small Mediterranean port. But here was no sea, this was still water, a great placid lake lying in the bowl of the mountains. Those mountains in the distance, the big blue ones across the water that he knew were in France, if one screwed up one's eyes and gazed blindly until they began to water, they were vaguely reminiscent of mountains in the Cape Peninsula. But of course the old refugee and his rented accommodation wouldn't have known the Cape mountains either, he'd seldom been out of the Transvaal veld until, that is, he began his great last journey into exile.

The flag-pole on the balcony was slanted at an angle of forty-five degrees and from it hung the familiar blue and white and orange colours. Very carefully Blanchaille lowered the flag to half-mast.

'Any more questions?' Trudy asked jumping up and smoothing the white coverlet on the death bed. 'Oh yes, I know – you're dying to ask me if I'm Gus Kuiker's mistress. So, then – do I sleep with Gus Kuiker?'

'No,' Kipsel protested weakly, 'we were not going to ask you that.'

'But I insist. Sleeping with Gus Kuiker means that once or twice a week he gets into bed beside me. I lie on my back and spread my legs. He puts a cushion under my backside because, he says, he doesn't get proper penetration otherwise, and then he pushes himself into me with some difficulty and moves up and down very fast because he gets penis wilt, you see. He can get it up but he can't keep it up. You can rub him, suck him, oil him. It doesn't help. While he's going he's O.K. The moment he stops, it drops. So about

203

two minutes later, that's it. Overs cadovers. So much for sleeping with Gus Kuiker. He's also heavier now, sadder, he drinks almost all the time and he seldom shaves. But, as you say, we do indeed sleep together. Though I hope next time you use the phrase you will think hard about its implications.'

Back in the cellar Blanchaille was gloomier than ever. 'What if I'm wrong and the Kruger story ends with this house?'

'It doesn't.'

'But say it did.'

'No, dammit. I won't say it did! You know the story as well as I. This is just another stage on the journey which began in Pretoria, went on to Delagoa Bay, touched Europe and Marseilles, and then moved on to Tarascon, Avignon, Valence, Lyons, Mâcon and Dijon to Paris, as Uncle Paul travelled Europe to win support for the Boer cause. He pressed on to Charleroi, Namur and Liège, he called at Aachen and Cologne and Düsseldorf, Duisburg and Emmerich, and then he went on to Holland, stopping at over half a dozen cities before pitching up at the Hague. December 1901 saw him in Utrecht, nearly blind, 1902 he was in Menton for the warmth. He was in Hilversum in the following year and then back to Menton for the sun. Only in 1904 did he come here to Clarens, to this house which he did not buy, but rented from a M. Pierre Pirrot – some doubt has been cast on the existence of this man – notice the similarity between his name and the French pantomime character with the white face, Pierrot. The picture we have of the solidity of this house, of his living here in exile, of the near-blind old man in his last days looking out across Lake Geneva to the mountains, it all sounds like a drama, doesn't it? Or a tragedy? And it suits the people to give the legend weight and durability, to make it solid and believable. The bourgeois respectability of this house aids that delusion. But it's not a drama, or a tragedy. It's a pantomime! Everybody's dressed up, everyone's pretending. For instance, he wasn't here alone, Uncle Paul. His family was with him, his valet, his doctor, countless visitors called. And he was by no means finished either. He had his plans. The last act of the pantomime was not yet played out. And he had to hurry. He came here in mid-May of 1904 and by the end of July he was dead. But in those short months he was busy, sick as he was, planning a place for those whom he knew would come after. He knew that many of his people would collaborate with the enemy. But he also knew that some would hold out, escape, and would have to be accommodated. He wanted a place, an ark that should be made ready to receive the pure

204

remnants of the *volk*.'

But a black passion had seized the ex-priest and he said stubbornly. 'Yes, but what if there is no such place?'

'Then,' said Kipsel, 'all I can do is to quote to you again the mad old Irish priest who knew a thing or two – if a last colony, home, hospice, refuge for white South Africans does not exist, then it will be necessary to start one.'

That night Trudy lay beneath Kuiker who was hissing and bubbling like a percolator and had his tongue clenched beneath his teeth in a frenzy of concentration as he entered her, trying to ensure that his erection lasted through the entry phase.

'I think,' said Trudy, 'that you are going to have to get rid of our guests.'

Kuiker did not reply. He had begun moving well and did not want to break his intense effort to remain upright and operational. Instead he shook his head, not to indicate his refusal, but to show her it was not the time to talk of these things.

'Now,' said Trudy, cruelly tightening her exceptional vaginal muscles.

Kuiker shrank, he fell out of her, he sat back on his haunches and said, 'Damn! That's lost it.'

'We can't hold them much longer, Augustus. Something is going to have to be done. They claim they don't care about us. They say they're above all this. But they might just give us away.'

But he was not interested. He considered his failed member. The brandy he had drunk had befuddled him and was making him very sleepy. He reckoned he had at least one chance to make it inside Trudy that night and he was going for it. Such determination, such single-mindedness had been the mark of his political success in the days when he was tipped as the next prime minister. Desperately he seized his penis and began rubbing it firmly. It stiffened perceptibly. There was no time to lose. With a grunt he pushed her back on the pillows, thrust his hands under her buttocks and rammed himself home.

'First thing in the morning,' he promised. 'Crack of dawn, I'll finish them.'

Downstairs in the cellar Kipsel was in a bad way. Trudy's knots cut so deeply into his wrists that the circulation had gone and try as he might to loosen the cord he only succeeded in cutting more deeply into the flesh and making his wrists bleed. He'd not been able to contain his bladder either and a pool of urine spread beneath the chair.

It was then that Blanchaille had a brainwave.

'Ronnie,' he said suddenly, jerking upright in his chair, 'Jesus what an idiot I am! I've been sitting here for days putting up with this crap and all the time I had a way out of here.'

Kipsel licked his lips weakly. 'Good. Only hurry, Blanchie.'

Sometime later Mevrou Fritz arrived with a pile of ironing. She grimaced at the sight of the urine and wrinkled her nose.

'Mevrou Fritz,' said Blanchille, 'do you get well paid?'

'Are you joking?' the concierge demanded. 'I work for the Department of Works, that's who this house comes under, through the Embassy in Berne, that's who I work for. I thought I told you. Do I get well paid? Bus drivers get better paid! Then there's my accommodation here, for free, so they dock the salary accordingly. Why?'

'What would you say if we disappeared?'

Her grey eyes stared into his unblinkingly. 'Hooray. That's two less to worry about, I'd say. This house isn't meant for people, you see. Not living people. At the moment I've got the attic full of guests, and you men in my cellar.'

'I think we can help you on both counts,' said Blanchaille.

A few minutes later they were on their feet and Mevrou Fritz was stroking the necklace threaded with Krugerrands with which Blanchaille had been presented in the Airport Palace Hotel by the beautiful Babybel – a key she had said which he would know how to use when the time came.

Mevrou Fritz took them to the front door but to the old woman's horror they would not go until they signed the visitors' book. Trembling she took them to the book and begged them to hurry before the big boss upstairs, as she called him, woke up and shot them all.

Very carefully, Kipsel wrote this message in the book: TO THOSE WHO COME AFTER US – BEWARE! THIS IS NOT THE HOLY PLACE YOU THINK. THIS IS THE HIDE-OUT OF ESCAPED MINISTER GUS KUIKER AND TRUDY YSSEL. THEY ARE LIVING RIGHT ABOVE YOUR HEADS. TELL OUR EMBASSY IN BERNE. YOU WILL BE RE-WARDED.

Blanchaille wrote simply: WHERE ARE THE KRUGER MILLIONS?

And then to Mevrou Fritz's intense relief the two fugitives slipped into the night.

CHAPTER 20

Now I saw in my dream how the travellers wandered the lakeside in the manner of those wild tribes who are said once to have populated the shores of Lake Geneva in Neolithic times. They looked, it must be said, no less savage being red-eyed from lack of sleep, tousled, dirty and smelling to high heaven.

It was fine weather all that day with the sky high and blue, full of rapidly scudding thick woollen clouds, and the shining freshness of the prospect increased the feelings of relief and freedom which Blanchaille and Kipsel enjoyed as they made their way along the lakeside towards the town of Montreux. Kipsel wanted to stop at an hotel to wash and eat a meal but Blanchaille allowed only a brief pause by the water's edge where they splashed themselves, dunked their faces, ran their fingers through their hair and Kipsel at last got rid of the strong ammoniac smell of the dried urine that clung to him. Blanchaille removed his underpants and threw them into the rubbish bin. This was after all Switzerland and the trim sparkle of the countryside insisted on respect. Nothing could persuade Kipsel to do likewise. 'I simply cannot walk about without underpants, it gives me the oddest, most uncomfortable sensation. Sorry, Blanchie, I know I pong a bit. Where to now?'

'Up into the mountains, above the town. Remember the readings from Kruger's book old Lynch gave us so often? Remember the story?'

And Blanchaille quoted exactly as he could remember, the passage from *Further Memoirs of a Boer President*:

'Travellers approaching their journey's end will find themselves as it were between heaven and heaven, one as deep as the other is high. They will think themselves close to Paradise, and they will be as close to it as faithful servants are permitted on this earth, for the country answers to the heavenly ideal in these several instances; to wit, it possesses elevation; it is a republic; it respects and honours the memory of John Calvin; and, not least, honesty prevailing over modesty requires the recognition that it has taken to its bosom this servant of his broken, scattered people, Stephanus Johannes Paulus

Kruger. That it is not the divine country itself but its reflection will be apparent to those who walk in its mountains and still lose their way. But help is at hand for those who seek their true homeland. Scouts will be posted by the camp kommandant as I did always when establishing a concealed *laager*, or Boer strong-point . . .'

'Between heaven and heaven, the book said,' Blanchaille pointed to the deep blue lake on their right and the bright sky above. 'I'm sure that's what he meant.'

'Scouts will be posted, I remember that.'

'Well, then, shall we start climbing? They'll be expecting us.'

'Bloody well hope so. You could wander in these mountains forever without a guide.'

Blanchaille surveyed the great blue lake, smooth as a dance floor. He saw the flat brown pebbles neatly packed beneath the clear surface, the brown ducks daintily dunking their heads, the roving sea-gulls, the sailing swans. At his feet miniature waves slapped tidily against the rocks. A few palms stood by the lake. Palms in this place! It cheered him faintly. Some sleek crows scavenged an old sweet packet and a sparrow carefully shadowed a gull and ate what it dropped. A duck dived and showed its purplish under-feathers, two swans pecked at each other viciously. The water of the lake began with pebbles and clarity at his feet and turned grey-blue under a gentle rippling surface and then still further out showed itself in pure grey slicks bounded by great shadows, flat and full it stretched into the mist of the further shore line where blue mountains reared; if he half closed his eyes they reminded him eerily of Africa. But this wasn't Africa: Africa was dead and gone for him. He was here now, and here he must keep his feet firmly planted. At his feet there floated a split cork from a wine bottle, several shredded tissues, a fragment of the *Herald Tribune*, a Pepsi-Cola can, several orange peels swimming in a bright school, wisps of swansdown, an old pencil, the filters of many cigarettes, and all the few small signs of life washed in by the tiny waves which arrived with gentle decorum. The lakeside was broken up by stone jetties and small coves and he noticed how cunningly the trees and shrubs had been introduced among the rocks: saw the ivy which crawled down to the waterside, the huge willow flanked by palms, those shrubs planted in pots and cunningly blended among the rocks, saw everything was arranged, everything cemented into place. The apparently haphazard grouping of rocks into natural stone piers and causeways was an illusion, he saw that they were actually propped with wooden stakes and iron bars beneath the surface. He could see the steel cables that held these structures in place. Everything was at once so natural and so skilfully arranged. Here was a country which lent itself to such paradoxes. Here, you felt, everything was allowed providing it could be properly arranged. A family, mother, father and two sons in a red paddle boat, with knees going like pistons, floated by. They waved. It was time to be getting on.

In Montreux they paused at a camping shop to buy two knapsacks which they filled with chocolate, bread and milk and a couple of bottles of cherry brandy – they also bought two stout walking-sticks, walking-boots and then struck into the mountains.

Here in this corner of French Switzerland they admired the clipped serenity of the countryside, its villages, vineyards, hotels and castles. They noted how well all things were accommodated, the way in which the country entered towns and villages in the form of carefully mown lawns and artful gardens, while the towns tiptoed into the countryside never disturbing the settled neatness. Here everything was made to fit but given the semblance of casualness. They passed orchards of heavily laden apple trees and burgeoning vineyards and had no qualms about raiding the fields of fruit, snatching apples and bunches of grapes as they went.

The road above the town of Montreux climbs steeply and soon leaves vineyards and orchards behind. The day was hot. They were soon pouring with sweat. The lake was now a long way below.

It was here, in the late afternoon, that they were met by four men wearing walking-boots, short leather trousers, thick red woollen socks and walking-sticks decorated with brightly coloured tin badges showing the coats of arms of all the cantons thereabouts.

The men said they were shepherds.

Kipsel rejected this and in fierce whispers told Blanchaille why: 'One, they don't have any sheep; two, they're carrying sticks and not crooks; three, this is cow country, you don't get sheep here; and four, they're countrymen of ours, right? Well, you don't get South African shepherds. I vote we be careful.'

Blanchaille secretly agreed. Something in the manner of these men reminded him of the policemen in their shiny orange mackintoshes who had stopped him on the road to the Airport Palace Hotel. Yes, he was fairly sure of it, their heavy and rather aggressive manner suggested representatives of the Force. Or at least ex-policemen, who were now going straight. But he confided none of this to Kipsel.

'Scouts have been posted,' he reminded his friend of the clues in the Kruger book. 'We can but hope.'

By way of breaking ice Blanchaille told the shepherds that they had helped themselves freely to grapes and apples and water from the streams along the route and he hoped that there was no objection. The shepherds replied that walkers had been coming this way for so many years and that some of them wandered for so long among the mountains that the owner of the big house to which they were bound, this was delicately put, had an understanding with the neighbouring farmers under which any of his people who came that way were free to help themselves from orchards and vineyards, in moderation of course, and providing no damage was done or camp fires lit, since the Swiss were a particular race and, like farmers everywhere, took a dim view of strangers tramping on their land. However, the procedure had worked well enough for many years and just as well for there were travellers who had come from great distances and who were tired and hungry and parched, not to say absolutely bushed and clapped out, by the time they got this far. And besides, the altitude got to one, if one was not used to it.

'Is this the road then to the big house?' Kipsel asked.

'Keep straight on,' came the answer. 'You can't miss it, set high on a hill in the last fold of this range of mountains, you'll know it when you see it.'

'How much further?' Blanchaille asked.

Here the shepherds were less forthcoming. 'Too far for some,' they said. 'Not everyone makes it. There are accidents.'

'What sort of accidents?'

'Climbing accidents. Heat-exhaustion in the summer. Cases of exposure in the winter,' said the shepherds. 'People arriving from Africa often underestimate the ferocity of the winter.'

Now I saw in my dream that the shepherds questioned them closely, asking exactly how they found this route, and how they'd come so far without maps, directions or luggage. But when they heard of Father Lynch, of the death of Ferreira, of the betrayal of Magdalena, they smiled and said, 'Welcome to Switzerland.'

The shepherds had fierce, flushed jaws, hard, cold eyes like washed river stones, hair blond and thick, necks thick too, and muscles everywhere. Their names were Arlow, Hattingh, Swanepoel and Dekker and they took the travellers to one of the travellers' huts which the thoughtful Swiss provide in the high mountains for those who need them. This they found well stocked with tinned food, a paraffin stove, blankets, bunks and all necessities, and here after a meal the travellers went to bed because it was

210

very late.

In the morning they rose and breakfasted on beans and bacon and although they had no razors and could not shave, there was running water so they enjoyed the wonderful luxury of a good wash. They breathed the clear mountain air and wondered at the fierce gleam of the rising sun on the snowy peaks of the distant Alps.

A little later the shepherds arrived and, taking Blanchaille and Kipsel back inside the hut, they drew the curtain and showed them slides on a small portable projector. 'We would just like to clear up a few points which may have been puzzling you boys,' they said. The first slide showed battle casualties fallen on some African battle-ground. The troops appeared to have been caught in some terrible bombardment, artillery perhaps or an air strike because they were hideously wounded, limbs had been torn away and there were many soldiers without heads. The soldiers, they noticed, were young, no more than boys.

Then Blanchaille said: 'What does this mean?'

And the so-called shepherds, who by this time had produced flasks of coffee and kirsch and were drinking heavily, replied: 'These are innocent boys who were called up to fight for their country and for Christian National civilisation and for the Regime and for God and for the right of all people of different races to be entitled to separate toilet facilities, which is the custom of that country, as well as for every family's rights to a second garden boy and for the freedom to swim from segregated beaches, and who now lie where they have fallen in the veld because on the day on which these pictures were taken the troops suffered a reverse and were forced to retire owing to the perfidy of the Americans who having persuaded the Regime to launch an invasion of an adjacent country then left them in the lurch and so these children lie here in the sun. What you see here is the death of a nation. Civilisations have died of old age, of decadence, of boredom, of neglect, but what you are seeing, for the first time, is a nation going to the wall for its belief in the sanctity of separate lavatories.'

'It is a tragedy,' Blanchaille said.

The shepherds nodded. 'And a farce,' they said.

Further slides showed the Kruger lakeside villa at Clarens they had so recently vacated. And the shepherds said, 'We wanted you to see crowds of deluded pilgrims visiting what they're told is Uncle Paul's last refuge abroad, though it was nothing more really than a stage prop. At the heart of their delusion is the belief that the

211

Regime is the true heir of Uncle Paul and will preserve the white man's place in Southern Africa forever. Whereas the poor sods are no more than tourists and the site they visit may be compared to an abandoned stage, or the deserted set of some old movie and the Regime of course is busy selling out everything and everyone in the service of the only reality it recognises, survival.'

In the pictures parties of the faithful arrived in coaches, flocking into the house with looks of awe and reverence. They wept when they saw the ugly bust of old Uncle Paul, they wept when they saw the death bed, they wept at the President's last message to his people, set in stained glass, encouraging them to look to the past, they admired the view from the balcony where the old man had sat, and they wrote of their feelings in the visitors' book. Examples of their messages were also shown in a variety of different colours of inks and hands: *Uncle Paul your dream is alive and well in South Africa*; *We will never surrender!*; *The Boer War goes on!* There were angry threats: *Kill the Rooineks* and *God Give Us More Machine Guns* and *We Will Die on the Beaches*; as well as more frivolous slogans such as *Vrystaat!* and *Koos Loves Sannie* . . .

At this point in the proceedings the shepherds, having become rather drunk on the large quantities of kirsch consumed during the slide show, withdrew to relieve themselves at a discreet distance from the hut and Blanchaille and Kipsel met each other's eyes and blushed to think that even they, who should have known better, had been unable to resist a visit to this empty shell of a house and had paid dearly for their foolishness by spending days under the whip of Gus Kuiker and his paramour.

Kipsel, perhaps to deflect attention from that humiliating episode, again expressed his suspicion of the so-called shepherds. And despite Blanchaille's attempts to dissuade him he met the four men on their return with these words:

'I don't believe you're shepherds at all. I've got a feeling for these things and I think you're policemen.'

And Swanepoel replied: 'If you're talking about what we were, you may have a point. But if we were all judged by what used to be then who would not be damned? Weren't you Kipsel the Traitor, once? The only thing that matters is what we are now.'

'And we're shepherds now,' said Dekker.

'Oh yes?' exlaimed Kipsel. 'In that case where are your sheep?'

'You are our sheep,' came the reply.

Blanchaille stepped in to prevent further embarrassment and told the shepherds that they were eager to continue their journey. Then

212

the shepherd Arlow said to the shepherd Hattingh, 'Look, since these guys are on the right road wouldn't it be an idea to give them an indication of their destination?' And Hattingh agreed, so they stopped at a typical mountain hostelry, perched on a promontory and called the Berghaus Grappe d'Or with a wonderful view of the mountains, where there was a telescope, as is the custom in such places. And here, after the insertion of one franc, they were invited to 'lay an eye against the glass'.

What they saw differed considerably. Blanchaille said he could see what he thought was a big house surrounded by a wall and it reminded him of a hospital, or perhaps a school. Kipsel said he could see no wall at all, but he made out a gate, a garden and many tall trees and a tall building 'like a skinny palace'. Then their time ran out.

Would the shepherds give them more precise directions?

'Keep on the way you're going and you can't miss it,' said Arlow.

'Look out for Gabriel,' Swanepoel advised.

'Our Gabriel?' Blanchaille was astonished.

'Ain't no bloody angel, that's for sure,' said Hattingh.

And the shepherd Dekker said nothing at all, just laid a finger alongside his nose, and winked.

CHAPTER 21

On that hot, never-ending Sunday beneath the Tree of Heaven, among the wreckage of Father Lynch's church, while the baleful yellow earth-moving machines baked in the heat, I slept again and dreamed of the two travellers, gipsy spirits one would have liked to have said, carefree, happy voyagers – except that they looked in fact like two increasingly tired, dirty, bearded and hungry men (a two-legged pear and his lightly furred friend), trudging through the Swiss mountains towards they knew not what – some great house or palace, or castle, château, hotel, hospital which they had glimpsed, or thought they had glimpsed through the telescope of Berghaus Grappe d'Or; some retirement home, or refuge, or whatever it is where white South Africans must one day fetch up, if they are to fetch up anywhere. What is the old joke? When good South Africans die they go to the big location in the sky. When bad South Africans die they go into government.

I saw how, as the climb grew steeper, the road winds back on itself to lessen the upward slog and gives a clear view behind and below. It was then that they saw another traveller straggling behind them in a queer sideways crab-like shuffle. Imagine their astonishment as he drew closer and they recognised Looksmart Dladla, last heard of in exile in Philadelphia.

Their old friend was smartly turned out in a dark blue suit and shining black shoes, quite unsuitable for the rough road he followed and he stopped every so often and knocked his forehead with his fist as if it were a door and he wished to be let in, or at least attract the attention of whoever was inside. He gave no sign of surprise, or of recognition, but Kipsel, all his old fears and guilt returning, had become terrified and had quite unashamedly hidden behind Blanchaille.

'Looksmart! What, you here? Hello, it's me, Blanchie!'

The black man peered. There was no surprise, no anger, not even a quickening of interest, merely a blank cursory inspection. 'I do not remember.'

'You must remember the old days.'

'Why?' Looksmart asked.

Kipsel, now bolder, stepped forward: 'Well, you remember me.'

Looksmart stared at him. Perhaps his eyes narrowed fractionally. But then his head was continually cocked to one side and he appeared to suffer from a facial tic.

Blanchaille seized his hand. 'For God's sake, Looksmart – it's Blanchie. How are you? I thought you were in Philadelphia.'

There was a slow nod of the head. 'Yes. I was in Philadelphia.' He spoke very slowly, as if searching for the words, rounding them up like wild ponies from the canyons inside his head. He spoke thickly, clumsily, with little whistles and splutters. It seemed there was something vaguely familiar about the two men who had stopped him, especially the one with the fish face, the thick lips and the agitated manner. He hadn't time now. He took a red handkerchief from his breast pocket, bent and polished his black shoes. Then he straightened. 'Goodbye,' he said. 'People are waiting for my news.'

What happened to Looksmart before and after his flight to America has been the stuff of wild rumour, legend and conflicting stories. But it was given to me in my dream to see the truth.

Looksmart escaped to New York on a ticket acquired by his brother Gabriel (as was his passport, US visa, and a pocket full of money), a step ahead of the police and unbeknown to himself, in the company of the famous Piatikus Lenski, the defence lawyer. This flight was ever afterwards regarded as having been *planned*. People marvelled at its audacity and gave credit for its brilliant execution to Gabriel Dladla. Gabriel Dladla, everyone agreed, was an absolute marvel. On the one hand he was a priest and so forbidden to take part in politics. On the other hand he was known to be openly sympathetic to the Azanian Liberation Front. Yet he continued a free man. In fact his political sympathies and connections, far from endangering Gabriel, increasingly won him admiration and respect. It was whispered in some quarters that if ever, and it was a big if, the Government were to attempt some form of dialogue with its sworn enemies in the Azanian Liberation Front, then Dladla might be the man to talk to, and through; there was widespread agreement that Dladla was the sort of man with whom one could 'deal'. Of course the official view was that there was absolutely no question of dialogue, or of dealing with the ALF and its murderous terrorist wing, the Azanian Strike Kommando No. 3. Even so, people felt obscurely comforted by the knowledge that if, and it was an enormous if (everybody always stressed this), the need should ever arise and the Regime should wish to talk to the Front, Gabriel was the man. The Regime were careful to discourage any such speculation. Bubé himself had given the official response, when, in the course of a particularly strident political meeting, he had responded to the repeated jibe of 'Yes – but what *if*?', with the remark that people could believe what they liked and the Regime could not stop people believing in fairy stories – but, speaking for himself, *IF* was a dangerous country which he did not visit. Everyone knew what he meant.

The famous defence lawyer, Piatikus Lenski, was equally unaware of Looksmart's presence – but the two were forever afterwards associated in the public mind. Thus do haphazard conjunctions become established as historical facts in the story of our country. Lenski had made his reputation in the trials of such notables as the saintly pacifist leader, Oscar Amandla and the martyr, Joyce Naidoo. Lenski's reputation stretched from the great show trials of the anti-pass laws demonstrators of the early years to the increasingly frequent hanging trials of black guerrillas which more and more occupied the courts as time went on. Piatikus Lenski defended his clients with passion and brilliance. He invariably lost the case but this never affected his reputation as a formidable opponent of the Regime. He was, as he himself said, if one was to judge by results, a complete failure. He never accused the judiciary of any bias. The judges, Lenski had said, were quite objective in their interpretation of the law but since the Regime was thoroughly perverted, corrupt lawgivers and objective judges made an unbeatable combination. He was a short, curly haired, vain little man with dark eyes and a high querulous voice which drove court officials to distraction and struck fear into the witnesses for the State. Nothing scared Lenski. When the prosecution scored a point he would turn to his junior and in his high, carrying tones exclaim: 'Now *that* was well done. But do we care?' He'd been terrorised by the usual methods applied to public opponents of the Regime. His house had been shot at, his children threatened, his wife abused – and he had yielded to none of it. Instead he gave an interview to the papers explaining how these efforts ensured that he would never falter in his appreciation of the lengths the Regime was prepared to go in order to get its way. Finally, Piatikus was placed under house arrest for 'associating with known terrorists and violent opponents of the State'. The Government thus found in his connection with his clients an unanswerable logical reason for banning him. And in so doing they had at last done really well, and even Lenski had to admit it, and did, by showing that yes, finally, they had made him care, for when the police arrived with the signed order of his banning at his gracious residence in the northern suburbs, Piatikus had fled.

On board the Pan Am flight to New York, Looksmart knew nothing of his illustrious travelling companion. He'd never flown before, he had got into conversation with the passengers, he was rather drunk, and the recent beating he had received had left him in a disturbed and agitated frame of mind. Besides, Lenski travelled first class, behind a beard and dark glasses, and his presence on the plane only came to light when they arrived at Kennedy Airport and the press thronged the concourse. Lenski left the airport immediately after the press conference for a secret destination in Colorado where he went to work on his memoir of the most celebrated of his deceased clients. Called *The Last Days of Oscar Amandla*, it was to become a minor classic. The American press, and through them the wider world, concluded that this eminent lawyer and the black activist must have escaped together. That was the impression Piatikus never chose to correct and Looksmart was never asked to do so. Not that it mattered for he was so incoherent with his rasping voice and the terrible roaring in his right ear since the cell beatings that he would have been unable to convince them otherwise.

Looksmart had left the country abruptly. His brother had collected him and taken him to the airport in a great big black Chrysler. Looksmart had tried to get some information: 'How –' he began.

'How did I get you the passport? These things can be done, my dear Looksmart. Of course your visa only gives you three months. You'll have to think of something else by then.'

'Yes, but how –' Looksmart tried again. His tongue sat wooden in his mouth, sluggish, thick and unable to respond to signals from his brain. 'But . . . how?' It wasn't quite what he had wanted to say, but it would have to do.

Gabriel said, 'How what? How did I do it? Please, give your brother some credit.'

'How?' asked Looksmart again.

'Forget it,' snapped Gabriel. 'Better you don't know.'

Here Looksmart wept. He didn't mean to weep but it had become an uncontrollable response after weeks of interrogation. Anyone raising their voice to him got that response from the tear ducts. There was a furnace in his right ear and a subterranean rumble which reminded him of the rockfalls on the gold mines which from time to time shook the city and set the cups complaining on the shelves and windows shivering in their panes.

He paused at the barrier at the airport and waved. Gabriel raised an encouraging thumb. Looksmart squared his shoulders and shuffled through fully expecting to be stopped and turned back but feeling in the face of Gabriel's efforts that he ought at least go through the motions, if only to please his brother.

Gabriel had this gift of making people want to please him. He had a honeyed charm, a lightness, a fleet delicate mind, he was little, gracious, winning, not at all dark but golden. There had always been this contrast with his brother ever since their days in Lynch's garden when he called them his greyhounds, his porcelain slave boys, his unlikely pages. Gabriel was deft and surefooted, Looksmart was heavy, solid mahogany, his lips pink and full as inflatables, a lump beside Gabriel's vaulting allure. Gabriel forged ahead effortlessly in the seminary towards ordination and a brilliant career while Looksmart stumbled and floundered in a bog of black theology, making passionate speeches about 'The first Kaffir Christ', and burning his Bible on the seminary steps as the white man's bank book, and thereafter departing in a kind of glory.

'My vocation,' Gabriel sweetly told friends, 'is the priesthood. Looksmart's is prison.'

Indeed it was. Looksmart proceeded there by the usual route: demonstrations, marches, plots, arrests and bannings and all the blood-warming activities which opponents of the Regime practised in the hope that somehow, someday, they might have some effect. At last grey and despondent he went underground and dreamed of bombs.

When Kipsel's bombs went off he would have been a prime suspect had he not had a cast-iron alibi. He was already in prison at the time, in the cells of the Central Police Station being beaten with a length of hosepipe by a blond young man called Captain Breek, that very same Arrie Breek who was later to become so close to wresting the world middleweight boxing crown from the American Ernie Smarf in their memorable encounter in the amazing amphitheatre hewn from solid rock in a newly independent black homeland cum casino, run by the Syrian entrepreneur Assad, before a ferocious crowd of 75,000. As Breek later told the papers, his heart had never been in his police work and this may explain why the young man with his great blond cows-lick and the open fresh looks of a serious young accountant should have so forgotten himself during the interrogation of Looksmart that he seized the prisoner's head and banged it repeatedly against the wall, a method as clumsy as it was inadvisable, since it broke the cardinal rule of police interrogation which is never to leave discernible marks on a live victim and on a dead one only such marks, bruises, lesions, or breakages as would accord with the kinds of fatal injuries the coroner could reasonably expect to find on a dead prisoner who has fallen from a high window, or down a steep flight of stairs, or has hanged himself in his cell.

This Breek was to go on to become a famous entrepreneur and promoter himself, with his own casino and his own homeland and his own international pro-am golf tournament.

Looksmart had been stretched to his limits by Captain Breek. There had been electric shocks to his testicles and when this failed, the current was passed from his nape to his coccyx to render him more pliable. Then he was taken swimming. In this procedure his head was dunked in a bucket of water for a period determined by the swimmer who could obtain release before he drowned by tapping the floor with his foot thereby indicating that he wished to talk.

His lungs burning, Looksmart tapped. Breek hauled him out. Looksmart took a few, deliberately deep breaths while Breek waited impatiently. 'I forget the question,' Looksmart confessed. It was true, although even if he could have recalled it he couldn't have answered. He did not know what Breek wanted, but then neither did the policeman. He kept demanding that Looksmart tell him all he knew. He swore that he would get at the truth. But what he wanted to know, and what he imagined the truth to be, he never made clear and Looksmart found it impossible to guess. Looksmart's tears mingled unnoticed with the water streaming from his nose and ears. Angrily Breek seized his hair and plunged his head back into the pail. Looksmart prepared to die. He would not tap. He waited for unconsciousness. He welcomed death. Deliberately he thrust his head further into the pail. His chest felt as if it were collapsing, he felt the terrible burning pressure grow. He could hear his heart firing away crazily. Just another few seconds, another few moments and he would open his mouth and suck water into his lungs. He would cheat Breek. He would die in front of his eyes. Breek realised almost too late what was going on. Furiously he yanked Looksmart's head from the pail and in his rage began banging it against the wall until Looksmart passed out.

The next day he was released, his head swathed in bandages, an eye closed, an intense burning feeling in his right ear, a deep rumbling groan deep in the eardrum together with a rather strange inertia of the tongue which simply wouldn't obey him, baulked at even easy words, no matter how he whipped it up to them, refused like a horse at a jump. He was recovering in Gabriel's house when the police came and asked about the bombings of the electricity pylons.

'He was in jail. How could he be involved?' Gabriel asked them.

The police went away.

The papers headlined the story. LUCKY LOOKSMART! 'JAIL ALIBI'.

The next day Gabriel suddenly said he must leave. He had heard that the police were coming back. That they were definitely after him even now, whether or not he had been in jail at the time of the bombing. They had other reasons for looking for him. He must skip the country.

'How do you know they won't arrest me as soon as I show them my passport?' That had been the question he had wanted to ask Gabriel. After all if the police were looking for them, then the airport officials would know and would turn him back.

But they did not. His passport was cursorily checked and he was waved through. An hour later he was airborne over the baked brown veld of Africa. This was even more puzzling still. For if the police wanted him they would have been watching the airport. Since they weren't, he had to conclude that they were not looking for him yet. Was it not a miraculous sign of Gabriel's power and prescience that he had known that the police would be looking for him before the police knew themselves? Thus Looksmart was long gone when the police issued a warrant for his arrest, citing information supplied which revealed that he had a hand in the maps showing the locations of the electrical pylons in the townships destroyed by Kipsel, Zandrotti and others.

DOUBLE BREAK FOR FREEDOM, the papers said. DLADLA – LENSKI, FLEE COUNTRY!

Now he stood on that Swiss mountainside did Looksmart Dladla, in his blue suit and black shoes and his odd mode of sideways locomotion, and his odder cranial rumblings, insanely beaming, turning on them a look Blanchaille later described as one of radiant ignorance. Had Blanchaille not seen examples of such deluded sweetness of temperament many times before during his years in the camps in old men and women who after their sufferings should have been eaten with rage and bitterness, he might have wept. Instead he turned patiently to Looksmart and asked about his time in America.

Looksmart beamed. 'In America I began as a humble student of history and rose to become president of several radio stations, a news magazine and a cable television station.'

'America is still the land of opportunity, then?' said Blanchaille politely, without the least sign of surprise at Looksmart's meteoric rise.

'Oah yes,' said Looksmart with another series of rapid smacks of the head as if to keep his word-hoard flexible. 'But it was never ambition that took me to these positions.'

'What then?' demanded Kipsel sceptically.

Again the seraphic smile. 'Patriotism. Oah yes! Without a doubt. I am part of the new order. Now I really must go. As you can see, I walk slowly. The result of an old injury. Now forgotten. And forgiven. I must give the good news.'

'What is the good news?' Blanchaille asked.

Looksmart produced a piece of paper from his suit pocket and waved it. 'We are saved. I have here a treaty signed by the President himself granting to me and my dependants a territory on the east coast of Southern Africa, in *perpetuity*.' He stressed this word with reverence.

'You're going home?' said Blanchaille. 'But, Looksmart, you're a wanted man.'

The other laughed delightedly. 'We are all wanted men. We are needed to rebuild our country again. What good does it do to hide in some mountain lair, some hospice, some institution set up on Boer charity for lonely exiles, frightened of their shadows? We must reinvent our country. Set out like Van Riebeeck in reverse to rediscover South Africa.'

'The only territory they'll give you back home is six feet deep,' said Kipsel.

Looksmart gave him a look which though no less joyous was tinged with pity and a hint of scorn. 'As his nephew wrote of the late great Benjamin Franklin, so with Looksmart, believe you me. "My resolution is unshaken, my principles fixed, even in death." ' – and he banged himself on the right ear for emphasis. 'We have been given our African Pennsylvania, in which we will found our new Philadelphia, a city of brotherly love, and from that perhaps we shall make a new Africa, a revolution like that of the Americans, a triumph of sensible, pragmatic, independent people. They did it. So will we.'

'We already have a Philadelphia,' said Kipsel. 'And plenty of Pennsylvanias. Only we call them Homelands and Bantustans, Tribal Reserves and Resettlement Camps . . . We tried it, Looksmart, and it didn't work. And we don't have any sensible people.

Never mind pragmatic ones. Looksmart, don't go back!'

'I have it in writing,' repeated Looksmart waving the paper again. 'It has been promised to me in exchange. Now you must not delay me, I am on my way to the place on the hill to convey the good news. Step aside if you will. This is the freedom route. They will cheer when they see me. "Come home with Looksmart," I will say. Permit me to give you a small memento of our meeting.' He handed them a coloured postcard showing a big brass bell with a crack in it. 'The famous Liberty Bell. I have seen it with my own eyes. Soon we will have one of our own hanging in our country.' And with a cheerful wave, the black man set off on his slow, shambling progress.

They watched him helplessly.

'Bell's not the only thing that will hang back home,' said Kipsel. 'Tell me, Blanchie, what is this new order he muttered about?'

Blanchaille remembered his meeting with Van Vuuren in Balthazar Buildings and the pathetic outcasts in the holding cells. 'The New Order is actually the old order, adapted. Under the old order they refused to compromise. Under the New Order there is nothing they won't compromise.'

And thinking these things over in their minds they walked on, soon overtaking Looksmart who moved at half their pace, boxing his ears, muttering and stopping to polish his shoes, but he showed no sign of recognition and they had soon left him far behind.

CHAPTER 22

Now I saw how our pilgrims, climbing ever higher, came suddenly upon a party of police manhandling a captive by the roadside. The prisoner was a plump, elderly tramp in handcuffs who must have been hiding out in the countryside for some time because he was very dirty and even more thickly bearded than Blanchaille and Kipsel. He was very frightened and kept crying that he was a diplomat of the highest standing and entitled to immunity according to all known protocols. The police, while not dealing with him harshly, bore him relentlessly towards a waiting police car. Despite the dirt, the beard, the matted, filthy hair, the travellers knew him immediately.

Blanchaille asked permission to speak to the prisoner and the Swiss police turned out to be perfectly amiable despite their appearance, for they wore rather a menacing grey uniform and carried large pistols in their belts. Perhaps it wasn't too surprising that Kipsel shrank back when one considered his dealings with policemen but I saw that it was the prisoner himself who most disturbed him, sending him scuttling for cover. Later, he was to claim that the need to relieve himself had carried him behind some large roadside boulders, but I think we know better. The wretched fugitive in the hands of the Swiss police was none other than Adolph Bubé.

Here perhaps it is fitting for me to pay tribute to the humanity and innate democratic sensibility of these Swiss officers who must have been hard put to distinguish between the large tramp who approached them and the hysterical hobo they had taken into custody. Perhaps they were influenced by their long experience in administering the Red Cross, as well as the admirable ideals enshrined in the Geneva Convention for the treatment of prisoners of war. In any event, the officer in charge granted Blanchaille's request for a few words in private with the prisoner and he and his men withdrew to their vehicles and occupied themselves by polishing windscreens and clearing the roadside verges of unsightly weeds and performing various other useful activities.

I saw in my dream an astonishing sight. The ex-priest and the former President cloistered at the side of the road in the attitude of a father-confessor and penitent, while Kipsel hid from sight and the Swiss police tidied up the landscape. In hoarse whispers Bubé made his confession while Blanchaille listened gravely, nodding at times and comforting the old man when grief overcame him. An odd couple, to be sure, but both men were experiencing the painful dislocation of reality which had pitched them onto this Swiss mountain and so felt a curious kinship and Blanchaille listened with every sympathy, stirring only to offer his handkerchief when the tears became a flood and once intervening to restrain the old man when he attempted to dash his head against a rock. And on another occasion, he drew something in the sand with his finger and the old man beat his breast and called on God to forgive him.

When at length they finished I saw Blanchaille lead the prisoner over to the police. And as he turned I saw, as did Kipsel, now bold enough to peer over the boulders, a sign on his back which read A. BUBI.

As the police car disappeared down the mountain road Blanchaille returned to Kipsel and told him the amazing saga of that unlikely renegade, former President Adolph Gerhardus Bubé.

'He's in serious trouble. He has committed the gravest offence this country recognises –'

'Wait, don't tell me,' said Kipsel raising his hand. 'He's broken financial regulations.'

Blanchaille nodded. 'Yes, but it's worse than that –'

'It's something to do with the missing millions, isn't it? The money Ferreira was looking for, the discrepancies in the books? The money he sent here?'

Blanchaille had to smile at his friend's naïvety. 'Heavens, Ronnie, that's no crime! Not here. It's widely expected that the heads of various regimes should squirrel away large sums in Swiss accounts against a rainy day, the sudden coup that will pitch them into exile, or just for insurance. Hell, no, the Swiss don't get offended about that. They consider it quite natural that foreign regimes should screw their people, empty the banks, siphon off the aid cheques into secret accounts in Geneva and Zurich. African regimes especially. And to them Bubé is just another African. No, what the Swiss have set their faces firmly against is anybody diddling the Swiss.'

Kipsel blew harshly between his teeth. 'Wowee!'

'Precisely,' said Blanchaille, 'though "Wowee!" hardly covers the complexities involved. It has to do with gold sales. We might have guessed that. You remember Himmelfarber telling us about the switch from the London gold market to Zurich in what he called the gilded days? Well Bubé was largely responsible for the move. And the Swiss bullion dealers were impressed. Some of his best friends were bullion dealers and they were very grateful to get our gold. Some of them were very grateful before they got our gold and showed their gratitude. As we say back home, they "thanked" the Minister.

'But when gold sales returned to the London market the love went out of Bubé's relationship with the dealers. It did no good to explain that it was the Swiss Government's fault for imposing the sales tax, thereby forcing the dealers to show their volumes of sales and upsetting our other friends, the Russians. As far as the dealers were concerned, one moment they had all the gold and the next moment they didn't. They insist Bubé gave them to believe that South African gold was here in Switzerland to stay. They feel aggrieved. And behind the dealers are the banks. Because of course they lent the money to the dealers. And as that pleasant young police officer from the Commercial Division of the Swiss police told me back there – in Switzerland when the banks speak the cantons tremble. The banks are very bitter. After all, they argue – who was it who arranged loans and credits to the Regime when no one else would touch them?'

'Then the stories about the President are true?' Kipsel asked. 'He has money stashed away?'

'Quite a lot. Perhaps as much as twenty million. Perhaps more. Bubé himself isn't sure.'

'That's a fortune!'

'That what I said. Bubé became pretty peevish. "You don't plan for a government-in-exile on peanuts," he said. "It's not like arranging a skiing trip." It's this money that is the subject of the dispute. The bullion dealers claim that it was amassed using their contributions, their commissions, so they're laying claim to it. Meanwhile the Regime, having got wind of it, is also after the money. They say it belongs to them having been improperly acquired. Bubé says he's sick to death of this nonsense. He says that there have long been plans to establish a government-in-exile should the Regime fall. It was, as Himmelfarber told us, just one of the options. Various South American countries have been selected as suitable where of course there are communities of the many descendants of those Boer exiles who originally fled to South America after the Boer War. Bubé referred to this money as a contingency fund. A hedge against the day when, like it or not, the Regime may have to transfer to Paraguay or Bolivia. What's more he says that everybody in the inner ring of the Cabinet has known of this fund for years, approved of it, encouraged it. Yet when he arrived in Switzerland he found the Regime was denouncing him for fraud. They were demanding his extradition – with all the money. And the Swiss bullion dealers are demanding that what they call "earlier undertakings" must be honoured and the banks are talking menacingly of this insult to the soul of the nation; this cancer in the body of the Helvetian State – this is dangerous stuff because the banks are to Switzerland what I suppose the Roman Curia is to the Vatican, director and guardians of the faith . . . Bubé's alleged crime is not only that he has injured Swiss banks, but by turning up in person on Swiss soil he has added insult to injury. Not only are they determined to get their money back, but they want to make an example of him. I expect he will be paraded in the market squares of all the towns between here and Geneva.'

Kipsel understood. 'Hence the notice.'

'Right.'

'I've got little sympathy for him,' Kipsel commented. 'But I wonder how firm their evidence is when they can't even spell his name.'

'It's very common in the German-speaking cantons of Switzerland to find names ending in "*i*" – Matti, Jutti and so on. That young policeman's name was Mitti. They've spelt it the way they heard it – BUBI.'

'How come you know so much about the Swiss arrangements, Blanchie?'

'Well, I was incarcerated for some time with a wild Swiss priest back at home. His name was Wüli. There's a case in point. Wüli had often been arrested in Switzerland and he was something of an expert on the subject.'

'What was he doing in South Africa?'

'Much the same sort of thing. Getting arrested. He had an overwhelming desire to expose his genitals to unsuspecting civilians. This simply didn't cut him out for parish work. So the Church confined him to one of those *gulags* in the mountains. But that didn't stop old Wüli. He was as fit as could be and would saunter off, up hill and down dale, like a bloody mountain goat in search of some sympathetic soul to whom he could make his personal revelations. Wüli warned me about the horror and detestation with which economic crimes were regarded in Switzerland. Each nation has its love, Wüli told me: the Regime dreams of naked black women; the English are a nation of child molesters; the Swiss have exchanged their soul for financial security, they worship the franc and hold sacred the bank account.'

'And Bubé has abased the sacred rites?'

'It's worse than that. The account was found to be empty, it's tantamount to religious blasphemy. He's in deep trouble.'

'All of it – gone? But Blanchie – where? How?'

'Bubé was very cagey about that. He kept trying to defend himself. Said he had no option. He was a victim. The Swiss would wring him out and hand him back to the Regime who'd spent so much time washing their hands of him they had to wear gloves. They were going to blame him for their own decisions, crucify him for saving his country. I put it to him straight. You've transferred the money to the other fund, I said. He was ready for this. He looked almost triumphant. There was a flash of the old Bubé, the truculent jeerer of the political platform, scourge of the press, whirlwind diplomat, baby creator – "How could I?" he asked. "There is no *other* fund." What about the Kruger fund, I asked. He laughed. "You don't believe that old story, do you? There were no millions, there is no fund."'

'Clever,' said Kipsel.

'The President's vanishing trick. Where are the missing millions? Now you see them, now you don't. Like Kruger, like Bubé. Clever, and inevitable,' said Blanchaille. 'The old man may suffer in the short term, because the Swiss are convinced he's got the money stashed away. But they won't find it since the other fund doesn't exist. And that's official. The Regime denies the story of the Kruger millions. The Swiss deny the existence of a Kruger asylum here. Therefore it's not possible for Bubé's treasure to have joined it. After a while the Swiss will convince themselves that the money Bubé owes them never existed. They never bribed Bubé and he never welshed on his promises to them. The banks will absorb their losses stoically and save face. The Regime will appreciate the value of this. If the money does not exist, nor the secret accounts, then neither does the fraud or the defection of the President, nor the plan for a government-in-exile.'

'Yes,' said Kipsel, savouring the beauty of it, 'and I won't be surprised if the Regime starts threatening anyone who tells these stories of the missing Bubé's missing millions. People will get into trouble for telling stories.'

'The chances are,' said Blanchaille, 'that Bubé will be completely cleared, his name will be incised on all the war monuments and the attacks upon him cited as further evidence of the Total Onslaught against our country. The missing presidential millions have their uses.'

Kipsel nodded emphatically. 'What would we do without them?'

They sat by the roadside and gazed down at the lake far below. A tiny white steamer moved in a wide arc across the still blue water, it followed a great circle, creeping round like the second hand of a watch. Running down the sides of the lake the vineyards seen from this height stretched out with a green and metalled regularity.

After some while I heard Kipsel ask: 'Blanchie, what were you drawing in the sand when you were talking to Bubé?'

In reply, Blanchaille drew in the dust the letters ASK 3. 'When I was in London, before Van Vuuren was killed, we met Father Lynch. He had been following us. Don't ask me how. We talked about death. His and ours and Ferreira's. Having explained to us why the price of shares fell after Tony's murder we asked if he knew who'd killed him. He said he didn't. But he said something interesting. What if the letters scrawled on the wall did not stand for the Afrika Straf Kaffir Brigade, or the Azanian Strike Kommando No. 3? What if those letters had not been written by his killers, or even by someone wanting everyone to think they'd been written by his killers? What if they'd been written by Ferreira himself? I remember his words, "If you can read the writing on the wall you may be close to the killer." Back there, when we saw the police with Bubé, something suddenly occurred to me. Look at the letters again – ASK 3. Now imagine someone writing them in a hurry, someone in a state of shock, in pain, someone dying. Maybe he would write clearly. Look at the number 3 – and remember that the people who saw it said they "thought" it looked like a 3. But say it wasn't. Say the dying man had been trying to write not 3 but B.'

'All right, say they were,' said Kipsel. 'All it does is to make the message even more mysterious. You can't make sense of B. At least ASK 3 can be made to fit the initials of two known organisations both of which were capable of murdering a Government official who had discovered something nasty about them.'

'Exactly,' said Blanchaille triumphantly. 'Those letters can be *made* to fit. Your words, Ronnie! And they were made to fit. They made possible a theory to explain Ferreira's death. So we grabbed it. But we were being too clever by half. We were forgetting the first rule in African politics, the principle which dominates the way we are.'

228

'Which is?' Kipsel asked, amused.

'That what begins as tragedy turns into a farce at a blink. That in all Government activities you must suspect a cock-up. We forgot that rule. Why should the letters on the wall stand for anything? Why shouldn't they mean exactly what they say?'

Kipsel jumped up and began to turn around in excited circles banging his foot on the ground as if to try and anchor himself, as if he might spin too fast and fly off the mountain. 'Blanchie! Of course!'

Blanchaille leaned forward and completed the message in the sand. ASK BUBÉ, the message read.

Kipsel stopped spinning and sat down. The little steamer now circled the lake like a racing car. He closed his eyes. 'And so you did just that. You asked Bubé?'

'Yes.'

'Well, don't hang on to it – tell me, who killed Ferreira?'

'I wish I could make this something you'd like. Something you could respect. I apologise in advance for what I have to say. Entirely typical. In a way I prefer the earlier theory of the political organisations. It's more elegant, more serious. And it makes the killing seem more important. Something to look up to. Hell, we *need* something to look up to.'

'Blanchie, please!'

'His killer was a small-time English thug named Tony "the Pug" Sidelsky, from Limehouse.'

'You're pulling my leg. From Limehouse, England?'

'I'm perfectly serious.'

'Then why are you smiling?'

'I can't help it. According to Bubé, Sidelsky drove to Ferreira's house on the appointed night knowing what he had to do. It was supposed to be professional, clean and quick. But it wasn't. Sidelsky, it seems, was none too bright. For a start he behaved as if he were going to knock off an old-age pensioner in Clapham. He didn't seem to realise that in South Africa houses are barred, wired, and fortified against night attack, that some of them even have searchlights. Now Ferreira didn't have all that security. He didn't even have a dog, which was most unusual and lucky for Sidelsky. But Ferreira was no idiot and naturally he was armed. Sidelsky found himself unable to enter the house without breaking a window. Ferreira was waiting for him. I don't know what Sidelsky expected. Perhaps he expected Tony to put up his hands and get shot. Instead he got hit himself a couple of times before he got Ferreira.'

Kipsel turned on him a look of intense suffering. 'But you still haven't told me – why get an Englishman to kill him?'

'It's really not so surprising,' Blanchaille said. 'Not when you think about it. English killers have been used for one job or another for many years in South Africa. It's almost traditional. Do you remember the shooting of the racehorse, Golden Reef? That was done by that bookie fellow from Ealing. Who was it again? Sandy Nobbs. He had been secretly commissioned, for reasons I don't remember, by the manager of the Tote. They caught him, remember? And then there was the killing of the fairy mining-magnate, what was his name?'

'Cecil Finkelstein.'

'That's right, Finkelstein. He was gunned down one night when he opened his front door. You remember the story?'

'Yes, I remember the story,' Kipsel said. There was immense weariness in his voice. And contempt. 'Years later some English guy in Parkhurst prison confessed to Finkelstein's murder after he got religion. Of course I remember the old story. It's the story of imported labour. It's the story of our country. Lack of muscle power in some areas, lack of skilled technicians in others. So you import them, engineers, opera singers, assassins. It's always the same – the butler did it, or the cook, or the gardener. Anybody but ourselves.'

'I said you wouldn't like it, Ronnie. I'm just telling you what I know.'

'Who ordered the killing? Bubé?'

'He swears not. He says that this was a *Bureaucratic* decision, as he puts it. He says the order came directly from Terblanche.'

'– who may not exist.'

'Correct. Bubé's story is strengthened by the fact that men from the Bureau were the first to arrive on the scene after the murder. I believe they probably expected to find Ferreira neatly dispatched and the place turned over and robbed so as to make it look like some sort of violent burglary. But what did they find instead? They find Ferreira dead, or damn nearly, and Sidelsky dying on the carpet. You can imagine the problem this gave them. I believe, at least Bubé says, they came close to panicking. You see it meant they first had to dispose of the killer and then return to the house and pretend to discover the body of the dead accountant. It was a very hairy business. Bubé's story had the ring of truth to it. You should have heard the way he sounded off about the Bureau. He says that the Bureau chose Sidelsky because he was broke and unemployed in England and they got a real bonehead for their pains. False economy. He says the money they saved on the contract then got eaten up by the burial costs of the dead Sidelsky and they couldn't even claim on his return ticket because they'd booked him Apex, or something like that. Cost-cutting costs money, Bubé told me, showing a flash of the old financial brain that made him the big wheel he was. He was absolutely scathing!'

'For Christ's sake, you can't swallow that! Bubé controls the Bureau. He is or was the President and the Bureau is his army.'

'In a manner of speaking that's right – but to say that is to say very little. What exactly is the Bureau? We like to think of it as the Secret Police, run by the mysterious Terblanche – who probably doesn't exist. Well, I've got news for you, Ronnie. Not only does Terblanche not exist, but neither does the Bureau. Not as a single entity; some super-secret unit. The Bureau is simply a term, a useful fiction which we use to describe a whole range of options – the police; the Hand of the Virgin; the Ring; the Papal Nuncio; the New Men; the New Order; the Old Guard; the Straf Kaffir Brigade; the Azanian Strike Kommando; the Department of Communications; the Bureau is all of them and none of them. It's Bubé and Kuiker and Yssel and the entire establishment which controls our view of reality. It exists so that we have something to fear. But more importantly, it exists so we have someone to *blame*. It is that force which the Regime as much as its enemies needs to believe in. It gives clarity and purpose to what is otherwise a long, ugly, dirty grab at power. We need the Bureau, we love the Bureau. We would be lost without it. You ask if the Bureau killed Ferreira? The answer you want is, yes. All right, the Bureau killed him, they paid the incompetent Englishman who pulled the trigger. But Ferreira stumbled on the truth and every new discovery was a nail in his coffin.

'Ferreira took three hammer blows to his faith. Firstly he believed in books, in fact, in figures. One day he was taking a routine look through the books. He began by checking the budget figures of the various departments of the Regime and in those figures he found discrepancies. Consider what this did to him. His whole life depended upon a single premise. The Regime might be mad, it might be stupid, it might be cruel – but it was sincere. It was honest. Tony believed that utterly. Well, the books told another story.

'To begin with he found that some of the monies listed in departmental spending had actually been channelled elsewhere, they appeared to him to have gone to Minister Gus Kuiker. It disturbed him. He went to Sidleman, the Government Accountant, and reported his discovery. Sidleman hit the roof. He was another Government man. He didn't understand why the official figures did not reflect the truth. Apparently he asked Ferreira if he was suggesting that elected officials were setting up secret funds of public money. Ferreira replied that he wasn't suggesting anything of the sort, but he wanted to know why the figures didn't add up. Sidleman went to the President who promised a full investigation. In the meantime he told Sidleman to call off Ferreira and to stop his enquiries. But that was impossible. He had to follow where the figures led. There was no stopping Ferreira. Everywhere he looked he uncovered further mysteries. Not only did he find, as he went through the files of the various Government departments, that there was money leaving the country for unexplained reasons, there were also funds reaching Government coffers which he couldn't account for. The figures led him abroad. To South America, Bermuda, France. He was shown houses on the Italian Riviera, farmhouses in the South of France and learnt they belonged to Gus Kuiker and Trudy Yssel. The Department of Communications was waging a foreign war against secret funds. He travelled on, to Rome, Washington and then Switzerland. Everywhere he went he heard the most astonishing stories. He heard of wild nights in Montevideo, week-long sex parties in Las Vegas, of private jets for American politicians and free holidays for British editors. He learnt about dummy companies set up in Bermuda and Panama which were used to buy up or buy off political commentators; he found deals as bizarre as the plan to arrange a tour of Japan by our rugby players in exchange for a tour of the casino nightclubs by Japanese sumo wrestlers and for the tour to be extensively covered by a Taiwanese news agency which would circulate the story as evidence of our racial tolerance; in Switzerland he found companies set up to translate South African currency into American dollars, apparently an expensive business, and he found that this accounted for some of the millions he had detected draining out of our foreign reserves; in Switzerland too he came across disturbing rumours of deals between important men of the Regime and the whole raft of currency manipulators, he learnt of promises not kept, of secret deals, secret accounts, gold sales and Russian contacts. Perhaps he unearthed the true story of Popov. By the time he got to London he was shattered. He got in touch with Zandrotti. Perhaps he needed to talk to a friend. He got drunk, he probably told Roberto more than he'd intended. Of course Zandrotti got it in one. Ferreira still didn't realise the full implications of his discoveries but Zandrotti did. I think with that wild, anarchic mind of his he probably got it in a flash, saw the horrible black farce it was. Ferreira was overwhelmed by the tragedy. But Zandrotti saw the joke.'

'And Zandrotti went home – to find out for himself?' Kipsel asked. 'He couldn't believe it.'

Blanchaille looked surprised. 'Oh no, he went home because he refused to believe it. I remember how he was in Balthazar Buildings after he'd been caught by the police. Zandrotti was broken, he'd lived his whole life in the belief that the Regime was genuinely, thoroughly, consistently and impressively, let's face it, evil. He grew up in that belief, he'd suffered for it, he'd gone to jail for it, he'd lived in exile for it. It was, when you think about it, a very high expectation. He had a worthwhile enemy. You can imagine what it did to him when Ferreira told him he was dealing with a bunch of crooks. He hadn't been a hero. He'd been a fool. He was not going to have that. My guess is that he booked his flight home and then saw Magdalena.'

'Who shopped him, of course,' Kipsel snapped.

Blanchaille understood the anger of his friend; how the business of Magdalena's betrayal still hurt.

'My feeling – guess – is that was just what he wanted. Heaven knows what came pouring out between bursts of the litany in the bar where Ferreira told Zandrotti his story. Some clue, perhaps, which gave Magdalena's double game away. And Zandrotti used her.'

'It makes a change,' said Kipsel.

'Ferreira believed in figures. He also believed in the integrity of the Regime. Mad it might be, but honest. Negative, but sincere. Narrow, but forthright. The Regime had set its face against blacks, Communists, Jews, Catholics, against compromise, liberalisation, democracy. This might be narrow, foolish even, but it was a question of principles. And he could admire people with principles, who would die for those principles. As for himself, well somebody had to do the sums, as he liked to say. He had kept the faith. Now he found the Regime dealing with the Russians through Popov and Himmelfarber –'

'And Himmelfarber's nephew, left in Moscow on deposit,' Kipsel reminded him gloomily. 'Blanchie, this gets blacker.'

'And Himmelfarber was supposed to be an enemy. But gold as we know is more important than principles. The Regime had dealt with Moscow when they moved bullion dealings from London to Zurich. In Switzerland he'd heard rumours that some big man in the Regime had cleaned up on the move. Then he discovered money going to the Israelis! Now the orthodox teaching was that at least half of the Regime was of the unshakable opinion that Hitler got a bad press and was really a sensitive, patriotic house painter at heart who became Chancellor and was looking for nothing more than sweetness and light and that any stories to the contrary were products of commy, pinko Jews, who wished to destroy the white man's way of life, his religious beliefs, and to sleep with his daughters – and yet here was the Government supporting whole teams of Israelis and concealing them in the countryside. Israelis who wore baseball caps the wrong way round and disturbed the peace of the countryside, cost a fortune to police and protect and then desecrated the Calvinist Sabbath by drinking and whoring in sleepy country towns. Most important of all, he'd been taught that the President was the father of his country and its stay and protection in times of trouble, that he would lead the nation in the flight to the beaches when, and if, by some horrible catastrophe, the savages prevailed and the last white tribe in Africa faced extinction. Then, with his back to the sea, the President would hand round the poison to the kids and begin shooting the women before the enemy troops arrived. That's what he believed, and then blow me down, he goes out and finds that the old fox has been salting money away for years in a Swiss account against just such a contingency, against that rainy day which might carry him off to Bolivia or Paraguay.'

'Then he goes back to his books and finds he isn't looking at figures, he's reading a horror novel,' Kipsel broke in. 'He finds not one financial nightmare but three or four. There are the funds creamed off the various Government departments and sent abroad secretly for Kuiker and Yssel's Department of Communications to fight its propaganda war. There is the money Bubé has been collecting in his secret accounts against a rainy day.'

'And there are the funds entering the country which presumably baffle the hell out of him until he interviews the brokers Kranz, Lundquist and Skellum. And his last and most cherished belief collapses. He finds out about the *Manus Virginis* with their strategic charity, how the Ring collaborates with them in tactical investments in the future of the Regime.'

Kipsel sighed. 'Poor Tony. Finding that the Church was in it too will have hurt more than anything.'

'Yes, but not for the reasons you think. What crucified Ferriera when he discovered the links between the Regime, the Ring and the Hand, with the Nuncio Agnelli acting as flyhalf, was that the Church really was powerful after all. Tony had never accepted Lynch's theories about the structure of power. He rejected the Church as played-out, ineffectual, unimportant. And he was wrong. Every-where he looked he found a policy of outright deception. There was the Church going around the country issuing statements about embracing its black brethren in Christ. There was Bishop Blashford publicly deploring the shipment of human populations to the transit camps and relegation of entire tribes to desolate "homelands", and defying the Regime to arrest him. There were the charitable bodies shipping in dried milk and penicillin and designing new churches in the beehive style and attacking the Regime for being in league with the devil and preaching that the programme of separate freedom for ethnic groups was a crime against humanity, an economic nonsense and a sin against the Holy Spirit. While this was going on, here was the Regime whose followers took an oath of loyalty to Calvin before they slept and believed the Pope feasted on baby meat and sucked the marrow from the bones of orphans, meeting with certain Italian Societies, and here were its loyal followers in that most secret of societies, the Ring, those ultra-Calvinists, sitting round a table with a bunch of genuine opera-loving flesh and blood holy Romans, fresh from the Vatican, representing the *Manus Virginis* and discussing share portfolios. One by one, every belief he held had been destroyed. Lynch had been right. And if Lynch had been right about the deceptions, he was right about all the other things too – including the missing Kruger millions, right about the house on the hill. It was in this despairing state that he phoned me.'

Kipsel was very pale. 'I didn't know he phoned you.'

'Just before he died. I was one of the last people to speak to him.'

'What did he say?'

'That I should get out. That he had found the City of God, or Gold. The line was bad. He was slightly hysterical, said he was planning a trip himself. He sent me money. Next thing I knew he was dead.'

'And here you are?'

'And here we are.'

Kipsel swore bitterly, then scrambled to his feet and picked up his stick and rucksack. 'Let's get on. I don't want to know any more. Tony "the Pug" Sidelsky! The whole thing's a horrid cheap little pantomime. Do you think it's much further?'

'I hope not, I hope not,' said Blanchaille fervently. 'I've had about as much as I can take. All my prayers are that God preserve me from any more of my itinerant, wandering, bemused, addle-brained countrymen, from policemen, rugby players, patriots, accountants, priests and presidents.'

'Amen,' said Kipsel.

CHAPTER 23

And so I saw in my dream how they hurried on their way, anxious to arrive somewhere, anywhere, elsewhere, the pear and the fish, strange partners.

Fearful imaginings crowded in on Blanchaille and left him weak and uncertain of his true direction, characteristic phobias, indigenous phantoms, familiar demons arose from the catalogues every South African recites before sleep and loves to recall with horror. Black men hunted with huge home-made knives beaten out of oil drums or made from railway steel ripped from the sleepers, flattened by a maniac, hammered, honed to a scalpel's edge, metal machetes called *pangas*, slicing the air; he remembered white boys, so huge, so long and lanky they reminded him of giraffes, against whom he had played rugby, boys with strangely dark complexions and moustaches, surely men, and not that *white*! They raced down the rugby fields towards you with that stiff-legged giraffe gait, their hooves wrenching the turf. These monsters were surely never the babies which loyal white mothers had had for Bubé? No, these boy giants were born with full moustaches – wearing rugby boots. Their call-up papers were delivered to the maternity wing, they leapt from their cradles, kissed their new mothers goodbye and went off to defend their country's borders against the Total Onslaught. Thus the dreams of misplaced, wandering white Africans, each with his own compendium of horrors, stories of *tokoloshes*, green and black mambas, murdered nuns. Each has his favourite, but most fearful for Blanchaille was the memory of a crop of graves he had watched growing in the camps. Growing and growing. If there was a symbol that scared him, it was not the gun nor the knife nor the snake – but the spade. In the camps he had learnt to dig. He had stood in the big trench grave and thrown red sand up onto the parapet, mounting higher and higher. He had felt he was digging in for a great war. What he now feared most as he slogged along an obscure Swiss track towards an improbable destination was not ambush or betrayal, but arrival. In the old story, the Regime was regarded by its opponents as utterly evil, by its supporters as divinely good. Everyone dwelt among absolutes and was happy. Now it seemed that the Regime was no better or worse than two dozen other shabby little dictatorships north of the border. He stole a glance at Kipsel, a tousle of curls falling over the shallow brow, the fish lips making their silent, pouting little *o*'s. Had it occurred to him that if the hell he had left behind wasn't as bad as they had believed or hoped – then might not the place to which they travelled be no better than anyone might imagine?

What do you do when you find that the world you imagined to be bad, decently evil and have judged this so by observation and report and legend, fact and figure, is none of these, but is instead flat, dull, ordinary and very much like anywhere else? You have believed in its evil, trusted in it, you have been convinced by friend and enemy alike of its horror, have had it whispered to you in the cradle, written on the bodies of men in the cells, the message is one which has reassured the condemned as they are led to the gallows and made for an enemy worth fighting against – but, what if everything turns around suddenly, turns upside down and becomes in truth, banal? When it reveals to you that thing which you can least bear? That it is, in reality, very ordinary? Well, what you do is to keep climbing, and to dream, and to come in your dream, as Kipsel and Blanchaille did now, to the crossroads.

And into my dream there now steps a strange figure, his perfect teeth flashing like a sword. The teeth are noticeable for they are all that can be seen behind the African mask he wears, a wooden mask with black lines incised on the cheek bones and a fuzz of hair made from sacking falling down almost to the eyes and where the ears should be.

The travellers stared at this strange figure. Their road was little more than a track. The tree-line was ending. The pines that had been climbing steadily beside them had grown thin and feeble and were now tottering to a halt. It was from behind one of these ailing trees that there stepped the figure in the mask and unsheathed its smile. The lake below was lost in a distant blue haze and might have been the sky. It might have been that the whole world turned suddenly on its head.

The creature before them was dressed in tribal finery of an African chief, though of which tribe neither of them could say, but certainly he looked very regal, war-like and confident, and most bizarre on that green mountainside. He was planted squarely on the spot where the roads divided. There was, it occurred to Blanchaille, something vaguely familiar about his costume though he couldn't put his finger on it.

'We're looking for the road to Uncle Paul's place,' said Kipsel politely. 'Perhaps you can direct us?'

Blanchaille examined this strange tribal creature. He wore a kind of cap of fur with the arms and tail dangling round his head, a monkey pelt across his shoulders, he carried a short stabbing spear and a cowhide shield. Beneath it all he wore a black morning suit and highly polished shoes.

'How would you describe the place you're looking for?' the stranger asked.

'A place of rest,' said Blanchaille.

'A holiday home,' said Kipsel.

'Retirement village, old-age home, hospice,' said Blanchaille.

'A home-from-home, hide-out, colony, camp,' said Kipsel.

The figure nodded. 'Follow me.'

And he led them along the road which turned to the right and passed along the shoulder of the mountain. The sun was setting and a small chill wind was blowing. They followed him in silence and so compelling was his presence that they covered considerable ground before they realised the road had levelled out and was beginning to descend.

'Wait,' said Blanchaille. 'This can't be right.'

'I'm doing you a favour,' said their guide. 'Don't argue. Keep moving. Don't look back.'

'But we're going down,' said Blanchaille. 'We're not supposed to be going down.'

'Where does this road lead?' Blanchaille asked.

The stranger stopped. He turned and confronted them and very slowly removed his tribal mask.

'Gabriel!' Kispel said.

'I tried to help. It's the least I can do for old friends. I want to help you.'

'Where does this road lead?' Blanchaille asked again.

'To Geneva, the airport and home.'

'But that's the way we've come,' Kipsel said.

'Of course it is. I asked what you wanted and you said home, hotel, hospice, guest house, retirement village. That's what you're wanting and this is the road that leads to it. This is the *only* road that leads to it.'

'That wasn't the home we had in mind.' Blanchaille objected.

'It's the only home you have. There is nothing where you are going. Believe me, trust me.'

Despite himself Blanchaille laughed.

Gabriel became angry. 'Yes, laugh! Maybe you won't get another chance. The joke's over. Come home with me. Face up to reality – or go on and fall off the edge of the world.'

'If you want to help someone, what about your brother? He's still wandering about here. He's got a piece of paper in his hand that he believes will give him the title to some fabulous strip of land where he'll be king and everyone will be equal and live happily ever after. Why not take him home?' Blanchaille asked.

'My brother is in a real sense quite unreachable,' said Gabriel. 'My brother's on another plane. He imagines himself as a great explorer. He thinks he can reverse history. He believes he can set out with his piece of paper and imagines he will discover the New World. Like he's Columbus in reverse. Or Van Riebeeck going the other way to rediscover the Cape of Good Hope. He plans to reopen the Garden of Eden, which he thinks has just been closed for repairs.'

'We saw the guarantor of his dream of Eden being led down the mountain in chains,' said Blanchaille.

Gabriel shrugged. 'Correction. You've seen Bubé in chains. What Looksmart sees is another matter.'

'You sent Looksmart to Philadelphia.'

'Another correction. I didn't send him to Philadelphia. He took up with some girl and landed there. All I did was to get him on the plane to America, one step ahead of the police.'

'So you warned him the police were coming?'

'Of course.'

'And who warned you?'

Gabriel shrugged.

'You don't deny it then?'

'Why should I?'

Kipsel who had been listening to this exchange in bewilderment now broke in. 'What are you saying, Gabriel? That it was you who talked to the police?'

'How else do you think I got him out? Sometimes,it's necessary to talk, to deal.'

'But the police hurt your brother,' said Kipsel. 'They nearly killed him.'

For the first time Gabriel showed signs of impatience. 'Jesus you guys are so tiresome. I've tried to help you before, Blanchie. I got you into Pennyheaven. To do that I talked to Blashford. But then I've talked to the Afrika Straf Kaffir Brigade and to the Liberation Front, in my time. But you guys won't have it, will you? I'm the only one who understood it wasn't enough to hear what Lynch taught us. We have to act on it! I am brave enough, desperate enough to do what's necessary, because we plan to win.'

'So do the other side.'

'Naturally this gives us something in common. So we talk to each other. It's a complex balance.'

'Gabriel. What are you saying?' Kipsel was aghast. 'People are dead. Mickey, Ferreira, Van Vuuren – friends!'

'Van Vuuren was no friend. Besides he brought it on himself. If you want to blame somebody, blame the Regime. You can't send policemen snooping around the Azanian Front. If the Regime wants to talk they know the way of getting through to us.'

'But he wasn't with the Regime. He was one of you!' Blanchaille cried. 'Kaiser Zulu sent for him. Van Vuuren came because the ALF called him in.'

'That's his story,' said Gabriel. 'I'm beginning to wonder if you guys have understood a damn thing.'

He left them then, striding away rapidly into the gathering dark.

Then Blanchaille remembered where he'd seen the tribal dress before. 'In Balthazar Buildings there was a portrait of Bubé hanging on the wall. He wore ceremonial tribal finery, the skins, the spear, the shield. He wore it to visit the tribes of which he was honorary chief. Gabriel was wearing the same get-up.'

'As a kind of disguise,' Kipsel suggested, ever naïve.

'No. Not a disguise. It shows Gabriel is presidential material.'

Kipsel said he wished he could identify the tribe from which it came.

Blanchaille said it didn't matter. 'They probably have a big box of fancy dress tribal finery, or a props cupboard and drag out some vaguely appropriate costume when a ceremonial visit crops up. Something that makes you look vaguely chieftain-like and impressive.'

'The only thing that worries me is that Bubé, of course, wore it when he made these visits to some wretched tribe who were about to be dumped in the middle of nowhere.'

'God, how he must have terrified them!' said Kipsel. 'Imagine Bubé stepping out of the presidential limousine in that get-up. Imagine what the God-forsaken tribe felt when they saw him. It must have been like getting a sign, the arrival of the messenger of doom,' said Kipsel.

'Remember the shepherds warned us about Gabriel,' Blanchaille pointed out. 'They said he was no angel.'

'I still say they weren't shepherds,' Kipsel insisted.

'Please Ronnie, is this the time to argue about shepherds?'

Kipsel agreed it was not perhaps the time.

And I saw in my dream how the two friends began the long haul, retracing their steps back to the crossroads as darkness fell.

CHAPTER 24

Blanchaille and Kipsel heard, rather than saw, Looksmart, for it was quite dark by the time they had regained their position at the crossroads, deeply regretting the distance travelled and the time lost in the vain detour into which Gabriel had tricked them.

They heard the scrape and scrabble of his dragging walk while he was still some distance behind them and they heard him muttering to himself. They heard the name 'Isobel'. They heard how he addressed himself in a language composed of grunts and clicks, in a dialogue between the foreigner and the lunatic.

'Here comes Looksmart,' whispered Kipsel. 'Poor bastard. If he saw Bubé it will have finished him. Let's wait.'

'Perhaps he really does imagine himself to be another Columbus. Listen how he argues with himself. Do you think he could be talking about Isabel of Spain? Didn't she send Columbus off to discover the New World?'

'Isabella,' said Kipsel. 'It was Queen Isabella and Ferdinand who sent Columbus off.'

Looksmart approached. 'Isobel,' he said firmly, 'who sent me to find America.' Here he took out a tiny, weak torch and examined their faces. What a strange couple, the big round one with a face like kneaded dough and the other, thin, big-lipped, with hands that sliced the air like fins. Though it was many years ago they still retained the familiar shapes of the boys he remembered toiling in Father Lynch's parish garden. In his curious click language he muttered their names.

'He really knows us now,' said Blanchaille.

Of course he knew them now. They were the altar servers whose heads Lynch had filled with stories of vanished millions, of Uncle Paul's promised land across the sea, of gold and secret colonies and lost souls, of the illusions of politics and the sole reality of power. Above all he remembered the pleasure he felt at seeing how hard those white boys were made to work in a garden which would never be got right, by an Irish priest leaning on an elbow on a tartan rug on a hot day drinking something from a thermos flask. But these memories returned in bits and pieces, now bright, now fading, like light glimpsed through a smashed windscreen. The work done by

242

the policeman Breek on Looksmart's head had been thorough, the damage to the brain irreversible, but these glimpses remained of the old days. 'Blanchie, and Kipsel . . .'

'Odd that he should know us by night and not by day,' Blanchaille reflected.

The weak, yellow flickering torch-light searched their faces, assembling sections for process and developing in the dark room of Looksmart's brain.

'Did you meet with the President?' Kipsel asked.

The torch went out. 'Looksmart saw him, oah yes. What a traveller! He must be on another diplomatic tour. He had been given a special police escort. I approached the car with my treaty and asked for ratification that this land belongs to me and my descendants, in perpetuity.' Looksmart had trouble getting the word out. 'The President looked at me. He pushed my pen away. "No need for me to sign. You have it anyway. You and your descendants, forever". Then he went away, the President and the police. Perhaps they planned to show him to the people of all the towns he passed through.'

'Perhaps,' said Kipsel drily.

Blanchaille felt his pity mounting. This shambling wreck in the darkness with his weak little torch and his insane ideas. This shadow of Looksmart. The real Looksmart had been a holy terror. This was a mumbling ghost. 'Who is this Isobel you're talking about? Tell us, please.'

On went the little torch again, probing their faces as if verifying the authenticity of this request. 'It's a good story,' said Looksmart. 'Oah yes.' And switching off his torch he began.

If Looksmart had been ignorant of his famous travelling companion, Lenski, on his flight to America, he had not wanted for company. In the seat beside him sat Isobel. And before we are too quick to condemn Looksmart for his failure to recognise the treachery of which he was a victim we would do well to remember the fate of other black exiles who went to America, reached New York, and later jumped to their deaths from sky-scrapers, or bridges; and the white exiles had come to no happier conclusions. Their patron saint is probably General Cronje, who earned a few dollars at the World Fair in St Louis in 1904 by re-enacting for gawping tourists his disastrous defeat and surrender at the Battle of Paardeberg. That Looksmart arrived in Philadelphia and discovered the roots of the American revolution was an advance due entirely to Isobel. That he drew strange conclusions from what he learnt must be laid at the door of the salvationist delusions of all South Africans.

Pretty Isobel, in her caftan, cowboy boots and soft generous ways had come to Southern Africa as a meré tourist intending to visit the famous game reserves including, of course, the Kruger National Park. Instead she had fallen into conversation with the man who carried her cases to her hotel bedroom soon after her arrival in the country and had been converted. This radical spirit had taken her on a tour of the townships, to the resettlement camps, had taken her to meet those who had been detained, mothers whose children had died in front of them, people under house arrest and discarded people of all sorts. The high point of her visit had been taking part in the great student march on the Central Police Station in the capital to protest against the detention without trial of student leaders. It was this that suddenly radicalised Isobel, plump, pretty and so pleasant, so cordial in her peppermint caftan and cowboy boots, who found herself sitting beside Looksmart on the flight to America. He had never met anyone so thrilled to hear he had been in prison. Her face puckered, she cried for some moments before pulling herself together and then defiantly ordered champagne. She felt utterly privileged, she told him. He liked her, too. She did not make his eyes water. Over the champagne he told her he was also fleeing the country. After that they never looked back.

Isobel carried his luggage and refused to comment on his behalf when the reporters encountered him in Kennedy Airport after their interviews with Piatikus Lenski. It had been Isobel who dealt gruffly with the surly immigration officers over the matter of Looksmart's presence in the United States. It was Isobel who got the tickets for the train to Philadelphia and who moved him into her apartment on Walnut Street.

It was Isobel who took him into her wide soft bed beneath the eiderdown decorated with signs of the zodiac and its sky blue sheets.

She removed his clothes, she took his penis between her breasts and massaged it. It had been Isobel who straddled him. She was an odd girl, he remembered thinking. Political commitment made her misty-eyed, stimulated her, while he looked on quizzically with his one good eye caught between the desire to help and the vague feeling that he ought to apologise, wondering whether this was quite the career Gabriel envisaged for him in America. She took his now rampant member and kissed it, crooning to it between kisses, pulling and patting the foreskin gently as if trying to get it to lie

244

down, as if it were the corner of a shirt collar she'd been ironing and which refused to stay neat. She took him inside her and began rising and falling, her face tightening with concentration, her forehead shiny with effort. He tried to move with her, to make some gesture of communion, but her knees gripped his hips and kept him still. He lifted his hands to her breasts but she took them down and pressed them flat on the bed, gripping his wrists hard. She had told him on the plane how she loved Africa, how joined to it she felt however vast it was and with this her grip on him tightened. He wished he were more substantial beneath her, he did not feel very large or even very African. She was riding him more swiftly now, her breath coming in short hisses. He realised that his role at this particular point anyway was to lie still. He realised from something in the movement of her body that what was happening was in some sort a further dimension of her tribute to him, both to his person and his cause, as she had taken it to herself, now she took him. Looksmart's good eye watched the triangular patch of pubic hair rising and sliding, felt the contractions of her vaginal muscles, felt himself swell and spurt within her as she came to a shuddering, panting conclusion, dropping her head onto his chest and resting on her arms which curved outwards at right angles to her body like staves, or hoops, cutting half moons out of the white walls behind her. Afterwards it was Isobel who told him that this was her commitment to a vision of freedom. It was a vision to which Looksmart felt he had been permitted to make only an involuntary contribution. It was rather like giving to some mysterious, distant charity, he decided. You felt better for it after you had done it, though you couldn't help wishing you had a clearer idea of where the money went.

A few weeks later it was Isobel who arranged their marriage by 'the turkey who lives on the hill'. The turkey turned out to be a pleasant young Methodist minister; the hill, Society Hill. It wasn't so much marriage, Isobel explained to him, as the question of his visa, his freedom to stay in the United States. She said this very delicately as if she feared he might take offence. Afterwards she took him to lunch at a fish restaurant called Bookbinders and ordered him lobster. The waitress produced a huge paper towel which she tied around his neck and Looksmart felt very embarrassed to be wrapped like a parcel. With his knife he tapped an anxious tarradiddle on the red beast's back. Isobel asked about his mother.

Looksmart's mother had been called Agnes. That much he did

remember. Up from the kraal, a raw farm girl, she came to the capital in search, not of work, but of her husband who worked on the gold mines. Which mine? No one knew. One day her husband's letters had stopped. Worse still, so had the money he used to send. So Agnes brought her sons to the city and failed to find him. She was told to go home and wait. But she couldn't do that, her children had no food. She looked for work. Those to whom she applied warned her, threatened her: she had no papers, no permission, no future, no business to be there. Tap, tap went Looksmart's knife on the lobster's gate of bone behind which the beast hid and would not let him in, knock as he might. The hot, salt, sea flesh inside steamed in his nostrils. He realised then what was to be done in order to eat a lobster, why the huge paper bib, the finger bowl. You were supposed to tear it apart with your bare hands. His mother would have fled from this monster. The lobster fixed him with hard, unblinking eyes. Never mind, he would outstare it, using his bad eye.

Agnes, Looksmart's mother, arrived at Father Lynch's front door clutching Gabriel's hand and Looksmart, then still a baby, strapped to her back. Lynch took her on immediately, impressed on the one hand by her inability to do any cooking or washing or ironing or sewing. These were deficiencies he approved of heartily. Coming into contact with the white madams who taught these things was the ruination of many a good person, he liked to say. Lynch was delighted by the impressionable enthusiasm she showed and her lack of bad culinary habits. He taught her to cook what he called Irish food, plain and solid, stews and roasts and soups and plenty of potato with everything, since that was the way it was done in Ireland, his country, God help it, a tiny island no bigger than the tip of a finger nail, and here he squeezed between thumb and forefinger the requisite area of nail for her inspection. A little place so full of priests it would sink beneath their weight into the sea one day.

So much for the wedding lunch and Looksmart's mother. It was Isobel who acknowledged that she would awake one morning and find him gone, having slipped away in the night, summoned by his comrades to return home and fight for the cause of freedom.

And it was Isobel, above all, who sent him out one day with instructions to cast an eye over 'our revolution'.

Down Walnut Street Looksmart scrabbled towards that amazing rectangle bounded by Second Street and Sixth, by Larch Street and Spruce, the launching pad of the American revolution. He visited the Declaration Chamber in Independence Hall along with a bunch of tourists. Their guide was a bluff young man who wore what looked to him like a scout's uniform, but who turned out to be a Ranger in the Parks Department. He discovered that the area of Independence Hall was designated a National Historical Park. How strange America was! In his country the national parks were full of animals; here, they were full of people. The crowds stood behind the railing which enclosed the sacred area where the furious debates about independence had taken place. They stared at the tables covered with green baize and the crowded, spindle-legged Windsor chairs, the papers, the quills, the inkstands. They saw the Speaker's Chair with its rising sun motif and heard how Benjamin Franklin sat day after day, during deliberations that led to the Declaration, wondering whether that sun was rising or setting. He gazed at the silver inkstand designed by Philip Synge for the Speaker's Table, he learnt that unlike most of the other furniture, the inkstand was original; from it had come the ink that had loaded the quills that signed the Declaration of Independence adopted by this rumbustious, Second Continental Congress of 1776. The tourists stared at the crowded tables and chairs in that silent, empty chamber and tried to imagine the bells, the bonfires, the cheers and the shots with which the revolution began. Most of them were dressed in jeans or slacks and had this shifty, almost guilty look about them, Looksmart thought, as if try as they might they simply couldn't imagine that such climactic matters had begun in this small place. Afterwards, Looksmart bought a copy of the Declaration Document and a postcard of Trumbull's painting, *The Signing*, with its bouquet of American flags and its serried racks of bewigged and utterly respectable gentlemen who beneath their composure and their wigs had proved to be wild and redhot revolutionaries.

Looksmart visited, that same day, the House of Representatives Chamber in Congress Hall, as well as the Senate Chamber. He stared at the great star-spangled eagle painted on the ceiling overhead with its claw full of arrows. He admired the creamy symmetry of the old Supreme Court Chamber and he walked across Market Street and joined the crowds thronging the Glass Pavilion where the Liberty Bell hung.

He arrived home that night loaded with papers. He had gone out a tourist and come back a recruit to the American revolution. Something had caught fire within him and the roar of its flames competed with the deep internal cranial rumblings and explosions inside his damaged head and sometimes, hallelujah! overcame them and drove them out, even quietened the continuous buzzing in his ear, warmed his stiff and stupid tongue, disciplined the feet that each went their stupid, separate ways. He carried brochures, postcards, maps, prints and an armful of books he had discovered on sale at the Visitors' Centre on Second Street. Isobel was amused by this enthusiasm. He lay there that night staring up at her sizeable breasts, swinging like bells. Later, while Isobel slept, he got up and went through his papers.

The next day he was back at Independence Hall. He admired the style of the ground-floor rooms which he now knew to be in the English Renaissance style, with graceful pilasters proceeding heavenwards in strict proprietorial order, Doric on the first floor, Ionic on the stair landing, Corinthian cornice beneath the tower ceiling. When the guide asked the tourists whether anyone could identify the rather skinny-looking chairs crowding the Declaration Chamber, Looksmart said right out loud that they were Windsor chairs, adding in his slow and rather baffling tones, that legend had it several of the chairs had been borrowed to accommodate the delegates who crowded into the Chamber on those heady days in July, 1776. The guide stared back at him, thunderstruck.

In the Liberty Bell Pavilion across the road, a plump lady in furs and dark glasses asked why the bell was cracked.

'It cracked when they rang it,' said the guide, an innocent girl staring with big eyes at the huge brassy bell.

Looksmart stepped forward. 'The bell has always been cracked,' he said, rejoicing that his tongue obeyed him. 'It's been cracked from the day it was born. Since 1752 when it arrived from England and they hung it up on trusses in State House Yard. It cracked on the first bang. Pass and Stow cast it again. But this time it didn't sound right. Too much copper. The third time –' Looksmart held up three fingers '– they got it right. The bell rang for the Declaration of Independence in 1776, and for another fifty-nine years until, in its eighty-second year of service it rang out for the death of Chief Justice Marshall in 1835, and cracked for the last time . . .' He leaned over and with his knuckle knocked on the bell. It gave off a dim and distant echo. His audience stared. It's doubtful they understood much of this explanation, for though he pronounced quite perfectly the words came out a trifle rough and slurred and sluggish perhaps. The tourists backed away from him. The guide and the plump lady in furs beckoned frantically to the two heavy gents in green standing at the door, doubtless the guardians of the bell, and up they came and very firmly requested Looksmart to leave the Pavilion.

Looksmart sat on a bench in Independence Square and read a copy of the Declaration of Independence and I saw in my dream how the scales fell from his eyes, poor fellow. America appeared to Looksmart rather in the way that the Angel of the Lord appeared to the Virgin Mary. In Philadelphia, the cradle of revolution, an idea of an African redeemer was born.

Of course he quickly realised that the American Declaration of Independence was a document so advanced in its political thinking that, had it been promulgated on that day in his own country as the manifesto of some new party or movement, it would have been shredded on the spot and its adherents exiled or arrested, banned, imprisoned, or tortured as wild men beyond the civilised pale. It rang with phrases, any one of which would have brought blood to the eyes of the followers of the Regime; it spoke of equality, of inalienable rights, of Life, Liberty and the Pursuit of Happiness. It spoke of Just Powers, and, most startlingly, of the 'Consent of the Governed'.

It must have been likely that in the years that followed the Revolution some news of its occurrence would have travelled abroad, even as far as Southern Africa. But to judge from all the evidence no such thing occurred. Of course it was not unusual nowadays to claim kinship in retrospect. It was put out by the Regime that they too had fought for their freedom against the Imperialists, to say that 'we were fighting for our freedom from the British at about the same time as the Yanks, you know.'

In fact they hadn't stayed to fight at all, they had not been set afire with a light of freedom. Instead, deeply unhappy about the loss of their slaves and chafing at the English overlordship, though they had settled the country with their first colonists at about the same time as the Americans, they put up with successive overlords for years – until damn busybodies got between them and their slaves, and the disgruntled Boers migrated northward with God as their guide and their guns loaded, set the whips cracking over the backs of oxen, and the covered wagons rolling north into the interior in search of fresh grazing, uninterrupted privacy, and plenty of servants, in search of a heaven in the middle of nowhere. A Garden of Eden free of English and full of garden boys. Over half a century had passed since the time the Massachusetts militiamen shot it out with the British at Lexington. But no news of these great events appeared to have reached the Boers. Or if it had, Looksmart suspected, they wouldn't have liked what they heard. The early Americans wanted a nation free and independent among the nations of the world. The Boers had no nation, distrusted freedom and cared nothing for the world. The very idea would have had your average Boer choking into his brandy. What he wanted was to be left alone and to put as much distance between himself and the English enemy as possible, to trek until he reached that magic land, the land of Beulah, where the game was limitless, grazing good and armies of black slaves kept him in clover. That was the cloud-capped summit of the dream towards which they had trekked. Trekked once more. And Uncle Paul had trekked yet again.

In the end they had to stand and fight. They found you could never go far enough. It wasn't just that the English were following them, it was history that stalked them down and chased them and in time overtook them and ran them to earth. They fought and lost. But when the Dutch farmers lost the war to the English rednecks at the turn of the century, and Uncle Paul Kruger fled into exile, it was the end of the Boers forever. Those who replaced them, that is to say those who remained, and never took the one-way ticket to the remote Paradise on the Swiss mountains set aside by Uncle Paul for his dispersed people, those who remained got wise. If you couldn't out-gun the English, you could out-vote the bastards. And they did. And scooped the board and so in exchange for the two Boer republics they had lost, they gained the whole damn southern sub-continent and as many servants as any reasonable man could wish to flog in a lifetime.

On through Philadelphia Looksmart trekked, to Betsy Ross House with its spinning wheel and its first American flag; then to Franklin's Tomb in Christ Church, to Carpenters Hall and to the Tomb of the Unknown Soldier of the Revolution where Looksmart laid a dozen red roses. And towards evening he set off back down Walnut Street, forgetting, as Isobel had prophesied he would, where home really was, to Penn's Landing where he fell on his knees to the amusement of a man selling pretzels and gave thanks for his salvation. And he began to plan in his mind his 'holy experiment', his own Pennsylvania, his own Philadelphia, City of Brotherly Love, which was to absorb him utterly from then on and dreamt in Franklin's words that he might one day set foot on its surface and say, 'This is my country.'

It was Isobel who remained loving and true even when he fell so deeply into these reveries that he forgot who he was or where he lived and spent the winter nights in the streets crouched over the iron gratings from which the hot wind blew, like any other bum. And of course it was Isobel who, when the invitation came to present himself at the Barclay Hotel where 'he would hear something to his advantage' encouraged him to go at once.

'You've heard of the wandering Jew, well you're the wandering African. Finding ways to go home.'

Isobel was a dreamer. And a bit of a dope. But she loved him. And though there are some who say that Looksmart would have learnt more of the genius of America in her arms than in all his researches into Benjamin Franklin, they forget how far gone he already was when he met her.

Looksmart's head had been repeatedly knocked against the wall by Captain Arrie Breek, who today imports famous crooners and entire Las Vegas girlie line-ups to perform in his Mountainbowl Auditorium, and arranges pro-am golf tournaments at his Palace in the Veld, with million dollar prizes, and his part in the little matter of Looksmart's head should not be forgotten. When you twirl a glass of water, the glass moves but the water stays still; unfortunately, when the head is struck and moves violently this rotation means the brain tries to move with it, with calamitous results for concentration, pronunciation, locomotion.

Looksmart crossed Rittenhouse Square in brilliant sunshine and went up to a suite on the tenth floor where he met a certain Mr Carstens and his friend, Estelle. Mr Carstens said he was an American with plenty of available capital. Estelle was a friend of his from Looksmart's country. Carstens wore a vivid green and orange shirt. Estelle was dark, authoritative, and her features were chiselled, determined and pert.

Now again, there are those who say Looksmart should have known the score. He should have spotted who Carstens was. And anyone who had looked at a newspaper in the months past would have identified Estelle as Trudy Ysscl. But Looksmart did not know the score and he did not read newspapers, not when he had the mountainous literature of the American Revolution to consume.

'Mr Dladla,' said Estelle, 'we are here with a revolutionary plan.'

'Mr Dladla,' said Mr Carstens, 'you may or may not know that there is in our country a new dispensation. A New Order. Changes are occurring.'

'Mr Dladla,' said Estelle, 'I have here a letter of introduction from your brother, Gabriel. He is one terrific guy. And a friend.'

Again, there are those who charge that Looksmart should have known Carstens was a phoney, that his accent was ridiculous, and, anyway the shirt he wore with its mango sun floating above some palms should have been a dead give-away. But Looksmart had long passed beyond the petty day-to-day treacheries of the Regime. He was out of all that. He had entered a new world.

And they overlooked the letter from Gabriel.

> Dear Looksmart,
>   This is to introduce you to a couple of friends of mine, useful contacts and deep down, I believe, supporters of the cause. They have proposals to put to you which I genuinely believe can promote our struggle for liberation. I urge you to listen carefully to what they have to say and to act quickly.
>   Remember me in your prayers.
>   Your brother in Christ, Gabriel Dladla.

'We represent a force so radical we cannot reveal ourselves,' said Carstens, 'so secret it speaks only through its appointed agents. The Regime wouldn't tolerate our liberal aspirations or pragmatism. The Americans will not believe them. We have a problem. We wish to invest in several of the communications media in this town to promote our message. A couple of radio stations, a closed-circuit TV station and a news magazine.'

'What can I do for you?' asked Looksmart.

'Scepticism, cynicism, downright suspicion of our intentions is what we have to combat. If we are to buy into these businesses, our enemies would cry foul. But if you were to bid, or to allow us to bid for you –'

'You want me to buy some radio stations?'

'We will do the actual buying,' said Carstens.

'We will do the actual paying,' said Estelle. 'But you'll be the owner.'

Looksmart stared at them, wonderingly. This they misinterpreted.

'Of course, we would make it worth your while. I understand you are a student of history here. We believe you wander the streets. Sleep rough.'

'I'm a student of revolution,' said Looksmart proudly.

'Aren't we all?' said Carstens politely.

'Don't want money,' said Looksmart.

'That's up to you. Maybe you want something else. You just tell us and we'll see if we can help.' Estelle smiled sweetly.

'Do you know anyone in the Regime?' Looksmart demanded. 'Do you know President Bubé?'

After some hesitation Carstens said he had met the President, briefly, on one of his foreign tours, he thought.

'O.K.' said Looksmart. 'Now this is what I want.'

In the darkness on the mountainside Blanchaille and Kipsel heard him waving what he had got, his slip of paper, his dream. 'Here it is! Here it is! Pennsylvania here I come!' The little torch was switched on, the light pale on the paper.

'You fool,' said Blanchaille. 'You idiot!' Blanchaille yelled. 'You'll never do it. Our country is already torn into independent kingdoms, homelands, reserves, group areas, Bantustans, casinostans, tribal trust lands and all you're proposing to do is to fucking well found another!'

'Mine will be different!' Looksmart's voice cracked and trembled. At Blanchaille's raised voice he could feel the tears beginning to start. 'We'll have no racial separation, no servants, no gold mines, no Calvinists, no faction fights. In my country the Boer will lie down with the Bantu.'

'Numbskull!' Blanchaille shrieked. 'They're *all* different. All these places. That's why there are so many of them. Everybody who is different has got to have one. The one thing we have got in abundance is difference. Difference is hate. Difference is death. I spit on your difference.' And he did, spitting noisily into the night. 'You've been gypped, by your brother, by the Regime, by yourself.'

They heard the scrabble of paper as Looksmart returned the precious document to his pocket. 'You can't scare me,' he replied through his sobs, 'I will continue. Oah yes, right on to the end of the road, as the song says. I will enter Uncle Paul's place and lay my case for a new republic before the lost souls. And they will hear Looksmart, and return with me to our homelands leaving you behind, Blanchie, like the last bit of porridge clinging to the pot.'·

Here I truly believe Blanchaille would have leapt at Looksmart and killed him if Kipsel hadn't pulled him off. The two friends turned to their path again and by starlight continued on up the mountain, soon leaving the sobbing, crippled, cracked visionary far behind.

CHAPTER 25

So I saw in my dream how they arrived by night at the high stone wall and the big iron gates and read by moonlight the name of the place:

BAD KRUGER

On each of the gateposts crouched enormous stone lions, much weathered; rain, snow and wind having smoothed away their eyes and blunted their paws; their crumbling manes were full of shadows. And I saw in my dream how priest and acolyte, or detective and aide, dish and spoon, fisherman and fish, call them what you will, pushed at a big iron gate which opened easily on well-oiled hinges and closed behind them soundlessly. Without any idea of the sort of place they had entered but too tired to stand any longer, they lay down on the grass and slept.

They awoke to a morning full of bird-song to find themselves in an extensive garden thick with flowers, ornamental ponds, gravelled walks, fountains and orchards and beyond, a small, thick wood. Kipsel identified several familiar blooms: blazing Red-hot Pokers, magnificent specimens standing five feet high, their full, tubular heads of red and yellow swinging like flaming bells; the rare Red Disa, Pride of Table Mountain, as it was called, with its little trinity of reddish-purple petals framing a third which turned the opposite way showing a cup veined in purplish ink. Blanchaille knew nothing of flowers but this identification of plants and blooms recognisably African excited him as the first definite sign that they had truly arrived. The water in the ponds was a cold green. The ponds were fringed with reeds and carpeted with blue water-lilies and these in particular made Kipsel exclaim: 'Amazing! You see them? Blue! *Nymphaea* those are, blue-ridged leaves! Blanchie, they barely exist any longer. You used to find them in the Cape Peninsula many years ago. But not any longer. To find them here . . . they're virtually extinct! And look – masses of Red Afrikanders. It's far, far too late for them, surely?'

'Virtually extinct,' Blanchaille repeated, wondering at Kipsel's floral knowledge and thinking that sociologists, like cold green pools, sometimes possessed hidden depths.

Small turtles swam across the lily ponds pushing a film of water before them. They watched a brilliantly coloured bird, its plumage a dancing gloss of green and purple, its bill and forehead in matching orange, its throat bright blue, hunting elegantly among the reeds and when it caught something it would pause to feed itself with its foot with the aplomb of a fastidious diner.

Through the small thick wood they pushed and came at its edge to a wide and well-kept lawn and across it saw a great building presenting a broad and sturdy front to the world. Here Kipsel and Blanchaille drew back into the trees, for walking on the lawn were groups of people. Some were in wheelchairs attended by nurses, some walked with sticks, others seemed fit and well and played a game of touch-rugby. The scene reminded Blanchaille of a convalescent home, of pictures seen of veterans home from a war, recuperating. Though the strains of music coming from the big loudspeaker mounted high on the pediment of the house gave to the scene something of the convivial quality of a village fête. Only the bunting was missing. They withdrew more deeply into the wood. At their waists were Kaffir-lilies, three-foot high at least with great trumpeting mouths of deep crimson; hip-high Chincherinchees, big white flowers with chocolate hearts; spotted velvet Monkeyflowers; and golden banks of the misleadingly named Snow-on-the-Mountain; all of which caused Kipsel further perplexity as such flowers were found only in African gardens. The music the loudspeakers relayed was a medley of light classics: Strauss marches mingled with traditional *boere-musiek*, or farmers' music, of which the old favourite 'Take your things and trek Ferreira' seemed very popular, with its wicked thudding refrain:

> My mat-tress and your blan-ket
> And there lies the *thing*!

If the music seemed appropriate to the establishment they'd expected, the house did not. It was a solid, assertive building: a strange mixture of grand hotel, railway station and museum, built on two storeys, squat, bulky and prodigiously solid, perhaps eighty feet high and crowned by a great dome of coloured tiles, pierced by oval windows. A flight of stairs in two graceful stages climbed majestically to the bronze doors. The windows on the ground floor were arched and comparatively simple while those on the second storey were flanked by columns and surmounted with medallions and above it all, and for the whole of its length, the pediment was crowded with statuary: Greek gods, perhaps; venerable old men with philosophers' beards; horsemen; griffins; wrestling cherubs and other fancies intended to give an aura of substance and dignity, but this was undermined by the big loudspeakers mounted on poles which framed the statuary.

They drew even deeper into the wood, aware of how strange they must look, two ragged fugitives, eyes pink from lack of sleep, bodies smelling of sweat, chocolate, cheese and brandy.

'We should go forward. Introduce ourselves. We should see if this is the right place after all,' Blanchaille spoke without conviction.

'Or we could wait until we felt a bit stronger,' Kipsel suggested.

Blanchaille appreciated his trepidation but knew it wouldn't do. 'We'll never feel as strong again.'

'Excuse me, but I need a swaz,' said Kipsel and disappeared hurriedly.

A swaz! How many years was it since he heard that expression? One had to admit it was precisely onomatopoeic, echoing perfectly the zip and gush against the rock in the dusty veld, or the business of drilling muddily into a garden bed, but it pained and discomfited here in its buzzing directness. Accuracy of observation, whether of the names of flowers or of the sonic effect of urination did nothing to help; what was needed was not description but meaning!

When Kipsel returned he challenged him accordingly.

Kipsel shrugged. 'Fall into a small pool of words early on and you'll spend the rest of your life splashing around in it. For example, I had a girlfriend once, by name Karina. She had five brothers, all cricketers. I think her father played, too. Her life was taken up with starching shirts, whitening boots and keeping score. As a result she was a child of the pavilion. There *was* no other world. Her bag of words came straight out of the changing room. She had no other terms of reference. Everything was described in cricketing language. Even sex. She was forever making jokes about maidens. When we were in bed she would cheer me on if I looked like flagging with cries of "only another sixty to go or you have to follow on"! And when she was coming she'd cry "how's that?" and stick a finger in the wind like an umpire giving his man out.' Kipsel banged his fist against his forehead to still the extravagant memories of these exhausting matches. 'Going to bed with her was like going into bat without a box. She took that as a compliment when I told her. See what I mean? It wasn't so much that she was really interested in cricket itself but it provided her with a life she could get hold of. And beat. Cricket was her way of living, her get up and go, her entry into the life of action settlers must have, because doing gives an illusion of winning. Her way of grappling with life.'

'And going forward,' said Blanchaille. 'No illusion is more precious.'

It is interesting to note that they themselves did not go forward at this point but walked away from the house until the music from the loudspeaker faded. They found themselves in an apple orchard. The fruit beckoned them, the crispness of the huge pale green apples tempted them. They must have eaten half a dozen each, tearing at the tight sweet flesh as if their systems needed it, as if it was some sort of antidote to the poison of too much travel, a diet of brandy, chocolate, cheese and a constant series of shocks to the system.

I saw also that there was a vineyard nearby and this, too, they invaded, gorging on the plump white grapes until they could eat no more. I watched Kipsel who lay on the ground with his fingers over his eyes to keep out the sun and let the juice run down his throat, spitting the pips into the air, even though Blanchaille had asked him politely to stop. And then with full bellies and pleasantly overcome by the walk they slept, restlessly muttering of home, heaven and angels and policemen, no doubt believing themselves safe in the privacy of their dreams.

Then I saw that they weren't alone.

He stood up among the vines. A big broad man in a floppy straw hat, waring faded and patched brown dungarees, with his thumbs hooked into his belt. He stood watching the sleepers from a little distance away, listening to them; a big man with freckled arms and a considerable tan, attending closely, taking notes in a small book with great rapidity. And when he saw me watching him, he looked up and smiled and said: 'What's so puzzling? They come here, they're tired and hungry, they eat, they relax, they sleep. In their sleep they talk. It's a habit of people like this, terrified of speaking aloud what they think, they confine their comments to this sort of dream talk. Dreams are the only underground left.'

'And you? Is your note-taking also a habit?'

He didn't answer me, but I had my suspicions.

So I saw when the sleepers woke they found the man watching them, though he no longer carried his pencil and notebook.

'Who are you?' Blanchaille asked.

The big man smiled, he rubbed his neck, he cracked his knuckles, he flexed the muscles in his freckled arms and he said: 'I'm a gardener. At least I help to keep the place up. Of course I've got under-gardeners with me. This place is too big for one man.'

'I hope you didn't mind us helping ourselves to your fruit,' said Kipsel.

The gardener smiled. 'That's why it's there. Only I wouldn't stay here very much longer, it's getting on towards evening. You'll be wanting dinner soon. The others have already gone in, the music has stopped.'

'Are they expecting us – up there?' Blanchaille nodded his head towards the big house beyond the wood.

The gardener nodded. 'Anybody who gets this far is expected. They'll be looking out for you all right. The worry always is that people who make it this far might get lost again.'

'We weren't lost,' said Kipsel. 'A few detours, perhaps. A few hedges and ditches to jump. But not lost.'

The gardener smiled. 'If you hadn't been lost, buster, you wouldn't be here.'

'What's your name?' said Kipsel.

'Happy.'

'Happy!' Kipsel laughed, genuinely rolled about. Blanchaille was embarrassed.

In fact it wasn't too difficult to understand Kipsel's amusement or his friend's sheepishness, since, after all, the term 'Happy' was used in their own country as one of the many derogatory terms in the rich vocabulary of racial invective the ethnic groups enjoyed directing against each other. Mutual abuse was a mainstay of political life. The pleasure of calling supporters of the Regime, Happies, with all the ironical strength the insult carried was matched only by the enjoyment with which the Regime declared its opponents to be Kaffir-loving Jewish Commies who should go and live in Ghana . . . Hence Kipsel's laughter and the embarrassed silence which followed.

The big man stood by impassively watching. 'There've always been Happies here,' he said. 'Ever since the old man started up the place.'

'I think I see what he means.' Blanchaille cleared his throat with the air of a man anxious to prevent misunderstanding. 'This word "Happy" I think is a corruption, or at least a mutation, of the name of Kruger's valet, a certain Happé. You remember? He was the one who was with Uncle Paul when they found whatever it was they found.'

'Came at last to the place in question,' said Kipsel.

'Quite.'

'Which was this place.'

'Very likely. Happé is supposed to have taken down the notes dictated to him by Uncle Paul, which became the *Further Memoirs*. Our friend says he's a Happy. I think what he means is that he descends from an unbroken line of the Happé family. Is that right?'

The big man did not offer to enlighten them. Instead he indicated where their direction lay with a jerk of his chin towards the big house. 'They'll be expecting you.'

He walked them through the wood; perhaps marched would be a closer description of their brisk determined progress.

As they came to the edge of the wood the windows of the big house scintillated in the afternoon sunshine which gave an equally rich lustre to its gutters and drain-pipes which Blanchaille realised with a start were made of copper and polished to this ruddy sheen.

'This is the place?' he asked, '*Bad Kruger*?'

'Is *Bad Kruger* the place?' Kipsel demanded more subtly.

He was more than a match for both of them. 'This is it. *Bad Kruger*. Of course it's the place. Where else would it be if it wasn't *Bad Kruger*? It's *Bad Kruger* or nothing.'

I saw how the gardener knocked on the door which was opened immediately and he handed over his companions to a pair of bare-legged attendants most curiously dressed in what looked like checked pyjamas; short pants, loose fitting shirts without arms and big white buttons. I watched as these two attendants took Blanchaille and Kipsel firmly by the hands and drew them inside, the enormous bronze doors closed behind them and the great house presented once again its look of massive solidity as it presided over the perfect lawn flowing past the front steps like a tranquil green river which the gardener now crossed, giving the occasional chuckle to himself as he went, amused no doubt at the foolishness of those who did not know the place when they found it.

Blanchaille and Kipsel were escorted through the great entrance hall with a vaulted roof. Old-fashioned iron lamps hung overhead from long chain pulleys; the walls were decorated with frescoes showing knights on horseback, boys on dolphins, dying dragons, naked maidens, castles, rivers, holy grails and mermaids wearing large golden ear-rings. The place was vast and silent; the only sound their own footsteps, for their barefoot companions made no noise at all. There was a very strong smell, too, a strange mixture of sulphur, mud, salt and above all of soap, and a certain peculiar dampness pervading everything. They made their way down an extraordinary corridor off which led handsome arcades flanked by tall Corinthian columns. The frescoes became more extravagant as they proceeded; angels struck rocky outcrops with golden wands and jets of crystal water burst into the light of day. The mermaids combed their long blonde hair on high rocky promontories, turning their angelic faces to the high-flung spray from the pounding seas below. Plump olive-skinned bathers with a faintly Roman or Grecian look to them, were shown taking to the waters, moving in stately fashion – noses rippling the surface like sea-lions, and their eyes shining like dates.

Blanchaille and Kipsel asked their companions where they were taking them.

'For a bath,' came the wholly unexpected answer. 'We are the bathing attendants here to introduce our facilities to all the newly arrived guests.'

Here they began to descend a steep flight of stairs where the smell of soap and sulphur was even more pungent and the damp, mouldering air of the place clogged the nostrils.

Kipsel began to show signs of panic. 'I don't need a bath,' he whispered furiously to Blanchaille, despite the fact that his need, and that of Blanchaille, had long been apparent and increasingly unpleasant, even to themselves. The stairs grew even danker and saltier until they issued at last in an enormous underground cave or bathing chamber in the centre of which was a huge bath, a large sunken swimming pool lapping at its tiled lips.

'Step into the water,' the bathing attendants invited, 'as if you were Roman emperors.'

Then I saw Blanchaille and Kipsel remove their heavy walking boots and Blanchaille took off his clothes, though it is true that Kipsel at first attempted to walk into the water fully dressed and had to be restrained and it was only with considerable difficulty, after assuring the attendants that he would undress only if they went away, that he could be persuaded to take off his clothes and, with Blanchaille, stepped into the water which proved far hotter than they had expected and took some time to get used to.

The attendants meanwhile had withdrawn to a small glass booth and were watching them steadily. These attendants in their barefooted, flapping obsequiousness reminded Kipsel of warders, he said, or actor convicts who'd escaped from an old Charlie Chaplin movie. Blanchaille said this was probably because they were dressed in some costume of an earlier period. Kipsel said that one of Blanchaille's less likeable traits was his pedantic streak. He christened the attendants Mengele and Bormann, a joke which

Blanchaille found to be in very bad taste.

Kipsel gained sufficient confidence to float on his back. 'Have you noticed how the water gets suddenly deeper? In some places I can't stand.' He drifted idly in the water with just his nose and his toes visible. Blanchaille stared at Kipsel's toes which were very white and seemed to fold in on themselves, reminding him of white roots, or of strange mushrooms. The two attendants in their glass booth continued to watch them closely.

When at length they stepped out of the bath it was to find their clothes had disappeared. The attendant stepped forward and Mengele explained that the clothes had gone, as he put it, for the burning. The attendants offered towels. They were shown the row of saunas, the Turkish baths and the Turkish showers which were followed by the freezing plunge bath one reached by climbing a steep steel ladder and then dropping into, breaking a film of ice. They were shown a choice of soaps, the hairdriers, the pomades, creams, colognes, razors, sponges, scrubbing brushes, loofahs, and invited to make use of some or all of these. The waters in which they had been bathing were highly effective for oto-laryngological ailments, said Bormann, radioactive of course and slightly odorous, and so showering was advisable after taking the waters. They might feel rather tired a little later, said Mengele, but this was quite usual. They should go and lie down if they felt tired. There would be a place for them to lie down.

After their showers they were directed to the relaxation room, a chamber of the utmost modernity carved into the rock, glass-walled, softly and luxuriously furnished with leather loungers and a variety of ultraviolet sunbeds. There was also on offer, it seemed, among the many therapies: massage, electric roller-beds, acu-punture, aromatherapy, colonic irrigation, physiotherapy, medit-ation and drinks, both hard and soft, as well as mud baths, a gymnasium, and, for those who felt they needed them, a valuable course of rejuvenating, fresh-cell injections. At short notice, the attendants also offered to arrange for inhalations and osteopathy.

These offers were declined. And as he stepped into the shower I heard Blanchaille put it with simple dignity, 'to be clean is enough.'

Afterwards, with their hair clean, freshly shaved, deodorised and shining, they were dressed in soft and fluffy cream towelling robes with the golden letters B.K. prominently blocked above the breast pockets. I saw them led back up the stairs and through the corridors and arcades and then up a further flight of stairs into the dining room.

Kipsel could not help trembling in his towelling robe as he stood in the doorway of the crowded dining-room feeling, as he confessed to Blanchaille with a half-apologetic, rueful smile, that he really hadn't believed that he'd ever see the light of day again when the attendants marched them into the sunken bathing hall. 'This notion of washing before entry is a bit bloody quaint, not so? I mean, you know Blanchie, it reminds me of going swimming, when they used to have one of those freezing foot baths with disinfectant you had to slop through. I hated that. I always hopped it.'

'There is no hopping here,' said Blanchaille briskly. 'Here I get the feeling that they do everything by the book. Unless you go into the baths you can't join the others.'

'It reminds me of Lynch's thoughts on salvation. Do you remember his Clean Living Fallacy?' Kipsel said.

Who could forget it? This was Lynch's answer to the morbid teachings of the Margaret Brethren on sudden death and inevitable damnation. The Margaret Brethren taught them that by going about in a state of sin knowing not what the day brought forth they risked the wrath of God: a motor car accident, a sudden electro-cution, asphyxiation, choking, or one of the hundred hidden ways in which God might strike and send the sinner to judgement un-shriven, unprepared and irredeemable. Death in the state of mortal sin would deprive the sinner of any chance ever again of heavenly bliss, and even a venial sin would plummet the sinner to purgatory where sufferings were just as bad and the period of confinement so vast that by comparison all the time which had passed since the creation of the cosmos to the present day seemed no longer than a millionth of a second. Lynch savaged this doctrine by pointing out that precisely the same fear possessed people who hoped, if knocked down by a motor car, to be wearing clean underpants. In the eschatology of the Margaret Brethren, Lynch explained to them, God was reduced to a bad driver, the human being to a hit-and-run victim and the soul to the status of an article of underwear.

This mere mention of Lynch made them both wonder and look around them as if hoping that they might spy the little priest lurking about. Perhaps they might ask him whether he thought people here lived by the book and if so whether the book was any good and life lived by it worth the trouble?

They were in the dining-room now, a magnificent iron and glass pavilion which looked rather like a huge bird cage. There were many tables and many diners. Obligatory portraits of President Kruger hung on the walls. In the centre a fountain kept its awkward watery balance in a great stone basin shaped like a giant baptismal font. All the diners wore the same creamy towelling robes and all looked freshly scrubbed. A short, square, capable looking woman in a dark blue uniform which gave her the look of a nurse, though there was also something vaguely military about her, stepped forward. There were black epaulettes on her uniform and silver stars that served as buttons and her bearing was upright and disciplined. Clearly someone not to be trifled with. But her smile was open and genuine and her welcome warm. She was smoking a short, thin black cheroot.

Though there were none of the faces they half-hoped, dared perhaps, in their wildest imagination to find, there were all around them familiar countenances. Surely that grey-haired old gentleman was a former prime minister who was said to have retired to his farm in Swellendam to raise bees? And was that a necklace of golden coins he was wearing threaded on a piece of string around his neck? (As they were to discover it was not string, but fishing tackle that served best for this purpose.) Here surely was the origin of the legend of the golden crowns which all who reached the last refuge would receive. Some of the women, with considerable ingenuity, had designed jewellery, elaborate harps or butterflies made entirely of gold coins, and some of the rougher looking men, perhaps farmers or rugby players in former lives and who could hardly be expected to go in for bodily decoration or for fancy jewellery, had fashioned their coins into large gold rings, chains, and chunky medallions which nestled in the thick black hair of their chests. A few held golden flutes and some played on them, rather badly but with great enthusiasm.

The matron followed their glances. 'Patience. We have such a wide variety of people in *Bad Kruger*. We are many things to many people – a club for retired gentlefolk, an old folks' home, an old boys' reunion, a retirement village, a sheltered accommodation scheme, a hospital, a shelter for the incurably desolate and an asylum for patriots. You are perhaps looking for people you know? It will take a while to recognise all those who are here, and not everyone comes down to dinner. Some stay in their rooms. You'll have time enough to look for them. *Bad Kruger* was never built to hold our present numbers. We must arrange two or three sittings for each meal – just as they did on the trains.'

The food was served and the wine went round. The meal was good, if rather heavy. Soup, followed by veal in a thick cream sauce, fried potatoes and solid wine which they took from a carafe at the table. The waiters wore black trousers and rather grubby white bunny jackets fastened with a single brass button, their black bowties were scruffy and they lounged against the walls and muttered things among themselves in the manner of waiters the world over, bored between courses. They looked as if they had once worked on the trains, Blanchaille thought. They had that characteristic air about them, a truculent and a rather rough *bonhomie*. Also there was a slight roll to the way they walked, as if the room were moving.

In the centre of the room the fountain played. Matron explained: 'The fountain is known as the *Afrika Stimme*, or the African Voice. When Uncle Paul arrived here with his valet Happé he found the place in ruins. It had been a spa once, it was to have been a palace of health visited by the crowned heads of Europe and was founded by one Pringsheim with casinos above, baths below. Built in 1875 at a time when the great spas of Europe were beginning to draw the rich and famous to them, Pringsheim knew of the link between wealth and power as well as the incessant interest aroused in rich and successful people by their bowels, their colons and their irrigation systems. He understood their obsession with health. He understood that the rich and beautiful and powerful needed to purge themselves of the grime which inevitably accumulated in mastering the world. This spa was founded upon an incredible hot-water spring. Such was its heat that it was known to the locals as the *Afrika Stimme*. You've seen the bathing halls below, those enormous, moist, echoing places. The curative properties of the steaming, radioactive waters were believed to be miraculous and have been known since Roman times when legionaries were said to have bathed here in the reign of the Emperor Diocletian. Pringsheim planned for these healing waters to wash away the sins of the worldly. Pringsheim was ambitious. He built wonderful new bathrooms, steam rooms, mud rooms, inhalatoriums. There were nozzles and sprays and dunk baths, plunge pools, massage rooms, radon chambers. There were waters for drinking, for irrigation, for warming, curing, strengthening, purging, saving. Alas, tragedy struck. The great casino was no sooner built, where we now sit, than the spring died. Stopped dead one day and would not flow again. Pringsheim shot himself. For a time the place was empty and I believe after that an asylum was established for a short while. However it was quite unsuitable for lunatics who drowned in the mineral water swimming pool, choked in the mud baths, strangled one another with inhalant tubes. The building fell into disuse, into ruin – and that is how Uncle Paul and his valet Happé found it.

'Uncle Paul did not hesitate. He knew the curative properties of the water, these had been analysed and found to contain various chemicals: lithium, manganese, phosphoric acid, fluorine, caesium, and even a tiny touch of arsenic, besides, of course, being radioactive. Fifteen mach units of radon was the measurement, good for the blood, for breathing problems, for arthritis, rheumatism, for just about anything you care to mention. He knew this, but that wasn't the main attraction. The main attraction was the hot spring, the African Voice. It seemed fated. Intended by God. It was a sign. Of course they told him that the spring had failed. That it would never flow again. The old man is reported to have said nothing, merely to have asked Happé to help him over to the base of the fountain you see there, and proceeded to strike it with his walking stick. And the spring flowed again. Those around him understood the significance of that gesture, they read their Bibles regularly, they knew the story of Moses striking the rock in the desert and finding water. They knew of the wanderings in the desert of the Israelites in search of the Promised Land. They knew the old man had made his choice. In a sense he had come home, he had realised his dream. The spring flowed again. He had made a home for others to come home to.

'Two events were crucial in driving the old man to this place. The story of the Thirstland Trekkers of the 1870 haunted Kruger, Happé writes. Perhaps you know it? The Thirstland Trekkers were not content even with a pure Boer Republic. Even there they felt the lack of freedom, even there they felt constrained, even there when they had what they wanted of Africa they dreamed of yet another Promised Land, a heavenly Republic beyond the horizon. They dreamed, in a word, of Beulah, the Promised Land, Eden, Shangri-La. It was a vision which drew this particular party of Boers to trek forever onwards to the sacred *laager*. It carried this small desperate party of six hundred or so men, women and children through the Kalahari Desert "dying as they went", according to one historian. The end is sad. The dream drew them not to Beulah but to a steamy, fever-ridden province owned, not by Jehovah, but by Catholic Portugal. They set off, as Uncle Paul told Happé, those poor haunted brave Boers in search of heaven only to end in the hands of Portuguese market-gardeners! The special significance of this trek, said Uncle Paul, exposed the vital character of the Boers. They were destined to trek, but the mistake of the Thirstland Trekkers was that they trekked away outward, whereas the true trek was not one which covered territory but one that moved forever inward. An interior trek, an internal journey to the centre of themselves. This was the paradox at the heart of the true Boer, that he must continue to trek and yet he could never expect to arrive in the Promised Land. Kruger saw the fate which awaited his people if the trek failed. He saw it in the two colleagues closest to him, he saw it in Smuts who turned from general to bank robber overnight, and, worse, went on to show considerable flair for world diplomacy. Kruger did not know which was the greater scandal. And then there was General Piet Cronje, whose defeat in the Battle of Paardeberg and his subsequent surrender to the British enemy had been one of the most cruel calamities of the war and hastened the end of the struggle against the British Empire. He saw his enemies, the foreign outlanders, the gold bugs, throwing parties and buying beers all round, inviting Boer generals to sit on the boards of their companies. And then in the final months of his life he heard of General Cronje's horrible plans in St Louis, Mississippi. For what was the old general preparing to do? He was preparing to stage, for gawping tourists, his Last Stand at Paardeberg. According to Happé this distressed the old man terribly. "Can you imagine it, can you imagine it?" he is supposed to have said. "Can you see, these Americans, queuing up to see this great disaster inflicted on our suffering people?" The knowledge tortured him. Visitors to the Kruger House in Clarens gave him graphic descriptions of the preparation for Cronje's little piece of theatre in faraway St Louis.'

The matron drew deeply on her cheroot and puffed creamy smoke. Her voice sharpened and quickened in an American drawl. 'Roll up! Roll up! See the *Boojers* meet the British in mortal combat! See General Kitchener's final triumph! See the Boojers digging nests of trenches! See the Lydite shells blasting their positions! Read Cronje's courteous request for a truce to bury his dead and for British doctors to treat his wounded. Listen as Field-Marshal Roberts pronounces his niggardly refusal. Then hear General Cronje's noble response, which was in essence, *Then bombard away. . . !* Now watch the great Boer military genius De Wet harassing the British from Kitchener's *koppie* which with supreme daring he has snatched from under their noses. See him command the strong point of Paardeberg for three days. But it is too little, too late. Now see everything lost. See General Piet Cronje and his four thousand men surrendering to Roberts. See him stepping down from his white horse, the Boer in his big hat and his floppy trousers and see the triumphant Roberts, neat and dapper, stepping towards him while in the shade Cronje's broken troops watch impassively from their wagons, and all around them sit the British in their khaki, wearing their funny hats with those strange protective peaks back and front to keep the sun off those long, thin noses, those red necks . . .' The matron's impersonation using hands and napkins impressed a number of the diners who applauded politely. She acknowledged the compliment with a nod of the head. 'You can imagine the old man's agony when he heard of Cronje's preparations at the World Fair, of his old friend's plan to make money while the bones of the Boer dead whitened on the slopes of the mountains their General had lost. But it spurred Kruger on. He told his doctor, according to a story that has come down to us, "You take care of the bodies, but someone must take care of the souls. We must make a little hospital, a little spirit hospital, ready for them." Well this is that little hospital. By July of that year, 1904, Uncle Paul was dead, but *Bad Kruger* was alive and well.'

'And what do you do here?' Kipsel was bold enough to ask.

'What do we do? We tell stories, of course.'

'More stories!' Kipsel protested. 'I'm tired of stories. Will we never get to the end of stories?'

Matron turned on him sternly. 'Never. And what would you do if that happened? Stories have brought you this far. From the most powerful member of the Regime to the lowest gardener, cook or nanny, we all need stories. We owe our lives to stories. Would I be here now? Or you? Or any of these people if it weren't for the stories of another place, of Uncle Paul's arrangements for the likes of us? Do not spit on stories, Mr Kipsel, or stories might spit on you.'

Kipsel hung his head. 'I'm sorry, it's just that we never seem to get to the end.'

'The end? Mr Kipsel – *we* are the end of these stories. I see you're puzzled. You fail to understand – even now.'

Sweets were brought, great big dishes of *koeksusters*, golden plaited sweetmeats oozing oil, and milk tarts as big as wagon wheels, fig jam, watermelon conserve, raw sugar cane, fly cemetery, coconut ice and, of course, peach brandy with the coffee.

'Fail to understand what, precisely?' Blanchaille asked.

'Everything,' came the laconic reply. Matron nodded her head towards the first speaker who had got up and was preparing to address them. 'Listen and you'll learn.'

A thin man with a nervous manner. His cream towelling robe

267

made him look rather like a chemist, a little drunk, and he tugged nervously at his ear-lobes while he spoke.

'My friends, my name you know.'

'I don't,' whispered Kipsel.

'It's Peterkin, Claude Peterkin, the radio producer,' said Blanchaille, 'from home, I knew him immediately.'

'From home!' Kipsel echoed in hot sarcastic tones. 'Where's that?'

Matron banged on the table with her spoon. 'Let him tell his story,' she ordered.

Peterkin bobbed his chin gratefully towards her. 'I was by trade a radio producer and rose in time to become Head of Broadcasting. My motto had always been – "choose the middle way". Useful advice to myself, working on the State radio you might say, since it meant I could steer between what was on the one hand a public broadcasting facility and on the other a Government propaganda service. You could say I'd been happy and moderately successful. Then one day I made a mistake. I allowed myself to be persuaded by Trudy Yssel that times were changing. "Produce plays," she said, "which display our adaptiveness to new political perceptions, which are modern, which are of today!" I went out and commissioned a play by none other than Labush Labuschagne. The Labuschagne you all know with his Eskimo wife and his interest in Zen and his quivering attacks upon the Regime's race policies and his impeccable Boer credentials, being a descendant of one of those heroes in Piet Retief's party who were murdered by Dingaan. And what did Labuschagne give me? He gave me an attack on the Catholic Church in Africa. Fair enough, you might say. The play was entitled *Roman Wars* – and not, let me stress, *not Roman Whores*. That was an incredibly stupid printing error. The same combination of bad luck and mechanical error which has pursued me all my life. Be that as it may, my intentions were good. Could I have made a better choice of playwright than Labush Labuschagne? His radicalism was unchallenged and yet his Government connections were superb. He wrote a play about a Church which is far from popular and he portrayed its missionary activity on our continent as hypocritical, self-serving and deceitful. What better way of encouraging a debate? Why then did the Regime put out a statement saying that while it was true they had differences with the Roman Church in the past, there was now no room in the new South Africa for religious or racial bigotry and they deplored the irresponsibility of those, they did not say whom, who attacked other religious groups? Now if this

268

wasn't enough, at the same time stories of my homosexuality began appearing in the newspapers. It was suggested that I had a particular taste for young police reservists. Readers' letters choked the columns of the newspapers demanding that this faggot be neutered on the spot. Then the Board of Governors of the Broadcasting Service put out a statement that I was considering, quite voluntarily, whether I shouldn't perhaps take early retirement. The first I knew of this was when I heard it on the "Six O'Clock News". Then the Chairman of the Governors organised a farewell party. And who do you think he invited? He got in Bishop Blashford, the Papal Nuncio, Agnelli, and half a dozen pretty young police reservists. And this was to be my retirement party – a surprise retirement party! I walked in and found myself on the way out. Of course the cameras were there and the whole thing was shown live on television. I was presented with a farewell memento. I have it here.' Peterkin reached inside his robe and withdrew a large knife. 'It's a hunting knife, for those of you not near enough to see it. It has a sheath of genuine kudu-hide, its blade is fashioned from a piece of steel taken from one of the original rails from the Delagoa Bay line which carried President Kruger to exile. Its handle is made of rhino horn. This is inset with four golden studs, representing the four major racial groups in South Africa. I accepted the gift. After that I was escorted to the door and shown into the night. And so I came here, like so many of you. One morning the gardener found me wandering in the vineyard, and here I am. I thank you for listening to me and most of all I thank our President who made this place ready for us.' And with that he lifted his glass towards the portrait of President Kruger on the wall. The old man with the tufty beard, the sashes, the rows of medals, stared broodingly down upon his displaced children.

Another then rose, a bulky man with a bristling moustache, a big belly beneath the robe. Of course they all knew him, Arnoldus Buys, the nitrate millionaire. Even Kipsel knew him.

'I was a Government man, through and through. I was amongst the chief sponsors and backers of the New Men in the Regime. I was something of a rough diamond, but I was modern, tough, pragmatic. I backed the new dispensation. I believed in the new vision. I supported the principle of Ethnic Parallels, Plural Equilibriums, Creative Differentiation, all the terms, all the ideas, all the words. I also believed that we could fight our way back into history. I was one of the original backers of Minister Kuiker and his Creative

Sterilisation Campaign. I backed the propaganda war. But my friends I was asleep. We have all been asleep so you know what I mean. I was asleep and when I woke up I found I'd been taken to the cleaners. My story is brief and tragic and may be encapsulated in a few words; I fell victim to our own propaganda, I believed in it because I was paying for it.' And here Buys, the businessman, sank back into his chair and buried his face in his arms and a sympathetic hush descended on the room.

Then there rose a man who Blanchaille and Kipsel knew immediately – and who would not? For here was Ezra Savage, the novelist, the most notable writer the country had produced, described by some as a sad, thin old lay-preacher. Savage was the dogged champion of a Christian, liberal multi-racial vision of the future, author of a shelf of books amongst which the most famous were of course, *My Country 'Tis Of Thee; Come Home Dingaan!; Our Land Lies Bleeding;* and *White Man Weep No More*. It was extraordinary to see him here. He who had proclaimed that *Emigration is Death*! A man who had stood up for years against the harassment of the Regime, had survived countless arrests, imprisonment and privation, had seen his house set on fire by gangs of white youths wearing ruling Party sashes, an attack which his asthmatic wife barely survived and which undoubtedly contributed to her death soon afterwards. A man who had withstood this and yet now stood here in this room full of fugitives.

'What the Regime had been unable to achieve, my daughter accomplished. Some of you will be familiar with the extraordinary events surrounding the elopement of my daughter, Mabel, with Sunshine Bwana, the black taxi driver. When Mabel and her lover set up house in open defiance of the laws against interracial cohabitation, the pressure on me of course increased. Some of you will perhaps have read my *Letters to a Daughter of the Revolution*, in which I tried to set out, as calmly and dispassionately as I could, the difficulties which her behaviour had caused me. Mabel's reaction was to give an interview to a Government paper in which she identified people like myself with "liberals who thought left and lived right". We owned large comfortable houses in the white suburbs, preached racial harmony to our black servants and were in reality the true enemies of the revolution. Mabel said she preferred the Regime to us, that if she were made to choose she would have found more in common with those who ruled the country than she did with these vague and sentimental politics, these liberal

270

chimeras, these values of a damp English rectory. But of course Mabel knew the thing was not to talk about the world but to change it. And so, though perhaps this is not widely known, my daughter Mabel led a second charge on her father's house at the head of a gang of black youths, and they attempted to set it on fire. Considerable damage was done. The Regime's newspapers took pleasure in reporting this, as you can imagine and there was a lot of speculation at the time, probably mischievously put about, that I was thinking of selling up at last, leaving the country and moving to a home for retired clergy on the Isle of Wight. It was then that I made my declaration – emigration is death! Well then, you must be asking yourselves, what is he doing here in this room full of fugitives? What drove him? I'll tell you what drove me. What I wasn't prepared for, what I think many of us were not prepared for, was the impact of what are called the Young Turks, or sometimes the New Men, or the Pragmatists, or whatever term you chose to designate that dangerous breed personified by the likes of Minister Gus Kuiker and Trudy Yssel. What was at the heart of their programme? It was to talk to us, persuade us, delude us into the belief that substantial changes were under way. It depicted a new deal in race relations in which people of goodwill and of good sense were seen working together in a society based on synchronised ethnicity, equal freedoms and plural balances. So it went. New names, old ideas. You might have laughed. I might have laughed. But my daughter accepted the challenge and that wasn't amusing. She took a job in Gus Kuiker's Department on the understanding that she was totally free to work for its destruction from within. She justified her job by saying she was genuinely interested in power and since this was the case it made sense to get as close to the centre of it as possible. If working for Kuiker meant getting her hands dirty, well that was too bad. Working with power meant coming to grips with it. That's what I didn't understand, she told me. That's what I was too frightened, too pure to grasp. Was there any greater test of a man's resolve than to realise he was fighting a regime ready to die for the sacred right to segregated lavatories? Well, yes, actually there was. As Mabel said: what I couldn't face was the fact that they had no intention of dying at all! Well, that's when I went away. You understand I couldn't take that. I think I would've preferred my daughter to shoot me, it would have been kinder than preaching at me from the Government benches.'

There were sighs all around the dining hall and an evident feeling of sympathy translated itself into an audible hum. Several diners

271

wiped their eyes with their sleeves. Savage sat at his table clasping and unclasping his hands, a look of intense puzzlement on his nut-brown, wrinkled, intelligent, simian face. Every so often he shook his head and they knew the rage to understand what had happened to him still went on inside him.

Next there arose two ladies who introduced themselves as the Misses Glynis Unterjohn and Moira Schapp, the noted lesbians. They rose, not to tell their own story, at least not then, but to introduce a third friend, the journalist Marie Hertzog, whose pioneering study of the working conditions of black domestic servants entitled *Matilda: Venus of the Servants' Quarters* had caused a considerable stir some years before. The study had been notable not only for its original work on the conditions in which black women were forced to live but also because Hertzog herself was a card-carrying member of the ruling Party. Her book, which revealed the women she studied to be serfs in a male-dominated world, victims both of their drunken, brutal husbands as well as of their white mistresses and masters, had been promoted by Trudy Yssel and Minister Kuiker, both at home and abroad, as an indication of the new mood of liberalisation and self-examination sweeping the country. The book was held up as an example of the way in which members of the Regime were turning the microscope upon themselves, fearlessly analysing their weaknesses, changing the system from within.

Marie Hertzog spoke in a low, angry growl. 'It was my feminist investigations that took me to the Misses Unterjohn and Schapp because they came and complained to me that their houses were being raided by the police. Imagine my horror one Sunday morning when I discovered a photograph on the back page of the paper. This photograph purported to show what was described as "an illicit love-in" in a house of sin. It showed leather-clad women scrabbling suggestively, and among the tangled legs and tongues and other phantasmagoric elements I glimpsed my own face. No names were printed beneath the photograph, I wasn't identified. But then it was hardly necessary. Those who printed the photograph knew I would recognise myself. Quite obviously someone had decided to discredit me and since they were unable to do so publicly – my uncle was after all Attorney General for many years, and my connections with the Party were good – they had turned to this means. Naturally I suspected the Bureau, for what reasons I couldn't be sure, but it smacked of their taste and planning. Naturally I said so, right out loud. I had no intention of keeping such news to myself. The Bureau immediately denied it and to prove their good faith to a loyal daughter of the Party, offered to investigate themselves. They did. And they produced the culprit.' Marie Hertzog's head drooped, she found it difficult to continue. 'It turned out to be my own domestic servant, Joy, whom I'd invited to the party believing that she was as much entitled to go as I was. It seems she took along a camera, just because she thought it might come in useful. And it was. The picture she took turned out to be worth a lot of money and poor Joy needed money. She had a sick mother, she was a working girl. What else was she to do?' Marie Hertzog threw back her head. 'Friends and colleagues, everyone of you has lived through a similar experience. That isn't what's brought us here. No, I'm afraid the trouble with us is that we've all expected to win. We're on the right side, we said, so we've got to win. Well that sort of dreaming is all right I suppose provided you win. You can say a lot of things about us. You can say we've been foolish, that we've been sentimental, we've been misled, we've been badly treated. Maybe all these things are true, but truer than them all, simpler, ordinary, horrible, is the truth that given the way things are – we've been dead wrong.'

Many were the stories they heard that night, terrible, heart-rending. Consider the tragedy of Maisie van der Westhuizen, a singer synonymous with local opera, a well-loved soprano, 'Our Maisie', a familiar figure, somewhat bulky in flowing electric blues and acid greens, with elaborate black bangs and her huge sapphires, a wonderfully successful artist, best known of our singers abroad, making regular appearances with the Vienna State Opera. Fame and a soft heart and an excellent command of German; thereby hung her tale and her downfall. For Our Maisie was one of the chief supporters of the Benevolent Fund for Forgotten Germans, which, as everybody knew, was a front organisation for the support of elderly Nazis, a group of demanding old pensioners for whom, generally speaking, holidays were difficult to arrange. To this end Our Maisie had founded a group of sunshine homes on the South Coast to which these loyal old soldiers could be flown for a few weeks, to bask in the sun in the evening of their lives. Maisie told her story:

'One day a party were turned back at the airport when they arrived. And the reason given? Because they were National Socialists. I couldn't believe my ears! So were half his Government, I told Gus Kuiker, who had signed the exclusion order against my old gentlemen friends. It did no good, they were turned back, flown out, sobbing some of them, back to their little flats in Düsseldorf and Frankfurt, to die of disappointment. And if this wasn't enough, when I returned to the country some while later to open the new opera house in the great University of Christian National Education I walked out onto the stage to discover all the front rows were crammed with Jews, wearing yarmulkas and carrying placards: SAY NO TO MAISIE'S NAZIS! My voice snapped like a pencil, I stormed off the stage, I walked to my dressing room, I fetched my car, I drove to the airport and here I am, as you see, finished . . .'

Then there was the pathetic little tale of Hans Breker, the long-service South African spy who had worked for years in London under cover of a stringer for Dutch and South African newspapers, passing back information, mostly pretty low-grade stuff, to Pretoria, without interruption for almost two decades. His material had been rather pedestrian, nothing in comparison to the jewels of information achieved by the likes of Magdalena. Breker had culled the newspapers for reviews and articles by South African exiles, photographed them secretly at political rallies, looked up information on suspect organisations, kept his eye on peripheral figures, supplied biographies, checked addresses, filed descriptions and generally carried on the boring everyday business of undercover surveillance. This loyal agent lived in a flat in Hackney and in the normal course of events could have expected to see out his time and return home and spend the rest of his life in a special settlement for retired spies on the South Coast, with his pension sufficient to keep him in gin and cigarettes. Alas, Breker had fallen in love with an artist. She taught him to paint. The results were fatal. He sold his large flat in Hackney and took a room in Chelsea. He began to be seen in art galleries. His shoes were hand-made. He entered paintings for the Royal Academy Summer Exhibition, he even began learning French. By this time the woman had left him, but the damage was done. Breker was seen around town frequenting the oyster bars, he even signed his name in a letter to *The Times* about the fate of the Turner paintings.

'In short, I committed the worst sin of an agent – I became known. When the Government ordered me back I refused. I said I wasn't going back to some holiday home for senile spies in Bronkhorstspruit. Well, that did it. I was as good as dead. I came here – where else?'

And many more were the stories they heard that night. Too many to be recounted here, though mention must be made of the odd little history of Bennie Craddock, C. C. Himmelfarber's nephew, whom Blanchaille had last seen in a photograph weeping in Red Square. No wonder! He spoke briefly and movingly of his arrest in Moscow and of his eventual freedom which was achieved when Popov was exchanged for several agents who had been held in the Soviet Union, to wit a Briton, two Frenchmen, an American and a German. This young man, with his thin face and shaking hands, gave no indication that he had once been on the board of Consolidated Holdings, his uncle, Curtis Christian Himmelfarber's right hand. He produced copies of the Regime's propaganda magazine *Southern Comfort* (free to all foreign embassies, colleges, doctors' waiting rooms worldwide), its cover-story the exchange of Popov in Berlin and he pointed to his uncle, Curtis Christian, among the smiling observers of what was widely regarded to be a sensational coup for the Western intelligence services and not least, of course, for the Regime.

It would be unfair not to mention also the appearance of the former opposition leader, Sir Glanville van Doren who didn't in fact tell his story at all but instead gave a repeat performance of his farewell speech to Parliament, the one he made before he disappeared. The speech ran as follows: 'With happy memories of a full and useful life, conscious of having fought the good fight, I leave this House now to return to my farm, Morsdood, near my hometown of Glanville, which those of you who know your history will remember was named for my grandfather – and there I plan to devote myself, as a good dairy farmer, to rebuilding my herd.'

Matron gave a little bow when she heard this. 'Brave words, and absolute utter nonsense. What he was saying was that he was a shattered man. It was only a question of time before he left his cows and came to us.'

So it was, in the silence that followed the recounting of these cruel events that Blanchaille had time for reflection. He remembered what Kipsel had said about the plants and flowers growing in the garden; it was that most of them were found only in Africa and some were extinct. Was there something on this mountainside, in the quality of the air, or the soil, or some strange trick of climate that enabled them to survive here and only here? He found himself remembering the balcony of Uncle Paul's other house in Clarens, his heart went out to the old prophet, sick and tired, sitting on his front veranda staring blindly at the blue mountains across the water, those mountains which looked so curiously African. How sharply they must have reminded him of home! And then he found himself studying the waiters, or stewards, or whatever they were (he didn't really like to give them any other titles or descriptions). Waiters would do. Waiters sounded safe. They stood there against the wall in their white jackets and trousers, observing the diners. He knew there was nowhere else to go now, this was where the Last Trek ended, in this refurbished bathing establishment, this decrepit one-time spa on a Swiss mountainside attended by a matron and surrounded by Happies . . . They had indeed come home, they had all come home. They had come home with a vengeance.

Now let it be remembered that in this great dining-room there were many hundreds of people; that Blanchaille and Kipsel were excited, disturbed and that the alcohol had had some effect on them; and let it also be said that the stories they'd heard moved them very deeply and unsettled them more than they wished to admit. For one thing it was quite clear that they too would be expected to tell their stories, if not that night, then soon. It was in this unsettled, bewildered state that one must treat Kipsel's extraordinary claim, made in a choked whisper to Blanchaille, that sitting in a small group of men near the door, a group who he had not noticed until they got up to leave the room, hadn't wanted to notice, hadn't looked at really, who were partly masked by the fountain anyway and had their backs turned . . . that in this group of men he had recognised Ferreira.

It was a claim which Blanchaille dismissed out of hand. And a short angry conversation was conducted between the two men in whispers which the matron pretended not to hear.

'Perhaps you were mistaken. It's the light. There were a lot of people in here. It could not have been Ferreira.'

'I tell you it was.'

'How do you know?'

'What do you mean – how do I know? Of course I know! I know Ferreira. As well as you do. I'm telling you it was him!'

It clearly excited and delighted Kipsel to think he'd spotted his friend. The implications were astonishing! If Ferreira was here then why not others? Why not Father Lynch (only to be expected, surely?), Mickey the Poet, Van Vuuren? Or any of those who had gone before.

The possibility excited Blanchaille too. If Kipsel had been right then they would find their friends here. Now a second realisation occurred to him which he preferred not to contemplate, which he put out of his mind almost as soon as it had made its insidious, chilling entry. For if Ferreira was here it told them something about themselves which Kipsel hadn't thought of yet. Because the point about Ferreira which really alarmed was not that Ferreira was there – but that Ferreira was dead.

Despite the implication of this he couldn't stop himself from scrutinising with ever great intensity the faces of his fellow diners.

'You are perhaps looking for somebody?' the matron asked.

Blanchaille nodded. 'A friend. A friend I knew once.'

'I'm sure you'll find many of your friends here.'

'Her name was Miranda, I knew her some years ago. She – she went away. Do you know if she's here?'

Matron blew jets of steely smoke from her nostrils. 'Regret I can't answer. I'm not at liberty to disclose the names of our patients. That's up to them. Rights of privacy are paramount in our little community. It's up to people themselves to decide whether they want to be known, or whether they want us to know who they are. And if they do, they tell us their story. In fact it's very often by telling us their story that we find out who they are and they find out why they're here.'

Then I heard Kipsel ask Matron a question which went to the heart of the mystery. 'Where did Kruger hide the gold he brought with him?'

On this subject she was forthcoming. 'Oh yes, the gold. Do you remember the scenes you so often enacted, where you played the old President in the railway saloon waiting to be taken to the coast and the ship which was to carry him off into exile? Well most conveniently he had with him a number of Bibles. They were big family Bibles. Very heavy. Each capable, I suppose, of holding a few pounds of gold – once the pages had been removed of course.'

Kipsel shook his head incredulously. 'He would never have done that! Never! Not in the Bibles.'

'Why not?'

But Kipsel would not bandy words, simply shouted, red in the face, 'Not in the books!'

She shook her head. 'You don't understand. You see for him the gold was no longer money, treasure. It was his sacred trust. He wasn't stealing it. As far as he was concerned he was safeguarding it. And where better to do so than God's holy book? Nobody would have thought of looking there, nobody would have thought of searching an old man's Bibles. Of course many realised that the gold had gone. The British knew it had gone. And when he was out at sea, on board the man-of-war, the *Gelderland*, a curious incident occurred. As they steamed between Cairo and Corsica five British men-of-war were sighted and they gave every impression of being about to attack. Certainly the Dutch captain thought so. He prepared to fight. But at the last moment the British ships turned away. The story is that somebody big in London decided to let it go. Perhaps even Chamberlain himself. They called it off at the last moment. It wasn't worth an international incident. It would have looked like the worst sort of bullying. "Let the old man have his few dubloons which he's tucked into his socks," Chamberlain is supposed to have said.'

'So he got his millions after all?' Kipsel asked.

'Not exactly. The amount has been grossly exaggerated. He collected a few hundred thousand in total when the gold was sold but hardly the fortune of myth and popular imagination. I hate to spoil a good story but the money didn't amount to that much. Not even with the sums flowing into the house at Clarens from Boer sympathisers and charities from all over the world. But it was enough for him to do what he had to do. Enough for him to buy this place. And remember he was a man of simple faith. He believed that once he had the place, the funds to keep it going would follow. And he was right.'

Blanchaille said softly, 'Then there never were any Kruger millions.'

She looked at him now, and she laughed, broad and rich. 'Oh yes, there were Kruger millions all right. Just that they weren't the sort you think. You see, we are the Kruger millions.'

And then I saw the whole company of diners stand up and quite spontaneously sing several verses of the National Anthem; after which I watched the Happies going around drawing the curtains of the great dining-room with its living fountain and its lost souls and I wished, as the curtains closed one by one, that I too was inside with that strange company of story tellers before I woke from my dream to find myself, as of course I knew I would find myself, alone in Father Lynch's ruined garden beneath the Tree of Paradise waiting for the earth movers to close in.

Perhaps one last thing should be added. Unknown to Blanchaille and Kipsel, a traveller arrived at the big wrought-iron gates and was met by the gardener. Looksmart Dladla produced his slip of paper ceding him the strip of land for his new colony in Southern Africa. The gardener took his piece of paper and asked as well for Looksmart's passport, and his pass, and his book of life, documents which contain between them every single item of information about what are often otherwise quite unremarkable existences. Looksmart innocently handed these over, explaining to the gardener that he wished to enter and make a short address to the inhabitants of *Bad Kruger*. Asking him to wait, and promising him speedy attention, the gardener made a telephone call while Looksmart confidently anticipated admission and ran through the speech he had prepared.

But instead, clattering out of the sky came a police helicopter and Looksmart was arrested. For what was he in the cold light of day but an illegal immigrant, a black man without papers of any sort, a refugee from justice, an African lunatic abroad on Swiss soil, a man suspected of a variety of currency offences, a man who gibbered incomprehensibly of freedom and liberation. The lips of the policemen tightened when they heard this tirade.

I saw Looksmart frog-marched to the helicopter and watched as the machine took off and headed down the mountain. And then I knew that poor Looksmart though he had read Jefferson the philosopher of the American revolution, and Franklin and others, was beyond saving. He had fallen into the extraordinary delusion that given energy, ingenuity, bravery and just a modicum of goodwill, a people of sufficient determination can survive and prosper, even in South Africa. And as I saw him turned away from the gates of Uncle Paul's great white location in the sky, expelled from the sacred Alp, I realised that it's a long way down at the best of times and that the pit may wait at the end of the American rainbow, or open beneath the feet in some seeming Swiss paradise just as surely as it does in the city of destruction where I was born.

Also available from Atlantic Books

My Mother's Lovers
Christopher Hope

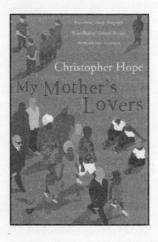

Once it seemed to Kathleen Healey th
Africa was empty and all of it belonged t
her. An aviator, big game hunter and knittir
devotee, she would land her plane wherev
and whenever she chose. She was free wi
her favours too, and her multitude of love
came from all over the continent.

When Kathleen dies, her only son Alexand
returns to Johannesburg to carry out her l
wishes. But then he meets Cindy Septemb
and Alexander must confront the final part
his mother's legacy – his capacity for love.

'Hope writes with extraordinary exuberance and invention. His narrative
like one of the great rivers of Africa, carrying everything before it, and da
zling the eyes with its glitter... This powerful, disturbing, scintillating no
confirms me in my view that Hope is one of the dozen best novelists in t
country today.' Francis King, *Literary Review*

'Remarkable... Grave and tender, savage and subtle.' Giles Foden, *Guard*

'Biting, outrageously inventive and peopled with memorable characte
Paul Hopkins, *Irish Independent*

'Exceptionally funny... Hope's novel is an addictive read.' Brian Mart
Sunday Telegraph

'This is a big novel, funny, sad, rumbustious, bitter... just like Africa.' Al
Massie, *Scotsman*

Atlantic Books
£7.99
ISBN 978 184354 383 1
www.atlantic-books.co.uk